sparks still fly

Love in LA Series
Book Two

cristina santos

This one is dedicated to you, mãe e pai.
Please, I beg of you, don't read this one, all right?
I'm so serious right now.
Amo vocês!

———

For all of the eldest daughters who take charge, know what they want and go after it…but still want to be told they're a good girl.

contents

playlist

1. Daylight - Taylor Swift
2. I Think He Knows - Taylor Swift
3. Like This - Jake Scott
4. Sparks Fly (Taylor's Version) - Taylor Swift
5. Falling Like The Stars - James Arthur
6. This is how you fall in love - Jeremy Zucker, Chelsea Cutler
7. Ceilings - Lizzy McAlpine
8. Would've, Could've, Should've - Taylor Swift
9. You & Me - James TW
10. You - Dan + Shay
11. The 1 - Taylor Swift
12. A Little Bit Yours - JP Saxe
13. Sure Be Cool If You Did - Blake Shelton
14. I'm sorry - Joshua Bassett
15. Would you love me now? - Joshua Bassett
16. Stay - Gracie Abrams
17. Are You Gonna Kiss Me Or Not - Thompson Square
18. I Remember Everything - Zach Bryan, Kacey Musgraves
19. Buy Dirt - Jordan Davis, Luke Bryan, Bluebird Days
20. I Want Crazy - Hunter Hayes
21. Somebody Like You - Keith Urban
22. Locksmith - Sadie Jean

23. The Good Ones - Gabby Barrett
24. Invisible string - Taylor Swift
25. What My World Spins Around - Jordan Davis
26. You're Still The One - Shania Twain

Get the playlist here!

a little note...

first of all, thank you.

I will never get over the fact that people want to read the stories I've written, and I appreciate you so, so much!

That being said, parts of this book may be triggering to you. I always want you to go into my stories knowing what to expect, but if you don't have any particular triggers and don't want any potential (*minor*) spoilers, skip the 'Content Warnings' page.

This is an 'open door' book, and that means that my characters have sex on the page, and things are described in detail. If that's not for you (or you're related to me), the chapters you should skip are in the 'Dicktionary'.

I hope Owen and Maeve's story makes you feel all warm and fuzzy and that it makes you believe in second chances.

xoxo,

-Cristina

dicktionary

Whether you want to skip it, or skip *to* it, here's where you can find the spice and whose POV it's in:

Chapter 6: Owen
Chapter 31: Maeve
Chapter 35: Owen
Chapter 38: Maeve
Chapter 39: Maeve
Chapter 41: Maeve
Chapter 42: Owen

Enjoy! (Or don't...)

content warnings

Please note that this book contains the following:

- Marine Corp MMC with some traumatic events mentioned
- Death of a parent
- Strained mother/daughter relationship
- Mention of death during childbirth
- Baby guardianship
- Mention of Marine killed in action (no details)
- Mention of hostage situation
- Open door scenes of the couple being intimate (in 7 chapters as mentioned on previous page)
- Panic attack
- Mention of another character's pregnancy

Reading this book might make you feel things, yes, but I never want to trigger negative thoughts or feelings, so please be kind to yourself.

part one
then

1 /

fuck me sideways.

maeve

may, 10 years ago

TODAY, I met the man I'm going to marry. Of course, he doesn't know, and I certainly won't be telling him or anyone else right this second because he's my best friend's older brother. But he's the one. I feel it with every fiber of my being. I may only be nineteen, but once I know what I want, nothing can stop me. And what I want is Owen James.

Some may call me dramatic, and they would be right, but the moment I saw his 6'4" frame walk through the door of our dorm, I felt it. A bolt of electricity ran right through me, and I saw sparks fly. It's not just because he's the hottest man I've ever seen, though that certainly doesn't hurt. It's because he's meant to be mine, and I'm already his. It's as inevitable as the sunrise.

WE'RE SITTING in a booth at our favorite Thai restaurant, close to where I live with my roommates—Elaina, who I call Bonnie, and my twin sister, Charlie. Owen is directly across from me, and he's been so polite, asking me and Charlie about how our first year at NYU has been, what we love most about the city, and what we miss about living in London.

I've been taking in every detail about him. The way his blond hair is cropped evenly all around his head, the way his throat moves when he swallows, the muscles in his arms moving as he brings his chopsticks to his mouth. His cheeks are perfectly smooth, and my fingertips tingle as I imagine what it would feel like to touch them, kiss him there.

I've done little except smile and occasionally ask a question as I fidget with my chopstick wrapper, turning it into a mini origami swan. It's something I started doing as a way of distracting myself during dinners as a child. My mum's third husband insisted we should try different foods and be exposed to all cuisines, and I always loved going to the restaurants that had chopsticks so I could practice making things like boats and hearts. But I always loved the swans most of all—there's something about how graceful they look, even in paper form.

Once I've successfully made four swans out of all the discarded wrappers, I allow myself to glance at Owen, my eyes pausing where he's twisting one of my swans around the table with his index finger and thumb as if the tiny bird is swimming along calm waters. It's soothing, watching the way his fingers move my little creation, and eventually, I allow my gaze to move back to his unfairly sharp jaw.

He seems more comfortable with Charlie because she smiles just about as much as he does, which is not very much at all. Ever the opposing twin, I've constantly got a smile on my face. I like to be happy, and I like to make other people happy, too.

Char is very direct with her answers. That's always been her style, and she's not one for theatrics. I, on the other hand, absolutely live for theatrics. It's why I'm going to become an actress. I love becoming someone new, thinking of new ways to express myself and really getting into my characters' minds. So, when Owen addresses me, I give him the full Maeve, which amounts to big smiles, loads of eye contact and pauses in all the right places. He smiles politely back at me, but it's the same smile he's given Charlie—small and tight—so I know he hasn't realized we're meant to be just yet.

That's fine, I can learn to be patient. Maybe. Hopefully. I mean, I've never done it before, but how hard can it be, right?

He pays for dinner, and we start the walk back to our dorm. Char and Elaina are happily chatting ahead of us, and that allows me to hang back a bit with Owen.

"How are you liking New York so far? Has it met all of your expectations?" I raise an eyebrow and look up at him as I ask this, and he glances at me quickly before staring ahead again.

"It's fine. I've visited before, but it's nice to see Lainey feeling so at home here." He shrugs as he says this, then looks down at me. "Thanks for being a good friend to her. She always writes about how great you and Charlie have been, especially after everything that happened at home."

The earnestness in his eyes knocks me off my game, and my *Maeve the actress* persona falls away faster than a car explosion in a movie after someone shoots the gas tank. I swallow hard as I think of everything my new best friend has been through in the last year. She fell in love and lost that love tragically. It took her weeks to open up to us about it, and she's finally smiling a little more these days.

"Oh." Suddenly, my eyes fill with tears for a reason I can't explain. I'm not a crier. I control my emotions like I control my eyeliner—with the precision of a brain surgeon. But when it comes to my girls? My sisters? I'm a goner.

Owen touches my arm, and I'm certain I stop breathing. "I'm sorry. I didn't mean to upset you. It's just nice to know she's got good people around her. I worry about her, you know?" He moves his hand away, and I stare at it for a moment too long, watching the imaginary sparks as they flutter around us.

"Of course. She's doing so much better, though, and you don't have to worry. We've got our Bon no matter what." I smile weakly up at him, and when he returns the motion with a deliciously crooked smirk, my step falters. My hands instinctively go out, and Owen's massive arm is there to catch me.

"You all right, Maeve?"

Oh god, he said my name. He said my name. It was the first time he's said it and I'll forever remember this moment as the first time he said my name, and I nearly fell on my face into a disgusting New York City sidewalk.

"Yep. Thanks!" There's far too much pep in my tone, considering I'm not sure I've taken a breath yet since he touched me.

Thankfully, Owen is much smoother than I am at this moment and diffuses the situation brilliantly. "Why do you call Lainey Bonnie? Or Bon? Where does that come from?"

"Oh, well, it's a nickname. It means beautiful. Because Elaina is beautiful inside and out, and that's easy to see from the moment you meet her." This is a fact. I have known Elaina for eight months, and she's one of the best people I've ever met. "She's a bonnie lass, that one. Charlie and I had this elderly Irish neighbor who used to babysit us sometimes, and she always called us that. I guess it felt natural to pass on to Elaina."

His rumbly chuckle makes my pulse race. "That's...very cute."

Cute? Oh, bollocks. Cute is no good. Not when I need him to see me as his future wife, or, at the very least, his next shag who will turn into his future wife.

"Well, you've been good for her. So...thanks. Again." One more time, the sincerity of his voice rocks me.

"No need to thank me. She's been good for me, too. And

for Charlie." We lock eyes for a few seconds. His eyes are green, like his sister's, but there's something deeper about them. They remind me of fir trees in winter on a sunny day after a snowfall. The light bounces off them, and they nearly sparkle.

I'm so caught up in thinking about his eyes that, for the second time today, Owen keeps me from slamming my face into something. This time it's the back of Charlie's head as they've come to a stop in front of our building.

His hand is firm and warm against my belly, and it drops away quickly, but not quickly enough for me to miss the warmth of his fingers as they wrap around my waist.

"Okay?" And that word. That one whispered word turns my brain into soup inside my skull. I don't respond. I can't. I'm floating away, and the only thing keeping me tethered to the ground is Owen.

"All right, Maevey. Why don't we let Elaina and Owen say their goodbyes?" Charlie takes my hand and looks at Owen with a small smile on her face. "Thank you for dinner, Owen. It was nice to meet you."

"Right. Thanks." Those are my parting words to him. To my future husband.

Crap on a cracker.

---

september, 10 years ago

I haven't told Bon and Charlie about my feelings for Owen because they'll surely think I've gone off my rocker, but Charlie instinctively knows. A twin always knows.

It's been a few months since that first meeting, and I've dreamed about him every night. I think of him often, which is why I've taken up working out to Zumba videos. I need the distraction.

The music is so loud, and the dance moves are so outrageous that it makes me forget about his bright green eyes and that reluctant smile. With that thought, I put on my headphones and push our minuscule coffee table out of the way to make room for my awkward arse shaking.

Sweat pours down my back and chest halfway through the class and I throw my fist in the air, congratulating myself for finally nailing the hip thrusts in 'Gasolina.' I turn around to find Bon twisted in her chair at the kitchen table; a slack-jawed Owen on her laptop screen. I throw myself on the floor, hiding from their prying eyes and hope I can just live here forever. I don't need to move ever again. I'll just go ahead and die of embarrassment right here on our shit-brown carpeted floor.

"It's too late. He already saw you." Bon's voice is so full of mischief, it makes me want to pinch her right on the nipple. She deserves it. She couldn't have taken her call with Owen elsewhere? She had to do it here? While the camera faced my arse?

Ugh.

"Don't let us stop you. I can see that the class isn't over yet." The low timbre of his voice has the butterflies in my stomach all taking flight at once and my skin breaking out into goosebumps even though I'm a sweaty mess. Every word is laced with amusement, but not in a way that makes me feel embarrassed. It makes me feel shy, and that's not a feeling I'm comfortable with. At all. I obviously don't mind an audience —I'm constantly on stage in front of crowds. So why do I feel like this?

His voice breaks through my muddled thoughts. "Come on. At least come say hi if you're not gonna keep shaking your ass for us."

My body reacts to his words quicker than my brain and before I can stop myself, I'm on my feet, waving at the screen.

I feel like Jim Carrey in *The Truman Show* with one hand awkwardly high above my head. "Hello, Owen."

His smile is wide and makes his dimples pop. I'm drawn to the sight of it like a moth to a flame. I know it'll be my demise, but I can't be stopped. Can't be helped. Wouldn't want to be, either.

"Hey there, tiny dancer." His voice is clear, but the deep baritone always hits me in the same spot. Right between my thighs.

I hover over Bon, smiling right back and hoping it looks casual, not frenzied. "Glad you enjoyed the show, O."

"Ew, you're sweating all over me. Here. Sit. I'm running late for class, but Owen should talk to someone other than me and Mamá, anyway. Not like he ever has a girlfriend he can call." She pushes my shoulders down so I'm sitting on the chair, then wipes her hands on her jeans, not masking her horror at my sweat on her palms, completely unaware of how many times I'm going to overthink that girlfriend comment. "Bye, O. Love you!"

"Love you, Lainey Banainey!" The nickname makes me melt, which only reminds me I actually *look* as though I'm melting right now. There's sweat everywhere, and my hair is stuck to my face and neck.

I clear my throat, attempting to wipe my forehead with the back of my arm. It's not helping. Everything is sticky.

His chuckle brings me back to the moment, and I remember he can see me.

Is this your first time on a video call? Of course he can see you, you twat!

Oh, fuck me sideways.

His laughter gets brighter, the sound bouncing around in my chest like a ping-pong ball. "I said that out loud?"

"You sure did." He cocks his head to the side, taking me in. I take a moment to do the same, noticing that the room he's in is dark. His hair is buzzed even shorter than when I met him. His brown uniform seems to be covered in some sort of pixelated camouflage pattern, a black T-shirt peeking out beneath the collar. A million questions hit my brain all at once.

What time is it there? What does the air smell like? Are you sleeping enough? Eating enough? Will you come back to New York to see us? To see me?

"You wanna go get some water? That was an intense workout, and you seem a little out of it." He's joking, though the smile is gone from his face. Even so, the pesky belly butterflies flutter at the fact that he thought to ask.

"I'm fine. I'd rather talk to you, anyway."

Fuck. Nooooo! Why did you say that? Idiot.

I clear my throat in an attempt to delete that last comment. I know. It doesn't work that way. "Where are you?"

He clicks his tongue. "Can't tell you that, sunshine. But it's really hot and dry here."

Sunshine? Did he just nickname me? Is it like a cute, flirty thing or a sisterly thing?

I can't think about it, and I don't want to ask him about his deployment. I'm sure he doesn't want to talk about that. He needs to think about happy things, so I naturally ask about the thing that always cheers me up.

"Do you ever watch *The Office*? I don't mean while you're deployed, but like when you're home?" I haven't a clue where this is going.

"Yeah, I love that show. And we watch it here sometimes." He shrugs, a small smile playing on his lips. "But we are talking about the American version, yeah?"

"Oh, god, yes. Of course. I mean, I love Ricky Gervais, but Steve Carell is a comedic genius." His smile widens. "I'm sad the show's ended, but I feel like I'll rewatch it over and over, you know? It just feels like one of those shows you never get sick of."

He keeps looking at me, smile still on his face, head still slightly cocked.

"The episode where Jim dressed up like Dwight has to be one of my favorites." I clear my throat and deepen my voice. 'Fact: Bears eat beets.'"

I pause, and when I get going again, I can't hide the delight on my face as we say in unison, "'Bears. Beets. Battlestar Galactica.'"

We both burst into laughter. I will quote every single line from this show if it gets him to laugh like this again. He looks so... light. Free. Nothing like the serious and stern guy I first met. Elaina has said that he makes a terrible first impression because he's not super friendly to strangers, but that once he warms up to a person, he's a big teddy bear, and maybe I'm starting to see that.

We're both nearly recovered, and he looks like he's about to say something when he looks off to the side, the smile immediately erased from his handsome face.

"Sorry, Maeve, I have to get going. But, uh...thanks. For staying and talking to me."

"Don't mention it." We're both quiet and unmoving, staring. He's completely still, and it seems as if the video is frozen, so I say the thing at the forefront of my mind.

"Please stay safe." Then I kiss my fingertips and touch them to the screen, where his lips are. I hit the red button to end the call, and half a second before the screen goes black, his eyes move to the camera, so it's as if he's looking right at me. My stomach dips faster than The Tower of Terror ride, and I clutch my chest in actual horror. "Noooo!"

Did he see me do that? After he saw me shake my uncoordinated arse all over the living room? After I sat here like a sweaty beast talking about a TV show? Did he see me do the kiss thing?

Charlie runs into the room with a giant textbook in her hands, holding it like a baseball bat, though I'm certain she wouldn't know the difference between a bat and a lacrosse stick.

"Get off her, you filthy beast!" I swear, ever since Charlotte saw her first NYC rat while leaving the subway, she's convinced they're out to get us.

"There's no rat, Char. Just a giant wanker." I close the laptop and walk toward the bathroom. I desperately need a shower and to forget whatever that was that just happened.

I hardly hear Charlie's "Ew! What? Why? Where? When? And whose?" She really just gave me the 5 W's. I cannot with this girl.

"It's me, Char. I'm the wanker!" I slam the bathroom door before she can reach it and immediately turn on the shower, drowning out the noise, but not the visions of two wide green eyes staring right into me.

2 /

tell me something good.

owen

october, 10 years ago

IT'S BEEN months since I visited Lainey in New York, and tonight, I'm keeping her company while she eats dinner with her roommates. Virtually, of course, since I'm still deployed.

Charlie is just offscreen, but Maeve is sitting next to my sister, somehow making eating a greasy pizza look borderline pornographic.

She keeps tucking her hair behind her ear, but it's no use. It just doesn't want to stay put, and every time her hand reaches up, I want to stop the movement and be the one to run my fingers through her hair. It's so shiny, and the color reminds me of the sand on the beach in the middle of a summer day.

I know she's trying to play it cool, and it's adorable. Every time I engage with her, she leans in a little closer to the screen.

I ask if the weather's been nice, because apparently nothing else worth saying wanted to leave my mouth. She nods, and that lock of hair comes loose again. I don't think I can take it anymore. I need to look at something else.

Anything else. I didn't expect my little sister's roommate to be so distracting. She's a nineteen-year-old university student. I'm a twenty-three-year-old currently deployed active duty Marine. We're not a match.

Lainey is going on about one of her classmates and how annoying she is, but my eyes keep going back to Maeve. She runs a finger up her forearm absentmindedly as she listens to a story she's likely already heard with a smile on her face. It's not lost on me how much she cares about my sister.

My mind goes back to the day I met her as we walked to their dorm after dinner. She nearly fell, but I caught her, and as my fingertips grazed her skin, I felt the surge of electricity between us. My heart lurched as if an actual bolt of lightning had struck me.

A moment later, she nearly walked into the back of her sister's head. I stopped the collision, grabbing her around the waist, and the memory of those touches has me feeling a little dizzy. This is not the time for my body to have a reaction to a woman. Nope. Definitely not the time.

―――――

november, 10 years ago

"Tell me something good, Maevey," I say. I'm so fucking tired today, and as much as I wanted to talk to my little sister, there was a big part of me that was hoping that Maeve would be the one to pick up. I know Lainey asked her to do that when she's not home so that I have someone to talk to, but on more than one occasion, I've called when I know Lainey has a class and Maeve might be home. Of course, I call Lainey more, but some days I just want to hear Maeve's voice. The way she says *bollocks* and *tosser* repeatedly anytime she brings up her theater studies professor always makes me laugh.

"I had an audition earlier, and I think I nailed it! Then on my way home, I stopped to get a celebratory donut, and when I looked in the bag, there were two, so it feels like a sign that today is a good day." This girl and her sweets. She probably eats one of Lainey's chocolate chip muffins every single day.

"What was the audition for? And then tell me about the donut. Fuck, I miss donuts."

I miss a lot of things. Donuts are low on the list, but if donuts also mean some sort of connection to Maeve, then I miss donuts a fuck ton.

She giggles at my answer. "It was for a low-budget rom-com a classmate told me about. Something light and sweet. The guy I auditioned with made it easy." My eye twitches at the mention of her auditioning with a guy.

Did she like him? Will she see him again? Did he ask for her number? He'd have to be an idiot not to.

Fucking college guys only have one thing on the brain, and it doesn't take 20/20 vision to see that Maeve is a knock-out. I want to ask about this fucker she auditioned with, but it's not my place. Maeve and I are just friends. At least I think we're friends, or on our way to becoming that.

"I always choose a sprinkle donut. It's the happiest donut and makes me feel like a little kid when I eat it."

I smile at the way her nose scrunches up, and we move on to talking about other things. Audition guy doesn't come up again, and I'm glad for it.

Before we hang up, she sends me off with her usual line. "Please stay safe." And once the screen goes black, I always feel a sliver of disappointment that she didn't kiss her fingers and press them to the screen again. I wait for it every time, but it never comes.

All I have is the memory of that moment.

That day, I learned that she cared whether I came home, and that knowledge felt heavy, like a boulder straight to the chest. I couldn't move. Couldn't breathe. When I looked into the camera to say something, anything, the call had ended. I missed my chance.

I close the laptop and walk out of the trailer and back into my very bleak reality, willing my brain to forget about her glossy blue eyes and the way her lips molded around her fingers when she kissed them that day. Just for now. I need to focus.

———

december, 10 years ago

"Favorite episode so far? And you can only pick one." Her eyes widen at my question, as if picking only one episode of *The Office* as a favorite is completely illogical. It is. But I want to see how she answers this anyway.

"That's—no, I can't answer that! I mean, how do you choose between the one where Jim and Pam finally become a couple or the one where they run a 5k and Michael carb loads right before, or the one when Michael and Jan host a dinner party or...You know what? I'm going to stop. It's not possible." She crosses her arms as she shakes her head, eyebrows scrunched together because she takes *The Office* very seriously.

"That dinner party one was pretty fucking awesome." I sing part of "That One Night" from the show, and that gets her arms to loosen at her sides and pulls a loud laugh out of her. The more loudly I perform, the more she laughs, until her head is thrown back and her skin is flushed.

It's the most beautiful thing I've ever seen. I want to bottle up this sound, bring it out when the nights here are long, when shit gets dark, when everything hurts and I need a ray of sunshine.

3 /
shania or faith?

maeve

february, 9 years ago

"AND you really think Faith Hill could out-sing Shania?" He winces at the shrillness of my voice, even thousands of miles away, but it's immediately followed by that crooked smile that tells me he's toying with me.

Mmmm. Owen toying with me—NO! Quit it!

"I mean, who doesn't love a good All-American girl?" He sticks out his bottom lip in a pout I'd like to bite, and it nearly distracts me from the blasphemy he's spewing.

"Ugh! Who doesn't love a small-town Canadian girl? You're out of your mind, Owen James."

"All right. You can only pick one: Garth Brooks or Tim McGraw?" His lips twitch in a way that tells me he's getting a kick out of this, and I respond with a loud gasp, clutching my chest in mock horror.

"I could never! Could you?" My eyes widen with sincere concern for his sanity because there's no way to pick.

He shakes his head, and my concern washes away, my hand lowering to the cup of tea on the table.

I raise a finger in the air. "Mmm! I've got one. The Dixie Chicks or The Judds?"

"Easy," he responds. "The Chicks. "Wide Open Spaces" alone solidifies that for me."

A giggle works its way up my chest at his sincere and quick response. "Wow, okay. Strong opinions on The Dixie Chicks. Noted." I smile brightly, a low chuckle still working its way through me.

Things go on like this for a while longer. We argue playfully about which '90s country music stars we love most, and the sound of his laughter slowly fills every crack in my heart. Even if just temporarily.

———

march, 9 years ago

"Tell me something funny." He's in a great mood today, and it's apparent in everything about his demeanour. His shoulders are relaxed, his smile is a little wider than usual, and his green eyes have an extra sparkle to them.

"Oh, you're not ready for this," I say. That gets his smile to grow impossibly wider. "My middle name is Charlotte." His smile fades, and his brows furrow in confusion. I give him a minute to catch up.

"What, like your twin sister's first name?" I nod. "Your middle name is your twin sister's first name?" I nod again. He sputters a laugh. "And what? Don't tell me… Charlotte's middle name is Maeve?" For the third time, I nod. He throws his head back, a laugh exploding out of him. All I can do is stare.

Blimey, he's beautiful.

What I wouldn't give to see this every day for the rest of my life—Owen James, laughing without a care in the world.

Once his laughter subsides, I explain the situation. "My mum said she had two girls' names picked out, and she was convinced one of us would be a boy since we're fraternal twins, and she couldn't think of any other girl names she liked enough, so...here we are." I shrug as if it's completely normal. "So, what's yours, O?"

He licks his bottom lip, and I have to cross my legs. The man is sex on legs. "Agamemnon." My vagina immediately shrivels up. That...is not what I was expecting. He's silent for a beat, giving it time to really sink in.

"Doug and Eva really did that to you? They named you Owen Agamemnon James?" I can't even find it in me to laugh. I feel a little bad for him.

"They really did. And somehow my little sister got Helen. A perfectly normal middle name." He shakes his head as he lets out a sigh.

"Looks like both of our parents did us dirty with the middle names." I laugh and breathe a sigh of relief when he joins me. I may not have a wildly traditional Greek middle name, but you better believe people made fun of Charlie and me as kids once they found ours out.

He hums a response, eyeing me in a way I've never seen before. He really is in a strange mood today. It's good, but it's not a side of Owen I've really gotten to experience.

"Tell me something good." God, I love it when he says that. It's so sweet and endearing and all kinds of cute. It's so at odds with nearly everything else about him, which is hot, sexy, and wildly sensual without trying to be.

"All right, well, I passed all of my midterms. That feels pretty good." It's lame. Who cares about my midterms? He's deployed somewhere in the Middle East, and I'm talking about stupid tests.

"Of course you did, sunshine. You're so smart." He smiles, and my insides turn into mush. I may be inexperienced, but the throbbing in my core doesn't lie. It tells me exactly what I want, and that's Owen.

Quit thinking with your minge and use your brain!

"What about you? Tell me something good." I've never turned it around on him before, always too afraid that it'll bring the conversation down when it feels like my only job is to try to bring him a little bit of joy. But with the playful mood he's in, today feels safe.

With a cute smirk, he looks straight into the camera and says, "I'm coming home next month."

Cue my jaw dropping to the floor.

---

april, 9 years ago

"Maevey, come on! Let's go!" Bon is impatiently waiting for me at the front door. Owen is coming to visit today. He just landed on American soil three days ago, and after a very quick visit with their parents, he's here. He's here. In New York.

He's here!

I check my hair and lipstick for the third time in less than a minute and run to the door before she leaves without me. We're meeting him at the airport, even though he asked Bon not to go to the trouble. She's too excited to see him, though, and I'm thankful for it.

I don't remember a single moment of our cab ride. I'm too busy making up all kinds of scenarios in my head for when we first see one another. Will he hug me? Will he care that I'm there? I can't hear anything Bon is saying in all her excitement to see her brother, and before we know it, we're walking toward Arrivals, where people are pouring through the sliding doors.

His buzzed blond head comes into view, green eyes

focused on where he's headed toward the doors leading outside.

"O! Owen!" Bon jumps up and down, waving him over.

He turns his head toward where we are, eyes brightening as a wide smile splays across his face when he meets his sister's eyes. It's so sweet, seeing them reunite like this.

In a few long strides, he's standing in front of us, hugging Elaina tightly and lifting her up.

"Lainey Banainey! You came!" He sets her down and ruffles her hair, as big brothers do. He looks up, and his eyes finally meet mine. My palms are so sweaty that I'm worried there are drips on the floor.

He reaches for me. My heart leaps inside my rib cage. I nearly black out.

"Sunshine," he whispers, so only I can hear. The hug is quick, but I register every moment. One hand around my waist, fingers gripping tightly. Another up my back, clutching the back of my neck. His chest against mine. His nose in my hair. The lingering hand on my elbow before he lets me go.

"Hello, Owen," I say dumbly, wiping my hand on my jeans as his smile widens. I swear he loves seeing me squirm like this.

"Maevey. Thanks for coming with her." He picks up the duffle bag he dropped when he hugged his sister and casually rests an arm on her shoulder. Bon is a few inches taller than me, but she's still nowhere close to Owen's massive height. "Where are we off to?"

As we walk out of the airport, Elaina rattles off all the places she wants to take Owen to. I hang back, just taking in the sight of him, floating in the relief that he's really here and he's safe. He looks happy, and that makes my heart beat more steadily and fills my lungs with a little more air. Things feel right when he's close by.

Still, I made plans to go out tonight because this isn't about me. He's here to visit his sister, and the more time I spend with heart eyes around Owen, the more likely I am to be noticed by Bonnie. It's too late for Charlie. She sees the heart eyes and calls me out on it with not-so-subtle head shakes, so that's just one more reason to stay away while he's here.

4 /

there she is.

owen

april, 9 years ago

AFTER THE GIRLS picked me up at the airport, Maeve took off to go to a, acting class, so I spent the afternoon sightseeing with Lainey. There was an exhibit she was super excited about at the MET, and I love seeing how animated she gets. We had dinner, then walked through Central Park, and having a conversation with her without a computer screen felt so good.

By the time we get back to their tiny apartment, which I'm noticing is barely larger than their dorm room from last year, I'm ready to sit my ass down and relax. Charlie chats with us for a bit, but then she heads to her bedroom to do some reading. She's not much of a talker, and I've always respected how well she sets boundaries for herself. If that girl doesn't want to do something, she simply will not do it.

It's 21:30, and Maeve stands in her doorway, looking like she's just walked off a runway. The curve of her hips sends my heart thrumming, and I'm forced to avert my eyes to avoid a sudden and ill-timed erection.

I need to get out more.

She saunters in, wearing a pair of hip-hugging pants that cling to her curves like a second skin. Her midriff is exposed, cinched tight with a shimmering belt, and topped with a cropped shirt that barely covers her chest. Thank fuck she's got a jacket on. I don't think I can handle seeing much more of her skin without having a very inappropriate reaction to it.

Her lips are a shade of red that matches her top, and she's wearing dark eyeshadow instead of the light pink she wears every day. Her normally straight hair is in curls that bounce down her back as she walks toward us.

She announces she's heading to a party nearby and throws a tiny purse over her shoulder. Before I can object, ask her to stay, go with her, or literally do anything that would keep her in the same room as me, she's out the door, blowing a kiss to Elaina over her shoulder that I definitely don't wish was aimed at me.

"You just let her go out on her own like that?" I point at the door and look at my little sister, who scoffs at my question.

"*Let her?* Have you met Maeve? No one *lets* her do anything. She does what she wants." She rolls her eyes when she sees my own widen in shock.

"But we have safety measures in place. Both of us always know where she's going and with whom. We can see her phone location, and she never ever has more than two drinks if I'm not with her." I finally take a full breath, thankful that they have this system. "Plus, she's probably meeting Cam there. It's cute that you've got the whole protective big brother thing going on with her, too."

Yeah, that is not *what's happening here, but I'm not about to correct Lainey. And who the fuck is Cam? And why would that make me feel better? And why does it make me feel like chasing after her?*

· · ·

CHARLIE JOINS us for a couple of rounds of Scrabble, but I lose both times. My head's not in it. It's with a certain blonde who left here one hour and forty-seven minutes ago. But who's counting?

THE GIRLS EXCUSE themselves to go to bed at 23:30, but I stay up. Lainey is rooming with Charlie because their couch barely seats two people, so I'll sleep in her bed tonight.

I'm distracting myself by messaging some guys I was on base with, just to check in, when I hear the click of the apartment door. I check the clock. 23:57.

"Hey. You're back early." I'm tempted to punch myself in the dick for not being able to think of anything less idiotic or obvious to say.

I see she's got a pink box in her hands, and my curiosity is peaked.

"I wasn't feeling the party tonight." She sets it down and turns to face me, but doesn't make a move to leave her spot in the kitchen. I stand and take a few steps toward her, reaching behind her to see what's in the box. And to be near her.

"Whatcha got here, Maevey?" I lift the lid and see half a dozen sprinkle donuts. The corners of my mouth lift into a smile. "Sprinkle donuts, huh? What are you celebrating?"

"Oh. Nothing. I get sprinkle donuts for everything. Joy. Sadness. Celebrations. PMS. They're perfect for all occasions." Her cheeks take on a shade of pink I'm suddenly obsessed with. She's fucking adorable. And sexy as hell. Goddamnit, this woman is tempting.

"And do you share said donuts?" I keep my hand on the counter, standing over her and taking her in from up close. Her makeup is intact, but her curls are loose now. I can still smell her lavender scent.

"Always," she whispers, then quickly maneuvers away

from me to get some plates from the cupboard, sitting them down next to the box without touching me.

I take two donuts and place them on the plates, and we silently make our way to sit at the breakfast bar. I raise my donut up, and she does the same as we toast with our midnight snacks.

"To you, *fengári mou*. To shining brightly." Even if she has no idea I just called her *my moon*, she doesn't show it.

"To you, O. To staying safe." Her voice is soft, and she doesn't meet my eyes.

"Always." I take in her perfect cupid's bow and chomp down on my donut, committing this moment to memory forever.

———

june, 8 years ago

"Don't tell me that's your dinner, Maevey." My lips turn down at the sight of her bag of potato chips and the chocolate-covered cookies she always has with her tea.

"That sounds an awful lot like judgment, O." She smiles as she slowly brings a potato chip to her mouth. She smells it first, taking her time chewing it, closing her eyes when her teeth first crunch into it. If I hadn't seen her do this exact thing several times already, I'd think she was just putting on a show. But no, this is how Maeve experiences the first taste of her food or drink. Slowly. Deliberately.

Before I can tell her that she should be eating something healthier, Clay, a fellow Marine and one of my best friends, sticks his head into the frame of the video.

"Don't listen to him. He had a cup of coffee for dinner last night because he didn't want the hot dogs I made." Clay pushes me out of the way so Maeve can see us both. "Hi,

Maeve. I'm Clayton." He does a goofy wave as he smiles widely at her. "Nice to finally meet you."

This fucker better not open his big mouth to say anything to her or I will punch that smile right off his face.

"Too good for my Walkers crisps and too good for hot dogs? I didn't take you for being so bougie!" My favorite pair of blue eyes sparkle, and I honest-to-goodness wouldn't mind having her take jabs at me for the rest of my life if it means seeing her like this. "Hi, Clay. O's told me a bit about you, so it's nice to finally meet you, too." She cocks her head to the side and smiles.

Stop staring at her like a lovesick teenager.

"The hot dogs were burned, Clay," I say, doing my best to calm my dick down. "Not just a little bit, either. They were black all the way through." Clay rolls his eyes dramatically as I talk. "And what flavor do you have today, sunshine? Prawn Cocktail? Come on. It even *sounds* disgusting." I scrunch up my face to show my obvious distaste of her British chips, and Clay laughs at the gagging motion I make. I can always count on him for a laugh.

"Don't knock it 'til you try it, mister. I could eat these day and night. You have no idea what you're missing," she says, holding up a chip.

I bet I could eat her *day and night.*

Jesus, Owen, what the hell is wrong with you? Settle down.

Clay seems to catch on to my thoughts and lets out a booming laugh. "I can see why he enjoys talking to you so much. You keep him on his toes. My girl would like you, too." He sighs. I know how much he misses Monica, and the thought sobers me a little. It's that heartbreak, that guilt of leaving someone behind to wait for you, that I never wanted. And I need to be better at reminding myself that Maeve isn't mine. I don't want her waiting around for me or worrying about me. She doesn't deserve that.

———

september, 8 years ago

The plane just landed back on base after too many days of intense rescue operations, and the fatigue of being awake for forty hours is becoming hard to ignore. I trudge through the hangar to my quarters and sink into a chair, my body begging for rest. Taking a deep breath, I slowly click the call button labeled 'Ma and Dad' and quickly fill them in before finally mustering enough strength for one more call. Lainey has heard nothing from me in weeks, and I know she's probably been worrying.

As the video connects, I send a silent prayer to whoever may be listening that Maeve is there, too.

Lainey picks up, smiling brightly.

"Big brother! Hi!" She shifts in her seat, like she can't be still.

"Hey, Lainey Banainey. It's good to see your face." And it's true. I'm so relieved to see her.

"So good to see you, O. How are you?" I don't know how to answer that. Not really.

"I'm... okay. It's been a tough deployment, but I'm all right." I swallow down the lump in my throat. "How are you? How are the girls?" I hope it's subtle enough, the way I'm clearly asking about Maeve.

"Everyone is great. Char is on campus, but Mae should be home soon. I'm sure she'll be happy to see you. She's been worried. I mean, Charlie too, but you and Maeve talk more often, and you're like friends now, so..." Her words make me feel both heavier and lighter. I don't want Maeve to worry about me, but the heaviness in my chest lightens at the fact that she thinks of me, talks about me.

I hear a loud thump in the background and Lainey looks up. "Oh, speaking of Mae, she's here."

Maeve is there. My heart doesn't know what to do in my chest. Does it beat faster? Stop altogether? Then she's in front of me, with a huge smile on her face, those baby blues sparkling.

"There she is. Hey, Maevey." She freezes, smile faltering as her eyes roam all over the screen, surely taking in how tan my skin is, maybe even the cuts on my face and the dark circles under my eyes.

"I gotta pee so bad. You guys talk. I'll be right back!" Lainey skips away, and Maeve sits on the chair in front of the laptop.

"Are you...Is everything...How—" Her eyes sparkle as tears fill them. Fuck, I hate that I'm the cause of those.

"I'm okay, Maevey. I'm happy to see you. And I'm sorry..." It's harder to get the words out than I expected. "I'm sorry if I worried you. We couldn't call from where we were."

"You don't need to apologize. I'm just so happy to see yo —to see that you're safe." It's my turn to take in every detail in front of me. The freckles on her nose. How her too-long bangs hang over her forehead. The curve of her lips.

"Tell me something good?" Though, I personally can't imagine anything better than this. Just looking at her.

"This is the best thing right here." And fuck, my heart does a full cartwheel in my chest hearing her say those words.

———

november, 8 years ago

"Tell me something unpopular," I say.

Her nose scrunches up in confusion, and her blue eyes twinkle with the afternoon sun in front of her. She's just so fucking pretty, I sometimes wonder if she's real. After two years of seeing her over a computer screen, the sight of her still makes my skin tingle.

"You know, like an unpopular opinion," I explain.

"Oh. All right. Ummm, well, I think pepperoni on pizza is absolutely rank. Americans really bungled that one up!" She sticks her tongue out, then scowls as if pepperoni pizza committed a felony against humanity. I laugh because between the fact that she just said *rank* and *bungled*, I'm pretty sure I'm becoming obsessively enamored with her. "They wrecked something so wonderful by putting the lowest form of salami on it. Yuck!"

My laughter grows, and it's been so long since I heard the sound that it startles me. We both seem to catch on to the fact that I'm laughing at the same time as we stop and stare into our respective screens.

"Tell me something crazy," she says, a small smile on her face as she sinks her teeth into her bottom lip.

The combination of how tired I am and how good it feels to see her, I don't think, and the words just stumble out of me. "If I was there right now, I'd kiss you. I'd kiss you until your lips were swollen. It'd be *my* teeth on that bottom lip instead of yours." She releases her lip from the hold her teeth had on it. Her eyes widen and her breathing is shallow. "If you'd asked me to say something true, I would have said the same thing." Her lips part, and she looks down at her hands on the table, head shaking gently as she mumbles something to herself.

"Maeve?" She doesn't look up right away, looking lost in her thoughts. I probably shouldn't have said it, but now it's out there. Maybe we should just move on. Pretend like I said nothing at all. "Tell me something." I swallow, feeling really fucking stupid for so obviously misreading our connection. "Anything…"

She finally looks up at the screen again, eyes gazing directly at the camera. "I wish you were here." I inhale deeply, and when my lungs fill up, I can't tell if it's oxygen or her words I'm breathing.

"I'd—" Her eyes shoot up somewhere around the room, and she freezes, then smiles a little too widely. "Bon! You made it."

"Hey! Did I miss him again? Please tell me I didn't." I hear my little sister's voice somewhere in the distance.

"No, you haven't. He's here." Maeve scoots to the side as Lainey comes into view. "Later, O." She smiles softly, eyes glistening. As she stands, she mouths *please be safe,* then waves. And then she's out of sight.

I do my best to engage in whatever Elaina is telling me, but all I can think about is her saying, *I wish you were here.* And the sad look in her eyes as she stood up. I wonder if I made a huge mistake. If my selfish choice just impacted her in a way I never wanted it to. I'm not available. Period. The Marine Corps is my life, and it's been that way for seven years. There's no room for a relationship. No time. I see what having someone back at home does to some of the guys, and I don't want that. I don't want a life of waiting for Maeve. I want her to be happy with someone who's available, who can make her a priority, and who can be there for her, with her, every day. I'm not that guy. Not yet.

Over the last few months, it's been harder and harder not to tell her how I feel. How much I think about her. How often I pull out that little origami swan she made the day we met. Even though I know I shouldn't.

I was selfish today. I said what I was thinking. And now, I wish I could take it back.

5 /

anywhere.
everywhere.

maeve

august, 7 years ago

THIS ISN'T how I imagined seeing him in person again, especially since we've spent the last several months avoiding the comment he made about kissing me.

His shoulders are slightly slumped, though he's trying to put on a brave face. His father died suddenly days ago, and I insisted on flying from Los Angeles with Bon. We moved there right after graduation, and I think this is the first time in the last three months that she's regretted that decision. She's been quiet, much too quiet, and I have a feeling she's shutting down.

My eyes are glued to Owen, even though it's Bonnie's hand I'm holding. His eyes are dull, and the scruff on his face shows it clearly hasn't been shaved in days. He's hardly looked up, other than when he gave the eulogy, which was heartbreaking. The urge to reach out to him is so strong, but he still doesn't know, and I'm on my own with this knowledge that we're meant to be. That I'm his in every way imaginable.

• • •

THE SUN IS JUST GETTING ready to set when I walk out to the backyard after ensuring Elaina is sound asleep in her bedroom. It was a long day for her, and I didn't leave her side until minutes ago when her soft snoring told me she wouldn't be awake again anytime soon.

I don't feel him until I've sat on the step, the chill chasing the warmth up my spine.

"Sunshine."

One word. That's all it takes from this man and the Earth ceases to spin. My heart threatens to beat through my ribcage. My grip on the edge of the step tightens as I hold my breath and listen for his footsteps. One heartbeat. Two. Then he's here and the wood creaks beneath his weight as he settles next to me.

"Hello, Owen." What a stupid greeting. "I didn't know you were out here. I can go, if you'd like some privacy." I move to stand, but he takes hold of my hand and keeps me low to the floor beside him, shaking his head. "Okay. I'll stay then."

He lets my hand go, flexing his fingers before running them up and down his leg as if he's scrubbing away the memory of touching me.

We're both silent for a few minutes. My hands are in knots on my lap, and his hang loosely as his elbows rest on his knees.

"Is Lainey asleep?" His voice is raspy and quiet, so unlike the roaring confidence I often hear on his calls with Bon, and when he talks to me, too.

"Yeah, she fell asleep about half an hour ago." We both keep our gazes locked on the backyard in front of us.

"You know, he taught me how to throw a ball right there." One finger rises to point straight ahead where we've been looking. "And he used to have a vegetable garden over there." He waves his hand over to the right, where a worn, raised garden bed sits. "He always made sure we grew potatoes. Said it made him feel closer to his family, to his Irish roots." His brows remain close together, his face so clearly full of tension as every muscle seems to tighten as he speaks. There's a tone in his voice I've never heard, not even when he seems to need cheering up while deployed. This feels different. It feels... painful. Hopeless.

"Go on." I reach for the hand closest to me, surprising myself, then further surprised by the fact that he lets me link our fingers together. It should feel monumental to be holding his hand like this, but all I feel is the weight of his loss. All I want to do is to take it away.

"He wasn't feeling well, so he went to have a nap while I took Ma to the store. The stroke was so massive, we wouldn't have been able to get him to the hospital fast enough even if we'd been there." He squeezes my hand a little tighter, and I squeeze back, shutting my eyes tightly when I hear his sniffle. "Fuck, he was the best dad. I don't think I ever told him that."

"He knew, Owen. Your dad knew you loved him." He turns his head and meets my gaze head on, those deep green eyes looking almost muddy with the fogginess of this loss clouding them. A tear rolls down my cheek, and he reaches up with his free hand to wipe it away. "I'm sorry. I don't know why I'm the one crying. I shouldn't—"

"Don't apologize for showing how you feel, Maeve. At least one of us is feeling something. Fuck, I haven't even cried yet. What the fuck does that say about me, right?" His broad shoulders tense, then drop slightly in a subtle shrug, his gaze darting back to the backyard as he turns his body. The gesture is slight, but it brings with it a subtle shift in the atmosphere as he inches toward me until his leg touches mine, our hands clasped together on my lap.

"It says you're not ready yet. And that's okay, Owen." I lick my lips, feeling completely unprepared and unqualified to comfort him, but my mouth keeps moving, anyway. "Your parents visited often. I really liked your dad. He was funny and kind, and I swear his eyes sparkled when he talked about you. The pride in his voice was a visceral living thing, like it had its own arms and legs. He adored you and Bon." I take a deep breath, feeling slightly unsure of how to speak about a man I only knew for a few years but who felt more like a father figure to me than any of the men my mum brought home when we were kids. "She was his princess and his best friend. He worried about her so much. Wanted to protect her, you know? But you, Owen? He was in awe of you. Inspired by you. He talked about you like you had been the one to lasso the moon and hang it in the sky yourself."

I'm about to keep going when he pries his hand away from mine and wraps his arms around me, turning me so my head is in the middle of his chest. His scent hits my nose, and I don't hide the depth of the breath I take. He smells like leather and wood with a hint of mint, and the combination shouldn't work, but on him, it's heavenly.

"Thank you, *fengári mou*." His heart is a steady thrum beneath my ear, and his arms pull tighter around me as his cheek rests on top of my head. Our size difference has never been as obvious as it is right now, but somehow this feels just right.

"All I want is to be like him one day. To make my kids feel as loved as he made me feel." My insides twist at the thought of Owen as a dad. I do my best not to imagine myself as the woman next to him and his brood of beautiful blonde-haired and green-eyed children, but I fail. We sit in the silence of a summer evening, listening to the crickets until Owen speaks again.

"Want to come somewhere with me?"

Anywhere. Everywhere.

I nod silently as we part ways.

"Meet me at my truck in a few minutes." He walks into

the house, and after a few seconds I do too, grabbing a sweater and my phone in case Bon needs me.

When I climb into the passenger seat, he tosses something into the back. We drive in silence, nothing but the low twang of country songs coming through the speakers as the sun sets behind us. Within twenty minutes, we're at a beach. Owen exits the truck, grabs whatever was in the back seat, and motions for me to join him.

We walk down a quick path together, and he has a red plaid blanket tucked beneath his arm. We place it on the sand and sit next to one another, still not speaking.

"I hope this is okay. I just like the sound of the waves sometimes. It's steady, but never the same, you know?" He keeps his eyes on the ocean as I look around, noticing we're the only ones here.

"Yeah. I get that." I expect him to go back to being silent, but his voice is clear over the waves.

"Do you think Elaina is going to be okay? Does she need anything?" The way his voice cracks nearly breaks me. This giant of a man, Marine, trained fighter, is here, sitting on a blanket, holding on by a thread because he's so worried about his baby sister.

"She's been working a lot, but she's also been seeing her therapist twice a week and doing yoga regularly. She's eating, and she seems to be sleeping okay. I used to check in on her at night after she opened up about her past, so I think I'll go back to doing that now." Maybe I'm saying too much, but with every word I say, his shoulders seem to relax a bit more.

"You'd do that? Check on her?" He turns his face toward me, the last of the sun's rays making his green eyes shine as he stares at me with an intensity I can't understand.

"Yeah. Of course. I remember what it was like back then, and I don't want her to go back to that dark place. She's incredibly quiet when she cries, and I won't have her doing that alone." I swallow down the self-conscious feeling rising inside me as he stares, unblinkingly. "Char calls her every day, so Bon will be well distracted with her tales of graduate school in London, and Charlie will let me know if she senses anything off about their conversations. If Bon stops taking care of herself, I'll step in. We both will." I seal that promise with a smile, hoping that it also communicates to him that I see his concern, his love for his sister, and his kind heart.

He nods, lips in a straight line, and I swear the man is going to need severe dental intervention if he doesn't loosen his jaw. "Thank you," he mutters.

We sit, letting the comfortable quiet surround us for a while, the sound of the waves soothing something in me. I close my eyes and hope it's having the same effect on Owen.

"I think about you every day, you know?" At first, I think maybe he's talking to his dad, so I stay still and quiet, but then he keeps going. "Your blue eyes and your smile are the last things I think about before I go to sleep. Every night. For the past three years."

My whole body goes stiff. He shakes his head lightly as if rearranging his thoughts, his eyes still on the water.

"I think about the day I told you I wanted to kiss you. I wonder if I made a mistake because you weren't ready to hear that, and sometimes I wish I could take it back. But I meant it. I meant what I said."

It's as if I've forgotten how to breathe, and even though the midsummer air is lukewarm, it's suddenly stifling. Too thick. My words are so quiet I'm not sure he hears them. "You didn't make a mistake."

The way his eyes immediately dart to mine tells me he heard what I said, but all he does is stare at me like I'm a puzzle he can't solve.

Not knowing what else to do in this never-ending silence and feeling too warm with my hair sitting heavily on my neck, I reach up to wrap it in a ponytail. I swear there is fire in Owen's eyes.

I don't have time to register the movement. Even if I had, the sheer force of his body slamming against mine stuns me.

His hand goes to my ponytail as his body pushes me until my back hits the blanket, my gaze forced to meet his as he tugs on my hair.

"What are you doing?" The words slip out on a gasp, and I close my eyes, suddenly unable to look at his face. Owen's body covers mine like my favorite heavy blanket during a London winter. I welcome the feeling of his body on mine like this. I relish the feeling of it. Pray he never moves away.

This is clearly some kind of dream. I must be feverish and hallucinating.

"I don't know what I'm doing. Trying not to lose my mind? Because when you look at me with those big doe eyes of yours, tell me you're taking care of my sister, and smile at me like you actually see me, all I want is to bury myself deep inside of you and never leave."

Bollocks. What have I gotten myself into? If I ever wake up from this, I'm going to write down every last detail and relive this dream as many times as possible. I'll write sonnets about it. Describe the way his breathy voice sounds with words like gruff, hoarse, throaty. *The way the sound goes straight to my core, the warmth of it spreading all over me like a wildfire.*

Feeling brazen because, if this isn't real, I might as well do what I want, I open my eyes. "What are you waiting for?" Our noses touch, and suddenly, he's the literal air I breathe. I expect his lips to crash into mine. I expect him to push off the blanket and walk away. I expect a camera crew to pop out from behind the trees and tell me this was all a very elaborate prank. I don't expect what happens next.

"Tell me you want this." His lips are so close to mine that I can feel the words on my skin as he says them.

I swallow, suddenly forgetting how to speak.

"Say it, Maeve. Or don't, and we'll leave right now and forget this ever happened. But if you say you want me like I want you, I'm gonna kiss you, and I'm not gonna stop until we're both out of breath. So, what will it be?" My mouth goes dry. My panties disintegrate. My mind goes blank.

"I want this," I somehow manage to whisper, and then his lips are on mine. They're softer, fuller, more demanding than I have imagined every night for the past three and a half years. He kisses me like I'm his lifeline, like he's been drowning and needs this in order to take his next breath, like he's been as desperate to feel this as I have.

"Repeat," he grumbles against my mouth, but I can't stop kissing him.

"I want you, Owen." He licks from my earlobe to my pulse point, sucking the spot as I squirm against him, looking for friction. "Please..." I'll beg, if he wants me to. I'll do anything to never wake up from this. He shifts us so we're both on our sides, and his hands slide up the bottom of my shorts.

Oh god, his bare hands are on my bare ass, and I don't know how to act right now.

We move in a chaotic blur, our bodies intertwined as we twirl around the blanket. Clothes are strewn every which way while we explore each other hungrily, never wanting to let go. We seem lost in a trance, like this must be a dream, and if we break contact, then all of this, us like this, will cease to exist.

And in the end, that's exactly what happens.

6 /
goodbye, not
goodnight.

owen

august, 7 years ago

THE WHOLE THING is chaos as we rip each other's clothes off. Fuck, I need her. It should scare me how much I need her, but I don't fucking care right now.

Once we're both naked, I pull back so I can take her in. Goddamn, she's perfect. The full moon casts a cool glow on her creamy skin, and I know this is officially a new core memory for me. Maeve, splayed out on a blanket, naked. And she wants me. She fucking wants *me*.

When I look back up at her face, the blush on her cheeks and the look of uncertainty washes across her features.

Oh no. None of that. Not on my watch.

"You're fucking perfection, *fengári mou.*"

I dive in, taking one of her pebbled nipples into my mouth, and her breathy moan nearly has me coming on this blanket. She arches into me and my heart beats even faster knowing she's giving in to this. Giving in to us.

"Are you wet for me, Maevey?" I ask as I switch to her other nipple.

"Yes!" she nearly screams when I nip her. Fuck, her body responds to every touch.

I move down her torso, tasting her skin, inhaling her scent. I leave soft kisses on her inner thighs, reveling in the way her knees spread wider for me. I rub the tip of my nose against her clit, and she gasps, bucking her hips. I look up to find her wide eyes on me.

"Okay?" I let my breath hit her soaking wet pussy. Something between a laugh and a moan leaves her mouth.

"Fuck, yes," she squeals, and I smile before running my tongue up her slit, sucking lightly on her clit as she squirms beneath me. I pause very, very reluctantly as her moans get louder.

"I'm gonna need you to be a little quieter for me, Maevey. We don't want any passersby getting curious and coming to check on what these noises are, now do we?"

A softer moan leaves her when I run my thumb over her opening, dragging her wetness to her clit and applying pressure there.

"Can you be quiet for me, *fengári mou*?"

"Yes, Owen," she whispers, blue eyes meeting mine.

"Such a good fucking girl." She whimpers in response, fists clutching the blanket as I feel the effect of my words, her pussy dripping at my praise.

I fuck her with my tongue until her pants become desperate. I push one finger slowly into her, immediately feeling my greedy cock ache with the need to be inside her. Her breathing slows as her body gets used to being stretched. She relaxes, and her breaths come back to a shallow pant. Then, I add a second finger, curling them both as I find the spot that will take her over the edge.

My tongue circles her clit again, and in seconds she's throwing an arm over her mouth, muffling her screams as she comes. Her other hand looks for purchase on my head, but my hair is too short, so she has nothing to hold on to. As her fingers relax and her legs drop on the blanket, I kiss my way back up her body.

I reach for my pants, keeping my body on top of hers, and pull out my wallet, thanking the fucking angels above for the condom Rafael put in there against my will. I make quick work of putting it on and line myself up to her core.

Checking in one more time because I need to know for sure that she wants this, I brush the hair off her face with one hand as I hold myself up with my other arm. "I gotta ask you one last time. Do you—"

"Yes, fuck, yes, I want this," she cuts me off, both hands going to my cheeks, and the desire in her eyes is clear. "I want this more than anything. I want *you* more than anything."

I definitely don't need any more reassurances after that. I push the head of my cock in, but fuck, she's so goddamn tight, so I pull back, watching her for any sign of discomfort. When I inch in a bit more, she tucks her face into my neck, sinking her teeth into my shoulder with a whimper.

"Fuck, you feel so good. Too good." Her body relaxes, another moan spilling out of her parted lips. "You like it when I talk to you." I don't ask; her pussy grips me tighter, and the way her moans become louder when I praise her tell me. "You need me to tell you how perfect and tight you feel? How badly I've wanted you?" Another moan, and I push in a little further.

When I'm in to the hilt, I kiss from her shoulder to her earlobe, giving us both a minute to catch our breaths. I brush my nose against hers, laying a soft kiss on her lips.

"Okay?" And fuck if her eyes don't light up at the question.

"Yes, Owen." Hearing those words for the second time, I know for certain that it's the best thing she's ever said to me. My new favorite words coming from her lips strung together. I want to hear, *yes, Owen,* every day for the rest of my goddamn life.

I pull out almost all the way and push back in slowly. Her lips part on a gasp, so I do it again, a little faster this time, gauging how she's feeling. "You're incredible, sunshine. Better than I've ever imagined." I kiss a spot under her ear, licking a slow circle there that has her mewling. "Perfect for me, like I knew you'd be."

My words spur her on, and she arches her back, then wraps her legs around me. We move in sync with one another, her moans growing louder as I lose a piece of myself in her with every thrust. No, fuck that. I freely give it away to her. She can have it all. All of me. I'm hers.

"Shhh," I whisper against her lips. Her eyes narrow in annoyance as they meet mine. I chuckle, loving her little display of defiance as her moans quiet.

"That's my girl," I say, nipping at her jaw. I speed up my movements, and she gasps as her fingertips dig into my arms. I swallow her moans with a kiss, keeping my thrusts unrelenting.

She breaks the kiss on a gasp. "Owen! Oh fuck, Owen." She bites down on my shoulder again. I feel her tighten even more around me, and I completely lose it. My orgasm hits me so hard that I see stars, growling into her neck, willing this feeling to last forever.

We come down from our highs together, remaining in our embrace, panting and holding on to one another. It's as if she feels it too, this need to be connected, to not let go, because if we do, reality will sink in, and the spell will be broken.

I move quickly to dispose of the condom. When I get back to the blanket, Maeve has already got her bra and panties back on. She looks up at me, and there's wariness in her gaze. I give her space to redress, and quickly throw my clothes back on, but when she tries to get up off the blanket, I gently grab hold of her wrist. Her vulnerability may as well be painted in thick, dark streaks on her skin right now.

"Come here." I lay back on the blanket and spread one arm out, motioning for her to join me.

She moves closer, but before she settles next to me, she looks down at the blanket. "We don't have to, Owen."

"Please," I add when she still looks unsure whether to stay or go, though I'm not sure where she'd take off to this time of night in a town she's unfamiliar with.

She nods, lying next to me with nothing but her head touching my body. I let out a low chuckle and pull her closer to me, pulling her leg over mine until we're a human pretzel. I let out a deep breath, and she finally relaxes onto me, her hand settling right over my heart.

"Thank you," I whisper and feel her smile on my chest. I know she understands what I mean. That I'm not thanking her for sex, but for this. For just being here with me.

We lie silently, staring up at the night sky while I run my fingers through her hair. It's even softer than I had imagined, and the smell of her lavender shampoo is so soothing I nearly doze off. It's the most relaxed I've been in a long time, being here with her like this. But the moment my heart starts to feel settled, a warning bell goes off inside my brain, reminding me that this isn't real.

I stiffen, and she moves her hand off my chest. I don't stop her because I'm an asshole. An asshole who can't give her everything I want to give her right now. Who can't give her a future or a promise of more because I don't know what my tomorrow looks like. I'll be across the world for months, and then who knows where after that, if I even make it back. I can't make her wait for me. I can't ask that of her, and I won't. It's bad enough that Lainey and Ma already do that. I can't have one more woman waiting for me.

I clear my throat and let the inevitable words come.

She deserves better, and fuck... it nearly breaks me in half to walk away from her, but I have no other choice.

"Maevey, you know I care about you, but this can't

happen again. It won't." Now she's the one who goes rigid, moving her leg off mine.

"All right," she says quietly.

"I'm being deployed again soon. I don't know when I'll be back. The best thing for you to do would be to forget about me. We got this out of our systems, and now we have to let it go."

God, I'm such a fucking asshole.

"Of course." She sits up and smooths her hair down. "I didn't expect anything more, Owen. Why do you think I didn't want to cuddle? This doesn't have to mean anything. It was just sex." Her blue eyes are icy, but to her credit, she looks right into mine as she says all of this.

She stands and walks to the truck, effectively shutting down while shutting me the fuck up.

Maybe having her once will be enough. Maybe this will make her hate me enough to move on and not expect anything from me. Maybe that's exactly what I want. Maybe I'm just so full of shit that I can't even stand the sight of myself right now, so I avoid my reflection when I walk past the truck window.

When we get back to my parents' house, she calmly exits the truck, shutting the door gently. Ever in control. Before she opens the front door, she looks back at me.

"Goodbye, Owen." I can't find the words to speak, so I just nod.

Goodbye, Owen. Not goodnight. She's fucking done with me. Fuck.

7 /

she feels nothing.

owen

september, 5 years ago

I SAW HER TODAY. Granted, it was on a movie screen, and I wasn't expecting it, but there she was. She looks older, and somehow still so much like the nineteen-year-old girl I met five years ago.

Five years. How has this much time passed already?

My chest ached the whole time she was on the screen. And when she wasn't, I just kept waiting for the moment she'd be back.

Watching her in a movie was like being in a desert with no water. So desperate for it you imagine a lake in the distance, running toward it like your life depends on it, because it does. But it's not real. It's a mirage. There's no way to quench the thirst, not without the real thing; and I've been thirsty for her ever since that night at the beach two years ago.

The only time we talked was when I visited or called Lainey. We never crossed the line into having each other's numbers or me calling her directly. Lainey was always the buffer, the reason we even got to talk to each other at all.

Now I can't talk to either of them. Lainey put even more distance between us, as if moving to California wasn't enough. Ma says she hasn't been back home. I know just the thought of being in Marblehead probably feels like a dagger in her chest. I can't shake the feeling that my sister blames me for Dad's death—that maybe I was the cause of his stroke. And honestly? I don't think she's wrong.

Everything has felt wrong these past couple of years. Everything but my decision to move away from ground missions and pursue cyber security, which keeps me away from lengthy overseas deployments and any kind of physical danger. It felt cowardly at first, but I had put in my time. I'd had tough missions, lost friends, and saw some dark shit I do my best not to think about.

Through it all, she was the moon pulling me in like the tides. She was the reason I wanted to stay safe, and now she's the reason I want to do more with my life. Seeing her make her dreams happen is the next push I need to make myself better. To figure my shit out before I can go back to her with more than an apology and a hope for forgiveness that I know I don't deserve.

---

january, 15 months ago

She's avoided me all week, and I know she knows I'm here. My sister is her best friend. Of course, she knows. Though when I asked Lainey about Maeve, she didn't say much and told me she's not getting in the middle and that I "better fucking fix this." I'm sure as fuck trying.

Maeve hasn't been around when I'm in the building, and she hasn't joined Lainey and I on any of our touristy days in London. Not that I expected her to want to come hang out with us, but I've been itching to see her. Talk to her. Touch her.

I'm fucking terrified of what her reaction will be after all these years, but I need to be close to her.

I know that after years of silence, it's going to take work, and with the lie I told her that night on the beach, I wouldn't blame her if she never wanted to talk to me again. But I'm not going to let fear of rejection stop me. I'll do what it takes to just get to be near her again. It's all I've wanted for years.

Once I left the Marines, I started Aegis with my best friend and fellow Marine, Rafael. He's been working on the West Coast, growing the personal security side of the business while I stayed on the East Coast running the cyber security wing. Last year, someone made us an offer we couldn't refuse to buy the cyber software I developed, and we officially shut that part of the business down.

Since selling, I haven't had much to do, so Rafael invited me to come to London with him, knowing my little sister would be here. Lainey and I just finally sorted through our issues, and it feels good to have finally come clean to her about why I was out of touch for so long.

All that time and space left me convinced that she blamed me for Dad's death—like maybe the stress of my deployments was too much for him and caused the stroke, but I've had doctors and my therapist confirm that it's not the case. I'm good now, but that shit messed me up for a while.

So here we are. I've mended my relationship with my mom and sister, but Maeve is the missing piece. She's the final piece of this puzzle.

While we're here, Raf is going to be Maeve's bodyguard, and I'll be with her co-star, Adam. Or River. Seems he goes by both names. I'm sure she has feelings about me being here, but the opportunity to contribute to our company, and be close to my sister and, therefore, close to Maeve was just too good to pass up.

We're meeting at Maeve's apartment, and I'm nervous as all fuck. I've checked out every corner of the building with

Rafael, but we have a few things to go over before I'm officially on duty with Adam. The building is very secure, but Maeve has had some fans do really crazy things to get to her lately, so we're taking extra precautions with both of them, and they've been laying pretty low until filming starts.

I know she has some douchebag boyfriend, and I wonder if maybe he's here, and that's why she hasn't been around. He's a scrawny asshole named Lionel or some shit. I've never met him, and I hope I never do, but I've seen him in pictures with her. I hate the way he smiles so smugly with her in his arms. Fuck. I can't think about that now. I gotta get in there and see her. For the first time. In seven years.

I knock twice, then wait a few minutes and listen for any noise. When she doesn't answer, I assume she's not here and use the key Raf gave me yesterday. I walk into the apartment as I pull my suitcase in behind me, the wheels loudly moving over the tiled floor.

"Hello?" I hear her voice, and every cell in my body responds. My skin tingles. My heart races. My mouth goes dry. "Is that you, Raffy? I was just—" She stops when she sees me.

Maeve comes into view, and I feel the tide rolling in as I'm again pulled to her. I don't think, I just do.

In three wide strides, I reach her and pull her up and into me, that lavender smell filling my nostrils, making me feel like I'm finally home. Her arms don't fully wrap around me, but I feel her hands on my back for a fraction of a second, and the sensation fills me with blind, reckless hope.

"Hey, sunshine."

She flinches at my use of the nickname, and I feel that hope leak out of me like air in a punctured balloon.

Fuck. This isn't off to a good start.

When we separate from one another, her face is blank, devoid of emotion. "Hello, Owen."

She seems to have her mask on, and it feels like we're back

to the first day we met before I flustered her enough to get the facade to come down—before I saw the sweet girl hiding under this veneer of coolness, decorum, and control.

Her arms are crossed across her chest, a clear way to say *fuck off* with her body.

"Hi Maeve. You look...You, uh—how are you?"

Sweet baby Jesus, save me. What the fuck am I doing?

"Fine, thanks. I assume the same is true for you based on what Bon's told me." I stand there, just taking her in. She's so fucking pretty still. Prettier, even. And everything about the way she's looking at me tells me she probably wants to be anywhere but here.

"I'm sorry, Maeve." It just slips out. I don't mean to say it, but I mean the sentiment.

"Excuse me?" She cocks her head to the side, confusion splattered across her face.

"I'm sorry about how things were left between us. I can tell that you really hate me, and I don't want that. I want you to know how sorry I am. I want you to know everything, and if you give me the chance I can expl–"

"No, thank you." She uncrosses her arms and sets them at her sides, elbows locked, hands in tight fists for a moment before she relaxes them again. "I don't need your apology or your explanations. And I don't hate you. I don't feel anything when it comes to you, Owen. You're my best friend's brother. We were... friends? I don't know. We talked occasionally while you were deployed, and we shagged once. It's done. It was a long time ago. I don't have any feelings about any of it, so please keep yours to yourself."

Fuck, this is so much worse than I thought. I'd rather have her hate me than be indifferent to me. She feels nothing?

We stand there for a while, just looking at one another.

"We obviously can't avoid one another any longer, seeing as how you've made amends with Bon. So, let's just be...civil. Cordial." She looks so different and yet exactly the same. This coldness in her eyes is new, though. There was always at least a little warmth hidden behind the wall of ice she used to protect herself, but now? There's nothing warm about the way she's looking at me. "I have no interest in being your friend, but your sister is important to us both. We can act like adults about this, can't we?"

I think I nod.

She clearly doesn't want to be here and doesn't want to be near me, and this realization has me questioning every decision I've made to get here. To get to her.

"Your place is across the hall. Adam will show you when he's back." She turns away, walking toward the living room. "The guys should be here soon. I don't think you need me here for your debrief, so I'm going to work out and get out of your way. Goodbye." She scurries off like the place is on fire, and I'm left staring at the door.

She doesn't hate me. She feels nothing for me.

Her words hit me all over again, like ice being dumped over my head and I have to remind myself to breathe through it.

I sit on the couch, waiting for the other two guys to arrive, and contemplate every second of my interaction with Maeve. She definitely doesn't want me here. I know we haven't spoken to one another for years, but she's gonna have to hear me out at some point. She needs to know how I feel and everything I've done to get here. Even if, in the end, she still doesn't want me, I have to give this my best shot. Somehow.

8 /
dig, dig, dig.

maeve

january, 15 months ago

IT'S NOT until I've reached the gym that I clue in to the fact that I don't have my runners or a sports bra on, so I settle for a bra-less yoga session and meditate on just how much distance I'm going to keep from Owen James.

When he touched me, my skin was on fire. My heart stopped beating at the way he said *sunshine*. I don't want to be this affected by him. I want exactly what I told him. To feel nothing. To be indifferent.

IT'S MOSTLY WORKING. In the last few weeks, we've had the occasional 'family dinner' together with all of our friends, but I keep away, making sure to say hello and ask how he is before promptly moving along to talk to someone— anyone—else.

I can always feel his eyes on me though, and I hate it. Every time he uses a nickname for me, I have to take a deep breath to calm myself down. But it's not like it used to be.

This isn't me having a teenage crush on my best friend's brother. This is me despising every last fiber of Owen James for what he did to me. For taking a part of me and then making it mean nothing. For how he made me feel when he left then forgot all about me. For how worried I was for him. For all the times I sat staring at the computer waiting for a call to come through.

Now I resent that he's here, breathing my air and making it feel like there's none left for me whenever he's in the same room.

———

december 31, 4 months ago

It's been eleven months, six days, and roughly nine hours since Owen walked into my flat in London. I've kept up my cool, calm, collected exterior. I've avoided being alone with him at all costs. I even nearly convinced myself that being around him could feel normal and not at all painful. Nearly convinced myself that what happened between us wasn't a big deal. Nearly.

There was one thing that made the facade slightly easier to maintain, and that was Lincoln, but I couldn't keep up that charade anymore. He wasn't even sad when I broke things off. He was angry at the way this would look right before he started promoting his next film, and he's been angry since. Dating fellow actors has its pros and cons. Pros: they get your insane schedule, need for privacy, and general lifestyle. Cons: they can take everything personally or, worse, take it as something that can affect their own careers. Lincoln did both.

Thoughts of Owen kept slipping into my head, competing for space among all the other chaos — Mum's latest man drama, the extra therapy, meetings with my agent about the kinds of roles I'm being booked for, trying to keep up with an unreasonable schedule, and Lincoln. I've at least eliminated one of those things for now. It had to be Linc, since Owen doesn't seem to be going back to the East Coast. Nor does he seem to be leaving my brain space anytime soon.

Lincoln will get over it. He'll find someone who cares about how expensive his latest sports car is and who likes listening to voicemails, because that person certainly isn't me. I know he knows it, too. We were never quite right. But the paps loved us. We look great together, I'll admit it, but that's not enough. Not nearly enough. Not when he's not a broody, 6'4" former Marine with green eyes and a dimpled sideways smile that lives rent-free in my thoughts.

Owen is making LA his permanent home, probably to be closer to Elaina, Rafael and the business. Seeing him constantly hasn't gotten any easier, and knowing he's going to be so close has me on edge.

Elaina just got engaged in the exact same spot where she met Adam last year—in my kitchen at my annual New Year's Eve party. That means Owen is here, and I'm back on my avoidance game. So far, so good. I've found a quiet spot to gather my thoughts before I go back to playing hostess.

Looking out at one of the flower gardens, I feel something like longing clawing at me. For what? I'm not sure. My best friend just got engaged to the love of her life, and I'm sickeningly happy for her. Truly, I'm so thankful Elaina and Adam found one another.

But...?

I feel goosebumps on the backs of my arms and brace myself.

"Hey." My ears would know that voice anywhere. And so would the rest of my body, which lights up at the rumbly sound. He steps closer and the heat of his body is suddenly next to mine. "Looks like you're deep in your thoughts."

"I was thinking about how happy I am for Bon and Adam. They're perfect." I force a smile, and it surprises me how genuine it is. Thinking about them always makes me smile, though.

"Yeah." He takes a deep breath, looking down at his feet. I still haven't looked up at him. I can't. "I thought this was where you and Luke were headed. You know, marriage, kids, the whole nine."

I roll my eyes. He refuses to call Lincoln by his name. I know he knows it, even if they've never met. "Those things weren't on the cards for Lincoln and me. They're not on the cards for me at all, actually." And then I decide to dig my own grave. "What about you, Owen? I thought you'd be wifed up with a whole brood of kids by now."

Dig, dig, dig.

He hums, his feet shifting the stones beneath them. "Me too."

Stunned doesn't begin to do justice to how his answer makes me feel.

He wants to be married? With kids?

"What's stopping you?"

Dig, dig.

"The one. She's not ready for me yet." He turns his head toward me. My cheeks heat, but I don't look up. He couldn't mean...

No, you idiot. He doesn't mean you. You're his little sister's best friend, the girl he slept with once, then walked away from without a second thought.

"You think she's out there?"

Dig, dig, dig, dig...

"Oh yeah. No doubt. When she's ready, we'll get to work on that brood." I hear the smile in his voice, but I don't avert my eyes from the lamppost I've been staring at since he arrived.

"You want lots of kids?"

Dig, dig.

"As many as she'll give me. I'll raise a whole football team with her, if she'll let me." His voice is more serious now, and I feel his gaze still on me. My hands are in tight fists, my nails digging into my palms to give myself a different pain to focus on because the one in my chest is so intense, I'm not sure I'll be able to take another deep breath ever again, because this moment? This is the moment I realize Owen James should never, ever be mine.

part two
now

9 /
the only thing that brings me joy these days.

maeve

My skin crawls at the thought of Catherine being here. My mother isn't warm and fuzzy. No, she is glacial and sharp. Where my best friend grew up with Eva James, baker of muffins and giver of cheek pats, which make you feel like the only person in the room, I grew up with a real-life ice queen.

Mum never wanted kids, but she ended up pregnant and without prospects, so she trapped the first rich guy she could find and pretended we were his. Since she was pregnant with twins, an early delivery was expected, and no one questioned the timing. The only dad Charlie and I ever knew was enamored enough to not question it, even if neither of us shared any of his darker features.

I hate thinking about what she did to him. About what she did to us when he finally left. All because she couldn't commit to one man for longer than a couple of years at a time.

She always wanted more, constantly reaching for the next exciting adventure as she called her always short-lived relationships.

Taking a deep breath in through my nose, I count to ten and release the air slowly, imagining it's all the resentment I feel toward the person who has never loved me and my sister more than she loves new, shiny things. I repeat a few more times until it actually starts to feel like the sad feelings are being expelled from my body with the air in my lungs.

I ignore her message, like the previous handful she's sent sporadically over the last six months.

Things have finally settled down for me since we got back from London, and though I no longer need a bodyguard with me 24/7, Owen was concerned about some creep who kept messaging me on all of my social accounts. Being the cyber security specialist, he's here now, making sure my Wi-Fi is secure and checking on the security system.

Right now, however, I just wish he would see himself out of my house. Out of my life. But nope. Here he comes, looking like he just stepped off a shoot for Sports Illustrated with his perfectly wavy, dirty blond hair. Yeah. Owen has hair now, and it's annoyingly always unintentionally perfectly mussed. I know men who pay hairstylists good money for hair Owen surely doesn't appreciate.

The front door shuts, and the smell of chocolate chip muffins fills the room.

"Look who I found trying to break in." Owen swings his hand over his shoulder, thumb pointing behind him.

"Oh, fuck off, you big burly beast! I know the code for the gate. It's not my fault you've changed it again, you overprotective bear!" Bon's sweet voice and colorful language might be my favorite combination, second only to the mix of dark and milk chocolates in her muffins.

"Mae, please tell your bodyguard to chill the fuck out."

She hands him the plate as she removes her purse, then takes her shoes off.

"Not my bodyguard. And he's *your* brother, love. I think you have a better chance of him listening to you," I say from my seat on the couch. "I've been trying to get him to cool off with the codes, but it's no use. Do you know he changes my Wi-Fi password constantly, too? I was trying to watch a sexy movie the other night, and I got kicked off right as it was getting good and raunchy."

I don't miss the way his ears turn red at the tips. Teasing Owen James might be the only thing that brings me joy these days. It sure is more fun than ignoring him all the time since his persistent ass doesn't seem to be going anywhere.

"That was you? I thought someone was trying to hack in. Those sites are littered with spam and viruses, Maeve!" he practically barks at me, then takes a muffin and walks toward the stairs. "Enjoy your girl time. I'm changing the password before I go home. Call me if you have any other issues with the security system, yeah?"

I nod and wave him off with a smile I hope looks convincing. I don't know how much more of this proximity I can handle. It's one thing to see him occasionally at dinners, but in my house? With no one else around? It's overwhelming. But he insists on being the one to handle anything to do with my security. He's like this with his sister as well, so I don't think much of it.

Bon sits next to me on the sofa, the plate of muffins on the coffee table. "Hi, Mae." Her face softens as she takes me in. I'm sure she can see the stress all over my face. I hear the back door click shut, and I know Owen will just see himself out once he's finished. "You ready to tell me?" I should have known she'd read it all over me. I've been an uneasy mess since Owen walked into my flat in London.

I nod, and she moves in closer, taking my hand in both of hers. Her green eyes are kind, patient, but worried. She sensed something was off so long ago now, and she's probably been worried for no reason, which makes guilt churn in my stomach.

"I'm not sure where to start, if I'm honest." I swallow the lump in my throat. "Everything feels...off lately. I've always thrived in this world of constant motion, constant change, but I'm finding myself wondering what it would be like not to be in LA, London or New York for once. I wonder what not having a schedule would feel like."

She smiles and takes a muffin for herself. I want to swat her hand away because these are mine, after all, but she made them, so I hold back. She remains silent, waiting for me to keep going.

"That little break in Malibu was nice, but it wasn't enough. I think I'm ready to take a step back. To reassess. I've always been married to my career, and I've loved every minute of it until..."

"Until you didn't?" Bon's kindness has the hot tears stinging my eyes wanting to fall. I hate crying in front of anyone, but the people I love most always seem to pull the tears out of me so easily.

"Yeah," I say. "It just feels like it's time for a change, but I have *no* idea what to do to actually make that happen, or where to start. And what if I take a step back, and I hate that, too? It's not like I know what I want to do to replace the chaos that is my life at the moment."

"Wanna make a list? It worked for me!" She looks at me wide-eyed and bushy tailed, probably with a notepad and pen stashed in her back pocket.

"I remember. It was my idea!" I chuckle as I shake my head. "I don't think I need a list, babe. I think what I need is to get so far away from my everyday life that I can figure out just exactly who I am and what I want, you know?" At this, her whole face changes, and she frowns, blinking rapidly.

"Okay. Wow. I don't think I saw that coming. I mean,

you're the most self-assured person I know, Mae. It's one of the reasons you keep succeeding at what you do, you know?" I see the worry in her eyes again, and I hate it. I don't want to be a burden to anyone with my existential crisis, or whatever this is. "You've always known exactly what you wanted, and look at you! You went for it. You made it happen."

"Well, things don't feel the same anymore. They haven't for a while, and I need to figure out what my next steps are going to be. I love what I do, and I don't want to stop making movies, but…" I look down at her hand, now grasping my own tightly and look up at her. "I don't think it's *all* I'm meant to do. I mean, what else am I doing with my life, you know? Am I going to be married to my career forever? It doesn't feel like there's room for anything else. What am I missing because I'm so busy all the time?" I sigh, hating the feeling of uncertainty that clouds everything.

"What can I do to support you?" My sweet Bon, always ready to step into action.

"You're already doing it. You're here." I shrug, but I mean what I say. I just want to be surrounded by my friends, my family.

My best friend nods, then we hug for a long, long time. When she leaves, I feel a little lighter having shared this part of my life with her. She still doesn't know exactly what happened between me and her brother, but since I decided to pretend it never happened anyway, I don't think she needs to. I hate keeping any secrets from her. It's been a heavy weight to carry all these years, but I'm not ready to put any potential cracks in our friendship over a man who blatantly told me he didn't want me.

10 /
he hugs me far more than i would like.

owen

YEP. She still hates me. She's civil enough with her *hellos* and *goodbyes*, but she won't be caught in a room alone with me. How else do I know she hates me? She just brought up watching porn. In front of my sister. I absolutely cannot get turned on thinking about Maeve watching porn while my sister is within 100 feet of me. Evil woman, that Maeve.

But here I am, changing her password for the tenth time this week, making sure she's being as safe as possible because some creep decided to start sending her dick pics on every possible social media platform. He somehow got a hold of her email addresses too. We know it's the same asshole because he's got her name tattooed on his Johnson. It's fucking weird. And if we ever find this idiot, I'll be the one to personally break his nose.

I've been trying to think of ways to be around her, but I'm pretty sure changing her password isn't gonna cut it. There has to be another way for me to cut through this wall of indifference she's built around herself.

My phone rings with an unknown number and I groan before picking it up. Raf loves to remind me that it could be a client, but I don't like talking to people like he does, so I avoid it at all costs.

I pick up reluctantly. "Hello?"

"Yes, hi, is this Owen James?" a strange voice asks.

"This is him."

"Mr. James, my name is John Perez. I represented Clayton and Monica Moore."

———

I DRIVE STRAIGHT to Raf's once the call ends. I don't say goodbye to Maeve and Lainey. I just take off and call him on my way asking if he has any cold beer because I'm gonna need one. Or five.

When I arrive, he greets me with an open bottle and his arms outstretched.

"I'm not ready for a hug, Raf. Can we just sit for now?"

He looks like a wounded puppy when I walk past him, but he follows me into his living room and sits on the chair while I take the couch.

"All right, so if you don't need a hug to go with your beer, what do you need?" Raf is the kind of guy you want on your side in all ways. As someone I was deployed with, as a Marine, as a business partner, and as a friend. He's just all-around good, even if he hugs me far more than I would like.

"I guess I just need you to listen, for now? I found myself in a…situation today." I pause, looking down at the cold bottle in my hand, peeling the label off. "You remember Clayton?"

"Yeah. Good guy. Intense as fuck, but he had some great dad jokes. And he was really good at karaoke. Remember when he did "My Heart Will Go On"? I'm pretty sure I cried." Okay, good. He at least remembers who I'm talking about. Clay was one of my closest friends when I was still a Marine.

Unlike me, he hadn't retired yet, and a few months ago he was killed in action.

"That's him, yeah." I take a deep breath to settle my heart-beat down, because what I'm about to say next doesn't feel real just yet. "Well, his wife was pregnant. Last time I spoke to him, he asked me to check in on her, which I did. She lives here in Cali, so that was part of the reason I wanted to be here. I knew she'd probably need some help now that she's a widow and about to become a new mom."

"That's really good of you, O. And I'm happy to help too, you know?"

"Yeah, man. I know. Thank you." I take a deep breath followed by a few gulps of my beer, needing the liquid courage for what's about to come out next. "Well, Monica died while giving birth. Apparently, she lost a lot of blood. I don't have all of the details yet." Raf looks up at me, wide-eyed as he shakes his head in disbelief. And I haven't even gotten to the crazy part yet.

"The baby made it," I continue. "But now she has no parents. No grandparents either. Monica was in the foster care system most of her life. So was Clay. It was how they met." My stomach starts to turn, my lunch from hours ago threat-ening to propel its way out of my body. "They didn't want the baby to go into foster care if anything ever happened to the two of them, you know?" I look up at Raf. He's still wide-eyed, elbows on his knees, waiting for me to get to the punch-line he has no idea is coming.

"They put me on their wills as the chosen caregiver for any of their future children. Clay asked me a couple of years ago when they got married and had decided to start trying for a baby." The lump in my throat is too big. I can't swallow it down. I can't breathe around it. I can't do anything but stare at the floor, trying to pull air into my lungs.

"Fuck, Owen. Are you telling me you just became a dad?" He looks as nauseous as I feel.

"Yeah, Raf. That's exactly what I'm telling you. The baby's a girl. She's healthy."

I haven't even finished the sentence before Raf is sitting next to me, both of his giant arms wrapped around me in the most awkward side hug of my life. I don't fight it. He's strong as fuck, and honestly, I should have seen this coming. After years of knowing Raf, and now running this business with him, I should have known he'd hug me one way or another.

"Owen. My dude. I know this is a lot, but you can do this. Wow. Shit, man. You're a dad now!"

I scoot as far away from him on the couch as I can, his words ringing in my ear.

"Well, it's not official yet..." I mumble into my beer bottle.

Raf rears his head back. "But you're doing it, right? You're gonna be her dad?"

I don't think before answering. "Of course, I am, Raf. I promised him. Swore to him I'd never let any kid of his go through the foster system like they did."

Raf sniffles, and I can't bring myself to look at him. He might be the softest man I've ever met, but the man is an absolute tank. "You're a good man, Owen. And you know I'm here for you. We'll all support you. Lainey, Adam, Maeve. Fuck, I'm sure even Chuck would step in to help. You're not doing this alone. All right?"

I nod, still unable to look up at him because now I feel my own eyes stinging with tears. "Thank you, Raf. Thanks for letting me come over and drop this on you. I haven't told anyone yet. Lainey was at Maeve's when I left there, but I didn't want to share this with both of them just yet."

"I get it. I'm here for you. You're my brother, you know that." And I do. Raf and Clay were my two closest friends when I was a Marine. Raf and I left at around the same time, but Clay never wanted to leave. I respected the hell out of him for it.

"Thanks, man. I'm gonna get going. Sorry to just drop in

like this and leave. I just need to get ready to drive down to San Diego tomorrow to start sorting this whole thing out." He pats me on the shoulder and takes my now empty beer bottle.

"No need to apologize. Do what you need to do, and let me know when you need anything. Anything, O. I mean it." Rafael stretches out his arms, silently asking if I need another hug, but I just shake my head lightly.

"Thanks, Raf. Appreciate you, man."

"Right back at you. Drive safe."

11 /
well, there's more.

owen

THE WHOLE EXPERIENCE IS SURREAL, like I'm watching myself walk into this hospital. I watch myself meet a baby who's a complete stranger to me but is also going to legally be my daughter one day.

She's so tiny and beautiful. I can't tell what color her eyes are yet, but I'd bet they'll be brown—just like her mom's—and she has Clay's blond hair. Holding her tiny body, something immediately shifts in me. Like this little baby just rearranged not only my external world, but something biological in me, too. I told Maeve I wanted kids, but I never imagined this. Obviously.

It's hard to digest all of this and I feel my stomach twist multiple times as if my body is actually processing this new reality in real time. It's a lot to take in.

I've been across the world, fighting battles not everyone agrees with, operating guns and vehicles most people wouldn't even dream of touching. I've cracked codes so complex entire teams of trained experts hadn't been able to. I've been held hostage. And yet, I've never felt so vulnerable, so unprepared, and so out of my league like I do right now as a lawyer and social worker talk at me about guardianship and diapers, custody and formula.

By the time I'm back in my truck, my brain feels fuzzy, so instead of driving home right away, I call the one person who's going to make this make sense. It rings three times, then her face pops up on my screen. Brown eyes with wrinkles around the edges that I've come to know as her happy Owen and Elaina lines because she's always got a smile for her kids.

"Hi, Mamá," I say before she has a chance to say anything.

"My boy. How are you? Where are you? In the truck? What's wrong? Your eyes aren't their happy green, they're a sad green. What happened *moro mou*?" It feels like my heart expands in my chest when I hear her call me that. *My baby.* She's always called me and Lainey that in her native Greek tongue.

"Before I answer you, can we loop Lainey in? I want to tell you both something." I start looking for my sister's contact before she can answer.

"*Skatá*," she mumbles. "Must be serious."

"It is serious. And I heard that, you potty mouth. I swear, you and your daughter–"

"Ma and her daughter what, Agamemnon?" Lainey picks up, effectively cutting me off from commenting on how much she loves her colorful language. "What's going on? Why did you call us both? Where are you? Are you okay?"

"Jesus, you two. I'm gonna tell you, if you ever stop with the questions." I huff out a breath, running my hand through my hair while I prepare to break this news to them. I'm met with twin scowls that quickly melt into twin worried looks.

"Ma, you remember Clayton? I brought him home with me once." Immediately, I see my mom's eyes soften as she remembers him.

"Of course. Lovely young man. Very serious, but then he'd

come out of nowhere with a joke! Your dad really liked him." She smiles at the mention of Dad. "Didn't he..."

"Yeah. He was killed in action a few months back." I swallow and force myself to keep going. He's not the only friend I've lost in the Marines, but he was the closest. "His wife, Monica, was pregnant. I've gone to visit her a couple of times." They both nod, still confused, but at least they're not interrupting me. "She, uh, she had the baby. A girl. She's so tiny." I'm getting off track here, so I clear my throat and get back to the point of this call. "Anyway, Monica, she didn't...didn't make it. There were complications during the birth and..."

"Oh, Owen. I'm so sorry." Ma reaches out her hand as though she can touch me through the screen, and even though she can't, I swear I feel her reassuring hand on me.

"That's so sad. What can we do? How can we help?" Lainey is always the first to jump into action when someone needs something, and right now, I'm just so thankful for these two.

"Well, there's more. Back when Clay and Monica were thinking about having kids, he asked me if I would be listed as the guardian for any of their future children. Both he and Monica were in the foster system, and they didn't want that for their own kids if something ever happened to them." I see both of their eyes widen as realization starts to sink in, as they assume what I'm about to say next. "Of course, I said yes. They were such good people. Anyway, I just met her. The baby. Julia. Her name is Julia." I clear my throat as Ma's and Lainey's eyes widen while they stand-by, waiting for me to continue. "Nothing's been signed yet, but I'm gonna... I'm getting... I'm gonna do everything I can to make sure she's taken care of."

Their sniffles are audible, Lainey openly letting the tears stream down her cheeks while Ma covers hers with her hands.

"Are you saying I'm about to become a grandma? A *Yia-Yia*?" My mom's voice cracks with emotion.

"I hope so. I can't let her go into the foster system. I can't." I shake my head, knowing that's simply not an option. I wasn't planning on kids right now, but it doesn't matter. She's as good as mine.

"Of course, not. We're here to help you, okay? Tell us what you need. What she needs. Anything."

"Thanks, Lainey. Honestly, I don't even know yet. Julia will be here at the hospital until she gets placed in an emergency foster home. The goal is for that to be very short term, just until I can take her home. I'm gonna have to come back here in a few days. I have to get some documents from home for the lawyer, and then we can get the ball rolling. I just needed to tell you two what's going on." The weight feels a little lighter now that I've told my mom and sister.

"Anything you need, my boy."

"Thanks, Ma. I'll keep you updated as things happen. I don't really want to tell anyone else about this just yet. Raf knows, so it's fine if you tell Adam but no one else, okay Lainey? Not yet?" The thought of Maeve hearing about this... Fuck. I've been trying so hard to get her to stop giving me the cold shoulder, and this definitely isn't going to help.

How am I supposed to convince her to give us a chance when I'm about to have a baby to take care of?

"Yeah, of course, Owen."

"Thanks. I love you both. I'm gonna head back now but I'll call you soon, all right?"

"Love you, big brother."

"I love you, *moro mou*."

I hang up the call and sit, staring at the trees lining the street I'm parked on. A million thoughts circling through my mind, and yet not a single particular one stands out. Everything I know is about to be turned upside down. At least I have a house to take this baby girl back to. A house I had bought with another intention, for another girl, for another kind of life, but this is my reality now.

I DON'T REMEMBER MUCH from the drive back to Ojai. I think I went into autopilot and let my brain focus on the road instead of all the jumbled thoughts inside my head. As soon as I step into my house, I'm heading for the shower. And once the hot water rushes over my skin, I feel my muscles relax for the first time all day.

I stumble into bed, letting my physical exhaustion from the driving and being so damn tense all day take over, dragging me into a restless sleep.

12 /
the icing on this insane cake.

maeve

SOMETHING IS DEFINITELY wrong with him. He walked in and grunted—actually grunted—at me. Owen is a pretty stoic guy. He's not smiley like Raf or even-keeled and generally nice like Adam. He's a little rougher around the edges with most people, but he's never been that way with me. Not once. Not until today.

He's only here because I texted him about the security system. Something started beeping and wouldn't stop, and he was adamant that I call him directly for these things, so I did. Well, I didn't call. It felt too personal, somehow. Too much like something we used to be, something we used to do. So, I texted. And now he's here in all of his grumpy glory.

"Can I do anything?" I ask his back, not at all watching how his muscles tense and ripple under his gray T-shirt. No. I would never.

He grunts a response, and my jaw drops in sheer disbelief. Maybe I made a mistake texting him. I thought we could handle this.

"I can call someone else, Owen. It's obvious you don't

want to be here, so don't worry about it." That gets his attention. He turns his head to glare at me over his shoulder, then immediately goes back to the security panel on the wall. The beeping stops, and he huffs out a loud breath, turning his body around to face me.

Neither of us speaks for several seconds, but I keep my stone face firmly in place.

"You will not be calling anyone else, Maeve. This is *my* responsibility, and I take care of my responsibilities. Got it?"

Oh, hell no, he did not just speak to me like this.

"No. I don't *got it.* This is not your responsibility. And *I* am *certainly* not your responsibility, so you can kindly see yourself out and not come back, thank you very much!"

He pinches the bridge of his nose with his thumb and index finger, shaking his head like he's the one who's pissed off. "Not today, Maevey. Please."

"You come into *my* house and speak to me like this, and now you want to make it seem like I'm the unreasonable one? I think not. I've tried, Owen. I've tried to be civil and nonchalant around you for over a year now, but you've just pushed me too far." I walk to the front door, noticing that he immediately follows me.

"And stop calling me Maevey. We're not friends anymore." I look up to see his shoulders have slumped, and I take in his face for the first time. He has dark circles under his normally bright green eyes. Today they're dull, devoid of their usual brightness.

"Do you mean that?"

Yes! No, of course not! Yes, absolutely. I can't stand to be around you and not have what we used to have, but I also can't do this. I can't not know what you're thinking and also not be able to ask you.

But I can't say any of that.

I settle for, "Yes, but only if you choose to keep up this

attitude. Ditch the angry bull act and I'll be nice to you again." I can see that it's on the tip of his tongue to question my choice of the word *again* because I haven't been particularly nice to him since we reconnected in London. But to his credit, he says nothing. And the more I look at him, the more I see that he's not angry. He's defeated, maybe. Exhausted, definitely.

"Yesterday was... There's just a lot going on right now. I'm sorry." His eyes travel over my face, and I hate that I feel saddened for him. I hate that my instinct is to ask him what's going on, to ask how I can help, to ask him to let me in. But I can't. I can't go there again. I won't.

"Okay." I swallow down all of the urges to make this more than a casual interaction between two acquaintances. "I hope... I hope things get better for you."

He nods, looking down at his feet, eyebrows scrunched together in a way that makes me think he's not hopeful that things will indeed get better.

"I'll see you in Vegas?" he asks when he finally looks up at me again. I nearly forgot we have Bon and Adam's bachelorette and bachelor party this weekend. No one is more surprised than me that they chose Las Vegas for this. I think it's some sort of act of rebellion for them both, though it is a joint party, so it's not like anyone's getting too rowdy. I wouldn't be surprised if those two nap before we go out and then call it a night before midnight.

I nod in response to his question. "Yeah. I'll see you in Vegas."

And with that, I let him go. The thought that there's something big going on with him eats away at me for the remainder of the day. The gut feeling that Owen needs help but won't ask for it nags at me, and it doesn't let up.

———

"I LOOK BLOODY RIDICULOUS." I screech as I look into the mirror in my giant suite. "I love it!" A laugh spills out of me as I take in my ebony wig, heart-shaped sunglasses and poofy white dress. The Doc Martens are the icing on this insane cake, though.

Bon insisted all the girls wear white dresses for her bachelorette tonight, so here we are. Me, Bon, Charlie, and Taylor, my stylist and friend for the past five years. Okay, so Taylor's not *technically* a girl, but he's far more interested in wearing dresses than suits.

"Maeve Howard, just what in the name of Dolly Parton is on your feet?" I knew Taylor would hate this, but I need two things tonight: to not be recognized and to be comfortable.

"Tay-Tay, you know I love you, but you've dressed me in skintight gowns and ungodly high heels for every single event in the last three months. Tonight, I want anonymity and comfort. And no one will suspect me in these boots, right?" His scowl softens a little, but only ever so slightly.

"At least your dress covers them." He tosses a hand over his shoulder, moving right along. "Mine, on the other hand, requires these fabulous heels. I am giving off major Beyoncé vibes in this fit." He proceeds to stare at himself in the mirror, duck face firmly in place. I chuckle as I walk out to the living room area, where Bon and Charlie are sitting on the couch, white dresses cascading all around them as they drink champagne and eat chocolate-covered almonds.

"This is just like that episode of *Friends*! We need a picture. Taylor! Get your cute bottom in here!" I rush over to the girls after propping my phone on a weird glass sculpture that looks oddly like a minge.

I turn and look at Bon, taking in her wide, happy smile, and wait for Taylor to settle into a spot next to Char. I click the timer and run to the sea of white, jumping in the middle as we all laugh. I feel it right at this moment: tonight is going to be one of the best, most memorable nights of my life. I'm with my favorite people, celebrating a love so big and beautiful I'm not sure it can ever be replicated. Yep. This is a night I'll never forget.

13 /
don't finish that thought.

THIS IS NOWHERE near where I want to be or what I want to be doing tonight, but there isn't much I won't do for my little sister. So, when she decided on a joint bachelorette and bachelor party in Vegas, of course I said I'd be here.

That was also before the lawyer called with news that this guardianship process wasn't going to go as smoothly as I anticipated. Apparently, I have to prove that I'm fit to take a baby home. Financially, it's a non-issue. But they want to make sure I'm emotionally stable. That means as soon as this party is over, I get to go back to Ojai to have my house and my life thoroughly looked into.

It seems that giving custody to a single male isn't favorable, especially since I'm not related to either of the baby's parents. As much as I get it, it's also bullshit because I could have gone and made a baby with someone, and no one would be checking in on me. Plus, they picked me for a reason, damn it.

"O, you might wanna wipe the scowl off your face before the bride gets here." I know Raf is right. Lainey already tried to give me an out. She told me she wouldn't be upset if I sat this one out, but we've already missed enough in one another's lives. I don't want to miss one more thing.

I try to put a smile on my face, and Raf winces.

"Harder. Try harder than that. You're scaring me, man." He turns and takes another swig of his beer. Smiling seems to come so instinctively to Rafael, but my face just doesn't naturally go that way unless I'm with my people. Unless I'm with...

Don't finish that thought.

"I'm going to get another drink." I get up quickly, walking to the bar while I practice relaxing my facial muscles. I take a shot of tequila and another beer, and when I start making my way back to Raf, I see a giant white blob out of the corner of my eye. It's moving toward the VIP section, where we'll eventually end up so Adam and Maeve can enjoy the night without being seen.

I do a double take when I see Elaina's happy, smiling face in the blur of white. I immediately spot Charlie's red hair, and Taylor has a very long brown wig on his head. I squint, trying to spot the missing piece when the woman with the raven hair turns and stuns me. It's Maeve. She must also have a wig on, unless she really committed to this thing and dyed her hair.

Ha! Doubtful.

"There. That's much better!" There's a hard slap on my back, and I turn to see Raf's wide smile. "You found your smile after all. Good job, my man." He follows my gaze, spotting the group in white and chuckles, shaking his head.

I didn't know I was smiling, but it makes sense. Lainey looked so happy, I must have smiled when I saw her. Not when I saw the blonde sporting the dark hair. Definitely not then.

I finish my beer, and Raf does the same, then we make our way toward the VIP section to get this night started. Adam is already up there. He wanted to make sure everything was okay before we went up, so we sent him with one of the bodyguards we have hanging around tonight just in case anyone recognizes the two celebrities and decides to do something stupid.

ELAINA IS ABSOLUTELY BEAMING. She's clinging to Adam like he's her lifeline as they dance and they're both all smiles. I'm finally starting to feel a little more loose and at ease as the countless drinks I've already had start to do their job.

Maeve is having a good time. She's been with Taylor and Charlie most of the night. At first, she would hardly look my way, but anytime she has her sunglasses on, her head swivels in my direction.

The Docs on her feet were an even bigger surprise than the wig, but she looks so at ease. Comfortable. I like this look on her more than her usual style these days. Lately, she's all polished nails and high heels. Never a hair out of place. Even when she's in leggings and a T-shirt, her makeup is done and her hair is perfectly styled. I know it comes as a part of her celebrity status, but it's gotta be exhausting.

"Looks like you lost your resting asshole face." Raf wraps a giant arm around me and hands me another shot, which I happily take. This is so out of the norm for all of us, I think we're all indulging a little more than usual tonight.

"Yeah, the drinks are helping," I say right before I take my shot. The fact that I don't wince tells me everything I need to know. I should have stopped at that last drink. Or the one before that.

"The girls are having fun. Even Charlie's dancing. Have you ever seen Charlie dance before?" I turn my head toward Raf a little too quickly, immediately regretting it for how dizzy it makes me feel. I swear I see hearts in his eyes as he cocks his head and watches the girls dancing together.

"She's so beautiful," he mumbles.

I don't have the brain power or the bladder control to process what just happened, so I get up and make my way to the bathroom, chuckling at Raf's dopey face all the way there.

Since I have to be responsible dad for the next several months—for the next rest of my life—I'm using tonight as an excuse to let loose. Who knows when I'll be able to do anything like this again without worrying about a little person and whether or not they'll need me. So at least for now, I'm going to drink until I can't see straight.

14 /

maeve james

maeve

AM I DYING? Maybe I'm already dead. Based on the throbbing pain behind my eyeballs and the fact that every muscle in my body hurts, I think I must be well on my way to deceased.

A deep growl from the other side of the room has me jumping out of my bed. Every cell in my brain hurts as they knock against one another like pebbles.

Is there an animal in here? How did it get here? Is it going to eat me? Oh bollocks. I'm not prepared to die. Especially not like this. I don't—

My thoughts are stopped short as I take in the legs moving on the chair obviously too small for the behemoth of a man sitting on it. My skin tingles in a most unpleasant way, the pebbles in my head still heavily and loudly banging against my skull. As fear starts to settle in, I look left and right, hoping my phone is within reach. No such luck.

I lay perfectly still, awaiting my fate. I could scream. Someone might hear me. But even the thought of loud noises right now makes me queasy. So I wait, and as he lets out another beastly growl, I take in the blond hair and eventually a pair of green eyes I know all too well.

Crap on a cracker. What the bloody hell happened last night?

"Maevey? What are you doing here? Ow, fuck, my back hurts." He stretches his body over the chair, looking like he could swallow the thing whole and I fight the urge to laugh.

Don't. That'll hurt, too.

"This is my room, Owen. What are *you* doing here?" I see my boots are thrown on the floor, my dress is still on and I'm thankful I didn't choose anything with a corset. This thing is actually super comfortable, and if I was ever to get married, I might consider this very dress.

"I think I'm still drunk." He hiccups and finally unfolds himself from the small chair, taking in the significantly larger couch right next to it with a groan.

The fact that I'm fully clothed and he slept on a chair tells me we definitely didn't do anything regrettable last night. He looks down at himself, wide-eyed as he pats his abdomen and legs, like he's checking to make sure he has clothes on. When he looks back up at me, I snicker.

"I had the same thought. Nope. No sex." I move on my bed, feeling around for my cell phone. "Not to worry, I'm fairly certain we were far too drunk to do anything we'd regret last ni—""

My words come to a screeching halt as I catch a glimmer of something shiny and gold on my finger. On my ring finger. Of my left hand.

Oh god, oh god, oh god. No, no, no, no, no, no. No. Oh, please, no. Fuck. Shit. Fuck, fuck, fuck!

Owen's chuckle brings me back into my body, because I swear I floated away there for a second.

"This is not fucking funny, you twat!" I get off the bed, marching straight toward him. He's ruffling his hair with his left hand and I rip it away, releasing it like it's made out of searing hot lava as soon as I take in the matching gold band on his ring finger.

I stumble back, tripping on the tulle of my dress and I'm about to accept my fate and the pain that is sure to follow as I fall flat on my ass when two big hands catch me.

"Okay?" he whispers, mossy green eyes looking worried and confused. The word alone makes me pull in a ragged breath and I move away from him immediately, his touch feeling like tiny needles pricking at my skin.

I shake my head, bringing both of my hands to my temples, hoping I can ease the pain of the fucking pebbles and the thoughts slamming into my skull like a freight train. This can't be real, right? Surely it's just a joke. Yeah, we must have just bought cheap rings and this is obviously a joke. I bet Raf, Charlie and Taylor all have wedding bands on this morning, too.

I walk on shaky legs to the small kitchenette, reaching into the fridge for a bottle of water. I grab a second one and toss it in Owen's direction as he follows after me.

"It's nothing. I'm sure this is fine. Of course we didn't get married last night. We couldn't. We wouldn't." I drink some of my water, pacing around the living room as my dress drags behind me.

I press two fingers to one of my temples, willing away the pain and willing back some memories of what the hell happened after we left that club last night.

Owen finishes his bottle of water, and pulls his phone out of his back pocket and squints at it. I take him in for the first time.

His suit jacket has been removed and is nowhere to be seen. His charcoal trousers cling to his legs, emphasizing his muscular thighs. His soft gray shirt is still tucked in but the tie is gone and the top three buttons are undone, revealing hints of tattoos I've never seen underneath. The urge to see what's hidden beneath his shirt is nearly unbearable.

He looks so relaxed, so far from the normally stiff and guarded posture he carries daily. It's not fucking fair that he's this easy on the eyes. He's just come off a night of binge drinking and he's still positively delicious.

No! Stop that right this instant! What is wrong with you?

I must still be drunk too, because I cannot be having thoughts like that about Owen.

I do a quick scan of the room, hoping my phone is in here somewhere, but I don't see the glittery gold case anywhere.

"Hey, Owen, could you call my phone, please? I need to check in with Taylor and Charlie."

He quickly taps the screen and I hear a buzz before "You" by Dan + Shay starts playing. I spin around quickly as the memories come rushing in like a tsunami, wave after wave of images of us. Owen and I giggling into a little white chapel. Him slipping a gold band on my finger as we both laughed. Us holding hands as we practically skipped outside. Stopping in front of a fountain where he set his phone down while this song played from it. The way he pulled me in, warm fingers splayed across my back as we danced and he twirled me, dipping me low as the song ended, a scorching kiss landing on my neck as he pulled me back up.

His wide stare tells me the same memory reel is playing in his mind, and when the song stops as his call goes to voicemail, we both jump into a panic.

"Oh fuck! Oh shit! Oh my god what did we do?"

"Did we get fucking married last night? Jesus, Maevey, how much did we have to drink? Did we each eat a whole pizza after?"

"I don't fucking know! Stop calling me Maevey! Oh my god, I need to call someone. We need to fix this!" I lunge at the cushion where I assume the music was just coming from and grab my phone.

"Do you want me to stay? What do we do? Fuck me, I so did not need this right now."

I whip my phone at him hard, hoping to inflict some pain after that last comment, but the asshole catches the phone like it's a fucking softball.

"Believe it or not, Owen, I didn't need to wake up married to *you* either, but don't worry. I'll get this annulled as soon as possible and we can be rid of one another. For good." He has the audacity to look wounded. Fuck him.

"Okay, Maevey. Maeve. Sorry. I'm gonna go. Call me if I can do anything, all right?" He runs another hand through his hair and starts walking toward the door.

I'm not doing it. I'm not feeling bad for what I said to him. I don't care how convincing his puppy dog eyes are.

I need to call my lawyer. I need to find Charlie and Taylor and ask them how the hell this happened. I need to sleep. I need to take this goddamn wedding dress off. I need a lot of things, but instead of doing any of them, I sit right there on the floor as a tear slips down my cheek.

I remember the nineteen-year-old who met a handsome blond with a buzz cut and emerald green eyes. The girl who practiced writing Maeve James in a notebook, but only once, because that felt like something only pre-teens do. I think of the girl who lit up at the sight of those green eyes on a computer screen for years. The girl whose heart was shattered after giving away something precious to her. The girl whose heart then hardened as it healed, whose mask had to become tougher and more convincing. I sit there, in *my wedding dress* and cry for that girl then and for this woman now.

15 /
hubby?

AFTER A LONG SHOWER, I shoved that forsaken dress back into its garment bag, ready to be delivered to Taylor for me to never see again. I've been laying in bed wrapped in my towel for so long that my hair is nearly dry now. Normally I'm someone who jumps into action when there's a crisis, but this... I don't know how to handle this. I've already left my lawyer a voicemail. No one will know about this until I've got some answers on how to get an annulment.

I check my phone quickly and I'm greeted with a headache-inducing message.

MUM:

Are you ever going to answer me?

That's a hard no from me.

Charlie let slip last night that Mum's divorced her latest husband. I believe this was number five. So typical. She leaves a man and comes crawling back to her daughters for money, affection, attention.

I learned a long time ago not to fall for her bullshit, and that's not changing anytime soon.

There's a quick succession of knocks at the door. I get up to see who's impatiently trying to bring the door down, and I see Bon through the peephole, Charlie and Taylor standing directly behind her. Something must have happened. I open the door quickly, ready to ask what the emergency is.

"You married my brother!" Bon's eyes are wide, her face a little pale.

Oh fuck, how does she know?

"Uh, hi. Come in?" I open the door a little wider as all three of them stalk into the room, Charlie giving me a knowing look as she walks past.

"Maevey! We're sisters! It's official!" Bon darts toward me, and I instinctively grab hold of my towel to prevent any potential embarrassment. This is definitely a situation we don't want turning into a real Vegas showstopper.

"Owen just told me. He's a bit freaked out by the whole thing, and I know you two haven't sorted through your issues yet, but I mean, this is classic forced proximity, right, Char?" Bonnie's so excited. I need to stop this. She seems happy that Owen and I got married, but it's not going to stick. No way.

"Mae, can you tell us what happened?" Charlie takes a breath and somehow remains perfectly calm, a quality of hers I very much appreciate right now.

"I-I-I I don't know. I don't really remember. We woke up this morning with these rings on and—"

"Woke up where, Mae?" Charlie's no-nonsense tone makes me feel a little like I'm being interrogated, but I still prefer it to Bon's giddy excitement.

"Here. I was in my bed and Owen was on the chair. Fully clothed. Nothing happened! I don't know why we got married last night."

"What do you mean you don't know why? Owen's—" Bon is cut off by the sound of that stupid song coming through my phone speakers again.

"Who has ringtones anymore? And what is this song?"

Taylor looks down at my phone, which happens to be right next to him. "Hubby?" He lifts an eyebrow and holds up the phone to show the girls.

Who the bloody hell did this to my phone?

"Owen, it's not exactly a good time," I say as I pick up.

"I'm sorry. I freaked out. I told Lainey. I'm sorry."

Something is very off with him. He's not the type to profusely apologize, and why did this freak him out so much? We can just get it annulled and go on with our lives as normal. Separately. Very much unmarried.

"Yeah. She's here. I'll call you back later, yeah?"

He lets out a sigh and hangs up the call. My phone rings again immediately, no love song streaming out of its speakers this time. Seeing it's my lawyer, I pick up right away.

"Lauren. Hi."

"Hello, Maeve. So you got yourself in quite a pickle, huh?" She sounds poised, not at all rattled by my news.

"Uh, yeah. You could say that. So how quickly can we annul this thing?"

"Well, Maeve, that's tricky. You see, we would have to prove that there are grounds for annulment, such as fraud, forced consent, or mental incapacity. I understand that you were under the influence when this happened as you explained in your message, but I think your publicist will ask me not to use that as the reason for canceling this marriage."

I scoff, knowing quite well Jen will be none too pleased with this little turn of events. I've always kept a clean image. I don't give her much trouble. She mostly has to clear up unfounded rumors. But this... this will be an interesting one.

"Okay, so what are my options, Lauren?" I feel all six eyes on me as I pace around the room, staring at my feet as they move across the floor.

"Well, if the person you married agrees to admitting they were too inebriated to make an informed decision, we can go ahead with this. I'm afraid that doesn't make either party look very good though, and this will be public record, so it's really important you think about this." She clears her throat and I know she's about to say something I don't want to hear. "Would you consider staying married for a little while? At least until we can settle on a no-fault divorce in a couple of months."

"A couple of months?" I practically screech the words, halting my pacing. "I can't stay married to him, Lauren. He's my best friend's brother!" I whisper yell into the phone, but I know these nosy Nellies are listening.

"Well, at least you married someone you know and already probably spend time with. Just stick it out for a little while. That's my best advice to you, because either way this will be public information and you'll have to answer to it. Which would you rather? Admit to a drunken night in Vegas or announce a divorce and ask for privacy on a personal matter?"

Damn, she's good.

"Are you sure you don't also work as a publicist? Because as much as I hate what I'm hearing, Jen would love it."

Lauren laughs, and it pisses me off a little that she can laugh at a time like this, but she surely deals with much more pressing matters than a drunken night filled with mistakes in Vegas.

"I'm just giving you my best advice. Do with that what you will and call me when you know how you want to proceed, okay? I can have a postnuptial agreement ready within a few hours."

"Yeah. Thank you, Lauren. Speak soon."

I drop my phone onto the couch and promptly settle my ass on it, too.

"I need to talk to Owen." I look to the three people still staring at me from the other side of the room.

"Might want to put some clothes on first, babe." Taylor

points at the towel barely covering my crotch and I shoot him a scathing look.

"I love you all, but I need you to leave now so I can speak with Owen about this. We did not mean to get married last night. Bon, I'm so sorry we did this at your bachelorette party." I look at my best friend, guilt gnawing at my insides, because what kind of best friend does this?

"Oh, Mae. I'm not mad. You two will figure this out." She smiles sweetly at me over her shoulder. "Let us know if we can do anything."

Charlie mouths, "sort this out," and then the door shuts behind them.

I shoot Owen a text asking him to come back to talk about this and quickly throw on a sundress.

OWEN:

Be right there

Within ten minutes, there's a soft knock at the door. When I open it, Owen is back to his usual attire of jeans and a T-shirt and his dirty blond hair is wet, falling in chunks over his forehead. And he smells... oh shit, he smells good. Like soft leather and mint.

Focus, Maeve!

I open my mouth to say, "Come in," but the words stick to the roof of my mouth. I give him a brief smile and an apologetic head tilt and close the door.

"I spoke to Lauren, my lawyer, earlier." I follow him into the seating area. I can see the slight bob of his head from here as he nods, but I need to see his facial expressions.

We both take a seat, me on the chair, him on the sofa. He still hasn't said a word, which isn't exactly unlike Owen, but I expected him to have more questions.

"She said it's unlikely that we can get this thing annulled. One or both of us would have to admit to things like mental instability, being under the influence of drugs or alcohol, or a slew of other unappealing scenarios." His green eyes are on mine, head still bobbing as I speak. "Since these are public records, she didn't think it would be wise for us to use one of those reasons. She recommended—"

"I need us to stay married." His jaw is clenched shut, lips pursed in a tight line as he peers intently at something on the far side of the room. His usual bronze complexion has faded to an unnatural pallor, and his eyebrows are knit together in a mixture of fear and worry.

Wait, did he just say we need to stay married?

"Maeve, we can't get an annulment. We can't just dissolve the marriage. Please. I know we're not friends, but I've never asked you for anything before. I'm asking you for this." He rests his elbows on his knees, head falling onto his hands as he runs his fingers through his damp hair. All I can hear is the sound of his labored breathing.

"Please, Maeve," he whispers.

I'm frozen to my spot on the chair not understanding his reaction. This isn't about wanting to be married to me. We hardly even talk.

After a few seconds of confusion, I need an explanation for this behavior so I move to the sofa, careful not to touch him. It's never a good idea to touch Owen. The sparks that I feel whenever we make contact are practically visible. I swear I hear their crackling sound in my ears every time.

I take a deep breath and steady my tone, despite the erratic beating of my heart. "Owen, what is this about?"

"I... There's... She's..." He's making no sense.

"Take a deep breath. Try again," I urge him on, placing my hand on his shoulder against my better judgment. He flinches at the contact, but takes a deep breath, then two.

"I'm going to have a daughter." I hesitantly pull my hand away from his shoulder, my fingers trembling. It's as if his words are made of fragile glass, on the verge of shattering from the sharp edges of our complicated relationship. My ears start ringing. He says something else I don't hear. Her name, maybe?

I'm going to have a daughter. A daughter. When did this happen? Who's the mother? Who's the person who gave him what he's always wanted?

"I should get custody or guardianship or whichever one it is I need to make sure I'm the one that gets to raise her. Her mom, she... she died giving birth to her, and her dad was a good friend in the Corps."

Her dad. Her dad. Her dad. Owen is not her biological father.

"Wait, back up. I need more information. This isn't making any sense."

He finally looks up at me, that look of defeat on his face making me want to lose all sense and do something foolish like hug him. I sit on my hands to keep myself from putting them anywhere near him.

Owen explains the situation with Monica and Clay, his eyes filling with tears when he talks about them. He looks at his lap as he continues the story.

My own tears threaten to spill, and I tell myself it's only because seeing a grown man nearly cry would make anyone emotional. It's not because seeing him hurting is making my chest hurt. It's not because the thought of him being this upset makes me want to stand in front of him and protect him from whatever is making him feel this way. That's not why I have to quickly wipe my eyes before he sees.

"I remember him," I say with a shaky voice. "I liked him."

"He liked you, too, sunshine." He wipes a rogue tear off my cheek with the tip of his index finger and I force myself not to close my eyes at the warmth of his touch.

A moment passes without any words and though it's subtle, I feel a shift happening. Like something consequential has changed between me and Owen. Obviously because we're married, but also because we haven't just existed like this in each other's presence in so long. Sure, before it was through a computer screen, but I forgot how comfortable simply being with him is. How comforting.

"I called the lawyer handling everything. He told me any change to my relationship status at the moment wouldn't be good for my case." He looks up at me then with a lifetime of sadness in his eyes. "Please, Maeve. I wouldn't ask if it wasn't serious. We fucked up. I know. But I can't let a drunken decision be the reason this baby's life is changed forever. I can't let her down. I can't let Clay down. I can't—"

My heart feels like it's splitting in two. He tries to speak, but a sob gets in the way instead and his chest starts to shake. His fists clench up by his ears as another cry shudders through him, and I rush closer to him with my arms outstretched. He curls into me, burying his face into the crook of my neck, and his trembling body seems to sink into the couch even further with each sob.

"Shhh. It's all right, Owen. I've got you. We'll sort this out." He wraps both arms around me so tightly it almost hurts, but I let him take comfort in whatever way he needs right now. I let one of my hands rest on his head, brushing his hair off his forehead, the other rubbing circles on his back.

I don't know how much time passes, but eventually he shifts, rubbing his fingers over his cheeks. When he moves to sit up, I give him the room to do so.

"I'm sorry. That's so fucking embarrassing. It's just been a stressful time and—"

"Please don't apologize for expressing how you're feeling, Owen. It's fine." Maybe he remembers the words I'm echoing, maybe he doesn't.

He nods, wiping at his cheek one last time before looking at me again. When he does, I feel the literal weight of his gaze. What he's asking me without asking me again. What I'm about to agree to even if it means breaking my own heart a little more in the process.

I nod. He lets out a relieved breath.

16 /
all common sense goes out the window.

owen

DID SHE JUST NOD? Oh my god, she nodded. She's agreeing to this completely insane thing I just asked her for.

Thank. Fuck.

I glance down my left arm to the golden band on my finger, and I can feel the heaviness of it weighing down my hand. The ring is simple, but unfamiliar, as if a strange growth has sprouted overnight. And now it's mine to wear for the foreseeable future. Until I'm officially somebody's father. Then we can do as Maeve wants and *be rid of one another for good.*

There's nothing I want less than to be rid of her, but I have to prioritize this new role. Maybe one day we'll get the timing right and I can try this again. I can start over with her. But that's not a possibility right now and the faster I get the thought of her being my wife permanently out of my head, the better.

She's still looking at me, eyes so wide I can nearly see when the leaden realization of our complicated reality hits her.

"So we'll stay married for a little while." She lets out a sharp breath.

"Listen, Maeve, I don't want this to feel like a one-sided deal. I'm sure you're gaining nothing out of being married to me other than a giant headache and lawyer fees, which I'm happy to pay for, by the way." She rolls her eyes at me, and I don't know whether to laugh at her dramatic display or be a little annoyed by her response.

"We both did this, Owen. It's fine. I already keep my lawyer quite busy anyway, so I'm sure this is not going to be much more than whatever she already charges me." She shifts her gaze to her feet, pulling her bottom lip all the way into her mouth and I know she's got more to say. "She did mention a postnuptial agreement, though. You know... Just in case."

"Just in case, what, Maeve? In case you want to take me for all I'm worth and make yourself even richer?" She scrunches her eyebrows and scoffs.

Huh. She has no idea.

"Yeah. Right, Owen. *I'm* going to try to take *you* for all your millions. Sure." She laughs, though there's no humor in it.

"Billions," I mumble. I remove an invisible fluff from my shirt, not looking at her when I speak.

"Excuse me?" Her eyebrows are high on her forehead as multiple questions play out in her eyes.

"It's billions. I sold Aegis Cyber for billions, not millions." I pause, looking up at her stunned face, and I'd be a damn liar if I said it didn't feel a little nice to see the shock play out over her features. I don't like talking about money, but she's my wife, so she might as well know.

"You... But... Wait, what?"

I ignore her rambling and continue. "I don't want a prenup, though." I let out a breath, doing my best not to be too much of an asshole about all of this. "But if there's anything you need, Maeve, anything you want, it's yours. Lainey mentioned you might want to get out of LA for a while. I have a house with a very detached, very private guesthouse. It's yours if you want it. I know it's not much, but..."

"It's not in LA?" She's found her voice, it seems.

"No, it's not. But it's not far. It's a good sized property with nothing but mountains and horses for neighbors, and I'm sure it goes without saying, but it's secure."

The corners of her lips turn up slightly. "I'll take it," she breathes out. "Please."

Sweet Jesus, did I just invite my wife to live with me at the house I bought for her? Fucking hell, what am I doing? Why does all common sense go out the window when I'm around this woman?

The thought makes me dizzy. I'm about to bring a baby home and now also a wife who once told me she never wanted to be married or have kids. This isn't the life she wants for herself, and yet here we are.

"Owen?"

I snap out of my mental freak-out and nod my head. "Yeah. Of course. I'll text you the details. I can have the guesthouse ready as soon as you need."

"Right. Okay. Thanks. Well, call me if you need anything. For the baby. Or for the lawyer. Or whatever."

I stand up, assuming we're finished talking about this for now. I need to clear my head. I need to get back to Ojai. I need to... I need to not be so near her right now.

"Yeah. Thanks. We'll talk soon, then."

With one final look in her direction I shove my hands into my pockets and walk away.

I pack my things and get out of Vegas. I need to prepare for the arrival of two girls and I'm not ready. Not even close.

———

JAMES FAMILY CHAT

OWEN:

Help! What do I get for a baby? Her room is empty and ready, but I'm just staring at it not knowing what needs to go in it.

LAINEY:

We got you, big bro! Can I make a shopping list and send you the links?

MA:

How do I add things to this list?

OWEN:

Can I just give you my credit card number?

LAINEY:

Ooooooh! Yes, please! Ready to go shopping on your rich son's dime, Mamá?

MA:

Can I be in charge of her wardrobe?

MA:

What about toys?

MA:

Are you going to be one of those millennial parents that only wants neutral colors?

OWEN:

Geez that's a lot of questions, Ma.

OWEN:

Also, excited much?

OWEN:

I don't care about colors. Can we please just not make EVERYTHING pink?

LAINEY:

Leave it to us. Ma, I'll call you.

LAINEY:

O, you go worry about other things. We got this.

MA:

This is so exciting!

OWEN:

I'm glad you think so. I was freaking out.

OWEN:

Thanks, you two. Don't know what I'd do without you.

OWEN:

I love you both.

LAINEY:

Awwww love you too, O.

MA:

S'agapó, moro mou.

———

I'VE BEEN MARRIED for two days. Since then, I've flown to San Diego again, sent Maeve my address, and wondered if she'd be at my house every time I pull into the driveway. As I reach the front of the house now, I can see that she's still not here.

What's taking her so long?

I still haven't been able to bring Julia home. Thankfully, Monica and Clay had her name picked out, so at least I didn't have to make that very permanent decision for her. Since I have no familial relation to either of them, it's a more complicated process than I originally thought it would be. It seems like it should be straightforward since Julia has no next of kin, but the court is so backed up that we need to wait for a hearing date. It's bullshit. They also need to meet Maeve, and I don't know how to bring that up to her.

. . .

I'M SETTLING in for the night, checking the security system one last time, when my phone lights up with Maeve's name.

MAEVE:

Hi. I know it's late, but I'm about ten minutes away. Is that okay?

OWEN:

Yeah, I'll have the gate open for you. Guesthouse is to the left.

OWEN:

I'll be up for a bit if you need anything from the house, the backdoor code is 1027. The code for the guesthouse door is 0523.

MAEVE:

Thanks. I should be okay. I'll see you tomorrow.

TWENTY MINUTES LATER, I see her Porsche Cayenne pulling in and then away toward the guesthouse. I consider going over there to check on her, to see if she needs anything. I know she doesn't. I had the fridge stocked with fresh produce and dairy. Glass jars filled with homemade jams line the shelves along with a few pre-made meals that just need to be heated up. A tray of colorful fruits sits on the kitchen island. The beds are loaded with pillows of all different sizes and firmness. The linen closets have plush, white towels and soft, woven blankets lining the shelves.

I don't know what she likes, so I asked for two of everything available. Overboard? Probably, but I'm trying here.

I stay inside but keep an eye on the guesthouse, just in case she needs my assistance. I want to make sure everything is perfect for her stay, because Maeve Howard might hate me, or be indifferent to me, but I could never feel that way about her. Not even close.

these are my favorite snacks.

maeve

I SLIP INTO THE GUESTHOUSE, taking in the large space. It has two bedrooms and two bathrooms, a spacious kitchen, a den set up as an office, and a huge fireplace in the living room. If this is Owen's guesthouse, the main house must be massive.

It smells like fresh linens and there's a faint smell of lavender in the air. I take a deep breath as I look out the window toward where I know there are mountains, even if it's too dark to see them. There are a few lights outside, but we're clearly in the middle of nowhere because I can actually see stars in the sky. This already feels nothing like LA, and I love that.

I can't even see the main house from here, so maybe this means I'll be able to ignore Owen's presence as much as possible while we live on the same property. I'll say *hi* tomorrow, then come back here and stay out of his way.

I open up the fridge, hoping to find some water inside, and am shocked to see it's completely packed. Flat water, sparkling water, three different kinds of juice, milk, some cut up veggies neatly stashed in containers, and every possible condiment known to man.

Grabbing a bottle of water, I walk further into the kitchen, noticing the kettle and container labeled 'tea' next to it. I immediately wonder if it's at the very least black tea.

I sincerely hope so.

I walk over and open the container, smelling English Breakfast. Excellent. Now all I need are some digestives.

With a smile on my face, knowing my morning tea will at least be the same as always, I open up the pantry. It's also stocked. Neatly arranged clear containers are filled with colorful snacks on the shelf at my eye level and my eyes widen when I see the Walkers bags. Just below it is a whole row of digestive biscuits, even the chocolate ones, and some Jammie Dodgers.

Oh my God. These are my favorite snacks.

Owen must have asked Bon what my favorite things are and then he stocked up the kitchen. I can't dwell on how that makes me feel, or on the weird way my stomach dips at the realization that he took time to prepare for my arrival. But maybe Bon had these sent here. I wouldn't put it past her.

Shutting the pantry door without looking at what else may be lurking in there, I grab my suitcase with my toiletries and pjs and head toward one of the bedrooms. I choose the one that faces away from the main house. Temptation be damned.

———

THE FOLLOWING MORNING, I wake up to the sound of birds chirping outside of my window. The sound is so foreign that I reach for my phone, attempting to silence a non-existent alarm.

As I pick up my phone, I see a few texts that came in while I was peacefully sleeping in this wonderfully silent place.

BON:

Did you make it to Owen's okay? Is he being
nice to you?

I quickly type out a response, even though I know she's
likely not awake yet.

MAEVE:

I'm here. Haven't seen him yet. Thanks for
the snacks!

The second name is one that has me scowling.

MUM:

I hear one of my daughters got married.

MUM:

I had to see it in a magazine. Since Charlotte
actually picks up my calls, she confirmed
that it's true.

MUM:

Hopefully you fare better with your first
husband than I did. Doubt it, though.

MUM:

Will I find out about the divorce through the
tabloids, too?

Whatever. I don't care. I refuse to give her any of my
energy. Though the thought that she's right, that my
marriage will end in divorce just as all of hers have, makes
me feel sick. Mum changes husbands faster than most people
change cars, and I've worked hard to ensure that I'm nothing
like her. No doubt, she'll hold this over my head for the rest
of her days.

The next message is from Owen about ten minutes ago.

> OWEN:
>
> Morning. Hope you slept well.
>
> OWEN:
>
> I have breakfast here in case you don't want
> to cook anything.

My stomach growls in response to his breakfast offer. I definitely don't want to cook anything. I never do. And I have to see him anyway, so I quickly get dressed in jeans and a lilac jumper, toss my hair into a low bun and make my way across the treed path to the main house. Out of habit, I put on my daily makeup and bright red lipstick.

You can take the girl out of LA, but you can't take the LA out of the girl…

I can smell the bacon from outside as I step closer, suddenly feeling very unsure as to whether I should knock or simply walk in.

I should knock. I don't live here, and we're not exactly friends. But then again, we're married now, so I could just walk in, right?

The door opens as I'm hovering a hand over the handle, still battling with myself.

"Were you going to come in or just stand there staring at the door?" I don't know what hits me first. Owen's leathery, manly smell or the sight of him in workout shorts and a perfectly fitted black T-shirt. I've never seen his legs before. I mean, sure, we were naked together once, but I wasn't looking at his legs. I could hardly see anything because it was so dark. All I could do was feel…

Maeve Charlotte Howard, get your mind out of that place right this second!

In an effort not to stare, I end up looking down at his shins, then back up to his face, back to the shins, up to his face, until my eyes get tired and land somewhere over his crotch.

Shit balls, this is no good.

I wince, feeling very caught in this game I'm apparently playing with myself, and when I look up at Owen's face, his eyes are wide, eyebrows high on his forehead, a small smirk playing on the corner of his lips.

"You done ogling me, Maeve?" This is the moment the asshole leans on the doorway, biceps straining against his T-shirt, tattoos peeking out beneath the fabric.

I want to trace those tattoos with my fingertips. With my tongue.

NO! You absolutely do NOT! What is wrong with you? Months of not a single sexual thought and one look at Owen, and you've literally got your tongue out?

I collect myself with one deep, calming breath and slip into the house, being careful not to touch him.

"What's for breakfast?" My eyes devour every detail of his home. The walls are creamy white, the furniture is a mix of worn woods and metals, the couches and chairs a mix of soft leather and neutral linens. There isn't much color, but it feels warm and cozy. It's a more polished version of the guesthouse with pictures on the shelves and artwork on the walls. He even has plants. Like real, live plants.

Owen walks past me, pointing straight ahead. "Kitchen's this way. Do you prefer the table or the island?"

I take in the place settings at the island, complete with mugs, glasses, and cloth napkins.

"I usually eat at the island, but if you want to eat at the table instead, that's okay, I just—"

I cut him off, shaking my head. "The island is great. Perfect." I chance a look in his direction, thankful he's not facing me as he takes the juice out of the refrigerator.

"What can I do?" I ask.

"Is orange juice okay?"

We speak at the same time, and I bite my cheek to avoid a smile as he turns, holding a jug of what looks like freshly squeezed orange juice and a plate of fruit. I nod as he sets them down in front of me, his shoulders relaxing slightly.

"Can I help with anything?"

"I've seen you in the kitchen, Maevey. You sit down, and I'll finish up." He looks up, and my eyes must show some of the shock I'm feeling at his easy-going tone.

He clears his throat. "Sorry. Maeve." His shoulders tense again as he turns to the stove, quickly pouring the eggs into an already hot pan. "Habit."

The silence in the kitchen is thick, the tension swimming in it and making me feel uneasy.

Do something. Say something. He's letting you live in his guesthouse and making you breakfast. Be nice!

I spot the plate of muffins on the counter. There's my in.

"I didn't realize muffins were an option."

He turns his head toward where the plate sits, brows furrowing slightly.

"Oh. Yeah. If you'd prefer a muffin instead, please go ahead."

Shit. No. That's not what I meant to say. Or how I meant to come off. Does he think I don't want or appreciate the breakfast he's making me now?

He begins plating the eggs, adding bacon slices to the plates.

"Lainey made me bring them yesterday, so they're still fresh. She sent chocolate chip just in case you decided to come. I guess she knew something I didn't." When he turns, I catch the way his brows come together ever so slightly, causing a crease to form between them. I want to smooth that crease. I want to soothe his insecurities. I also want to make him sweat a little because I am, after all, still more than a little sour about...well...everything.

"Wow. She sent muffins and snacks? I'll be sure to call and thank her."

His brows furrow further as he tentatively sets the plates down on the island.

"What snacks?" He doesn't move to sit, but rather waits for my answer, standing next to me where I can smell the delicious bacon he cooked.

"Um, I opened up the pantry last night. I saw the snacks she either sent or told you I liked."

Owen walks to the teapot I hadn't seen and carefully picks it up, bringing it over to where I'm sitting. He sets it down slowly, standing closer to me than before.

"Lainey didn't send the snacks, Maeve." My brain cannot compute this. Did he talk to Charlie? Who else would know my favorites? I open my mouth to ask, but he cuts me off.

"*I* got those for you. I know what snacks you like, *fengári mou*." He leans closer to me so we're face-to-face. "You forget I spent years talking to you, seeing you through a computer screen." When my eyes don't meet his, he lowers himself further, which also brings his face closer. "I know what you like, Maeve." His green eyes drill into mine, and just when it feels like he's sucked all the air out of my lungs, he straightens and turns to his stool, sitting as he lets out a loud breath.

"Plus, I remember the obscene noises you made every time you ate one of those disgusting Marmite chips on set last year." It's barely audible, but I hear every word he says.

I turn to catch him shaking his head, like the memory needs to be jostled out of his mind. "They are not disgusting. You've just never given them a chance. That and your American palette is stunted, obviously."

He chuckles, and something warms inside my chest. I hate it.

"Obviously," he mumbles as he reaches for the muffins, placing them between our plates. Unceremoniously, as if we've done this every morning, he pours tea into my cup first, then his. He continues the ritual, adding two teaspoons of sugar and a splash of milk to mine, mixing it then sliding it toward me. He doesn't add anything to his own cup.

He knows how I take my tea, too?

I bring the cup to my mouth, inhaling deeply before taking a drink. That first sip of English Breakfast tea in the morning is sacred, and this one also happens to be perfect. A satisfied hum escapes my lips, and Owen shifts uneasily in his stool, filling the silence with a throaty cough.

I take in the absolute feast before me and wonder if he does this for himself every morning. Something tells me the answer is no, but I don't allow myself the indulgence of dwelling on that thought.

"Dig in before it gets cold, blondie." He smirks as I roll my eyes at the nickname.

"What is it with you and nicknames? It's Maeve. Just Maeve."

Says the woman who hardly calls anyone by their first name...

"Mmhmm," is all the response I get as he begins eating his bacon, forgoing his fork. I certainly do not watch as he brings the slice to his lips, or as he licks his fingers, or the way his throat moves when he swallows, or how his fingers wrap around his mug in lieu of using the handle. I don't notice any of those details about him.

here we fucking go.

owen

ONCE WE'VE FINISHED EATING, which happens mostly in silence, I don't immediately get up to clear the dishes, and I wonder if I should.

Maybe I should talk to her later.

No, it needs to be now.

"I hope this was okay," I say.

"Thanks for this," Maeve says at the same time, a clear a sign as any that we're both struggling to act normally around one another. As if knowing I won't be the first to speak, she goes on. "This was lovely. Thank you."

Her cheeks instantly flush, and it's not a sight I'm used to seeing. Not anymore. The version of Maeve I've come to know is the proper Hollywood celebrity who always knows just what to say. She doesn't blush; she doesn't get flustered like this. The reaction goes straight to my cock, and the realization jolts me, so much so that I nearly jump off my stool. Now we're both blushing with embarrassment.

"I uh... I need to ask you something." My palms feel clammy, like I'm some teenage kid about to ask a girl to the dance. Nope. Just a thirty-two-year-old man trying to ask my temporary wife to pretend to like me.

"All right. Ask away," she says.

"Since you're my... wife now, the social workers need to meet you. They have to do these checks to make sure everything is all right at home and all that. They'll have to run a background check on you." I rub the bridge of my nose with my thumb and forefinger as I exhale a heavy breath. "I'm sorry. I'm sorry that you have to do this."

"Right. That's completely fine. I assumed we'd have to do this, and I actually wanted to talk to you about something as well." She pours herself another cup of tea from the pot. I follow the action like I'm hypnotized, and maybe I am. Even her hands are perfect, her movements so fluid, likely from years of practice, expertly digging up the exact amount of sugar and pouring the exact amount of milk into her cups of tea.

I nod as I pour some tea into my cup, forgoing milk and sugar to drink it like I drink my coffee: black.

She purses her lips, as if she just can't help it. The sight of my tea, no milk or sugar in it, likely annoys the shit out of her.

"We're being quite awkward around one another." I raise an eyebrow at her, and she responds with an eye-roll. That eye-roll stirs up those bits of hope that linger in my heart. Because an eye-roll is a sign of my old Maeve. The one who's comfortable enough to be herself around me.

"You know I'm right," she continues before bringing her cup to her lips again.

I look away and nod my agreement. She's right. Our interactions often swing between moments of complete awkwardness and comfortable ease, but that's usually when we're not talking. The silence between us is shockingly not awkward. No, it's... comforting. Familiar.

"And we can't have that, Owen. Not when it could cost

you your friend's baby girl." I stiffen at the mention of Julia. We haven't talked about her. She catches the movement and lets out a soft sigh. "The social worker is going to assume we know how to spend five minutes having a conversation without one of us freezing up or talking over one another."

I look down at my cup to avoid watching her as she brings a piece of muffin to her lips. I know she's going to lick the crumbs off her bottom lip, and I can't handle that right now. I count to fifteen and look up, hoping it's enough time. When I do, I see her staring me down, waiting for my response.

"What's the point you're trying to make, Maeve?" My grouchy voice makes the edges of her lips twitch as her smile tries to break free. She doesn't let it.

"I think we should spend more time together." My eyebrows push their way up my forehead. How does she think us spending *more* time together is going to help?

"Hear me out," she goes on. "You don't seem to be working all that much anymore, and we're going to have to be seen together. We need to be convincing." She looks down at her muffin, which is nearly falling apart, and finally bites into it.

My eyes track the movement as she licks a crumb off her lip.

Fuck, can she just stop licking her lips already?

"We should get used to being around one another without our friends as buffers. Because I might be able to pull out my acting skills when we're being watched, but I'm not as confident in your abilities." She looks up at me, then says, "No offense."

I chuckle but nod my head—because she's right.

"They'll know something's up if you look like you're scared to touch me. And, I mean, we're sort of stuck with one another anyway. Even after this marriage ends. We have Elaina, and she doesn't deserve us acting like a pair of twats."

She lowers her eyes, brows bunching together at the mention of my sister.

"Yeah. You're right. Lainey deserves better." When she puts it that way, it solidifies two things for me. One, I'm a selfish prick. I've only been thinking of myself with this whole thing. I haven't even considered my sister. Two, Maeve really wants nothing to do with me outside of her loyalty to my sister, and her agreement to help me while this guardianship hasn't been finalized.

I see it clear as day now. I needed this bucket of cold water dumped on me.

"So how about we go for a walk later? I haven't seen the property yet, and I don't want to go alone because I'll likely get myself rather lost." She shrugs, and I'm sure it's hard for her to admit she wouldn't be able to get back here if she went off on her own.

"Sure. Yeah, I can show you the stable if you want." The first reason I bought this house.

"Stable? You have a stable? How come we can't see it from here?" She's doing a terrible job hiding her excitement.

"Yeah. This used to be two separate properties, so there's a whole other house near the stable. The guy who takes care of the horses lives there."

"*Horses?*" Her voice cracks, and I can't help the laugh that slips through.

"Did you think the stable was empty?" I allow myself another laugh at the incredulous look on her face.

"Well, I don't know. I'm still trying to get over the fact that there is one. That there are real, living horses in it is a surprise I wasn't prepared for!" Maeve told me one of her stepdads had horses, so she spent a few years around them until her mum divorced him. She always said being around horses made her happy.

"Real, living horses. There might even be one or two calm

enough for you to ride." That gets her to stand up and start clearing the food dishes off the island.

"Can we go right now?" She turns around from her spot at the sink. I stand too, picking up our plates and cups. "I mean, it's all right if you're busy. I don't want to assume you're free right now. I just—"

"We can go right now. I'll just text Arthur and let him know we're coming." I set the plates on the counter and pull out my phone. She quickly takes them and places them in the sink as I send the message. I know he won't mind me coming down, so I don't wait for a response.

"I'll help you wash these before we go," she says. Without thinking, I reach around her to turn the tap on. At the same time, she bends to grab the dish sponge and soap, and as she does, her ass bumps directly into my crotch. I jump back, and she straightens quickly, trying to move away, but she loses her balance, knocking her knee on the cabinet door. To keep her from toppling over, I grab her hips, but she startles again and tries to jump away from me, slipping on the floor. I wrap my arm around her waist to keep her standing, pulling her into my body.

Her back is flush against my front, my right hand splayed on her abdomen, the left holding on to the countertop. She lets out a relieved sigh, likely out of gratitude that her ass isn't on the floor, and her head rolls back to rest on my shoulder.

We could stay just like this, with the scent of her shampoo surrounding me, her body flush with mine, our breaths quick and hot. But I know we can't.

"Okay?" And that question has her head jerking forward as she pushes away from me. I step back to give her space, to give myself space.

She doesn't want this. Never forget that.

"I'm going to get my phone from the guesthouse. I can

come back and do the dishes later." She doesn't look at me before she walks away toward the door.

I change out of my workout shorts and into jeans, then head back to the kitchen to load the dishwasher. When Maeve walks back into the kitchen, I'm just rinsing the last plate.

"Oh. Thanks. Should we go, then?" She turns away from me again, walking toward the door. I catch up to her quickly, taking her wrist gently to stop her from leaving.

"Hey. Wait." Her eyes move to look at the spot where my fingers wrap around her small wrist. I let go, hoping she won't take off again. She doesn't. "We gotta figure this out, right? How to be more than just civil when we're in the same room? So let's talk about this." I pause as she nods and turns to face me.

I huff out a breath. "Okay, we can start with Arthur. He doesn't know anything about us. I don't even think he knows I got married. He's not much of a talker." Before I can ramble any more about Arthur and give away the fact that I'm lying, I stop myself. "Anyway, he might think we're weird if we don't know how to be around each other, but his opinion doesn't matter. He's not making any decisions about either of our futures, so he's a good test subject."

Lies, lies, lies. Arthur knows about Maeve and why I bought this house with horses I hardly know how to ride. But he'll be a good test subject because he'll tell me the truth. I can always count on him for that.

"So you're saying we should start now? We should pretend to be a happily married couple in front of Arthur?" She crosses her arms, but not in an act of defiance, almost like she's protecting herself.

"Only if you're comfortable with it." I put up both of my hands in a motion of surrender, and to my shock, she nods.

"Yeah. Okay. Let's test this out on your pal Arthur, then."

Here we fucking go.

this is a very, very bad idea.

maeve

I GUESS we're doing this thing now. Like *right* now.

It's fine. I can do this. I can handle touching and being touched by Owen, just as long as it's not my arse touching his crotch.

Once I'm outside, I turn around, realizing I don't know where we're actually going. Owen is a few feet away staring at my white trainers.

"You wanna drive there so you don't get those dirty?" He points at them as if I don't know what he's talking about.

"No. They're just shoes." He raises an eyebrow at me, and I roll my eyes. "Go on, cowboy. Lead the way." That gets his lips twitching, but seriously, all the man needs is a cowboy hat to replace his baseball cap. He's got the tight T-shirt, worn jeans, and boots look down.

"If you say so." He walks past me and... yep... his bum looks positively biteable in those jeans. It's entirely inappropriate. Sort of like my thoughts.

We walk past the garden—there are several raised garden beds that look ready for some vegetables to grow in them but are currently empty—and my heart tightens a little at the sight, remembering what Owen told me about his dad the day of the funeral.

"Do you think you'll ever plant anything in those? Some potatoes, maybe?" I wave a hand toward the garden beds and look up to see Owen smiling softly.

He chuckles, and the sound makes me feel lightheaded. "Yeah, I was hoping for some potatoes, strawberries, too since Lainey loves them." He seems so at ease here, and with the fresh air and mountains in his backyard, I can see why.

I consider telling him that his dad would be so happy to see the garden beds full, but I stop myself. It feels too intimate. Too close to the conversation we had on that night; the one I've tried time and time again to wipe from my memory.

"So… Why Ojai?" I settle for a rhyming question, which makes me cringe on the inside.

"Lots of reasons, I guess. The mountains, the small-town feel, being just far enough away from LA…" It seems like he has more to say, but I don't push it. It doesn't surprise me that Owen picked a place like this. He's never liked LA, but this way he can visit his sister and work with Raf whenever he needs to.

We arrive at the edge of a wooded area, a wide path cut out in front of us. Owen looks at my feet again. "Last chance to change your shoes or drive." I nod at him, and we start walking through the trees side-by-side.

"It's not very far, but sometimes this path gets really muddy. In case you want to come out here on your own, ever. Arthur wouldn't mind. You'll see. But, uh, don't go alone at night, all right? It's not dangerous or anything, but I wouldn't want you getting lost. These woods go for a lot of acres, and some of the paths here just take you in big circles, so if you don't know—"

"Hey, Owen? Take a breath." He does. "I won't be walking through the woods alone. K?" The worry eases off his face as he gives me a small smile before looking straight ahead again.

"So, how many horses are there?" He seems to relax further, hands no longer in fists at his side.

"Uh, six, I think. Arthur said something about getting some more though." I can't believe he lives in a house with a view of the mountains and horses next door. It's my literal dream, and he just shrugs as though it's perfectly normal to live on a property like this. I suppose for him it is.

"Wow. I can't wait to meet them all." A smile spreads across my face. My insides bubble up at the thought of being near horses again. As we walk, I swear I can smell the shift in the air. Like we're crossing over some invisible threshold. But as we take a few more steps, the stable is right up ahead, and there's a bulky sort of man leading a horse out.

Owen walks in silence, and I walk trying not to squeal at the sight before me. As we get closer, the man I assume is Arthur, waves at us, then goes back to his task with the horse.

"Should we be, like, holding hands or something?" Owen rubs his hands on his thighs, and I wonder if he's nervous about this whole thing, even though it was his idea.

"Sure." I hold out my hand, and he takes it gingerly, linking our fingers together.

This is a very, very bad idea.

Neither of us speaks as we approach Arthur.

"Hey, stranger. Haven't seen your ugly mug around here for a while. What brings you by?" Arthur's brown skin glistens in the sun, and when he takes off his hat, his hair glistens, too. It's so black it almost doesn't look real as the soft waves fall over his forehead. He stretches out a hand toward Owen, who releases me to greet his friend.

Something feels oddly familiar as I watch the two men hug one another. It's not the kind of hug you often see between men, and something about it warms my chest.

As they step away from one another, Arthur finally looks at me. "I'm Arthur. It's nice to meet you, finally."

Finally? Does he know who I am? Did he say that because he knows me from my work or because Owen has talked about me? Is he going to hug me, as well?

Owen interrupts the twenty questions currently floating through my head.

"Art, this is my... This is Ma—She's my... This is wife. My Maeve." He lets out a frustrated huff as Arthur, and I take in the spectacle of Owen trying to introduce me. "This is my wife, Maeve."

Woooooow, that was painfully adorable to witness.

"Never done that before, have ya?" Arthur laughs, looking at Owen, then extends his right hand to me. I take it, holding in my own laughter as Owen shakes his head beside me.

"Pleasure. In case you didn't catch that, I'm Maeve. His Maeve. His wife." I hide the complete body shiver that comes over me with a laugh. I meant for that to be funny. Just a little joke at Owen's expense. But hearing myself say *his Maeve* and *his wife* is almost as jarring as hearing Owen say it.

"Want to come meet some horses, Maeve?" Arthur claps Owen on the shoulder, another action that looks oddly familiar.

"Arthur, have we met before?" I don't think we have. I hardly ever forget a face, even if I'm awful at names. Arthur shakes his head, brows furrowing in confusion.

"Hmm. Something just feels so... familiar about you. The hug with Owen, and now the shoulder clap thing." That gets a small twitch of the lips from Arthur that slowly grows into a very unexpected smile.

"You know my brother. Rafael. Owen here is still coming to terms with the fact that the Machado men are huggers." It shocks me how the two relatives look nothing alike, but the mannerisms are all there. That easy affection Raf imposes on everyone he meets in the sweetest of ways. It's not quite as casual with Arthur, but it's there.

And now it makes sense that he said *finally*. Obviously, it was Raf talking about me, not Owen.

"Of course. Goodness, it's so obvious now that you say that! You two must be close." The smile that lights up his face falters so slightly it's almost invisible, but I catch it before he turns around. I look up at Owen, wondering if I said something wrong, but he shrugs, then places his hand on the small of my back to guide me into the stable.

The moment I set foot inside, it's like I've been transported to a time in my childhood when I remember actually feeling happy. The four horses immediately turn to look at us, and though I want to rush to all of them to say hello, I wait for Arthur, who knows these horses best.

"These four are very friendly. The two on the right are sisters. Willow and Scout. And the other two are Billy and Jasper. The ones outside are the rowdy ones. You can meet them another time. They're being assholes today." I chuckle as Arthur keeps walking into what I assume is the tack room.

I walk over to Willow first, and she immediately shoves her nose into my hair. I laugh, giving her a pat before heading over to Scout, who's a little more shy and simply nudges me as I rub the top of her head.

I don't even feel time pass as I go from horse to horse, asking Arthur questions about them, helping him get them fed and occasionally giving some of the carrots I found in a bucket to my new friends.

It could be minutes or hours later when I hear a throat being cleared next to me. I look up to see Owen leaning on the doorway to the stall I'm in. His arms are crossed in front of him, green eyes anchored on me. "Hi," he says with a small smile on his face. "Whatcha doing, Maevey?" The smile, paired with the nickname, has me a little weak in the knees, and I'm thankful for the horse I'm currently leaning on.

"Just giving Scout a brush. Want to try?" I pick up a second brush on the ledge behind me and give it to him. The easy, slow movement of his body toward mine makes the hairs on the back of my neck stand up. Owen James is like some sort of Gaelic Greek god, if such a thing existed—and it should. With those green eyes sparkling with golden flecks, he takes the brush from me and gently places it on the mare in front of us.

"Like this?" His eyebrows shoot up on his forehead, and I fight off a giggle.

"A little more pressure," I say as I place my hand over his to show him how it's done. "Always in the direction of hair growth. Use long strokes, like this…" My cheeks heat up a little, maybe from the contact, maybe from saying *long strokes*. Thankfully, Owen keeps his eyes on the horse, but I don't miss the way his throat bobs.

I move my hand away, opting to work on Scout's other side. When we're both just about done, I chance a look at Owen, who's already looking at me.

"We, uh, should get going soon." His voice is so low I hardly hear him, but I nod my agreement, turning into the mare in front of me and nuzzling her.

"See you soon, pretty girl," I whisper, hoping only she can hear me. When I go to walk toward the door, Owen is already there.

I take the brushes we've been using and drop them into a bin, then make sure to close the stall door properly.

"Can I just say goodbye and thanks to Arthur quickly?" Chancing another look at Owen, I take in the frown on his face.

He points toward the tack room with an annoyed look on his face. "He's in there. I'll wait for you outside." He purses his lips and looks away.

When did Owen get so grumpy? Geez.

I knock gently on the door to the tack room to let Arthur know I'm coming in.

"You two heading back?" He looks up from his task at the

small folding table set up in the middle of the room. It looks like he's doing some reorganizing.

"Yes, but I wanted to come say thanks." I take a moment to assess whether or not to say what I want to say. I settle on *yes*. Like always. "I'd love to come back, if it wouldn't be a bother. I'd be happy to help with whatever you like. I know horses well as I grew up with them, and I'd just like the chance to be around these ones while I'm here."

The look he gives me is a mix of confusion and amusement. He looks at a spot behind me, but I know Owen's not there because I can't feel his eyes on me.

"Do you ride?" he asks simply.

"Yeah. I don't do it as often as I used to or as much as I'd like, but yes, I can hold my own." His lips twitch into an almost-smile.

"We have stable hands. They're just out running some errands right now, but you can meet them next time. You're welcome anytime, Maeve." There's a twinkle in his eye that tells me he knows something I don't, but I don't know him well enough to push the subject.

"Great. I appreciate that, Arthur. And I'll be sure to make myself useful when I'm here." I give him a small smile, much smaller than the giant grin bubbling up inside me. "I'll see you soon."

He does that cowboy nod with the tip of his hat, and I turn on my heel. The second I'm out of his sight, I do a little happy jig, letting that smile burst out of me with a quiet giggle.

When I look up, still smiling like a fool, Owen is standing there, slack-jawed, staring at me. My smile doesn't immediately fade, but when my brain registers who's looking at me, I go back to my neutral expression.

"Why are you just standing there?" I roll my shoulders back, pushing back the excitement about the horses until I am perfectly alone.

"I was coming to see what was taking you so long." The look on his face is almost apologetic. "I didn't mean to intrude on your moment."

Yep. Of course he has to be nice to me when I was just snarky with him. Damn you, Owen.

"It's fine. Let's go." I walk in front of him like I have even the slightest clue how to get back to the guesthouse, or how to find the entrance into the woods from here. I don't.

Owen lets me have my moment of stubbornness and only casually walks ahead of me, pointing to the left when I'm very clearly about to head in the wrong direction.

We walk in silence, but it doesn't feel natural anymore. We walk side-by-side, but it's like there's an electrical current flowing between us.

Owen takes a deep breath and I catch the movement of his head turning toward me. "I'm sorry, Maeve." I wait for him to continue. For him to say sorry about what happened in the kitchen, or for his suddenly grumpy attitude, but he stays quiet.

"What for?" I don't take any chances assuming to know what he's thinking. Ever.

"Everything. The last seven years. Fuck, the last ten years." He takes his hat off and scratches the top of his head then shoves it back on roughly. "I was such a selfish asshole. Still am. I never wanted to hurt you. I wanted to spare you a life of waiting for someone who couldn't guarantee you a future. But I went about it the wrong way, and that night at the beach, I... Fuck, that never should have happened, but I'm so selfish that I can't bring myself to regret it, Maeve. I can't regret any of the time I had with you because those were the brightest moments of my life. You. You're the brightest thing in my life."

We've stopped walking now. I'm not sure my limbs have any blood flowing to them. It all seems to be in my temples, pulsing rapidly and loudly. He opens his mouth to continue because I'm not responding.

"Don't," I beg. Tears try to push their way out of my eyes, but I don't let them. I look around at the trees and will my heart to slow down.

"Maevey, I—"

"Stop!" His lips immediately close into a hard line. "I need a minute."

20 /
there aren't any left
for you.

owen

I DON'T KNOW how much time passes, but we stand there looking at the dirt, the trees, anything but each other.

"What makes you think you can make any choices for me? Or that I would have sat around waiting for you?" She pauses, still not looking at me. I can't tell if she's asking me the questions, or if she's just asking the trees, not really expecting an answer.

"I don't think I can make any of those choices for you. Not anymore. I was young and fucking dumb. And I have no idea if you would have or not, but, sunshine, I couldn't take that chance. Do you understand that? I could never take that chance with you."

She shakes her head so hard that some of the hairs fall out of her bun. Her eyes close tightly for a few seconds, and her face scrunches up as if she's in pain. She probably is.

"But you said we were just getting it out of our systems."

"I didn't mean it." I could say more. I could tell her right now that all these years later, she's still not out of my system. That I'm not sure that's even possible.

"So, what was it then? You were sad about your dad and

just needed a fuck?" Over the anger in her words, I see a flash of regret pass across her eyes as she looks at me. Her words deliver the intended punch, though, as I feel the air rush out of my lungs.

Jesus, is that what she really thinks? I'm such a fucking asshole.

"No, Maeve. That's not... it was never... that had nothing..." I take a deep breath, willing my next words to help me make sense of this mess. "Okay. Fuck. Yeah, I was sad and totally fucked up over my dad, but I wanted you before that." I pause, my heart thrashing in my chest with the force of my admission. "And I wanted you after." Her breathing is quicker now, and she's still staring at the trees like she's going to find the answer to all the questions undoubtedly bouncing around in her brain.

"You just left and forgot all about me." The way her voice cracks sends a sharpened arrow straight into my heart. I know I hurt her, but seeing the hurt, hearing the pain in her voice, it all makes me feel like I'm suffocating under the weight of my regrets.

"I never, not even for one second, forgot about you, *fengári mou*. How could I? You were in my blood, under my skin, like you embedded yourself in my DNA. I couldn't get rid of you or the memory of you even if I had tried." She opens her mouth to retaliate, but I don't let her. "I wanted you there. Always. Even when it hurt to think about you, I wanted you."

"So why, then? Why ghost me after? I waited for you. I waited for your call. I waited for you to send news, even through Bon, but you never did." Her face crumples, and all I want to do is wrap myself around her and take all these insecurities and questions away. "And I thought perhaps I deserved it. I told you it was just sex, after all. But your sister and your mum didn't deserve your silence, Owen."

"You're right. They didn't deserve that and neither did you. That's exactly what I didn't want. For you to wait. For you to hurt." That's apparently the wrong thing to say because she lunges at me and pushes her hands into my chest, trying to hurt me.

Good. I fucking deserve it.

"Well, I did it anyway, you arsehole. I waited because I thought I loved you! I was worried every day and every night for nearly two years, and for what? You didn't even care enough to send a sign of life!" She keeps pushing at me, and I step back, letting her think she's actually capable of moving me even though I have a whole foot and at least a hundred pounds on her. "Your mum eventually sent news that you were alive. We were all worried sick, Owen. You didn't even care!"

I wish I could explain it. Tell her that because of the secrecy of the mission, no contact was allowed, so when I went missing, not even my mom knew about it. I wish I could take it all away and make sure she never went through this, that Mamá and Lainey never went through it either. Something lodges in my throat and no words come out. I can't even look at her, even if I know I deserve to witness this. I deserve to see exactly what I did; the pain I caused.

"Why won't you answer me? Tell me! I deserve to know!" She's yelling now, and I hope that it actually makes her feel even a fraction of relief, to let this all out.

"It's complicated," I say gruffly. "A lot happened right after I deployed and... I can't..." It's impossible to get the words out. To relive those days and weeks, everything we lost.

"Well, fuck you, Owen! I fucking hated you for what you did to me. I hated you for the way you made that night seem meaningless, and for being the guy who left without ever looking back. I hated you. I... I hate you." Her voice breaks on that last word, and I catch her before she hits the ground. A sob has her bending nearly in half as she collapses, followed by a wail. I never thought I'd see Maeve Howard cry, let alone like this.

The sounds of her cries makes my heart physically ache, as though someone is taking a rusty serrated knife through my chest. But her words make my stomach turn. She hates me. I thought she might, but hearing the words makes it real.

I don't let her go as she cries, whispering *I hate you* into my chest. Words I deserve to hear and feel, especially given what she just confessed to.

When her breathing slows, and she pulls herself away from me, I take her face in my hands, brushing my thumbs over the tears still streaming down her cheeks.

"Maevey. I know what I said that night was so fucked up. You have to know that I didn't mean it. You have to know how sorry I am."

Some of the fire is back in her eyes, and I'm relieved. "You're really good at saying sorry, do you know that?"

"Yeah, well, I have a lot to make up for. Even more now, it seems." She shakes her head, brows furrowed in a look I can only describe as disgust. Or maybe disappointment. I take a step back from her, letting my hands fall at my sides. She hugs herself like she still needs the comfort I obviously wasn't able to provide.

She's trying to process, trying to understand, but there's a huge missing piece that I haven't given her. And if I do it now, I may just seem like I'm fishing for sympathy.

"I want to tell you, Maeve. And I will. Just not today. Not right now. Okay?" Her body stiffens at my question. She doesn't answer.

In a swift move, she starts to walk away from me, clearly being able to see where the wooded area ends and where the paths back toward the guesthouse and main house are. Her little legs move fast, but I keep up, staying just two steps behind her. When she reaches the bottom step to the guesthouse, I call out to her.

"Please?" I implore. She turns her head, looking in my direction over her shoulder.

"What?" she asks and slowly turns to face me.

"Please give me a chance to tell you. It's okay if you still hate me after, Maevey, but please... just give me a chance to tell you what only a handful of people know." I'm grasping at nothing here, but I refuse to give up on her.

"Don't try to pull at my heartstrings now, Owen. There aren't any left for you." Her blue eyes are red-rimmed, and I hate that I did that. I caused that. Today, and so many other times all those years ago.

"I know. I don't expect anything. Just know that one day, when I'm ready... When you're ready... I'll tell you. Please." I half expect her to tell me to fuck off again, for her to pack her shit and leave.

"I need time to just... think." Another tear falls down her cheek, and she wipes it away angrily.

"Yeah. Of course." I shove my hands in my pockets to keep myself from hugging her again. "See you tomorrow, then?"

She nods and turns, walking into the house as I stand there staring at the door, wondering if I've just made another huge mistake. It feels like I just can't figure out the right thing to do with Maeve.

As if the universe knows I haven't had enough bullshit for one day, my phone buzzes in my back pocket, and I take a deep breath before accepting the call from my lawyer.

———

I DIDN'T SEE Maeve the next day. Or the day after that. I used that time to prepare Julia's room with the things that have been arriving for her, and I'm glad I've had something to do other than dwell on not seeing Maeve. Not talking to her. Lainey's coming over today though, so maybe this is my chance.

A minute after I hear the gate opening, my sister's

laughter floats in through the front door, the pitter patter of Frankie's paws and Adam's deep voice behind them.

"We're here," he shouts. "In case we didn't make enough noise on the way in."

"More like 'in case you didn't already spy on us with your ten thousand cameras everywhere.'" Lainey's giggle is immediate, and I wait a few extra seconds before making my way to them, knowing they're likely in some sort of cutesy couple embrace I don't need to see right now.

I walk toward the sound of Frankie's bark, and when I turn the corner, I'm met with a strong set of arms around my torso.

"Hey, Lainey Bananey." I hug her back, and as if sensing something is off, she pulls back and looks up at me.

"You okay, big bro?" Her eyebrows furrow, and I give her a nod with a smile that hopefully looks reassuring and not manic.

Adam lays a hand on my shoulder with a squeeze. "Where can I leave the muffins?"

I chuckle as I point toward the kitchen. Of course Lainey baked more muffins. Not just for me, for Maeve, too.

Maeve.

The thought seems to summon her as she knocks on the door twice and walks in, peering around the door. My sister rushes to her, also hugging her tightly, then asking her the same question she just asked me, replacing *big bro* with *bestie.* I take in her yellow sundress and the braid in her hair, the white sandals and the pink polish on her toes. She gently toes off her shoes, taking a couple of deep breaths as she does.

I drink in every drop of her as if I haven't already memorized every inch of her. The curve of her waist. The gentle sway of her hips as she walks. Her delicate fingers brushing a strand of hair behind her ear. Each detail calls to me, beckoning me closer until I'm consumed by the desire to touch, to be near, to surround myself with her.

My feet carry me closer to her without my knowledge, and when I look up, she's standing right in front of me. My heart races, and I stand there speechless as if my feet are glued to the floor.

Her eyes scan over my features, but they never quite reach my eyes.

"Hello, Owen." She walks around me swiftly, leaving behind the usual smell of lavender I've never been able to figure out, despite buying dozens of bottles of lavender shampoo over the years.

"So, uh, how's married life?" Adam's smile is so genuine, it's hard to be mad at him, yet I feel the scowl forming on my face. Unfortunately for him, Maeve is not in a question answering mood, and she turns quickly toward the kitchen without answering him.

"Do I smell muffins, Bon?" Maeve darts toward the container, popping the top off and taking a deep breath. She's always done this thing where she smells her food. It's adorably weird.

Better shut out all thoughts of Maeve being adorable now, asshole. She hates you.

"Yeah, I made both your favorites. Adam, could you please help me get something from the car?" Lainey takes Adam's hand and drags him out of the kitchen. I can hear her whispering something to him as they speed walk to the door. I take a deep breath when I hear it shut.

"We're gonna have to get better at this, Maevey." Her shoulders stiffen, and she slowly turns to face me. There's nothing but disdain and sadness painted in bold strokes across her features.

Letting out another sigh, I face her. "They're not gonna come back until either we go get them or they hear yelling. So, if you want to let out whatever's in your head, I'm gonna suggest you do so quietly."

"Fuck. You." The words cut through me like a sharpened

knife, but it's nothing compared to the icy contempt that's etched on her face. Her eyes are narrowed and cold, her lips down-turned in disgust, and her jaw is tight with her barely contained anger.

"Maevey, please, I–" She bolts from the room as if it's on fire, her bare feet slapping against the hardwood floor. Her hurried steps and trembling hands make it clear that she's desperate to flee the conversation and me.

"You can come back now. I know you didn't forget anything, Bon!" Seconds later, I hear the door close again and their hushed voices. I walk out of the kitchen and into the living room where the three of them are standing.

"O. What's going on? Why do you both look like you haven't slept, and why is the tension so thick in here I can hardly see through it?" Lainey's eyes, bright green like mine and our dad's, are pleading and full of concern.

"Do you know, Bon?" Maeve looks at me, then at my sister. Her hands in fists at her sides.

Adam's hand comes to rest protectively around my sister's shoulder, as though he can sense the danger of Maeve asking a question through clenched teeth.

"Know what, Mae?" Lainey's concerned eyes don't leave her best friend.

"Why Owen ghosted you. Us. Everyone. Because he won't tell me, and I'm tired of feeling this angry about it." I can see how red her eyes are, and I wonder how much sleep she's lost these past two nights because of me. I'm so sick of being the reason people are tired or stressed.

"Yes. I know. But it's not my story to tell, Maeve." Lainey looks at me, and there's sympathy in her eyes. Despite not knowing what happened with Maeve and I all those years ago, she understands everything that happened after. "I will say that if that's all this is about, then you have nothing to be angry at. You two need to talk this out. And if us being here is going to be this awkward, we can go."

"No," Maeve responds. "Please stay." She takes a deep breath in. "Maybe we can go and see the horses again? Do you think Arthur would be okay with that, Owen?"

Her face grows expressionless, her eyes closed off and distant. She inhales deeply as if to lock away all of her emotions. Her fists ball up tightly until her knuckles are white, then relax as she exhales, all evidence of turmoil gone. I don't know how she does this.

"Of course. They're your— We can go see the horses anytime you want, Maeve." My eyes are heavy, my head is pounding, and my thoughts are a jumbled mess; every word I've spoken to Maeve in the last few days has been replaying in a loop in my mind.

My chest aches as I fight the urge to blurt out what I'm feeling. Clearly, therapy has been working a little too well if I can go from being completely shut down to ready to spill my guts. Now I know the price I had to pay for my silence all those years ago. And I'm not willing to eat that cost ever again.

I'm not sure if Maeve is even ready to hear it, but the words are poised on the tip of my tongue. They always are with her. And yet nothing comes out. Not the right things, anyway.

Unaware of the battle waging inside my brain, Lainey turns to me. "Shall we?"

I nod in response. "Let's drive over. It looks like it might rain today." It's rare, but it does rain here.

"I'll drive myself so I know how to get there." Maeve doesn't miss a beat. "I'll just grab some proper shoes quickly." In a flash, she's gone, and I feel like all the air has been sucked out of the room. Lately, it feels hard to breathe when she's close by, but it's nearly impossible when she's far away.

"Shit. I'm sorry, Owen. I did *not* read the room well before I asked about married life." Adam scratches his head, giving me a pitiful look.

"Not your fault, man. She hates me." I try to swallow past the words, but it feels like there's a tennis ball in my throat.

"She doesn't. She's just angry because she doesn't understand. You two had gotten close before Dad's death, and then everything changed. Just talk to her." I shrug my shoulders, but I don't have a clue how I'm going to do that. I thought I did, but when I'm near her none of the words I had prepared in my head make sense. Especially not now.

Maeve comes back, sticking her head through the door. "Ready?"

She's swapped her sandals for tall riding boots under her dress, and the large package that arrived for her yesterday makes perfect sense now. We all move toward the door and something eases inside me knowing she'll at least be happier around the horses and my sister.

since when are you the town grump?

owen

ARTHUR:

Maeve was here again. She's really great with these horses.

ARTHUR:

When are you going to tell your wife these horses are hers, you big wuss?

OWEN:

Mind your own business, old man.

ARTHUR:

I'm literally one year older than you, asshole.

ARTHUR:

And seriously, you gotta tell her. She loves these horses almost as much as I do, and you know I'm bordering on an unhealthy amount.

ARTHUR:

Does she know how long you looked for this house for? What you did to get the place? Have you told her anything?

OWEN:

I repeat: mind your own business.

ARTHUR:

You sure are grumpy for a newlywed. At least
your wife is nice. And she shares her snacks
with me.

Another day's gone by, and it's been nothing if not complete, blissful torture. She mostly stays in the guesthouse, and I find stupid reasons to check on her.

The weather is supposed to cool off tonight. Do you have enough blankets?

How's the Wi-Fi out here?

I'm going into town for groceries. Do you need anything?

Don't mind me. Just watering the garden. Again.

Even though I know there are extra blankets in every room.

Even though I made sure the signal was strong weeks ago.

Even though I know I had her fridge and pantry stocked.

Even though it had rained the day before.

I am a pathetic excuse of the man I claim to be. Around Maeve Howard, I can't be held responsible for the stupid things I say and do. Like when I admitted to knowing what her favorite snacks are. She thought Lainey got them for her, and I just had to correct her. I couldn't leave well enough alone.

I don't know what's worse at this point. All the time I had to spend away from her, or knowing that she's a hundred feet away almost at all times and not being able to do anything about it. It borders on painful, this closeness. She's my wife, for fuck's sake. My *wife!* I still can't believe that I got drunk enough to let that happen, and it pisses me off that I can't remember more than a few moments of that night.

But I got as drunk as I did thinking that I'd have a baby girl here with me by now. Except that's not going according to plan either, with how backed up the California courts are. Regardless of the roadblocks, though, I'll fight for her. Clay and Monica wanted me to raise her. And that's what I'll do. Somehow, this baby girl feels every bit mine as Maeve does, except neither actually is.

Yet.

After I've deep cleaned the fridge and taken out the trash, I know I have no other chores to do around the house. I took time away from helping Raf with Aegis Security since he doesn't really need me anyway, and I really need to figure out what to do with all this time on my hands. There aren't any deliveries coming for Julia today, and the things that have arrived from Lainey and Ma's shopping spree are already set up.

I kind of want to get out of here. Go somewhere.

Maybe Maeve would like to come?

That's a stupid thought. She wouldn't want to go for a drive somewhere. Not with me. Unless she would, because she's also been cooped up here with nothing to do but stare at the mountains for days.

Fuck it.

I grab my wallet and keys from the table by the door and make my way to the guesthouse.

As I step up, I hear what sounds like a frustrated grunt coming from the back porch that faces the garden. I opt to look there before knocking on the door, and Maeve is sitting on a chair, a book so close to her face there's no possible way she can see the words. Her shoulders are tight, pulled up close to her ears. I knock on one of the posts to get her attention and she spins around quickly, throwing the book at me.

"What the bloody hell, Owen!" I catch the book as it flaps somewhere near my knees, chuckling at her reaction.

"Sorry. Sorry... I didn't mean to startle you." I hold back another laugh as she purses her lips.

"It's fine. I was trying to read by osmosis or willing the words to actually make their way into my brain somehow. I can read a whole script in one day, but a book? Fucking impossible." She huffs out a frustrated breath and stands to face me.

"Well, I'm going a little stir crazy here myself, so I'm going for a drive—" Before I can continue, she cuts me off.

"That's nice. Enjoy." She turns back, clearly annoyed. Man, this girl is impossible. She just admitted to trying to read a book I'm certain she has no interest in because it's some shit self-help thing I had sitting in the guesthouse.

"I was going to ask if you want to come with me, but if you want to stay here and read about how to..." I flip the cover over and bite my tongue to fight a smile. "...*Ask for What You Want*, be my guest."

Her eyes widen for a second, and she grabs her phone, walks toward me, and takes the book from my hand, tossing it behind her. The thing nearly takes off, pages flapping everywhere as it lands on the floor.

"This doesn't mean I'm not still upset. I just... need to get out of my head." She starts walking toward the driveway, and of course, I follow. "So, where are we going?"

I don't watch the way her legs move in front of me, or how her muscles flex, or how her hair blows behind her and sends the smell of lavender straight to my nostrils. I don't think at all. I just follow her and get in the truck.

As it roars to life, I remember I haven't answered her question. I was just going to drive, but I had already made a mental list of places I thought she'd like here in Ojai.

"If you want to get a book you'll actually want to read, there's a great outdoor bookstore close by. I don't think anyone will bother you there."

Her seatbelt clicks, and she looks up at me. "Oh. Are you

sure? I don't want to put you out if you had anywhere else to be."

I drive past the gate and turn onto the road, shaking my head. "Nah. I was gonna just go for a drive. Stop and look at the mountains. Catch the sunset or something. But I could use a new book myself."

I keep my eyes on the road, so I can't see her expression, but her voice comes out with a level of excitement I haven't heard since I told her about the horses.

"Sunset? Can we still do that?" She fixes her hair and faces her body toward me. "I mean, we don't have to do both. But I'd really like to do the mountain thing."

How is she this fucking cute?

"Yeah, Maevey. We can do the mountain thing. We can do both." I catch myself far too late using the nickname she specifically asked me not to use, but she doesn't scold me or make any of her usual sounds of distaste, so I count it as a win.

Twenty minutes later, we arrive at the bookstore. It's a pretty well-known spot, but not super busy this time of year or in the middle of the week, so I don't think Maeve will have an issue with being recognized. Still, I'd rather be safe than sorry, so I take off the baseball cap I had on and hand it to her.

"What's this for?" She takes the hat and looks at it with a puzzled look on her face.

"For you. If you want to put it on, you know, for a disguise or whatever." I run my hands through my hair, which is the longest it's ever been. Maeve tracks the movement, then clears her throat as she puts the hat on her head, adjusting it.

"Thanks," she mumbles. I smile and wave a hand in front of me, signaling for her to walk in first. She does, and though I do my best not to hover, I don't let her out of my sight as she walks through the maze of shelves.

I'm thankful I had the hat to give her to wear, but I wish I could see her eyes. I'd bet those blue eyes are wide and sparkling. I can tell just by the way she smiles as she flips through a book. She looks so much like the girl I met when she's this unguarded and vulnerable. And it doesn't escape me that she's like this because she doesn't know I'm watching her. She's not like this with me.

Not anymore.

I quietly browse some parenting books while keeping an eye on Maeve. Giving her enough space to choose something without me hovering, reminding myself she agreed to this outing because she was bored, not because she wanted to spend time with me.

When she turns around and spots me, I shove a hand in my pocket and raise up the books I selected for myself in a dumb, awkward wave that makes no sense. She waves her book back and starts walking toward me.

"Why don't you head back to the truck and I'll get these? There are a couple of people by the desk." I gesture toward the two young women who don't seem aware that Maeve is here, but who would likely recognize her if she was standing next to them.

She hesitates for a moment, then hands me her book and takes the keys dangling from my other hand.

After I finish paying, I get back into the truck and put the bag of books in the backseat, reaching for my seatbelt almost immediately. Maeve and I haven't said much to one another. She's been taking in the view through her window, and I can't come up with anything worth saying, so I've stayed quiet too.

"Thanks, Owen," she finally says. "For stopping at the bookstore. And for the hat." She takes the hat off and moves to hand it back to me.

"Keep it." The look of confusion on her face is instant. "In case we go back there, or anywhere else in town."

We. Why did I have to say we?

"Will you be coming as my unofficial bodyguard again, then?" The teasing tone in her voice puts me more at ease as she places my hat back on her head, her golden hair fanning out around the edges, just skimming her shoulders. I grip the steering wheel a little tighter, not thinking about how her hair would feel in my hands. I never ever think about *that*.

The color of her hair now reminds me of honey. It's a warmer blonde than it used to be all those years ago when I mostly saw her through a computer screen.

"We still have some time before the sunset. There's a honey company close by that sells loose leaf teas. That's where I got the English Breakfast for you, so we can pick up some more." I'm on a real roll, so I just keep rambling. My sister and I don't have much more than our green eyes in common. That and our ability to ramble like absolute idiots at the worst of times. "They have these honey stick things you'd probably like. I think they're meant for kids, but they're really good. They didn't have any left when you got into town or I would have left you some. Wanna try them?"

By the time I finish, the small smile on her face is a full-blown grin. I can't look for too long. I'd never look away. Thank fuck I'm driving.

"Sure, O. Let's go." Goddamn, I love it when she calls me O. Fuck, she could call me asshole, and I'd probably still love it.

I thought we'd drive in silence again, but the bookstore seems to have loosened us both up enough to have a conversation.

"How long have you lived in Ojai?" She plays with the hem of her shorts, looking straight ahead.

"Just a few months. It took a while to find the right house."

"Hmm. And you like it here?" She looks at me, but just as

fast as she turned toward me, she's back to looking out the windshield.

"Oh yeah. It's a great little town. And I'm not too far from Lainey or Raf, so it's kind of perfect." We get to The Honey Place quickly, but I wish we had a longer drive now that she's talking to me.

"Seems like it." There's something different in her voice, but I don't have time to ask about it as I'm pulling into the parking lot. Not that she would answer me, anyway.

We quietly exit the truck and walk into the shop through the creaky wood door.

"Owen! You're back!" Josie, one of the owners, waves as she sees me walking in. At over six feet tall, her hug packs some force when she comes over to me. She slaps me once on the cheek by way of greeting, and I scowl. She just laughs, mumbling *grump* under her breath.

"Hey, Jo. How you doing?" As I look up, Maeve has her lips between her teeth, clearly enjoying this little display.

"Oh, I saved you a box of that English Breakfast tea you got for your super special lady friend last time. It's the last one!" My cheeks heat as she produces said box from somewhere under the counter.

Maeve takes the box before I can, opens it, and holds it up to her nose, breathing in deeply. Her eyes close and she makes that damn humming noise I can't get out of my brain.

"His super special lady friend thanks you. Your tea is absolutely delightful." Maeve smiles brightly at Jo, which doesn't surprise me at all.

"Josie. But Jo's fine, too. Really nice to finally meet you." Jo wipes her hand on her apron and sticks it out for Maeve. I can't decide if Josie has no idea who Maeve is, or she truly doesn't care. Either way, I appreciate her a little more at this moment, despite the fact that she just outed me.

"Maeve. Pleasure." Maeve shakes her hand, still smiling.

"You know, Owen, if you weren't such a grumpy bastard, I might feel bad about this." I roll my eyes at her, but considering she's married to the grumpiest man I've ever met, I know my attitude doesn't faze her in the least.

"No, you wouldn't, Jo." I reach for the pack of honey sticks next to the cash register. Then I reach for a second as Jo laughs.

"Just your usual, then?" I nod and give her a few bills that I know more than cover everything. She used to argue with me, but now she calls it her compensation for putting up with my terrible personality.

"See you next week, then," Jo calls as I walk back out toward the door. I like that I don't have to bother with small talk here. I don't like most people, but the folks of Ojai have slowly managed to crawl under my skin, and I might be a little less grumpy with them than I am with the LA crowd.

"Thank you," Maeve calls out as she follows me out.

Once we're back on the road she turns to me again. "Since when are you the town grump?"

"Since I moved here, I guess?" I shrug, not thinking much about her question. I've always been told I'm closed off and grumpy. This is nothing new.

"I don't understand. You've always been a bit serious, but... grumpy? Not a word I would have used to describe you until recently." She laughs again, and the sound makes something expand in my chest. It's not a tight, heavy feeling. No, this is light and feels an awful lot like relief.

"People like you, my mom and Lainey don't often see this side of me. Not like the rest of the world does." There's a quizzical look on her face.

"What does that mean?" I really need to learn how to keep my mouth shut today. We're on a straight stretch of road, so I chance a look at her for a second longer than I might otherwise.

"People I'm comfortable with. People I like. I'm not

grumpy with the people that make me happiest. It's easy to smile when I'm happy."

She opens her mouth to speak, then closes it again. She looks down at her hands, then out the passenger window. "Oh."

22 /

blink once for yes.

maeve

I'M NOT *grumpy with the people that make me happiest. It's easy to smile when I'm happy.*

How am I supposed to think about anything else? I mean, I know Raf has called him a grumpy asshole forever, but I thought nothing of it. Like, maybe it was a joke, because I've never thought of Owen as grumpy before. He's always smiled pretty easily when I'm around. Except that first day, but I chalked that up to him just not knowing us yet. I could see how easily he smiled at his sister. I just figured he was like this with everyone. I didn't see *I'm not grumpy with the people that make me happiest* coming. Not by a long shot.

Words suddenly fail me as I think of this new-to-me version of Owen. This revelation of a man who bought me my favorite snacks and tea. Who told the lovely Jo about me. Who bought honey sticks because he thought I'd like them as much as he does.

It's hard to wrap my brain around this contradiction. This man who once made me feel so seen, so happy, so free to be myself. Until he called what we did meaningless and never reached out to me again. It's difficult to rationalize how this is all the same person.

And yet I find the wall of ice I'd purposefully built between us melting a little more every day. He still hasn't explained himself, but Bon wouldn't lie. If she says there's a real reason, I believe her. I just can't fathom what it might be.

He seems content to let me be in my thoughts for the duration of the drive, and while I'm looking out the window most of the time, I don't register that he's pulled into a gravel patch and stopped the truck.

"Okay?"

Anything but that word. Anything at all.

I close my eyes and take a deep breath, scraping up my feelings, shoving them all back in that box I keep under lock and key in the darkest, deepest, furthest corner of my heart. The one I never allow myself to open. Not ever. The one that Owen seems intent on prying open every single time he speaks.

Without answering his question, I take off my seatbelt and reach for my door handle. He does the same, and while I'm busy recollecting the pieces of myself I'm not willing to share with him, he takes a bag out of the backseat.

We walk in silence, him ahead of me, through a small path.

"It's not too far," he says as he looks down at the heeled, backless shoes on my feet. "Is that all right?"

"Mmhmm. Fine." I keep my eyes on the path as I answer. I can walk in pretty much anything, so a few pebbles don't scare me.

Owen eventually stops ahead of me, and the view nearly knocks the breath out of my lungs. We're up high, but beyond the valley in front of us, there are mountains, green and lush, and the sun is slowly making its way behind them.

Just off the path, a log has fallen in a perfect position for us to sit and take in the vista before us.

It unsettles me just how comfortable it is to simply exist next to him. How easy it's always been, and how confusing it is that this fact has not changed all these years later.

He hands me a little plastic tube.

"Just bite off the top. I dare you to eat only one." He smirks, and I do as he instructed, biting off the top of the honey stick. My eyes immediately widen as I taste its contents. It's honey, only somehow better. Not sweeter, but richer, flavored with something I can't describe. Before I have time to figure it out, I'm sucking the last of it, putting my hand out for another from Owen.

He smiles that deadly smile and gives me two more. We sit, drinking honey and watching the sun disappear. I don't immediately feel the smile that blooms on my face as I take in the pink and purple sky, but I do feel Owen's gaze on me.

"This is stunning, Owen. Thank you for bringing me here." I dare a quick look at him, his green eyes shining with the golden hour.

It's a strange feeling, being this close to him and not feeling as much of the anger that I have held onto for so many years. He must sense my unintentional vulnerability because he reaches a hand up and tucks a strand of hair behind my ear.

"You're welcome." I shiver at the contact and also because as the sun sets, its warmth disappears with it.

Owen reaches behind him and produces a gray hoodie. Without asking, he puts it over my head, the thing nearly swallowing me whole. It smells like him, and I force myself not to take the deep breath my lungs are begging me for. His hat falls off my head in the process, and he takes that, too, putting it back on my head backward.

His pupils dilate as his eyes rake over me, from my legs to my arms poking through the sleeves of his sweatshirt to the top of my head.

"You look good in my clothes, Maevey."

Hello, universe? Anybody out there? Am I dead? Have I entered an alternate reality? Is Owen James currently giving me sex eyes and telling me he likes me in his clothes? Blink once for yes.

The arsehole smiles and turns back for something else behind him. He produces a blanket and places it gently on my lap, then returns back to gazing at the sunset like he didn't just spin my entire existence upside down. Like he hasn't been doing so for weeks now.

Why did I agree to this? Why did I have to accidentally get married to the one man I have never been able to keep out of my mind? Why did he suddenly have to be so nice to me? It's not fair, but we came here for a sunset, and I'm going to enjoy this fucking sunset if it's the last thing I do.

With my elbows on my knees and my face in my hands, I get Owen out of my peripheral line of sight, but then I breathe in, and his scent is everywhere. It's infuriating and delicious and I want none of it, but also so much more of it.

Once the sun sets, I allow myself to sit back.

"Wow," I whisper. I did manage to take in the colors, even if only for a few minutes. Now the sky is a mix of blues and pinks and purples, and though my fingers itch to reach for my phone so I can take a picture, I know it would never do justice to the real thing.

I look up at Owen and wouldn't you know it, he's looking at me again.

Or still? No, he couldn't have been looking at me this entire time.

"Do you think we can do this again sometime?" I don't know what possesses me to ask the question, other than the fact that I need to experience another of these sunsets while I'm here.

"Anytime you want. I can take you to a few other spots, which are even better than this, but they're a little farther away." He shrugs, eyes steady on me.

"Really? You'd do that?"

"I know it's going to take more than books, honey, and a sunset for you to realize this, *fengári mou*, but there's nothing in this world I wouldn't do for you. Not a damn thing." His eyes bore into my soul, and it should be too much. I should be running, like I usually do when anything beyond platonic civility happens between Owen and I, but I don't move. I can't.

I feel my body being pulled and pushed by an invisible force. My head feels light, like I'm floating on the current of his words. He has me in the palm of his hand, swaying back and forth like a leaf on a branch in the breeze.

His hand comes to my chin, his thumb brushing against my lower lip, the heat of his touch burning me in a most luscious way. Just before I give in to the touch, his hand is gone.

"Shall we? Before it gets too dark." He stands and puts a hand out to help me do the same. I still feel like I'm off balance, so I take his hand and know I've made a mistake immediately. His touch warms my entire body, and the blanket almost feels too hot now. Owen's face gives nothing away, though, and his lack of reaction sobers me.

He pulls me up, grabs the remaining honey sticks and the several empty ones we plowed through, then places a hand on my lower back, guiding us back along the path, which is darkened, but not completely.

I keep his blanket on me as we drive back to his house. We're silent the whole way again, and I allow myself to doze off for a moment as the blur of streetlights and darkened mountains fly past us outside.

When I open my eyes again, Owen is opening the passenger door, looking at me with a tenderness I surely must be imagining in my sleepy state.

"Come on. I'll walk you up. Unless you want to sleep in the truck tonight?" His lopsided smile makes my stomach flip and that wakes me up enough to jump up in my seat.

"All right. I mean, no. I mean, all right to walking me to the guesthouse, no to sleeping in the truck." I move the blanket off my lap then all of a sudden realize my error. The night is chilly, and the wind is ice cold as it hits my legs. I wrap the blanket back around me, hearing Owen's deep chuckle next to me. We walk down the paved path surrounded by flowers, and when I reach the door, I turn to look at him.

"Thank you again. This was such a lovely evening." Owen nods and hands me my book and an unopened box of honey sticks.

"Don't mention it. I'm glad you got to see a little Ojai magic tonight." We stand silently looking at one another for several seconds, and it dawns on me that he probably wants his things back.

I fumble the items in my hands, attempting to unravel the blanket from around my body, remembering I still have his hoodie on.

"Oh, your things. I'm sorry. Here—"

"They're yours, Maevey. I don't want them back." He catches my book just before I drop it and places it back in my hands, his hands closing around mine with a gentle squeeze.

"Have a good sleep." His hands release mine and he turns, putting both hands in his pockets as he walks away from me.

I don't dare watch him walk away. I slip into the house and immediately rip off the blanket, sweater and hat. I leave the book and honey sticks on the table by the door and rush into the bathroom for a shower so I can wash the smell of Owen James off me. I put on fresh pajamas and vow to go straight to my bed, but before I do, I find myself in the hall, turning his hoodie over in my hands and slipping it on over my head, allowing my lungs that deep breath they begged for earlier.

I slip into bed with the hood up and the neckline of his

sweatshirt pulled up to my nose, and know there's a stupid smile on my face right before I fall asleep with images of pink and purple skies, and green eyes looking intently into mine. The words, *there's nothing in this world I wouldn't do for you,* play on a loop as I doze off.

i remember everything.

maeve

THE MORNING LIGHT streams through the curtains, and I feel the soft fabric of Owen's gray hoodie enveloping me. With a deep sigh, I wrestle with the pang in my chest that has been there since I started living in his guesthouse. I roll onto my side and push away the blanket, hating myself for finding comfort in something that smells like him.

I know we need to talk. We need to figure this out before this visit with the social workers. Though I'm not officially on the paperwork for the baby's guardianship, I am his wife, so I'll need to be a part of this process too and I don't want to mess it up for him with the awkwardness between us.

I send off a quick text to see if he's at home.

MAEVE:

Can I come over now for a talk?

His response is immediate.

OWEN:

Of course.

I have the decency to swap his sweatshirt for one of my

own, brush my teeth and wash my face. I pile my hair on top of my head and make my way toward the main house. The door is ajar, so I take that as my invitation to walk right in.

The moment I do so, the smell of tea permeates the air. Owen is at the kitchen island setting down a plate topped with a dozen donuts with all kinds of sprinkles on them. Three things happen when I see this. My stomach twists at the thought that he remembers, then it turns at the same thought, then it rumbles again because I'm absolutely starving.

"Hello." If my face is puffy from oversleeping, Owen's is gaunt from the exact opposite. But I'm not thinking about whether or not he's been getting enough sleep. I don't care.

Okay, I do care, but I'm trying really hard not to.

"What's all this?" I ask, waving at the donuts, coffee, eggs, bacon, and pastries covering every surface of the countertop.

"I thought you might be hungry, but if you're not, we can just leave this stuff, and I'll toss it later." He shrugs, and I lunge for the plate of croissants he had started to lift.

"No!" I take a quick breath in and settle myself. "I mean, no, that's okay. I could eat." He places the plate of food on the counter and gestures for me to take a seat on one of the stools. His normally vibrant green eyes are dull, almost lackluster. I perch myself on the edge of a stool as he turns away.

Once we're both seated, I reach for a sprinkle donut, sitting it on my plate. "Do you remember the first time we ate these together? Well, I suppose that was the only time, really." I look up and find him looking down at me, the look on his face softer than before as he surely plays the same distorted memories over in his mind.

After a beat of silence, I chance looking at his eyes. "I remember everything, Maevey," he whispers.

My body is at war with itself. The instinct to fight *and* flight is simultaneously strong. How do I escape this hell of reliving memories with a man I thought I loved? How do I find the strength to stay and face these truths I know I'm not prepared to hear head on? It's an impossible situation, so I settle for taking a bite of my donut.

"I need to know now, Owen." I look down at my donut, half expecting him to have changed his mind. Half hoping for it. "Even if you might not be ready. I need to."

"Yeah." I look up at him again, and it's as if somehow the circles under his eyes are darker, his skin ashier.

He begins, hardly taking a breath before speaking. "I left a few days after my dad's funeral. It was just me and three other guys on a special mission we were going to be briefed on once we arrived, but we never made it to base." He looks down at his hands, which are in tight fists on the countertop. The urge to take his hand in mine is strong, but I hold back.

"The four of us were taken hostage." My mouth gapes open, and I inhale sharply as my mind races to process what he's said. My head spins, either from the shock of his words or the quick burst of oxygen I just took in.

"We were in a cell for weeks. We couldn't see the outside, so I didn't even realize how much time had passed until we...Until I was out. They couldn't tell my mom, and when I got back, I wrote her a fucking email saying I was on a secret mission and had just got back. I couldn't face her. Not in the state I was in." His fists somehow tighten, and this time I don't hesitate. I take one of his hands in mine and the other relaxes as I intertwine our fingers.

"Lainey didn't even know about the abduction until last year when we started talking again." His breath comes out choppy before he continues, "Four of us went in. I was the only one that made it out. And a couple of the guys on the rescue mission didn't make it either." He shakes his head. "I can't give you any more details than that, Maeve. Please don't ask me to. I can't."

Four in. One out. People died to save him. He's carried the weight of this for years. Years. Alone.

I hold my breath to keep the sob trying to break through inside.

I turn so that my body is facing him, but he doesn't move. "I won't," I whisper. He licks his lips and takes a deep breath.

"I was so fucked up after that. I had to go to so much counseling, so many doctors. It was months before I even started to talk about it. Before I talked at all. I was angry." He huffs out a humorless laugh. "No, I was... I was gone. I had nothing left but hideous memories and guilt to eat away at me. If I didn't have my psychiatrist and Raf, I don't know where I would be right now."

"Owen, I'm—"

"I don't want your pity, Maeve. I don't need you to feel bad for me or treat me like I'm made of glass. I'm good. I'm okay. For a long time, I didn't think I'd be able to say that, but I am." He moves to look at me, unshed tears sitting in his eyes that make my own threaten to spill over.

"I believe you." It's impossible not to. Since he came back into my life last year, he's shown no signs of PTSD, though I've purposely kept my distance, so what would I know anyway.

"I need you to know that I cut everyone off because I didn't know who I was anymore. I didn't recognize myself. I thought I had nothing left to give." I smile gently, thankful that all of those sentences were in the past tense.

"One day, my psychiatrist gave me a puzzle. A code to crack. I wasn't talking about what happened, so I guess she figured it would give me something to do. I took it back to my room at the facility they had me in and worked on it for a few hours. I brought it back to her the next day and asked her if she had any more. She told me it should have been nearly impossible for me to solve it. That she'd only ever seen one person come close after months of trying. Apparently, she wanted to give me something to work toward. To keep my mind busy with something other than reliving the hell I somehow walked out of." I can feel the ache in my chest building as he speaks, but then something changes. He takes another breath, less strangled this time, and shrugs one shoulder.

"I started cracking more codes. I knew I wasn't going back on the ground, so when the doctor cleared me, I moved into cyber security and did that for the Marine Corps until I left. That's when Aegis was born. Raf left at the same time as me, and we needed something... anything... to keep ourselves occupied. And... I think you can fill in the gaps. I went back to the East Coast, made amends with my mom, and eventually Elaina. And now I'm here. With you."

He faces me then, my knees fitting in between his, our hands together in the middle of us. Two hot tears roll down my cheeks as the weight of his words hit me. The anger is still there, still nagging at me, but it's not taking up as much space as before. It's been replaced with sadness, guilt, and what feels oddly like helplessness. None of us knew about any of this, so no one was able to help him through it other than his doctors and whatever colleagues he let in at the time.

When more tears come, he brings both hands up to cradle my face, tipping it up as he brushes away the wetness with his thumbs. I will myself not to think too hard about why my tears flow so willingly with him.

"Don't cry for me, *fengári mou*. It's over now." One of his hands goes to the seat of my stool, and he pulls me closer to him. He tucks some hair behind my ear, and as more tears silently fall, he kisses them away with a reverence I've never felt from anyone. And when a loud sob racks me, he pulls me close, cradling my head on his chest. My arms go around his waist, holding on tightly and the connection to him soothes something in me. He's here, and he's safe now. He didn't leave me.

After we've spent some time just holding on to one

another, and once my tears have stopped, I pull back, struggling to look at him.

Eventually, I do bring my eyes back to his and say the only thing I can think of.

"I'm so sorry, Owen. I'm so, so deeply sorry." He shakes his head, brows pulling together in disagreement with what I've just said.

"There's nothing for you to say sorry for. I'm the one who needs to apologize, Maeve. I'm the one who should be groveling and begging for your forgiveness. You didn't do anything wrong."

"Other than the way you left things, neither did you, O." My words surprise him, his eyebrows lift, and his eyes widen. If he really feels that even after everything that happened, I blame him for the rift between us, then I have a lot to explain to him.

"You didn't," I repeat. "Yes, it was unfortunate timing, and I spent a lot of time being angry with you, but you were in an impossible situation. I see that now."

We sit in silence for a little bit, and I soak up the moment, going over everything that was just said in my head.

"So where do we go from here?" I may as well be asking him *what are we*, but I don't care. I just want to know where he thinks we stand.

"Anywhere you want, Maevey. I know our marriage isn't real, that I come with more baggage than anyone should, and that I'm about to add even more to my plate with a baby. I know this isn't what you wanted, and fuck, I don't even know if *I'm* what you wanted, but here we are. At least for now." He relaxes his shoulders, bringing his hands to my arms, and his forehead to mine.

"Just please, please don't hate me anymore. I don't think I can take it." His voice is a whisper, and the words travel slowly, like dripping honey from my head to my toes. The hurt in his voice is crystal clear, and it dissolves all the anger I had left.

"I don't." The words spill out faster than I can register them, but I don't take them back. I shake my head and lift it up to look at him, swallowing back a lump in my throat when I see more unshed tears in his eyes.

"I don't hate you, Owen. I'm sorry I said that. I was angry, but I didn't mean it. I hate the anger that I felt. I hate that I didn't understand why things happened the way they did. But you?" I shake my head again, willing my tears to stay put, but they don't listen to my silent plea. Owen catches them with his thumbs and brings his face closer, so close our lips are nearly touching.

Please. Please, please, please. Kiss me senseless. Please.

Our lips brush as he says, "Thank you." And when I think he's about to give in, he pulls back, moves his hands to my shoulders, closes his eyes and takes a deep breath. My skin tingles and vibrates from the loss of his touch as I try to make sense of the roller coaster of a conversation we just disembarked. My stomach churns, and my head swims as I sway in my seat, trying to find solid ground beneath me once again.

What the bloody hell? Why did he stop? Why did he get so close in the first place? Why do I want him to kiss me?

"We should eat." His voice is rough. He clears his throat and reaches for the bacon.

"Oh. Right." As if on cue, my stomach rumbles and I catch the corner of Owen's lips lift up at the sound.

"You still like sprinkle donuts best, Maevey?" He looks at me, one eyebrow raised in question.

"Mmhmm." I reach for another donut and before I can bring it to my mouth, he raises his, holding it toward me. I freeze as the memories rush in.

"To...us. To figuring this out." He touches his donut to mine, and I nod dumbly.

"Yeah." I can't think of anything else to say, so I bite into my donut, hoping the sugar rushes to my brain and puts some cohesive thoughts back in there.

24 /
you should take a picture.

maeve

SOMETHING'S UP. Owen basically ran away from me for some mystery meeting earlier, and he hasn't done his usual inspection of the gardens around the guesthouse. I don't know when he'll be back, so I head to the stable to see the horses.

When I drive up, there are a few more cars than last time I came by, letting me know the stable hands are all here today. I figure I'll just say a quick hello and see my favorite mare, Scout, before I get out of everyone's way.

"Hi, Miss Maeve," Paige, a sweet young woman, greets me.

"Just Maeve, Paige." I smile at her as her cheeks turn pink. Arthur told me she's been dying to ask me for an autograph but doesn't want to bother me. I've got a massive package coming for her as a surprise.

"Scout hasn't had any carrots yet today. I waited to see if you'd come before she got any treats." Paige smiles ruefully, then continues on her way to the tack room.

"Thank you. That was thoughtful." I stop at Scout's door, smiling when she immediately nuzzles up to me.

"She really took to you." Arthur's booming voice comes from behind me.

"She's a lovely girl. Loves everyone," I say as I run a hand along Scout's neck. "Thanks for letting me just show up here anytime, Arthur."

He lets out a sigh, and I look up at him. He rubs the back of his neck, and it feels like he has something to say. I've gotten that feeling every time I've seen Arthur. "You really love horses, right?" I nod. "And mountains? Wine? Wide open spaces?" I repeat the movement. "And you can't live too far from LA because of your job, so Ojai is kind of a perfect place, isn't it?" I feel my eyebrows bunch together on my face, confused by what he's saying. "And Owen, being your husband, knows all this, yeah?"

"Arthur, what are you getting at?" Because there's no way he's saying what I think he's saying.

He takes a deep breath. "It's not my place to say anything outright, but Owen knows next to nothing about horses. He looked for a house with a stable or enough room for one for months. He paid out of his ass to buy this place, negotiated for weeks, and made sure I had everything I needed to keep these horses in the lap of luxury." He scratches at the stubble on his face. "All I'm saying is, I'm not *letting* you show up here. You can come anytime you want. And not just because we like having you here. All right?" His eyebrows jump up on his forehead, and I nod dumbly again.

With that small bomb he just dropped, he tips his hat and turns on his heels.

Owen bought this place for me.

I feed Scout a few carrots as I brush her, but my mind is busy mulling over the fact that Owen did this. That he didn't say anything. He keeps so much to himself, and I think now I understand that it's because he doesn't want to burden people. It took him years to tell me about his hostage situation. It took years for him to tell his sister. He waited until he felt he'd fully healed before mending their relationship and now ours. Is that what he's doing here, too? Waiting for the right time?

After dropping the brush for the third time in an hour, I put it away and drive back to the guesthouse.

I can tell that Owen is in the gym because it faces the guesthouse. He doesn't have any music on, but I heard the drop of a weight a few minutes ago.

I put some workout clothes on and pace around the entryway for a minute, working up the courage to walk in there.

I practically stomp into the gym, intent on confronting him for nearly kissing me and buying me a house, but whatever words I had ready quickly dissolve on my tongue at the sight of him. He's bent at the waist, gripping a barbell as he does deadlifts in front of the mirror. His back ripples with effort as he lifts and lowers the heavy weights, grunting with each repetition. From my vantage point, his well-defined thigh muscles are easy to see, flexing beneath his shorts.

The cords of muscle stand out in stark definition against his tanned skin. But it's what I see when my eyes travel up his torso that has my mouth going completely dry. The tattoos I've peeked at beneath his T-shirts are now a lot more visible with the cut-off shirt he's wearing. The ink travels up his right shoulder and onto his chest, though I can't see them from here.

"You should take a picture. I hear they last longer." He sets the weights down, making me jump at the sound.

"Huh? What? Hi." I clear my throat and snap back into myself.

What the fuck was that shit?

"I wanted to work you. Work in you. Work in *with* you. Bollocks! What the hell have I just said?" I wipe my forehead and look for any version of myself that isn't this babbling fool, but she's nowhere to be found.

The asshole in front of me chuckles. "You said a lot of things there, blondie."

"Oh, whatever. You could hardly introduce me as your wife to your friend. I haven't seen a real-life sweaty man in front of me in quite some time, so excuse me if I temporarily lost my wits." I pull at my ponytail, hoping the tightness will bring blood-flow back to my brain, away from my vagina.

He smirks, but then his face goes back to the neutral, emotionless expression he seems to greet most people with. I hate that it's aimed at me now. And the sight is so at odds with the easy grin on his face when he told me to take a picture that I immediately opt not to confront him. I want easy-going Owen. I want banter and almost-kisses that hopefully turn into real kisses.

"You want to use the gym, it's all yours. I'm done anyway." He wipes down the area he was just using and cocks his head as he walks toward the door. Without thinking, I grab his forearm as he walks past me.

"Wait." I gasp at our contact, remembering that touching Owen James is a bad, bad idea. I release his arm and look up.

Why does he need to wait again? Oh yeah. We're supposed to be able to be around one another...

"I thought we needed to be able to be around one another. We haven't been doing that. And you haven't given me an update on the baby in a while. And I'm feeling a little out of sorts here, living in your guesthouse, riding your horses, eating your food..." I pivot so my back rests on the door frame, and Owen does the same. "Just... talk to me. Please."

"Her name is Julia." He swallows as his brows come together. "You're riding the horses?" He crosses his arms, and I curse my eyeballs for following the movement, pausing on his biceps for a beat too long.

"That's a pretty name." A warmth spreads across my face, and a small smile blooms on my lips as I imagine Owen rocking a baby to sleep in his arms.

I shove the thought away, moving on to the next topic. "I've been riding a couple of the horses, giving them some exercise." The smile on my face remains now because these horses have given me more peace than I've felt in a long time.

"But listen, tell me more about Julia. What's happening? How are you doing?"

"Uh, I was gonna talk to you about that, actually. I talked to my lawyer earlier and they're coming here tomorrow." He swallows and brings the hem of his shirt up to wipe at the sweat on his face.

Congratulations, eyeballs! You didn't even sneak a peek at his abs!

"I know it's not ideal, and you don't want anything to do with this, but between the system being backed up and the delays with the court, we really want to do this as soon as possible." I hate seeing him look this defeated, and I hate that he just wanted to deal with this alone.

How long has Owen been dealing with all the most difficult parts of his life on his own?

"I'm here for you Owen. Literally. I am here to help you, so yes, of course I'll be there. I'm doing nothing else, so please call on me, all right?"

"Yeah. Thanks, Maeve."

Hmm. No Maevey. After the joke about taking a picture, he went serious.

He looks down at his shoes, shoulders slightly slumped, and it makes me feel a little sick to see him like this. I want the playful Owen back. I want the confident, take-no-shit Owen back. I want things with us to not feel so fucking hard all the time.

"Do you think you have time to stick around and spot me?"

Where the shit did that come from?

"If you think you can handle being around me and not run away again, that is." I say the words and immediately regret them. I look at Owen, whose eyes widen in surprise; his mouth slightly agape as he processes what I've just said.

Crikey, Maeve, you really need to know when to shut the fuck up!

His hand shoots out, and he grabs the pockets of the hooded sweatshirt I'm wearing. His sweatshirt. He pulls my body roughly against his, and when he speaks, I feel his breath on my neck.

"It's gonna be hard to handle being around you when you're wearing my clothes, Maevey."

Maevey. There he is.

It's too close for comfort and not close enough. I want to step back, to create some emotional distance between us, but I can't bring myself to move away, the physical pull is too strong.

I step back, and he lets the hoodie go. I pull at the hem, pulling it up above my head.

"I guess I won't wear it, then." I reveal a bright pink sports bra with delicate straps crisscrossing up the back, the fabric stretched tight across my chest. My matching shorts give me plenty of stretch to move around. My skin burns under his gaze. The muscles beneath my skin clench. "Better?" I'm taunting him, I know, but my vagina seems to be making all of my decisions for me.

"No." His green eyes are dark, and it's a look I haven't seen in a very long time. It sends a shiver through me, and he smirks when he notices. Now he's the one taunting me. I don't fancy it. I much prefer being the one in control of this situation. "Cold?"

"No." My body feels warm and tingly, but it has nothing to do with exercising.

I walk over to the bench and start to remove weights from the bar, though what I'm left with is likely still too heavy for me. "Just do what I asked you to, please."

"As you wish." He grins, standing at the head of the bench, waiting for me to begin.

I manage to get through the first three reps just fine on my own, but by the time I get to the fourth one, I'm grunting my way through it. He lets me struggle for a few seconds, and I manage to finish it. On the fifth rep, he has to help me, and as our hands brush, I nearly drop the entire bar on myself. He catches it.

"I've got you," he says. And I hate the way the words land on my sternum, soft and slow.

I walk over to the squat bar, again removing many weights as Owen easily has a hundred pounds on me. He helps me lower the bar so it's at a comfortable height for me, and I get into position, well aware that I'm about to squat directly in front of him.

This time I make it to seven reps before needing any help, and on the eighth one, he squats behind me, his crotch lining up to my behind, and by a sheer miracle, I manage to actually come back to standing. When we're both standing up straight, I feel him hardening behind me, and my eyes close as I take a deep breath in.

My libido is a feral beast threatening to make me do crazy things, like reach behind me and feel his length in my hand.

Absolutely the fuck not, Maeve Charlotte!

When I open my eyes, I catch his in the mirror, and it's clear that he knows that I feel it. There's no embarrassment, no shyness, but he also doesn't move at all.

"Are you done?" His voice is as rough as sandpaper, grating against my skin.

I whisper a yes and he steps away. The loss of his body heat, of his erection on my back has me swaying on the spot.

He turns and walks straight out the door, but I hear his grunt, and I don't miss the way his right hand reaches forward to fix himself before he walks out.

I take a step back and examine my reflection in the mirror.

A wide, triumphant smile stretches across my face as I feel an immense sense of satisfaction course through my veins.

I get back to the guesthouse and reach for a chocolate chip muffin, because I'm a grown woman, and I do what I want. I figure I should probably release some of the tension coursing through my body and enjoy some quality time with my vibrator. Maybe an orgasm will have me thinking straight again and not about the feel of Owen behind me. On top of me. Beneath me.

Bollocks. I had better get started.

i rub my magic lamp and you appear?

maeve

WELL, the vibrator idea was a colossal failure. I kept thinking of Owen, and his muscles, the way he smelled of mint and sweat, and how delicious he felt behind me. I couldn't let myself come with those thoughts. It's not right. We still have too much unresolved between us.

All for the best anyway. Especially as halfway through my failed attempt at an orgasm, I got a call from my assistant reminding me that I have an awards show to attend, and I'm being strongly urged to bring Owen with me. It's in two days. I completely forgot about it, focusing instead on resting, processing my feelings for Owen, and riding those beautiful horses he has. But my publicist won't let me live this down if I don't at least ask Owen, so I'm on my way to do that now.

I knock on the door twice, but hear no answer, so I peek my head in. I can't hear anything, and I call out Owen's name. His truck is in the driveway, and I don't think he's gone anywhere. I step inside, calling out to him again. After a moment, I hear a faint sound, so I walk further into the house. I haven't been further than the living room and kitchen.

When I hear another sound coming from upstairs, I walk up the stairs, calling Owen's name for the third time.

No response.

A groan sounds from somewhere down the hall, and I follow where it came from to what must be Owen's room, based on the dark bedding and the fact that the whole room smells just like him. His shower is running, and I fight the urge to strip myself down to nothing and walk in there, begging him to make me come, to touch me, to make me lose my mind just for a little while.

Where are these thoughts coming from?

I know this is a bad idea, but his next groan has me stepping closer to the bathroom door, and when I reach the threshold, I see him, finally.

His back is to me, water falling on the very muscles I was looking at earlier, except now there's nothing covering them. Through the almost perfectly clear glass, which somehow hasn't fogged up, I see him. He has one hand braced on the wall above his head and I can't see the other. His head is hanging low, but slowly it comes up until it rolls back as another strangled sound leaves him.

It hits me then that he's touching himself. Alarms ring in my brain.

Get out! Leave! Don't let him see you!

But then something happens that has my feet glued to the floor. All of his muscles tighten, and I watch every movement. His back, his glutes, his arms, all tightening as a grunt leaves him and then… and then…

"Maeve!" It's loud and clear. He's just moaned my name. I close my eyes, trying to collect my thoughts. "Maeve." Again. And this time my mouth works faster than my brain or my limbs.

"Yes?"

Ohhhhhh shiiiiiiiiiit. What?

He turns around, eyes wide like saucers, both hands

coming up as if he's about to punch someone, but when his eyes land on me, they widen further before softening again. His hands go to his hips, not an ounce of embarrassment visible on his face. He knows that I know exactly what just happened here.

"Are you some sort of genie, blondie? I rub my magic lamp and you appear?" His lips quirk up in a small smile, and I take the opportunity to clear my throat as I take a few steps toward him.

"Yeah, but my trick is I only appear after you come, and that's not really any fun, now, is it?" I don't let my eyes roam over his body. I keep them set on his bright, emerald eyes. Okay, so maybe I glance at his lips for like a second or two, but no lower.

"The beauty about my lamp, sunshine, is that it's always ready to go." His eyebrows raise in challenge, and I do let my eyes roam then. I don't bother to let my gaze travel over his body the way I want them to. I just focus my eyes straight on his softened cock, and with a victorious grin, I have my retort.

"Could have fooled me." His own gaze moves to where mine just was, but I don't take the time to drink in the expression on his face. I spin on my heels and saunter out of the bathroom.

"Well, you gotta give me a minute!" I chuckle at his response, but keep walking.

"I need to speak with you about something. I'll be downstairs waiting for you to be done playing with your lamp, Aladdin." His only response then is a loud groan followed by the water being shut off. I hope he takes his time so I have a moment to cool off and recover.

Owen was touching himself while thinking of me. The sound of his gruff voice keeps playing over and over in my mind already, and I wonder how long this memory will last. I wonder if it'll be seven years and counting, like the last memories of what he sounded like when I last heard him come. I wonder if I'll be haunted by visions of this for years to come now.

His footsteps coming down the stairs within minutes, and I brace myself for having to look at him again, silently praying for my façade to stick, for the mask to remain intact, and for him not to see any trace of how just being near him affects me.

Owen comes into view as I sit at the island, peeling a banana. It occurs to me this is either the best or worst fruit I could have picked from the basket.

"You needed to speak to me?" He stands on the other side of the island, hair wet, T-shirt sticking to his body where he clearly didn't dry himself off well enough before getting dressed. I bite off a piece of the banana without breaking eye contact, and he groans. "Really, Maevey? A banana?"

I shrug, taking my time swallowing. "I was hungry." He raises one eyebrow at me, defiantly. "Anyway, I came to ask if you'd like to escort me to an event in two days. My publicist insisted I ask, so I'm asking because she knows when I'm lying to her, so just go ahead and tell me no so I can let her know and move on."

"I would like to escort you." The shock of his response has me nearly gagging on the too-large bite of banana I just took, but I manage to keep it together. He seems to register my surprise and continues, "I would like that very much, actually."

"Oh."

Ladies and gentlemen, award-winning actress Maeve Howard.

I clear my throat. "You don't even know what the event is."

"I don't care what it is. As long as it'll be me on your arm and not that slimy Liam. I'm your husband, so yes, Maevey. I'll be there." His stupid green eyes are steady and clear, not a trace of a lie on any of the words he's just spoken. I don't correct him. Lincoln's name isn't important right now.

"Fine then. We need to get you a tux." This is the best I've got after he threw me completely off by saying he wants to go.

"Got one. Never worn it before, but it's custom." Blimey, he's got an answer for everything hasn't he? "I even have my own shoes, if you can believe it." He winks, and I want to hate the sight of it, but I want more.

Nope. Get those thoughts the fuck out of here.

"Right. Great. I'll text you the details. Meet me in LA on Saturday. I'll be getting ready at my house all afternoon. Our car will leave from there. You can stay at my guesthouse. It'll be a nice change in our dynamic." I swallow back the lump in my throat, which tastes a whole lot like uncertainty. "Time to put on the performance of your life, O—pretending to be madly in love with me." I don't give him time to quip back with any other smart remarks. I take my banana and hop off the stool, making my way toward the door.

hello mr. and mrs. james.

owen

THE SOCIAL WORKER is going to be here in fifteen minutes, and Maeve still isn't here. The nervous energy is making my heart beat too fast and I lower to the ground quickly to do a few pushups to see if I can get this out of my system.

"Honey, I'm home!" Maeve's sing-song voice comes from the back door, and by the time I get back on my feet, she's standing in the living room gaping at me. I fucking love it when she does that.

"Hey." I wipe my hands on my thighs and then it's my turn to gape. She's in light jeans, and a tight white shirt tucked into them. Her hair is in a loose bun at the nape of her neck with little pieces falling around her face. The light brown blazer she has on is big, and the sleeves are rolled up to her elbows. No red lipstick today. Her plump lips are a soft pink.

"Uh. Hi. What are you doing?" She cocks her head to the side as a curious smile plays on her lips, and I'm nearly winded with the force of déjà vu.

Shit. How am I gonna pretend that her looking at me like this, standing in my house, is perfectly normal?

"Me? Just…you know…nerves and shit. I just…" I clear my throat, hoping actual words form in my brain. "I just needed to let out some nervous energy."

"Right. Makes sense." She pulls her bottom lip into her mouth, nodding as she looks around the room.

Is she nervous?

"You look great." I walk closer to her, feeling the temperature rise with every step I take. Her eyes travel from my face to my feet and back up again.

"You, too."

As I get closer, she keeps her gaze on my chin or my chest, not meeting my eyes. When I'm close enough to touch her, I let my hands graze her arms until they reach her neck. And when they do, I gently pull her face up so she has to look at me.

"I know this isn't ideal. This isn't what you wanted to be doing. But I need you to know how much I appreciate this. How much it means to me." She nods, releasing her lip, and God, all I want is to take her mouth. Her sky-blue eyes roam over my face, landing on my lips. I lower my forehead to hers, and just as they're about to touch, I hear the ring of the gate, letting us know the social worker is here.

Maeve practically sprints away from me, adjusting her hair and her clothes even though nothing is out of place. She looks up at me briefly, and I try to reassure her with a smile that this is okay. We're going to do fine.

"Okay?" I ask. She stiffens, plasters on her practiced smile, and starts walking toward the front door, where our guest will be standing any moment now.

Maeve waits for me there, waving a hand to indicate I should be the one to open the door, and I do. I'm trying my best to look casual, but that little moment between us is throwing me off.

"Hello," I say to the nice-looking lady at the door. She's smiling, which feels like a good sign.

"Hello Mr. and Mrs. James. I'm Jessica, your caseworker." A sharp intake comes from Maeve when Jessica addresses her, and I smile widely at Jessica, feeling pretty pleased with the greeting myself.

"Owen, please." She takes Maeve's hand next, but when Maeve doesn't say anything, I jump in. "My wife is keeping her last name, given her public status. We reserve Mrs. James for a more…intimate setting, don't we, sunshine?" The way Maeve's cheeks immediately turn pink is far more satisfying than it should be given what we're doing, but I need her to relax a bit.

She shoots me a quick glare then turns to Jessica, that practiced smile on her face. "Just Maeve is fine. Please, come in."

Once Jessica is inside, we lead her to the living room. "Can I get you something to drink, Jessica?" Maeve asks. She's playing a role now, I can see it.

"I'd love a glass of water, if you don't mind?" Jessica smiles at Maeve and continues to follow me into the living room. I can see Maeve in the kitchen, being that this is all open concept, and she's frozen in front of some cupboards. She opens one up, but there are no glasses in it. Another, still no.

I excuse myself and walk in to help her. With a hand on her lower back, I guide her to the correct door and open it up, pulling out a glass and setting it in front of her. She takes it with a shaking hand, and I lower my mouth to her ear.

"Don't stress. We got this." I kiss her temple and move back to the living room, where Jessica is cautiously watching us.

By the time I sit down, Maeve is walking in with the glass of water, setting it down on the coffee table.

"Sorry about that. I just moved in, and I'm still figuring out where everything is." Maeve sits next to me on the couch, keeping several inches between us.

"Oh, you didn't live together before getting married?" Jessica doesn't seem to be making any kind of judgments based on our answer, but you never know.

"We waited until we were married." I move closer to Maeve, wrapping an arm around her. "But I bought this house hoping she'd come live here someday. And here she is." I smile down at Maeve, whose blue eyes are so wide I have to bite my tongue in order to not laugh. Arthur has already told me he spilled the beans without actually saying the words. The more time that goes by, the less I care about keeping my feelings and intentions from Maeve.

"How romantic!" Jessica brings a hand to her chest, and I imagine a big green check above our heads. We're winning her over for sure.

"Well, Mr. Ja—Owen. I'd love to know a bit more about the living arrangements for Julia." She gives us a tight smile. "I know someone's been here to see the house, and things seemed more than adequate in that department. You've prepared well for Julia's arrival. We just needed to meet Maeve and understand how you plan to care for Julia togeth-er..." She clears her throat and looks down at the notebook in her lap. "...since Owen's name is the only one on the guardianship."

"Yes, Owen's name is the only one on the paperwork. I didn't get the chance to meet Monica, unfortunately." Maeve looks at me, and then quickly looks away again, a look of uncertainty in her eyes.

"I understand. Do you two plan to adopt her?" Jessica asks. Maeve opens her mouth to say something, then closes it again, her eyes lowering to a spot on the floor.

"I don't believe that's what we intended to discuss here." I take a deep breath and bring my hand to Maeve's shoulder, squeezing lightly. "We're talking about my guardianship, yes? Not any future plans for adoption?" I glance at Maeve, who is still staring blankly at the floor.

"Right. We just know acting means a lot of traveling and a busy schedule. It makes being present for a child difficult, I'm sure. This is a major life change. For both of you." Jessica's eyes dart between me and Maeve, but I don't sense that she's meaning to be intrusive. I know she's just doing her job, but this fucking sucks.

Maeve looks up and speaks directly to Jessica. "Of course I'll be present in her life."

"Of course." Jessica makes some notes and continues with a few more lifestyle questions. Maeve doesn't speak again for the remainder of the meeting, and I don't dare take my hand off her.

Something caused her to shut down, and now my thoughts feel muddled, and though I manage to respond to Jessica, I know I'm not as engaged as I should be. I want to know what Maeve is thinking.

By the time Jessica leaves, Maeve can't even look me in the eye. As soon as Jessica's car is out of sight, she takes off, back to the guesthouse.

Every time I feel like we have an opportunity to come together, to get back to the us that we used to be, to take a step forward, something sets us ten steps back. I know she doesn't want marriage and kids, but those damn specks of hope I can't seem to get rid of keep pushing me to keep trying with her, anyway.

Logic tells me to stop now, to not bother trying, but love keeps telling me not to give up.

27 /

love you most.

maeve

I FUCKED IT UP. I'm sure of it. The nice social worker asked about adoption and my work schedule, and I froze. She was asking about me being a mum, and my brain completely shut down. I wouldn't be surprised if Owen was rethinking staying married, having me here, and just generally being near me.

After nearly running out of his house, I slammed the guesthouse door shut, and I've been standing with my forehead pressed against it for so long that I know I must have a mark on my face. I'm spiraling. This doesn't happen often, but with everything happening lately, this was only a matter of time. I came here for a break from my hectic schedule, and I got that. It's been amazing to be with the horses, breathe fresh air, and look at mountains without smog covering them up. But the constant calls from my mum, followed by texts asking why I'm ignoring her, have my heart racing every time. Add in Owen and this whole situation, and I'm feeling unsteady, which isn't something I like to feel. Ever.

I've always been the kind of person who performs best under pressure, but lately I feel like I'm crumbling beneath it.

I can't keep my cool. The mask of confidence I normally have on is slipping off, and I'm not sure how to fix it back in place.

I push myself off the door and turn around, sitting on the floor and dialing the person who understands this better than anyone. After two rings, the most familiar voice in the world comes through the speaker.

"Tell me everything, sissy. I'm right here." Charlie's voice is softer than her usual formal one, and I'm immediately thankful for her twintuition.

Blowing out a deep breath, I begin. "I think I messed up Owen's meeting with the social worker. I'm not sure, though. I was feeling so sure about it, and all of a sudden it was like the confidence just washed away, and I was this fumbling, mumbling twat. And of course, Owen was perfect. He talked to her so confidently and kept a reassuring hand on me the entire time, as if I'm the one who needs the support." Charlie listens quietly while I gather my words. "And Mum's been calling. More than usual. She couldn't have worse timing, you know? I mean, I'm trying to get away from the things that bring me stress, and yet she waltzes into my life via text messages and phone calls that I ignore, but they still bother me. She asks about Owen, makes comments about how I've made a huge mistake and how I'm just like her. She told me I'm an idiot for getting married and for pretending that being a wife to someone will make me happy."

Tears sting my eyes, but I don't want to cry over my mother. I refuse to. She doesn't deserve the tears.

Charlie hums. "She's wrong. You're not like her, Mae."

Before she can go on, I'm already arguing with her. "Aren't I? I'm a total phony. I got married to someone and it's not even real. And there's an innocent child in the middle of it all. Isn't that exactly what she did?"

"No!" Charlie's voice is forceful, and I don't dare interrupt her this time. "You're not Mum, Maeve. She married Dad knowing we weren't his. She tried to trap him, and she lied.

For years. That's not you." I don't miss the way she says Dad in reference to the man who married our mum thinking we were his. Poor fellow stuck around for years, treated us like we were his little princesses, and then he found out my mum didn't even remember who our biological father was. The only dad we ever knew left us when we were three years old. Sure, he also left us a trust that more than paid for our university education, but still, he left. I don't even blame him. I wouldn't want to spend a lifetime with my lying, cheating mother either. "You and Owen know what this is. You're not going to walk away from his life or his baby's. You two are tied together forever because you and Elaina are tied together forever. So sure, this marriage may be temporary, and it may not be real, but you both know the terms. You both came to the decision to stay in it for the sake of this innocent child. It's not the same, Maeve. Don't catastrophize this. Take it from someone who constantly sees the worst-case scenario."

She goes quiet, breathing a little harder than before because, clearly, my sister has thought about this before and had her mind made up about my situation with Owen. Of course she did. Charlie is always observing, always taking in people's body language, studying those around her.

"Did you hear me, Mae? This is not the same situation. She doesn't get to make you feel like this. This isn't the same situation. And it's not permanent."

"What if I want it to be, Char?" My voice is wobbly, and the words come out in a whisper, but based on Charlie's sharp intake of breath, I know she heard me.

"You…you want to stay with Owen? Do you still love him?" Her voice is softer again. She knows better than anyone how hard this topic is for me.

"I—I don't know. I don't know. I mean, I definitely feel *something*. And—"

"But he hurt you, Maeve. He left after you slept together and didn't say a word about it." Charlie may be younger by twenty-nine minutes, but she is my protector. She's always struggled with the way Owen left things all those years ago.

"Yes, he hurt me. And I can't tell you more because it's not my story to tell, but Char...he didn't have a choice. He was thrown into an impossible, horrendous situation, and he's had a lot of healing to do over the years." I wait for her to stop me, to tell me that I can't forgive him, but she doesn't. "He's done the work, Char, and now he's here. And he's sweet, kind, attentive, and still so fucking hot. It's impossible not to want to be near him. It's like all those old feelings have resurfaced. I thought they were gone, but I think I just tucked them away, and one by one, they keep popping back up."

"Oh, Mae..."

"What do I do, Char? Tell me what to do." I feel the familiar sting of tears yet again. "Please."

"Sissy...I can't. You know that." Charlie sighs into the phone and continues, "I'm sorry. I wish I could, but you and Owen are the only ones that can sort this out."

I know she's right. I know she can't actually fix this for me, but right now it's all I want. For all of these complications to just go away.

"How much longer are you staying with him?" I can hear the wheels turning in Charlie's head. She's thinking this through already.

"The lawyer recommended giving the whole being married thing a couple of months, but I start shooting on location in Colorado in six weeks. I don't know if Owen wants me here for that long, but I also can't see him kicking me out, so... I guess I have six weeks with him. I suppose we could divorce after that. No one would question that; my schedule is a good enough reason to not want to be with me." My heart constricts just from thinking about leaving Ojai. It's been days, and I've already grown attached to this peace, the horses, Owen's closeness.

"Don't do that. You're allowed to have your career, a relationship, *and* a family, if it's what you want. You don't have to choose between them. Understand?" I can't help the small smile spreading on my face as my sister puts me in my place, reciting words I've heard for years, whether from her or because I was saying them to myself. Since the beginning, I've set goals and made them happen. A permanent relationship and children were just never a part of the plan because…well, because if it wasn't Owen, it was no one. That, and the thought of quite literally becoming my mother, has kept me from allowing myself to picture a life with a husband and kids. Even if it's what I dreamed of as a little girl. A family. A house full of love. Kids making a mess, and a partner who adores me. I wanted everything I didn't see as a kid, but then I grew up, and I learned that it's not that simple.

"This wasn't part of the plan, but Mae, if it's what makes you happy, you owe it to yourself to go after it. Don't stay stuck and unhappy just because it's a part of the path you once laid out for yourself. You can still change your mind. You can still do and be anything you want." Her voice breaks, which is not typical for Charlie, and I feel the hairs raise on the back of my neck. My twin is going through something, and I've been so caught up in my own world that I haven't seen it, haven't sensed it, until now.

"Charlie. What's going on?" She goes quiet, and I allow her a moment to gather her thoughts. "What do you need?"

"I…I want to get out of London for a while." She normally stays at my house in LA when she visits a few times a year. "I've been looking for a place in LA. Your house is way too big, especially when you're not there, and I want something that's mine, you know?" Her voice doesn't waver, so I know she's made her mind up. She's thought about this because Charlie doesn't do anything without thoroughly thinking about it and considering all the possibilities.

"What about Robert?" I try to not roll my eyes when I ask my sister about the man-child she's gone out with off and on for years, but who refuses to commit to my sister because he's a complete wanker.

"I need a break from him. I need a break from everything here." I can tell she's not going to elaborate, but knowing my sister needs a change and that she'll be living so close to me for the first time in years is enough for now.

"I'll look for something for you. I can ask Taylor and Jen if they know of anything in a nice area of the city. All right?" I won't even offer to buy a place for her because I know exactly what she'll say…

"I don't want you to pay for it. I need to do this on my own." She clears her throat. "But I'd appreciate any leads. Maybe something furnished as I don't know how long I'll be staying?"

"You got it. And Char?" She murmurs a response. "I'm here, all right? I'm always here."

"I know, Mae. Thank you." She lets out a sigh, and I send a silent prayer that she's okay. I hate being so far from her. "Anyway, what else have you been up to in Ojai, other than reconsidering all of your life choices?"

I laugh because she's right, and her boldness is one of my favorite things about her. "Well, I've been riding horses again. I'm sure we can go see them when you visit. Rafael's very tattooed, very quiet, very tall, dark and handsome brother runs the stable." I make no mention of my last conversation with Arthur. I'm not sure I've fully processed it yet.

"Other than his unfortunate familial relation, I like him already." The sass is back in her tone, and the relief washes over me. She's okay. We're okay.

"Come to LA soon, all right? You don't have to stay at my house if you don't want to, but the sooner I get to have you staying close by, the better. I can't wait to see you, Char."

"I will. And me too. Love you most." I can hear the smile on her face as she says our typical goodbye to one another.

"Love you most."

Charlie hangs up first, as she always does. I make the decision to not overthink every single thing that has happened here in Ojai. To do what feels good in the moment, regardless of what my 5, 10 and 15-year plans are supposed to look like. Because I never planned for Owen. I tossed out those plans long ago and gave up on the possibility of anything but mutual civility being the norm between us.

But it seems like that could change. Maybe. If Owen even shows up in LA tomorrow.

28 /
i'm right where i want to be.

HER CAR IS GONE by the time I wake up in the morning, but it's fine, because I woke up with a renewed determination to not let the opportunity of tonight's event slip by. I'm gonna keep showing her what she could have here. With me. And if in the end, she decides that she doesn't want it, then fine. I'll learn to let her go. But she's going to know exactly what she could have before she makes the decision.

If there's even a small chance she still wants me like I want her, I'm taking it. Because I've seen the way she looks at me and how flustered she gets. The blush on her cheeks gives her away every time. She might be able to put on a mask for other people, but not for me. I know her. And I'm going to do everything I can to keep her.

I check the rearview mirror for what must be the twentieth time since I left Ojai to make sure my tux is still hanging up in the back seat. I keep running through the list of things I needed to bring, wondering what I forgot, but there's nothing. I pat my pocket to make sure the one thing I didn't want to forget is here. It is.

Lately, I just seem to live in this constant state of mild anxiety. But I've got everything. I did what I needed to do.

I rub at my sternum, trying to ease the pressure there. It seems to be coming from everywhere, this compulsive weight trying to pull me under, but I'm determined not to let it.

The closer I get to LA, the more nervous I get about tonight. I haven't heard from Maeve since she took off after the meeting with Jessica yesterday, and her words to me after the shower incident keeps playing over in my mind.

Time to put on the performance of your life, O—pretending to be madly in love with me.

She has no idea I won't have to pretend. No. My plan for tonight is to act exactly how I want to act around her. Touch her the way I constantly need to, without holding back.

THERE ARE a few cars in her driveway when I pull into her house. The gate code is the same as the last one I changed it to, so I make a mental note to amend that as soon as possible.

The house is oddly quiet as I walk through the front door, so I call out her name. No response. I decide to call her, knowing that her phone will ring loudly after I set her ringtone the night we got married. That much I remember. And it does. Our song starts playing.

I take the steps two at a time to get upstairs and follow the sound, still not hearing any voices or signs of life. I walk into a room full of people. Maeve stands in the middle of it with her phone in her hand and a look on her face that's somewhere between disappointment and annoyance. She's looking at the phone screen, but she hasn't picked up the call yet. It stops ringing as it goes to voicemail, and she lets out a sigh, eyes closing briefly.

I clear my throat and all eyes turn to me at once, but I only see one pair of blue ones, wide and clear, looking straight into mine.

"You're here?" She sets her phone on the table next to her, and I walk slowly toward her, trying to read her deer in the headlights reaction.

Did she think I wouldn't show?

"Where else would I be, Maevey?" There's an audible sigh from somewhere in the room at my use of her nickname. She still hasn't moved, but I'm standing right in front of her, my hand going to her waist, where her silky robe is tied.

"I thought when you called—I thought maybe you changed your mind or—" I pull her closer to me, and she doesn't fight it. Fuck, that feels good.

Focus. She was scared you weren't coming. That's why she didn't want to pick up the phone.

I shake my head and reach for one of the perfect curls framing her made-up face. "I'm right where I want to be." I lower my head, then whisper so only she can hear, "Where you go, I go *fengári mou*. Always." I leave a quick kiss just under her earlobe. "Don't want to mess up your make-up," I wink as I lift my head, knowing the strangers in the room are still watching my every move. They're not the audience we need to put this on for tonight, but it doesn't matter. I'm taking every chance I get to be close to her.

She nods and swallows, taking a small step back from me. A sly grin spreads across my face, a familiar feeling of satisfaction bubbling up inside me. I can sense the flustered energy radiating from Maeve, her composure shaken and unraveled. Watching her in this state has always been a source of pleasure for me, and I relish in being the one to provoke it.

I take a few steps backward, still smiling at her. "See you soon, beautiful." I wink and turn on my heel, leaving the room. There's a squeal and a chorus of *ohmygod* as I walk down the hall.

I hear a faint, "That's the most beautiful man I've ever seen." And then, "It's as if Jensen Ackles and Chris Evans made a baby, and that baby grew into a man…" I stop listening after that. I don't know who those dudes are that they're talking about, and I'm not about to stick around and find out.

TWO HOURS LATER, I hear the last of the cars leaving the driveway. I've been dressed for thirty minutes, not knowing for sure what time we'd be leaving. I got dressed in the guesthouse then came back to wait for her in the main house.

"Ready?" I turn at the sound of her voice to see Maeve adjusting her dress, her heels in her other hand. She's breathtaking. By the time I stand, she's already making her way to the front door. "The car's here, we can—"

"Maeve. Wait." She stops and slowly spins, her brows furrowed as her eyes meet mine for the first time since I surprised her upstairs. "Come here." To my complete shock, she does. She walks straight toward me. Her dress is almost the same color as her skin, strapless with tiny ruffles on the skirt that goes to just above her ankles. Her lips are bright red, and her eyes are lined in a way that makes the blues look even lighter, like a cloudless sky on a sunny day. "Wow," I whisper as she gets closer.

I run a finger up her arm, not missing the goosebumps that follow or the way she holds her breath. "You're beautiful, Maevey." She blinks, and her eyes move over my body, taking in the tux, shiny shoes, and probably crooked bowtie.

"Thanks." She reaches up to my tie and adjusts it with one hand. I take her shoes so she can use both hands, and she smiles in lieu of a thank you. I can't help but imagine what life would be like if this were real. If I was her forever date to these events. If we got ready together, so I could zip up her dresses, and she could fix up my ties while we smile at one another, thinking of when we get to come home and take everything off again. Slowly. Deliberately. Or quickly. Urgently.

Fuck. Stop. Remember what thinking about Maeve naked got you last time? Getting caught red-handed in the shower.

How could I forget?

Maeve clears her throat and takes a step back, her mask of indifference firmly in place. She nods once and starts to head back toward the door, slippers on her feet, which I'm assuming are far more comfortable than the six-inch heels I'm holding.

"Do you need a purse or something?" She doesn't even have her phone on her.

Without looking back, she pats her hip. "Nope. Hidden pockets. Taylor always makes sure I have pockets. Whenever possible, anyway."

The driver opens the car door for her, and I recognize him. She pats him on the arm as she says hello, and I tip my head as the man who looks to be about twenty years older than me sizes me up. I respect that.

"Hi, Gary. Nice to see you again." He hides the surprise of my greeting well.

"Mr. James." He nods, keeping the door open until I'm inside.

The drive is quiet, but once we get there, waiting in line behind several other limos, Maeve lets out a shaky sigh.

"Okay?" Her eyes close and she takes a deep breath. When she opens them again, she's obviously nervous, but as always, she's determined not to let it show.

"We'll take a few photos on the carpet. There won't be any interviews, so we don't need to talk to anyone or answer any questions. They might ask me for a few photos of just me, so someone will pull you aside to wait for me. Sorry. It's a little awkward, but necessary. Jen assured me we don't need any major show of affection, just some hand holding and smiling. You know, look happily married and all that."

She still won't look at me, so in the middle of her mono-logue, I gently take her left hand in mine and slide a shim-mering ring onto her finger. Bringing her hand up to my lips, I place a gentle kiss on the back of each knuckle before gazing into her wide, astonished eyes. The deep green emerald, encircled by sparkling diamonds, glints in the light next to her simple wedding band.

"Owen… What… I don't… What…" Her eyes flicker from the ring, to me, and back to the ring again.

"It was my mother's. My dad didn't have any money when they got engaged, so she never had an engagement ring. When he got tenure at MIT, he had finally saved enough to get her whatever ring she wanted. This is what she chose. She said she wanted something that reminded her of him, so she picked a stone that matched his eyes." I look up from the ring to find Maeve staring at me with a scowl, her eyes glis-tening with unshed tears.

"Owen! You cannot make me cry right before a red carpet. What is the matter with you?" She waves both hands in front of her eyes, fanning away the moisture in her eyes. I'm sure she's deflecting because seeing that ring did something to her. I know it did because I felt it, too. I've imagined her wearing my mother's ring countless times.

When she's finished covering up her emotions with feigned anger, she blows out a breath and adjusts the ring on her finger. "Thank you. It's beautiful. I promise to take very good care of it until it's time to give it back."

I swallow down my response once. Twice. Three times.

I don't want the ring back. Not ever. My mom gave me this ring when I admitted to her that I was in love with Maeve. I've had it for months. This ring is as much Maeve's as it was Mamá's.

well done, owen.

maeve

I'M NOT sure how much more of this I can take. He shows up to my house, quells my panic at the thought of him not coming with *where you go, I go.* Then the whispered words, and kiss on my neck. I was wrong about Owen not being able to handle pretending to be my husband. That was some perfect husband material.

After talking to Charlie, I felt better, but that nagging voice in my head keeps repeating the same few things: This is temporary. Julia isn't mine. This life, this house, this dream aren't mine.

Every insecurity I've ever had about being just like my mother is coming out, and I'm annoyed and confused by it all.

Am I selfish like her? Am I unable to love like she is?

And now… now this ring. It's the prettiest thing I've ever seen, and the green happens to match his eyes perfectly, so now I have a daily reminder of one of my favorite things about Owen on my ring finger. Until it's time to give it back, that is.

I wonder if his next wife will wear this ring.

I've already nearly cried in this car, I can't do it again. He's been silent since he slipped it on my finger, and according to Jen, who just texted me, it's nearly our turn to get out there and smile for the cameras.

"Ready?" Jen asks us as she pokes her head into the car. Her eyes travel from my face to Owen's, who looks perfectly relaxed. Her gaze snags on my left hand, her eyes narrowing as she smiles. "Well done, Owen." She points at the ring with an appreciative look on her face, but all Owen does is nod, his lips set firmly in a straight line. I don't think he's a huge fan of Jen's.

Owen exits first, lending me his hand to help me out of the car now that I have my heels on. As if I've forgotten how to walk in anything that isn't a riding boot or runner, I trip on something and my shoe slips off, almost sending me face first onto the red carpet. Owen gently rights me, and I silently beg him not to ask me, not to say that one word. He doesn't.

As I bend to look for my shoe, so does Owen. When I turn around, he's on one knee, holding my shoe in one hand as he inspects it, as if it's the shoe's fault I've forgotten how to walk. He pats his thigh, asking for my foot, and I place it there as he gingerly puts my shoe back on. It's a real-life Cinderella moment. A real sight to be seen, Owen James on his knee in front of me, his ring on my finger, his fingers wrapped around my ankle as they move up my calf.

He sets my foot back down on the ground and I gather myself with a deep breath, checking that my phone is still in my pocket, looking to Jen for direction as she looks on wide-eyed and slack-jawed. I've never seen that look on her before. She's not easily fazed.

Owen straightens his jacket and offers me his arm so we can walk in together. Thankfully, it looks like our moment was relatively private.

. . .

AS WE MOVE along the carpet, I easily slip into my role, all smiles and small waves to fans with signs, posing for the cameras as Owen stands with his back ramrod straight, no longer looking relaxed, but downright angry. At one point, I chance a look at his face and he's actually scowling. The sight makes me laugh, and at the sound, he looks at me, face immediately softening, green eyes taking in every inch of my face and pausing on my lips not once, but twice.

I clear my throat. "You good?" The man has the audacity to smile. Really, really smile. At me. I can handle the flashes and bright lights, but this? This has me going a little weak in the knees, and since nothing gets past Owen, he notices. His arm snakes around my back, and he pulls me into him, emerald eyes sparkling with mischief and something I haven't seen in a long, long time.

Desire. *Lust.*

His head lowers to mine, but he dips further, his warm breath on my neck. "I'm always good when I'm with you, Maevey." Then he kisses me in that same spot as earlier, but this time, his tongue swirls in that sensitive place below my ear, and my traitorous eyes close in response. My grip on his forearm tightens, and before I have time to gather myself, he straightens, looks out at the sea of flashing lights, and smiles while tucking one hand in his pocket.

I struggle to look away from his handsome face. It's always been difficult to look away from Owen, but like this? Looking suddenly at ease in a situation so foreign to him with his arm around my waist? He makes it impossible to focus on anything else, but I catch Jen on the sidelines waving at me to move along, and Owen follows as I start walking again.

"Show us the ring, Maeve!" "Where's your ring?" "The ring!"

It's clear what they want to see. Owen lifts my left hand gingerly, bringing it to his lips as he lays a chaste kiss on my hand, his eyes glued to mine the entire time.

Someone turn this charm off. Is there a switch on the back of his neck I can flip? It's too much.

The cheering is nearly deafening as we stand there, staring at one another, our hands suspended so they can take photos of the ring that has only been on my finger for the last half hour, but that feels like it's exactly where it belongs. Even if my brain loves to remind me the ring isn't mine, the man isn't mine, for this one small moment, I let myself feel like it is, like he is.

And then Jen calls him over, so I can stand alone with my hands on my hips, smiling like this is where I belong. The reminder that this is my reality, and not the stolen moments with the man I once thought would be my forever is jarring. But it works. It works to help me keep my emotional distance for the rest of the evening.

BY THE TIME we get back to my house, I've become numb again. Back to that place where indifference takes over, and the shields around my heart go back up, keeping me safe. Owen says *goodnight*, but I barely register it, needing to block his voice, his face, his ring, his words. I need to lock it all away. Back into that deep, dark corner. Back into that box with chains and locks. It all goes back in there, because it's not safe for feelings or memories to live out here in the world with me. Not when I can't guarantee that I'd ever be enough for him, for Julia. Not when the fear of getting hurt again has a death grip on my heart.

I've managed to get myself to where I am by keeping my career and my goals at the very top of my priority list. I don't know how to make room for anyone else, let alone a family. And Owen deserves someone as thoughtful and kind as he is. Someone who can be present as a partner and a mother, like his own mum was. He deserves the best, and so does Julia. I'm not that.

there's a flying rat in the guesthouse.

owen

I TEXTED her to ask if she wanted anything for breakfast. No response. I texted her to ask if she was still at her house. No response. I texted her to let her know I had to go to a meeting with Rafael before heading back to Ojai. No response. I thought that last night changed some of her indifference toward me, but I'm quickly losing hope. So, I repeat the mantra I've been replaying in my head over and over when I need to remember why this can't go anywhere, anyway.

She doesn't want this. You're about to have a daughter. This isn't the life she wants.

So far, it hasn't gotten me out of doing anything too stupid, like giving her my mom's ring or kissing her neck in public. Hopefully, it's easier to act like a regular human being and not a fucking horn dog when Julia's guardianship is on the line because dozens of cameras did not stop me last night.

ONCE NIGHTTIME ROLLS AROUND, I haven't seen or heard from Maeve, but I know she's back in Ojai and in the guesthouse. I'm just about to turn off the lights and head to bed to sleep away all memories of last night, when there's rapid pounding on my door. It has to be Maeve, because no one can get in here. I rush to the door and when I swing it open, she crashes into me so hard she nearly knocks the wind out of me.

"Oh my god, Owen. There's a flying rat in the guesthouse! Help me!" She's holding on to me for dear life, and something is jabbing into my hip. She must have her phone in the pocket of her sweatshirt.

"Wait, what? Flying rat?" I hold her by the shoulders and pull her away from me, needing to check that she's all right as her whole body is vibrating. "What the hell is going on?" Her hair is in a mess of a bun on top of her head, she has no makeup on and she's not wearing shoes. Or pants. The only item of clothing on her body is my sweatshirt. The same one from before. I like the sight of her in my clothes far, far too much.

What the hell am I being punished for?

"Maeve, start over. What happened?" I focus on her face, which is pale.

"I was just lying there, ready to start..." She looks at me, shoves her hands in the pocket of the hoodie and continues, "I was just lying there, and then I heard a noise, like something flapping, and then there was a screeching sound, and then I saw this giant fuzzy rat flying at me, and I threw a pillow at it and ran out the door, and now here I am."

"That sounds like a bat, Maeve. Did you see a bat?" I keep my eyes on her face. Her eyes are darting all over the place, like she's looking for the flying rat, which is probably a bat, in my house.

"I don't know! I didn't stick around long enough to ask its name and what species it was, Owen! I ran out of there, and now I'm here, and I'm not going back there, and you can't make me. I won't do it!"

I cradle her face in my hands and angle her head so she can look at me. "You're all right now, Maevey. You don't need to go back. You can stay here." Her eyes immediately soften, and then widen in surprise.

"I can?" Her slender fingers encircle each of my wrists, binding us together.

"Of course you can. I'll go check things out there tomorrow. You stay here tonight. I have extra rooms." She takes a small step closer toward me and winces. I look down and notice she's holding one foot off the floor. My arms move to her waist, and I lift her, walking into the kitchen. It happens so fast I hardly register her hands on my shoulders or the gasp she lets out when I set her down on the countertop.

"Ah! Cold." I ignore the reminder that she's not likely wearing very much under my hoodie and move to look at her foot, which is bleeding.

"You're bleeding. Stay here." I walk to the bathroom and grab the first aid kit, willing my heart to slow the fuck down because it's just a cut on her foot, and because she's fine. She's fine.

I set the kit on the counter next to her and prop her foot on a stool as she watches, wide-eyed. It's a minor cut, so I clean it quickly and bandage it up.

"You'll need to clean that tomorrow and change the bandage." I close the kit and walk to the trash can to dispose of the wrappers.

"Yes, Doctor." There's a teasing tone to her voice, which goes straight to my dick.

"Why didn't you use the flashlight on your phone so you could see where you were going? Might have avoided the cut." When I look back toward her, she's shifted on the counter to face me. She still has her injured foot on the stool, the other dangling as she tugs on the hem of the sweatshirt.

"I don't have my phone. It was too far to grab, so I just ran." My brows furrow in confusion.

"What the hell is in your pocket, then?" I point toward where I assumed her phone was.

Her eyes go wide, and her cheeks flush as she shoves both hands into her pocket.

"Nothing."

"What's in your pocket, Maeve?" She shakes her head, not answering me. "What was in your hand when you left?" I try to come up with a list of things of what it could be.

"Come on. Show me." She shakes her head again, but now my curiosity's got the best of me. "Is it the TV remote? It's okay if you watch television, Maeve. Everyone does it. I think even Hollywood stars do." I smirk, and she responds with a scowl and another shake of her head.

"Were you shaving your legs? Is it a razor? Because that's not safe, and you shouldn't have that in—"

"It's my vibrator, Owen!" She takes a deep breath, then looks me dead in the eyes.

That was not on my list.

"What were you doing before you left, Maevey?" I swallow hard, unsure of whether I want the answer to that.

What if she was thinking of some other guy? What if she was getting off to the memory of some idiot who had her while I was trying to get my shit together?

"Oh, don't be dense, Owen. I think you know what I was about to do."

"About to? You hadn't started yet?" I quickly decide that I want every single detail. Whether it'll stop all the blood in my body from racing toward my cock is yet to be determined. She shakes her head, and her leg stills. "What were you about to do with your vibrator in your hand and my hoodie on your body, Maeve?"

Her breathing quickens, but she still doesn't answer me.

"Were you going to get yourself off in my clothes, Maevey? So you can smell me on you?"

Goddamn it, if she doesn't answer me, I might just lose my mind.

She keeps her eyes on me, those baby blues wide and bright. And then she fucking nods. And it's not a small movement like the others. It's clear as fucking day that she's nodding.

"I wanna hear you say it, Maeve." My hands are itching to be near her, to touch her, but I know that I can't. This is already too much.

"Yes, Owen." She pauses. "I was about to get myself off wearing your clothes, so I could smell you on me." She pulls her hands out of her pockets and sets them on the countertop behind her. The sweatshirt rides up her thighs, and my eyes immediately track the movement.

Thank fuck I had the good sense to tuck my dick up into my boxer briefs when I went to get the first aid kit, or I'd be pitching a tent big enough for the two of us to sleep under right now.

Maeve's eyes move to my crotch, and she smirks, not missing the way this interaction is affecting me. Well, I'm ready to play now.

"What were you thinking about?" I ask.

There's no hesitation in her answer. "Your mouth. I was thinking about you trailing kisses down my body until your tongue was on my clit." She spreads her legs a little further. "I wondered what it would feel like for you to kiss my pussy the same way you kissed my neck the other night."

"Fuuuuck." I rub a hand down my face and bring my eyes back to her. Her legs are now spread even further apart, and she's practically panting, taunting me with her words and her smirk. She may act like she's indifferent, like I don't affect her, but clearly, that's not true. Now I need physical proof.

"Are you wet right now, Maevey?" She pulls her lower lip into her mouth and her head moves up and down repeatedly. "Let me see." Her breath hitches, and her eyes widen. She brings her other foot to rest on a stool, one hand slowly pulling up the hem of my sweatshirt to reveal a scrap of pink cotton that is clearly soaked.

A strangled groan leaves my body, and my hands ball into fists next to me, but I can't touch her. I'm afraid that if I start, I'll never stop. I want her too much. I want to pick her up and take her into my bed and not leave it until she's had so many orgasms she can't walk. Until all she can see, think, feel is me. But I can't. So instead, I shut it down.

"I can't believe I'm fucking doing this," I say with an aggravated grunt. Berating myself for letting it get this far in the first place, I walk away and head upstairs, stomping down the hall.

"Your room is the first door on the left," I yell down. Then I walk into my room and slam the door, locking it, not because I think she's going to come in here, but because I need the additional barrier between me and the urge to rush back into my kitchen to do exactly what she just described.

I lock the exterior doors of the house from my phone and turn the lights off in my room, reminding myself that she might be my wife, but she's not mine to keep.

She doesn't want this. You're about to have a daughter. This isn't the life she wants.

sweet dreams, maevey.

maeve

THAT ARSEHOLE THINKS he can just leave me here all wet and bothered like that? I think not! I hop off the counter, careful not to slam my foot down too hard on the floor and march to the bedroom he deemed to be *mine*.

I turn on the lights and pace around the large bedroom, barely taking in the furnishings. After muttering a string of expletives, I shove my hands into the pocket of the sweatshirt and settle on my plan of action.

I click the switch for the lamp on the nightstand, turn off the overhead lights, and settle into the king-sized bed, which is made up with white bedding and as many pillows as the bed in the guesthouse. I set my vibrator on the bed and toss my panties on the floor, leaving me in nothing but Owen's hoodie.

I cycle through the settings, finding the one I know I like most, with not too much suction. This little guy really provides the best of both worlds, clit suction and G-spot vibrations.

I'm still soaked from my little moment in the kitchen with Owen, and now that the memory is back at the forefront of my mind, I struggle to rip myself away from reliving it all. I don't want to think about him, but I can't seem to help myself these days. The way his eyes narrowed and his jaw ticked when I told him I was about to masturbate while wearing his sweatshirt pretty much had me coming on the spot.

Leaving the vibrator next to me, ready to be used when I need it, I start with just my fingers, spreading my wetness around and pressing into my clit, flicking it in a way that has my nipples hardening and a strangled moan slipping past my lips. Bringing a hand to my breast, I pinch a nipple between my thumb and index finger. My moans are uncontrollable now. I'm so wound up, my orgasm rests just below the surface, and its ripples travel along my skin.

An image of Owen's green eyes pops into my mind, and I don't fight it. I shut my eyes tightly as the orgasm breaks through and takes over. At the same moment, the bedroom door bursts open, and when I look up, Owen is standing there, hands balled into fists, eyes dark as night and boring into me.

My body trembles as I reach the peak of my pleasure. My breaths come out in short gasps, and my back arches off the bed. His intense gaze only intensifies my orgasm, making it feel like it will never end. A small whimper escapes my lips before I finally collapse back onto the sheets, panting heavily.

He's not watching my hand. No, his eyes are glued to mine as his jaw clenches tightly. When I catch my breath and relax from my climax, he stalks toward the bed with a predatory gait. He towers over me as I lay there, still holding onto my pleasure with one hand between my legs.

"Did you just make yourself come while thinking about me, Maeve?" He does allow his gaze to rake over my body then, but I close my legs before he can get a good look at what's going on between them.

"No," I lie.

"Liar." He narrows his eyes, which are once again focused on mine.

"I didn't," I lie again.

"Then why the hell were you moaning my name so loud that I have to worry about Arthur hearing you at his house?"

Shit. I moaned his name? That wasn't planned.

I shrug and reach for the vibrator, which is actually closer to him than it is me. He's faster and gets to it first, examining it as it pulses and vibrates in his hand.

"What do you think you're doing? I wasn't done!" I sit up, keeping my legs together still.

"What, one orgasm wasn't enough for you, Maevey? You need more?" He licks his lips, and my clit throbs at the sight. It wasn't enough. I do need more. "Will you be moaning my name when you come again?"

I shrug defiantly, but I know there's only one answer.

YES, YES, YES!

"Try again, or this little toy is coming back to my room with me." He holds it up as if to prove his point.

I take my time, engaging in a staring contest of sorts with him that I'm sure I'll lose. I don't want to win it, though. The only way I'll win is if I get to come again, and the only way that will happen is if I'm thinking about Owen. So, I'll happily lose this game, only so I can win my orgasm.

"Yes, Owen." The growl that comes out of him has me clenching my legs together even harder, trying to alleviate the need building at my core.

"That's right. Now spread your legs like a good girl."

My knees move without my permission, as if his command is all they need.

He sits at the edge of the bed with the vibrating toy in his right hand and stares at the spot between my legs that screams for his touch.

"So wet for me." My body might be giving in, but not my mouth.

"It's not for you." The stupid shakiness in my voice gives me away too easily.

"You're gonna have to stop lying now, *fengári mou*." He puts the vibrating end on my still sensitive clit, and I nearly jump off the bed, gasping. My legs instinctively shut, and he moves the vibrator away.

"Tsk, how am I gonna make you come if you don't spread those pretty legs?" He doesn't touch me, doesn't even get too close. My legs open for him again, wider this time, and he smirks before bringing the vibrator back to my center, not applying nearly enough pressure.

"Now tell me. Whose name will you be saying when you come?" I shake my head, and he moves the vibrating tip around my clit, never hitting the spot I need him to. He hums, moving so slowly that I feel as though I might explode from the need. The want.

He looks up, and our eyes meet, his brow quirking up in question as he moves the tip to my entrance, but again, it's too subtle. The touch is barely there.

I can't take it anymore. "Yours. I'm going to say your name when I come." He doesn't say anything else, but I feel his groan as intensely as I feel the vibrating end enter me and the suction on the other side finally hitting my clit perfectly. I gasp and fist the sheets, my hips bucking with the intensity of the invasion I needed so badly.

"Tell me when it's in the right spot, sunshine." His voice is soft, barely audible as he shifts the vibrator inside me ever so slightly, as if he can tell that it hasn't hit the right place yet. He does it again, and I moan loudly, my skin tingling every-where, feeling too hot and not hot enough all at once. I need more than the weight of his clothes on me. I need the weight of his body.

He pushes a little further in, and I gasp. "Right there," I mumble through more moans.

"Mmm." His hum morphs into a groan that I feel as

intensely as the vibrations in my body. I'm about to go off like a firework. He keeps the vibrator perfectly in place even as I writhe on the bed. "That's my girl, taking what you want. Now come for me."

And again, as if my body responds to all of his praises and commands, I do. I detonate while incomprehensible words leave my lips along with moans. And his name.

When my leg twitches as my clit is once again too sensitive to be touched, he slips the vibrator out of me. A final moan tumbles out of me as my entire body relaxes, sinking into the mattress. My vision is blurry, but I see the movement as the covers are gently placed over me.

Owen turns off the vibrator and stands over me. "I'm taking this with me. If you're gonna scream my name when you have an orgasm, I'm gonna be the one giving them to you." He turns off the lamp and walks away. "Sweet dreams, Maevey." The door clicks shut, and I'm left stunned, speechless. But also perfectly sated and sleepy. So I let sleep come and decide to deal with Owen and how I'll get my vibrator back tomorrow.

32 /

completely,
ultimately,
relentlessly.

owen

I HAVE DEFINITELY LOST my fucking mind. But how could I not? She was moaning in the room next to mine, and whether she was doing it on purpose to drive me fucking crazy, or she's really just that clueless to how loud she is...

My mind goes back to that night at the beach. I guess she's still loud.

It was too much. Pure torture, having to listen to her after seeing her like that on the kitchen counter.

Now I'm standing here with her vibrator in my hand, reliving the last twenty minutes in vivid detail, which is most definitely not helping the very hard situation in my pants. I allow myself another minute before springing into action.

Walking to my bathroom, I wash her vibrator and leave it on the countertop on a clean towel to dry while I have my second cold shower of the day. Once I'm clean and settled the fuck down, I put the toy in the drawer of my nightstand and collect some things for Maeve: a toothbrush and paste, a T-shirt and pants. She won't have clean clothes, and I sure as fuck don't need to see her nearly naked again.

Except you absolutely do need to see her naked.

I shake off the thought and leave the bundle of clothes just inside her door. I decide to try to sleep this off, knowing full well there is no sleeping off what I feel for Maeve.

IT'S STILL DARK when I roll over in bed, momentarily relieved that I actually managed to sleep a little, but incredibly frustrated by the fact that I dreamed of Maeve the entire time.

Despite the fact that the clock tells me it's just past 4 a.m., I go through my morning routine of washing my face and brushing my teeth before throwing on workout shorts, a cut-off shirt, and my running shoes. I can hopefully get a workout in before Maeve wakes up. I need to let out some of whatever the fuck this is that's making my entire body hum and vibrate.

No such luck for me today, though, because as I walk into my kitchen, there she is. My pants rolled at the waistband and still almost falling off her hips, and my T-shirt tied into a knot at her waist. Her hair is a tangled mess, and her feet are bare as she pours tea into a cup. God, she's fucking perfect.

"Fancy a cuppa?" she asks without turning back to look at me.

Something between a groan and a growl leaves my mouth, and I clear my throat. "Yes. Please." She nods in response and takes the cup that was already next to hers to fill next.

"How d'you take it? And don't say black because that's just disgusting." She's still facing away from me, moving slowly. In her tired state, her voice is groggy, and her British accent comes out to play more than usual.

"Same as you, then," I respond. That gets her head swiveling toward me, but she doesn't make eye contact. Facing the cups in front of her, she nods again, pouring a small amount of milk and sugar into each cup.

Then she pivots around. Both cups of tea in her hand, her eyes down on them as she concentrates on not spilling any of the precious liquid. Her face is slightly flushed, and she sucks her bottom lip into her mouth as she walks. Damn it, it's impossible not to want her. Especially like this. When she lets down all her guards, takes off all her armor, strips off the makeup so I can really see her, that's when I want her most. That's when it feels like loving Maeve is inevitable. Inescapable.

When she sets the cups on the island, she finally looks up at me, sitting and spinning on her stool to face me. I keep my body against the island but twist my head to look at her. My hands stay firmly on my cup, not needing the additional temptation to touch her.

"How'd you sleep?" She smirks, so completely enjoying my blatantly obvious discomfort with this whole situation. She doesn't wait for my answer. "*I* had a great sleep. I guess I was sort of tired last night after the whole flying rat thing, you know?" She runs her finger along the handle of her cup, then looks up at me again, her blue eyes shining.

"Though, I suppose the orgasm care of the Greek Irishman who broke into my room last night probably had something to do with it, too." She doesn't break eye contact. Her voice doesn't crack, and her composure is unwavering. It almost feels practiced.

"How long did you rehearse that line in the mirror before you delivered it just now?" My question has her teetering, but only slightly. Her eyes narrow, and I know she won't answer me. "Better question. How many times have you touched yourself while you think about me?"

She takes a quick breath in. "I'll answer that question as soon as you do, O."

Her sass, and her calling me O, get me to turn in my seat and I pull her stool closer to mine, just like last time we were sitting here like this. My legs cage hers, her knees brush against the insides of my thighs.

"I've lost count because it's every time. Every. Fucking. Time, Maevey." I watch as her eyes widen, pupils dilating.

"Why do you say things like that to me?" Her eyes flick to my lips, then back up, as if she's trying to catch me in a lie. She won't.

"Because I mean them. Because I'm not just trying to fuck with you like you're trying to fuck with me. Because I don't have a reason to resent you and make you pay for mistakes made years ago. Because it's always been you, Maeve. Always. Everywhere. I can't escape you, and I wouldn't even if I could. I say those things to you because I'm yours. Completely, ultimately, relentlessly. Yours. I always have been." I can't tell if she's still breathing. I'm not sure I am. "Do you have any other questions?"

Her chest heaves with the quick breaths she finally takes in, but to her credit, her eyes never leave mine. After finding whatever she's looking for, she nods, swallows, and then sits up straighter. "So many."

"Ask away. I promise to answer you honestly." I rest my hands on her hips, maybe to steady her. Maybe to steady myself.

"Do you really think I resent you?"

I nod, looking down at my lap.

"I don't," she says simply. And I believe her, because it feels like Maeve and I are finally done lying to each other about our feelings.

"Do you think you were ever in love with me?" The question comes out in a whisper, her voice barely audible. I look up at my favorite pair of blue eyes, finding them swirling with uncertainty.

As is usually the case, my brain shuts down around this woman, so my mouth moves and words come out without any deliberation. "I've never not been in love with you. Not since you nearly did a face plant on a New York City side-walk. Not since I saw you dancing very badly on a computer screen. Not since you first said *be safe*, kissed your fingers, and brought them to the screen."

"You saw that?" Her blue eyes widen in a comical way, and it makes me want to laugh, but I know that if I do, this moment will be gone.

"I saw it, and I wished you'd do it again every time after that. For years, I wished you'd do it again." Her hands are gripping her knees so tightly I'm afraid she's going to bruise herself, so I gently take them both in my hands. "Okay?"

She shakes her head as tears well in her eyes, her lips tremble, and a soft sob escapes from the back of her throat. Her face twists into an expression of pain, and she desper-ately tries to turn away, but I take her face in my hands, bringing her gaze back to mine.

She fills her lungs, steadying herself once more as I wipe the two tears that have fallen down her cheeks.

"Do you ever want to kiss me?" Her voice is so sweet that I can almost taste it as the words land on a whisper against my lips.

"Only when I'm breathing."

A breath leaves her mouth on a sigh. "Then kiss me, Owen."

I don't have to be told twice. My lips are on hers faster than I can pull her into me, and when I do, she shimmies herself right onto my lap, straddling me. Our kiss is hungry, because when you go seven years without a taste of the thing you love most, of the person you need most, it's impossible not to lose control.

My tongue swipes at her lips, and she opens for me on a whimper.

"Oh fuck, please make that sound again," I say into her mouth. Instead, she rolls her hips until we're perfectly aligned. Even through all our layers of clothing, I can feel her heat, and I have no doubt she can feel how hard I am.

She rocks into me again, and I grab onto her hips as I suck in a breath, holding it.

"You've stopped breathing. Must not want to kiss me anymore." Even now, she's taunting me. And I fucking love it.

"I want to do absolutely unimaginable things to you." I take in her flushed cheeks and the way her lips are parted.

"Like what?" Her gaze stays focused on my lips.

"Things that have you moaning and writhing underneath me. I want to touch, kiss, and taste every inch of your skin." I tease that spot under her ear that makes her close her eyes and moan. "I want to do whatever it takes to have you waking up next to me every morning so I can worship your body. So, I can do all the things that make you feel wanted, loved, and cherished. Things that make you come with my name on your lips again." She rocks into me again, and I don't hide the groan that builds in my throat. I want her to know exactly what she does to me. She opens her eyes, meeting my gaze. "I want to do everything with you, *fengári mou.*"

"Okay," she whispers. "But you really need to stop talking now, or I'm going to come on your lap before we get to any of those things." She's panting, lips parted, and eyes focused on my mouth, where a smile takes over my face.

"I'd really rather you come when you're naked and in my bed, but if you must..." I take her hips and move her over me one more time, grinding my teeth at the feel of her body melting onto mine.

"Owen," she moans. "We shouldn't." My whole body seizes up at hearing those words.

We shouldn't. What? Why?

I swallow the words down and reposition her so she's sitting on my lap and not on my throbbing erection. As I look down at where my hands rest on her hips, her hold on my neck tightens, and she pulls my face up. I greedily take in her flushed cheeks and sapphire-blue eyes.

"Not because I don't want to. Because look at me... I'm dry-humping you and practically coming in my pants. I just..." She shakes her head and closes her eyes tightly. It's so rare to get a moment where Maeve doesn't know what to say or how to react, so I give her some time to process.

As her fingers scratch at the hair on the nape of my neck, and she exhales a slow breath, she opens her eyes again and they're clearer now. Less fuzzy with lust.

"This is very complicated, whatever this is between us, and I need us to have a clear head about this. You've just said a lot of things, and I think maybe I need to say some too, and we should probably not be so close when that happens, but God, the thought of not being like this with you, of not being so close to you that I can feel you breathing makes my skin hurt." She rests her forehead on my shoulder, and I nod in agreement because I don't want to go back to a world where she doesn't touch me so easily. "But we won't talk if we stay like this. We'll kiss, and we'll fuck, and we'll come, and then we'll do it all over again. And I want that. Blimey, I want that so fucking badly, but I'm afraid if we don't do this now I'll bottle it and make a dog's dinner out of this whole thing, so—"

She suddenly straightens, jerking her body away from mine in a swift motion when she hears my laughter. Her blue eyes twinkle as she surveys my face, and a musical laugh escapes from her lips. "What's funny?"

"You just went full on Brit on me there for a second, blondie. Slow down." I run my hands down her arms, hoping it helps her relax a little. "Why don't we take our tea to the living room? We can even sit on separate couches if you want."

She smiles before pulling her entire bottom lip into her

mouth, releasing it before I have a chance to beg her not to do that when we're supposed to be talking.

"All right, but you can't call me sunshine. Or Maevey. Or blondie. And definitely not *fengári mou*. I can't be held responsible for what my lips do to yours if you say any of those." She's so serious, but I can't hold back the chuckle that comes out as I nod in agreement to her terms.

"And you can't suck your lip into your mouth like you just did, deal?"

She smiles so brightly it nearly knocks the wind out of me. Maeve hasn't smiled like this in years. Not at me, anyway.

I don't even get a chance to commit the moment to memory before she's pushing herself up and off my lap, taking her cup of tea to the living room, giving me a moment to adjust the now painful erection in my shorts.

i'd rather have you for now than not at all.

maeve

IS *Owen James in love with me? I think Owen James is in love with me. Oh my God, my husband is definitely in love with me!*

MY HANDS ARE SHAKING SO BADLY, I'm certain some of my tea has spilled out of the cup I'm not so carefully putting on the small side table next to the big comfy chair in Owen's living room. As I sit, silently promising my vagina some form of release after that torturous but delectable dry-hump in the kitchen, the weight of Owen's words begin to settle on me.

I had wanted him to love me for so long that, for a while, I'm not sure there was anything else I wanted more. Not even my acting career. I always wanted him more than I wanted a role or any kind of success. But then I let him go. And I allowed myself to want those other things again. I allowed myself to want my career as much as I had wanted him. If anything had to take his place in my mind and in my heart, I'm glad I chose acting.

I've prided myself in being someone who goes after what she wants for my whole life. It's been my purpose, my mission, and my biggest source of self-worth. I've never given up on anything except Owen. *That* was a dream I let go of a long time ago. A dream that I thought was permanently washed away. A dream that I work hard to push away every single moment of every single day because I've known for quite some time now that it's the only one I absolutely cannot have.

But here he is, all but telling me he loves me. Telling me there's nothing he won't do for me. Telling me he wants me.

The man I resented for so long has washed away all of those ugly feelings by opening himself up to me. The same man who has given up so much of himself for other people. And he keeps doing it. Julia isn't even here yet and already he's committed to this guardianship role as though he was made for it, and I have no doubts that he was. Whatever plans he had surely didn't include Julia, but he's changing his life for her, regardless. Never complaining.

How can I possibly ask him to take a chance on us when he already has so much going on? How can I ask him for anything when I don't know the first thing about being a good wife or mum? Especially not being a *mum*.

The thought sends pins and needles all over my body as the uneasiness of it seeps into my skin. My breathing starts to feel too shallow, and a headache starts at my temples.

"Maeve?" Owen's soft voice pulls me out of my spiraling thoughts. When I look up, clearly panicked and no longer in a lusty haze, he practically jumps over the coffee table to get to me, kneeling down in front of the chair.

"Hey. No, no, no. Whatever it is that's going on in your head right now, whatever's trying to talk you out of having this conversation and finally fixing things between us, please tell it to shut the fuck up. Please." He kisses my cheeks, wiping at the tears that are falling freely. "Just tell me what it is, and we'll work it out, Maevey." My gaze locks onto his emerald eyes, and I can feel the raw truth emanating from them, so intense that it pierces my soul with a pureness like no other.

A single sob shakes me, and several others follow, causing my shoulders to hunch, my body instinctively wanting to cave in on itself, to protect my aching heart that simply can't take any more beatings.

Owen is the kind of man who could make me believe I could break whatever generational curse makes it so the women in my family are incapable of sharing anything but their bodies with a man. He makes me want to believe I could start anew. He makes me want to believe I could be different from my mother and my grandmother, who were incapable of loving their husbands or their children more than they loved their pretty things and their so-called independence. But I know that's not the truth.

His hands move to my back, roaming cautiously in an attempt to soothe an ache he doesn't know exists.

"I can't do this." It slips out quietly between sobs, and for a moment, I'm not sure he heard me. Then his body stills, and I know even without looking at him that he heard.

"What do you mean?" His hands rest on either side of me, no longer touching me and I feel as though I'm drifting away without an anchor.

"Your *daughter* is going to be here soon, and I'm not... I'm not going to be her mum. That's not..." He nods, brows furrowed as he swallows, and my heart drops to my feet. He's not saying anything. "I didn't have a sweet, loving mum like you did, O. I don't know anything about babies, or how to raise them. I don't know what makes a good wife. I don't know what a good mum does or says. I just can't. I'm so sorry, Owen," I say on a whisper. My sobs have subsided, but my eyes are leaky taps with no way to fix them. I wish I could know what he's thinking. What he's feeling. If it's disappointment or relief. But there's nothing. I can't get a read on him.

"Why are you apologizing?" His face scrunches up in confusion, and the look in his eyes is unreadable.

"Because we've only kissed for the first time in seven years, five minutes ago, and now I'm doing *this*. Because we're married, but we don't even remember how it happened. Because we can't stay married. Because this is a mess, Owen! And we can't complicate it even more with flirting and kissing and orgasms!" More tears stream down my face as Owen straightens so we're face-to-face, but he still doesn't touch me.

"All right. I'm not even gonna touch the comment about you being a mom, because I get that it's a lot. I get that it's not something you ever wanted." I want to correct him, to tell him that I did allow myself to want it once, before he broke my heart. Before I saw that I'm a lot more like my mum than I wanted to believe. That like her, I'm always chasing the next goal, and that I put my needs above everyone else's. But I don't because it seems pointless to talk about Catherine. It seems counterproductive to bring up what happened so many years ago.

With eyes steady on me, Owen continues, "So I'll ask this: what *do* you want, Maeve?" Such a simple question, but my mind is so muddled with everything that's happened that I don't even know anymore. "Okay, how about this? Do you want to be with me?"

I wipe at my face and nod, whispering, "Yes. Always." Something like relief washes over his face.

"Then be with me. I know this is complicated, and it's not what you want, but just... be with me. For however long you're here. Be my wife for whatever time we have left. Whether it's a few weeks or forever—just be with me."

Now it's my turn to look confused, but thankfully, he

keeps going. "Please. I'd rather have you for a short time than not at all. Having you close by, it's the only thing that's felt right in my life in a long time. Please. Stay." He slowly moves his hands up my arms, stopping temporarily at my neck, then gently cups my face. "We're going to be in each other's lives anyway. Elaina would murder us if we ever made shit weird, and we've managed to handle it just fine for well over a year now. I ignored every instinct I had to kiss you and touch you, and if you asked me to, I'd do it again. But not yet. Not right now."

I consider this option, one I hadn't thought of before. "So you're saying…what? We try this out, you know, kissing, dry-humping, etc., for now and when it's time to part ways, we just do?"

He shrugs, looking down at the floor. "If you want… I mean, if forever isn't on the cards, I'd rather have you for now than not at all."

Charlie's advice echoes in my head.

If it's what makes you happy, you owe it to yourself to go after it.

Nothing has made me happier than being with Owen. Ever. It's a truth I've avoided and denied for too long. And if I'm the girl who chases after what she wants, this should be no different. Right?

His lips curve into a small smile as he studies me intently. It's as though he can see the response forming in my mind, the one that comes so easily it should terrify me. I sniffle and take a jagged breath in, letting his warmth sink into my skin slowly like summer rain after a drought. "All right."

There's a feeling in my chest akin to steam being let out of a pressure cooker. It's fast and loud. Everything we've just said is now out here, in the air all around us, and I'm no longer bottling in these thoughts and feelings all by myself.

"This is crazy." The words fall out of my mouth in a half sob, half laugh. He smiles so wide that his eyes crinkle at the corners. "Are we really talking about a temporary marriage? And not just for show?" I shake my head at how absurd this whole thing seems. Is. It is absurd.

Right?

He brings our foreheads together, sighing. "Yeah, Maevey. We really are."

A ridiculous smile blooms on my face, the force of it unstoppable as I allow myself to have this dream again, just for now. Because I'm chasing happiness, even if it's short lived.

He pulls in a quick breath. "I've waited seven years to see you smile at me like that again."

"And?" I tease.

"So much better than I remembered." He tucks a strand of hair behind my ear, and I press forward, gently touching my lips to his. His fingers immediately wrap around the back of my neck as our kiss deepens, but this time it's not desperate like the last. Now he's taking his time letting our lips get reacquainted with one another. This time, I feel everything. Like the scrape of his stubble on my chin. The way he explores with his tongue and angles my head where he wants it.

Owen doesn't lose control like last time. He keeps our kiss soft and sweet, and I feel every ounce of the tenderness he's pouring into it.

When we eventually pull apart, I collapse onto him, my head resting on his shoulder. A loud yawn leaves my lips, and he chuckles. I feel the sound in my bones and shiver. I'm a morning person through and through, but I lied when I told him I slept well. I didn't. And now I'm exhausted.

Owen's arms wrap around my back and as he stands, he pulls me with him. My legs wrap around his waist. As much as I want to be absolutely wrecked by this man, I have no energy left and just as I'm about to protest about getting naked in his bed with him, he sets us both down on the couch so I'm on his lap.

"You should get some rest. You obviously haven't slept off those two orgasms yet." He winks at me as he runs a finger over the bridge of my nose, and I snuggle into his chest. Before he has a blanket draped over me, my eyes have already closed.

i only got special ones today.

maeve

WHEN I WAKE UP, my legs are tucked up into my chest. Something soft is brushing against my cheek, and my lips turn up at the corners at the memory of Owen's warm hand at my back as I fell asleep. A hum of contentment rolls through me.

The soft chuckle coming from somewhere in the room has me startling awake, and when I open my eyes, I'm met with the most beautiful sight. Owen James is holding a box of donuts and smiling at me. And it's not just any smile. It's a smile that has his whole face morphing into what can only be defined as joy. It's a smile I haven't seen in so long, I thought it no longer existed. But here it is, right in front of me.

I push the blanket off me completely and swing my legs over the edge of the sofa. Before I can get up, he's sitting next to me with the pink box on his lap.

"I only got special ones today." He opens the top to reveal a dozen donuts with sprinkles in every color imaginable. There are heart-shaped sprinkles, and star-shaped ones, sparkly sprinkles, and the big round ones that are nice and crunchy. These are gourmet sprinkle donuts, and there's no way he got these from a random place in town.

I can feel my eyebrows lifting as I inhale and open my mouth to ask a question, but before the words are out of my lips, he's already speaking, stopping me mid-thought. "I told Don weeks ago that sprinkles were your favorites, and he got tired of me getting a box of the same generic sprinkled donuts every day, so he stepped it up. It's almost like he knew today was different." His cheeks flush, and when he looks at me, I see a much younger version of Owen in front of me. Not the always self-assured, brooding man, but a vulnerable boy with kind eyes and a little shyness about him.

"What do you mean every day?" My face falls, and so does his. His blush deepens.

"I've ordered these every day since you got here. I usually pick them up early in the morning, after my workout and before watering the gardens. I guess I just hoped we'd have something worth celebrating together at some point, or if you needed cheering up, I'd have these ready for you. It's stupid, I know." He chuckles and runs a hand through his hair, shrugging.

This man. He's bought donuts every day? He knows my favorite snacks? No wonder I can't keep it in my pants.

Truly, I thought the tea and the snacks were sweet and thoughtful, and here he is buying the donuts I told him a lifetime ago that I liked. A lifetime ago. The last time we even really talked was so long ago now. Nothing is the same anymore. We're not the same.

Are we?

I look down at my lap, and the words running through my mind slip out. "I'm not sure I'm the same person you knew anymore. We don't even really know each other."

"Maybe not," he says as he tips my chin up so I can look at him. "But I want to know you, Maeve. All of you. I want to learn all the ways you've changed, and I want to relearn every part of you that has stayed the same."

All these years, I thought he didn't care, that all our tiny moments that added up to some of my most meaningful and beautiful memories had meant nothing to him.

He looks down at the box of donuts on his lap, closing it and setting it on the coffee table. "You don't like sprinkle donuts anymore?" He looks embarrassed, and my heart breaks a little at the sight.

"No, I still love sprinkle donuts, O. I just don't eat them as often anymore." I place my hand over his, and he turns his head toward me.

"Sorry, I just thought—"

"Not because I don't like them, but because they made me think of you too much. Made me miss you too much. And I didn't like missing you. I didn't want to miss you." His green eyes shine as his lips settle into a frown. "But it's been nice getting to enjoy them again. With you."

I watch as his lips tip up into a small smile. "Yeah?" His earnest tone melts me, and when his head moves an inch closer to mine, I stand up quickly and move to sit in the chair I was in earlier.

As I settle into it, I look up and see Owen looking rightfully confused.

"I can't kiss you again. I want to. Badly. But remember what I said earlier? We won't stop, and we still have things to talk about." I fix my hair and pull it back into a ponytail, then I reach for the box on the coffee table because those donuts are calling to me.

"What do we need to talk about, Maevey?"

"No! I told you, no nicknames allowed. I meant it, Owen!" I take a big bite of the donut with purple and pink sprinkles and send a few flying onto my lap with my less than graceful eating. Owen rubs a hand across his jaw, covering what I'm sure is a smirk beneath his hand.

"We need to sort out what we're doing here. We don't speak for several years, then we get married, and now you're about to become someone's legal guardian. Not to mention there's the issue of our friends and family, who know this whole thing was a big drunken accident, and now we're...what? Dating? Are we together? Or do we not have a name for this yet? And how do we do this when we're already *bloody married*? What happens when we get divorced in a few weeks? And what, do I keep living in your guesthouse and only occasionally come here to make out with you or when I need an orgasm?" Another big bite of donut gets shoved inside my mouth as I try to breathe through my thoughts. I'm pretty sure there's sweat beading on my forehead, and as I wipe at it and look up, I find a perfectly calm Owen sitting across from me.

"You want a name for what we are now? I'm yours. There. Call it what you want. That's a fact." His elbows are casually resting on his knees, and he licks his lips while I continue to inhale this exceptionally large and delicious donut. "I don't want to get a divorce. I won't want to. Ever. If we hadn't gotten married in Vegas, I'd be begging you to marry me as soon as possible. Today. Tomorrow. But like I said before, if all I get is a short time with you, I'll take it. I'll take whatever you want to give me." Without breaking eye contact with me, he takes a slow breath and smiles. "I don't expect you to want the same things as me, Maeve. I just need to make it clear to you that this is where I stand. I don't really know what happens beyond this." His smile grows more confident, he clasps his hands together, and I swallow the last bite of my donut. "And you could move in here right now. Sleep in my bed and make it ours. Or stay in the guesthouse. Drop by whenever you want to make out. I'll make you come any way you like. I'll give you whatever you want because if we're together, everything else will fall into place."

"You really believe all that?" The tears at the corners of my eyes sting, and I stare at him unblinkingly so they'll stay put.

"Every word, *fengári mou*," he answers simply. My heart thrashes wildly inside my chest, its quick but steady beats like a kick drum inside my ears as it sends all the blood in my body directly to my core. I'm a living, breathing contradiction of feelings and emotions. I want him. I want him so wildly and completely that it hurts not to be near him, and I'm also terrified of getting too close. I'm so scared of the unknowns, of not being enough for him, of being too much. And the love that was there, that never left, that I just kept hidden far, far away is now peeking through. That love is like sunshine trying to be kept out by flimsy curtains. It finds a way to peek through the cracks, and while I'm not ready to open them up all the way yet, I'm feeling very tempted.

"I'm scared," I whisper, my voice cracking.

"I know," he answers steadily.

"You're not?"

"Oh, I'm fucking terrified of a lot of things. Of failing, of losing you, of not knowing how to care for a baby. But of being with you? Of falling more in love with you every day? Not even a little bit." With a shake of his head, he sits back on the couch, and I lunge for him, landing on his lap. He catches me with strong hands on my hips as the air whooshes out of his lungs.

what even is my life?

owen

SHE BURIES her face in my neck, hugging me tightly as she straddles me and God, it makes me feel whole. Complete. I pull her close, my fingertips digging into her skin through the soft fabric of *my* T-shirt that she's still wearing. The warmth of her skin against mine is a comfort I haven't felt in so long I almost forgot it. Her scent, now mixed with mine on my clothes, fills my lungs, and I close my eyes, savoring every sensation, so I'll never forget what this feels like again.

Her grip on my shoulders loosen, and I already miss her warmth before she pulls away. I prepare myself for the loss of her heat, but she readjusts, her soft lips brushing against my neck. Then her head shifts, and her lips are on my skin again, gentle kisses landing everywhere they can reach until they start to move up to my jaw. Without a word, she trails kisses to my lips, her tongue immediately seeking entrance to my mouth, which I freely give.

We stay like this for a while until her hips shift, and I hiss at the contact. I've been so desperate for her that even the friction through layers of clothing feels like it might be my undoing.

"There's something I've wanted for a very long time. Will you give it to me?" She shifts again, whispering the words in my ear. I grab her ass with both hands, holding her still.

"I'll give you anything you want." I feel her smile on my neck, and then she's moving down my body, hands roaming over my chest and stomach as she kneels on the floor in front of me. Her hands go to the waistband of my shorts, fingers sliding beneath my boxer briefs as she tugs. My eyes go wide, and I shake my head. She smirks and nods, licking her lips and tugging down again. When I lift my hips, she pulls my bottoms down to my ankles. I'm helpless. Hopeless. I can't say no to her. I don't want to.

Of course, I'm already rock hard, my dick proudly standing to attention for Maeve. Her lips part and eyes go glassy and wide, and she stares at it, then up at me. I shake my head again, and her eyes soften.

"Please," she whispers her plea, and I feel her warm breath land on my dick. My head falls back, and I groan. If a puff of air is setting me on fire, her mouth will surely kill me. She runs a finger up my length, then wraps her hand around the tip, spreading the bead of moisture there with her thumb.

"Fuck, yes." And that's all the permission she needs. Her lips wrap around me, her tongue perfectly warm as she takes me partially into her mouth. And then she fucking moans. My head jerks up at the sound, needing to see her. I've dreamed of this, imagined it, let it take me over the edge countless times as I jerked off, but nothing could have prepared me for the sight that is Maeve Howard with my cock in her mouth. Nothing.

She looks up as she takes me deeper, sucking so hard her cheeks hollow, and my hands immediately reach for her, one landing on her shoulder, and the other on her ponytail. I don't apply any pressure, I just need to tether myself to her, feel her, make sure she's real and this is really happening.

She moans again, blue eyes sparkling up at me with mischief and desire.

With a pop, she removes her mouth from me. "Tell me what you like." She licks every inch of me before wrapping her hand around me again. Then she sucks one of my balls into her mouth, and I swear to fuck, I levitate.

"Shit. Oh, fuck. That. I like that." She groans, and I feel the sound travel like lightning through my veins. Her hands start working me up and down in a torturously slow rhythm, but when she moves her mouth to my other testicle, she picks up her pace.

"Gah, ffff, oh my...Maeve, wh—" I growl, and she laughs. Every nerve ending on my body feels like a live wire right now, responding to every sound she makes. I pull at my hair with both hands, needing something else to focus on for a moment before I tether myself back to her.

"Fuck. I'm not gonna last. You feel so good." I'm panting, never taking my eyes off her as she moves again, taking me back into her mouth. She's faster this time, using her mouth and her hand together. I watch as her other hand reaches into her pants, and her eyes dart back up to mine.

"Are you touching yourself, Maevey?" She nods, blue eyes watering as she takes me deeper. And that does me in. She moans as I spill into her mouth. My grip on her shoulder is so tight that I worry I might bruise her. When she feels the last of it, she swallows and grabs onto my thigh as her whole body tightens, and she whimpers my name. Her hand moves from inside her pants to rest on her own thigh as she collapses on top of me, her head resting on my stomach. We're both breathing hard, and my brain can't seem to register what just happened.

"Did you just come while sucking me off?" Her eyes tell me everything I need to know, and she sucks in a deep breath through her nose. I scoop her up by her arms and lay her on the couch, hovering above her. I crash my lips to hers and taste myself on her tongue, making her whimper beneath me. "You're fucking perfect, you know that?" She smiles and pulls me back down to kiss her again.

I pull back, nibbling on her bottom lip. "Now, is it my turn to taste you?" She shakes her head, and I rear back, confused by her response.

"Bon, Adam, Charlie, and Raf are going to be here soon, and I don't think they're prepared to walk in on us while your head is between my legs, darling."

Nothing else even registers. Just one word. *Darling*. She's never called me anything other than my name or O before, and I fucking love the sound of this new name for me on her lips. I don't know how long I lay there, replaying the way her mouth moved around the word before it dawns on me that she just mentioned people coming over.

"Wait, did you say my sister and our friends are all coming here?" I come back to reality and find Maeve smiling and nodding.

"They're bringing lunch. I thought you knew."

Did I know? Maybe Lainey told me, but I've been so caught up on all things Julia and Maeve that I can't be sure.

My phone beeps with a notification, which I know is the front gate being opened, and we both jump up at the sound.

"Blimey, do they have impeccable timing, or what?" Maeve laughs, and I stand and pull her up with me, then I tuck myself back into my underwear and shorts, patting down my hair, which is surely standing up on all ends right now from the way I pulled on it.

Maeve rushes to the bathroom, keeping the door open as she washes her face and fixes her hair, and I clean up the donuts and rearrange the pillows on the couch. I'm a man who is confident enough to say I like throw pillows, and I don't care what anyone has to say about it. Even if my sister picked them out for me.

My sister. Who is about to walk through my front door any second. Minutes after her best friend gave me the best blowjob of my life. Minutes after my wife sent me on an out of body experience with her mouth.

What even is my life?

36 /

must have been a really hard workout.

maeve

I'VE JUST FINISHED FIXING my hair when the front door opens, and Bon's voice comes floating in.

"O? You in here?" I step out into the hallway where Owen is standing in the kitchen, staring toward the group walking in the door like a deer in headlights.

Oh bollocks. Here we go again!

I suppose it's nice to know that while he can make me weak in the knees with a kiss on the red carpet, I can render him speechless with a blowjob.

"Hiya!" I walk toward the four of them still standing by the front door as they take off their shoes. I catch what must be the tail end of Charlie and Raf trying not to rip each other's heads off.

"And I told *you* that I can't help the things I do in my sleep! If you really didn't like my head being so close to yours, you should have moved, Red!" Raf's voice is low, but I can hear the exasperation in it.

"I was also asleep, Rafael. On *my* side of the car. Away from *you*. Next time, please keep your drooling to yourself."

Charlie kicks off her shoes a little bit too forcefully toward where Rafael is standing.

"All right, *gata*. You win. I'll keep my drooling face away from yours as soon as you keep your hands to yourself. Deal?" Raf's smirk has Charlie's face going so red I'm worried she might burst. I peek at Bon and Adam, who are watching the two with rapt fascination.

"Stop calling me names," Charlie hisses as Raf's smile gets wider.

"Uh, you two should probably stop fighting now." Adam's voice is gentle, and both Raf and Charlie roll their eyes in his direction.

"Yes, Dad," they say in unison, and Bon explodes with laughter. Adam chuckles at their antics, and eventually, even Charlie looks less pissed. Bon turns and catches sight of me.

"Mae! You're he— Why are you wearing my brother's clothes?"

Oh, bloody hell. Leave it to Bon to just say the thing that pops into her head.

I love her for it, except when it serves to point out the thing that Owen is quietly flipping out about in the kitchen.

I go to her and give her a hug, laughing lightly as I do. "Well hello to you too, bestie!" I hug Adam next, then Raf, then I spend an extra few seconds hugging my sister tightly, and her body relaxes as I do. She whispers a *thank you*, and I nod, stepping away from the group and into the kitchen where we always seem to congregate.

"Owen, why is Maeve wearing your clothes?" Bon looks to her wide-eyed brother, a look of pure mischief on her cute face.

"Well, uh, you see, there was this, uh, thing, in uh..." Raf's laugh booms out of him as he leans over slapping his knee. I pull my lips between my teeth, so I don't accidentally join him, and Bon narrows her eyes at me conspiratorially. I shake my head at both her and Charlie, for good measure. Who knows what'll come out of their mouths next.

"There's a bat in the guesthouse. I kind of freaked out last night and ran here, and since I didn't have my own clothes to sleep in, Owen let me borrow his." There. That ought to shut them all up.

"That seems rational," Adam says as he nods. "Have you been back to see where the bat is?"

Damn it, Adam.

"Uh, no. I uh... Well, you see—" I can't take any more of Owen's nervous babbling so I interject again.

"Owen was working out, and I didn't want to go back there by myself, so we haven't been over yet. I have absolutely no desire to see that ugly thing again." I keep my eyes on the small group currently smiling at us like they know something we don't.

Little do they know just how little they know...

"Did you just finish your workout, O? You look a little flushed. Need some water?" Raf's eyebrows bounce on his forehead, the little shit.

"Uh...yeah. I did." Owen swallows hard and reaches for a glass in the cupboard behind him, filling it with water straight from the tap and downing it.

"Must have been a really *hard* workout. Your hair looks like it's been pulled in all directions." The little jerk laughs again.

I love Raf, but I might kill him today.

Owen spits out his water, coughing as he sits the glass down loudly on the countertop.

"You know what, why don't the three of you go check on the flying rat in the guesthouse and let us get lunch ready? Not to feed into the patriarchy but go take care of the big scary thing while us women converse in the kitchen, please." I start to shoo the three of them away from the kitchen, shooting a glare at Owen that hopefully communicates *get it together, man.*

The three of them walk out, and I catch the reassuring clap on the back Adam gives Owen as he looks back at me, and I wave my hand, signaling for him to keep walking.

"So I take it you've seen your husband's dick, then?" None of us have much of a filter, but Charlie was born without one, especially when it's just the three of us.

"Gross, Char. That's my brother!" Bon pretends like she's throwing up, making an awful sound as she does. Then she looks up, bright eyed. "But, I mean, without giving us any details of the how and when, did you?"

"Oh my life, Elaina soon-to-be Holm! I cannot believe the nerve! Both of you." I point at the two of them who look at one another with eyebrows raised.

"She did," Charlie says matter-of-factly.

"Oh, she *sooooo* did!" Bon is practically bouncing, which is hilarious and alarming.

"Oh, stop it, you two!" They high-five beneath the countertop as if I can't see exactly what they're doing. "I saw that!" I turn around to get myself a glass of water.

"We know," they say together, breaking into a fit of giggles.

I take a large gulp of water and sit the glass down gently, looking at a random spot on the counter. "Yeah. I did." I swallow, suddenly needing more water as I think of everything that happened before the hottest moment of my life took place on Owen's couch.

The girls pick up on my change of tone and still, sitting on the counter stools in front of me. I can't seem to find the words or the right way to start telling them what's happened between us since I moved into his guesthouse.

"Has Owen told you how he feels, Mae?" Lainey reaches out to touch my hand, and the simple touch soothes me enough to take a deep breath and look up at her. I nod and watch as her eyes fill with tears. "Oh my God," she whispers, bringing her other hand to her lips.

Charlie takes over, laying a hand on Bon's shoulder as our friend lets a few tears slide down her cheeks. "So, you know why he went silent, but have you two talked about your situation?" I nod again, drinking some more of my water. Char cocks her head to the side taking me in, and I know she's assessing whether I'm about to join Bon in crying or if I'm okay. Surprisingly, I feel all right.

Seeing that I'm not going to break down, she continues, "And does he know about what's been going on with you?"

"Not completely. He knows I needed to get away for a while, but not that I'm questioning everything. I need to digest that a little more myself, I think. Everything is so... muddy. There's no clear path ahead of me, and I'm not used to that. I've always had a plan and stuck to it." I look between the two women in front of me, one who shares half of my DNA and the other who might as well have been another sister. Charlie sticks out her other hand toward me, and we sit there, the three of us holding on to one another for a moment in time not needing any words to communicate. The physical connection opens something up in me, and if there had been any weight left in my chest, it's lifted now. Now that they know and understand what this means. "But I'm chasing my happy, Char. Like you said. I'm trying not to dwell on my plans, my goals, and whatever it is I thought I should be doing by now."

"Are you ready to talk about what's next for you two?" Bon's green eyes search mine. She never pushes too hard, never tries too hard to force a conversation, but also always lets me know she's there to listen, whenever that time may come.

"Not yet, but I'm..." I blow out a breath, trying to articulate the feelings floating in my chest. "We're going to see how things go for now, and I'm going to take it day-by-day for once. No five-year plan or goals for right now other than just enjoying the time we have. As unconventional and crazy as our situation is, I still feel settled, peaceful, and... happy, I think." Bonnie's sniffles have me turning my hand over so I can give hers a squeeze. She lets out a wet laugh and looks at Charlie, who gives her a warm smile.

"It's about time, sissy. You deserve this." Even Char's eyes are looking a little glassy. This level of emotion simply isn't something I can handle at the moment, so I pry my hands away and clap them together.

"Now, let's see if my husband has any good wine, shall we?" It's meant to be playful, but the words *my husband* fall out of my mouth far more naturally than they should.

37 /
holy motherfucking bats!

owen

"SPILL THE BEANS, James. What the actual fuck was that all about?" Raf walks ahead of us so he can turn around and walk backward, no doubt reading every minuscule change to my body language and facial expressions. It's part of what makes him such a great head of security for Aegis. He can read people better than anyone else I know. He sticks his arms out, eyebrows raised to the sky, impatient as a toddler.

"I don't fucking know." I shrug, trying to play it off, even if I know it's no use with him. He knows me far too well.

"Yes you do. You're in love with your wife. And something most definitely happened because you were giving her the eyes, and you actually *blushed* at one point." He stops talking to laugh and nearly trips on a bush. He recovers and proceeds to walk backward, clearly not learning his lesson. "Blushed! You!" He starts laughing again, and when I hear a chuckle out of Adam, I give him a glare. He has the good sense to stop laughing and gives me an apologetic shrug. This guy might be the nicest dude I've ever met. Next to Raf.

"Does she know, Owen?" The question comes quietly from Adam, walking beside me. I never even considered the fact that one day I might become friends with my sister's future husband, but of all the people she could choose to get engaged to, she picked one I really like being friends with.

"Yes. She knows I'm in love with her. I mean, I said it without flat out saying it, but, yeah." Raf jumps up in the air then sticks his hand up, waiting for a high-five. He doesn't get it from me, so Adam takes pity on him and slaps his palm.

"I'm so happy right now! So you two are gonna stay married then, right? Oh, this is great. And she's cool with Julia and everything? Are you gonna adopt her together?" My breathing speeds up at each question Raf shoots at me like a pitching machine, each one getting a little harder with a curveball thrown in at the end.

We arrive at the guesthouse, and Adam lays a hand on my shoulder. "You don't need to answer any of those questions. Raf's just excited, but he's gonna tone it down a notch, right Raf?" Adam sends his version of a stern look toward our friend.

Rafael nods and pretends to zip his own mouth shut. We walk into the guesthouse quietly, and I take in the little things Maeve had left out when she booted it out of here.

There's a blanket on the couch that's still rumpled, and the book she got the other day sitting face down next to it with an empty plate on the coffee table. We walk further into the space, but if it was a bat in here, I doubt we'd see it in the light of day.

"Let's just go straight for the attic and see if there's anything up there." I walk down the hall toward the room with the attic access, and the guys follow.

"Can I go up?" Of course, Raf wants to be the one to go. He's always the first to offer help. I pull the ladder down and wave a hand forward, letting him know he can go ahead, and he does—with a huge smile on his face.

As he climbs, Adam turns to me. "You all right, Owen?"

"I'm good, man. There's a lot going on, but I'm good."

"I can hear you, shitheads. Owen, don't you dare tell Adam anything before I get back down th—Holy mother-fucking bats!" There's a thud, then a high-pitched screech and the next thing I know, Raf nearly tumbles back down the ladder. He stands facing us, panting, then lets out a nervous laugh. "You've got a bat problem, my dude. There's like a whole family of them just chilling up there."

"What was that screechy sound up there? Was that one of the bats, or was that you?" Adam chuckles as Raf scowls at him, and I can't help the smile on my own face.

"I don't wanna talk about it." Raf turns and shoves the ladder back into place. "But Maevey can't stay here, man. She will flip the fuck out if she knows how many of them there are." He looks at me, hands on hips as protector Raf is firmly in place now. I smile and clap him on the shoulder.

"I got it man. I can take care of my wife." That gets a chuckle out of him, and he fakes a punch to my stomach with a big smile on his face.

"Your *wife*, huh?" He smiles at Adam then back at me, and it loosens the strain in my chest that my friends are happy for me. That they support me. I guess that also loosens my tongue.

"She hasn't said it yet, but I think she's in love with me, too. I don't have all the answers, but I think we'll figure them out. I think we—" I don't get to finish my sentence because Raf has his big meaty arms around me in a hug I didn't ask for.

He pulls away and steps back. "I know you hate hugs. Sorry. But you're two of my best friends. I'm just happy for you. I smothered Adam when he told me he was in love with Lainey. And you remember me at the engagement party. I didn't stop hugging them all night. I just like seeing my friends happy, man."

I give Raf a shoulder squeeze, thankful for this big teddy bear with a heart of pure gold. "Thanks, Raf. I appreciate it."

Adam steps closer. "And are you, Owen? Happy?"

I feel the corners of my lips quirk up immediately. "Yeah. I'm happy. I'm… relieved. I've spent a long time loving her on my own, and now she's here, so yeah. I'm happy."

"And what's going on with Julia? When will she be able to live here with you?" Adam's voice remains even as he tucks his hands into his pockets.

I let out a loud breath. "Soon, I think. The courts are super backed up and there was a request in the will to make sure I was financially and emotionally stable enough to be Julia's guardian." I rub at my chest, thinking about Clay and Monica having to make this decision, never knowing just how soon this would all happen. "My lawyer keeps me posted every day, even if there's no change, but it's a matter of days now. She'll be home soon."

I look up to find both of my friends smiling at me, and for once, Rafael doesn't say anything.

Adam nods, then asks, "You'll let us know if we can help with anything, yeah?" I nod, meaning it. "All right, then. You wanna pack Maeve a few things so she doesn't have to come back here?" Ever the considerate one, Adam makes a great suggestion, so I head into the other room before he can finish his sentence.

I'm not prepared for the sheer amount of stuff Maeve brought with her. You'd think she was moving in, and the thought of that happening makes me want to toss all of these things in the back of my truck and haul them into my house. Our house.

AFTER I'VE THROWN a few things into an empty suitcase, I roll it back into the house and find the girls setting some plates around the table, each with a glass of wine in their hands.

"We're back!" Raf's voice booms through the space.

"Did you find it and gently place it back into its natural habitat?" I laugh at Maeve's question. She didn't sound like she cared about anything's natural habitat when she came running in here last night.

Last night. How was that just last night?

Walking up to her, I place a hand on her lower back and practically beam when she relaxes into the touch.

"No. There wasn't only one, unfortunately, so it might be best if you stay here until we get this taken care of." She stiffens, turning to face me and I expect the worst. She's going to want to leave. She's going back to LA because being here with me is too much too soon. She's changed her mind.

"There was *more than one*?" Her eyes go wide and her jaw drops. "You can bet your ass I'm staying over here, then!"

She's gonna stay? Holy shit, she's gonna stay!

I smile, putting my other hand in my pocket to keep from touching her because I can feel all eyes on us right now. "I packed a few things for you, so you don't need to go back there if you don't want to."

She pats my chest and smiles brightly up at me. "That was nice of you. Thank you, darling." She walks away, stopping to top up her wine glass, and I look up to see Adam's knowing smile. "I'm just going to get changed quickly then." I stand there staring at her retreating form, heart pounding in my chest as the way she called me *darling* and the fact that she's going to stay here take root in my brain. The little specks of hope inside me are like seeds being planted into the ground and blooming.

"Owen?" Lainey's voice is loud next to me, and I turn to find her grinning from ear to ear. "I called your name three times. You want a beer with lunch?"

"Oh. Yeah. Sure. Thanks, Lainey." I run my fingers through my hair and go to find something to do that isn't obsessing over Maeve. I walk to the pantry fridge and grab some cans of sparkling water for the table. I have a feeling these girls started on wine early and haven't had anything else since.

We all settle onto our chairs, and Lainey smiles, taking in everyone gathered around the table. I know what she's thinking. It's been a while since we've done this, and it's never been here.

"Okay, so wherever you sit, that's what you get. We ordered six different mystery sandwiches then you can grab whatever sides you want. The bread and the chips are made on site, and the salad is fucking incredible—I've been trying to get the recipe for the dressing from the owner since the first time I came here." She sets her napkin on her lap, then looks up again. "And I'm really happy we're all here together. For the last time without a little baby! Eeeek! Now let's dig in. I'm starving!"

We all laugh and start unwrapping our sandwiches. As I'm about to bite into mine, opposite me, Charlie is scowling at hers and mumbling something I can't hear. Raf looks up and hands her his plate with his sandwich on it, which gets a small smile from Charlie. These two are such a mystery. Raf leaves his new sandwich untouched and fills his plate up with chips and salad.

"Rafael, what's the deal with your super-hot brother?" Charlie's eyes twinkle with mischief, and it's a look I only see on her when Raf is around. This is gonna be good.

"Ooooh, which one?" Lainey adds fuel to the fire, and I love it.

"Wait, there's more than one?" That's my wife's voice I hear, and I *don't* love that.

"Well, I'm asking about the one with the arm tattoos who manhandles horses all day. God, that's hot." Charlie doesn't look at Raf, so she can't see that his face is going a little red as she moans into her sandwich while talking about his brother.

"So hot," Maeve agrees.

The fuck?

"So, soooo hot." My sister nods as she agrees with her friends.

"What the fuck?" The question comes out as a chorus as Adam, Rafael, and I all ask it at the same time. The girls break into a fit of giggles, and the three of us shake our heads at one another, annoyed that they managed to mess with us.

WE CHAT about what's new and catch up on each other's lives. When we're all cleaning up, I watch Raf wrap up the sandwich he took from Charlie, handing it to me. "Maybe you wanna have this later? I wasn't very hungry." He's lying. Raf is quite literally *always* hungry.

"Sure. Thanks, man. What kind of sandwich was it?" Curiosity gets the best of me. There has to be a good reason for him not to eat. Raf is the guy who will eat other people's leftovers without second thought. Joey from *Friends*? Yeah. That's Raf.

"I got the veggie sandwich." Before I can respond, he walks away to clear some more things off the table. The veggie sandwich has mushrooms. Raf is allergic to mushrooms.

AN HOUR LATER, Lainey and Maeve are dancing in the kitchen, while Charlie's in the living room, completely unbothered, reading a book. Raf took off to see Arthur, and Adam's being lured into a dance with his fiancée.

Lainey must have let Maeve pick the music because "Somebody Like You" by Keith Urban is currently playing, and my sister has had enough wine to not care that she's dancing to country music, which she claims to dislike.

"Come on, husband. Won't you dance with me?" Maeve reaches out her hand, and since I'll never deny her anything, I take it. She pulls me up to her, and I'm not sure if it's her doing the pulling or if it's her gravitational force. My moon, calling me to her.

Her hands go to my hair, tugging lightly in a way that makes me groan. I shake my head at her. She knows exactly what she's doing.

"Tiny dancer, have you had any water?" She giggles and pulls me closer, so I wrap an arm around her waist.

"Yes. I had the water you so diligently put out with lunch. But, I've definitely had more wine than water, though." Another fit of giggles has her throwing her arms up in the air and belting out the lyrics.

I wrap both arms around her as she sways and sings completely off key. Seeing her this happy and carefree makes me laugh.

She brings her arms down, fingers back in my hair, right where they belong. "I want to love somebody like you, Owen. I really want to." Her blue eyes sparkle like the ocean on a sunny day. They're clear, even if I know she's more than a little tipsy on wine at the moment.

"I know, sunshine. I know you do." She tugs on my hair and pulls me down to her for a kiss. Her lips are soft and sweet as I taste the rosé on her lips. The moment is sadly cut short by my little sister.

"Whoooo! My best friend and my brother are kissing, and it's the cutest fucking thing I've ever seen!" Lainey's shout has us quickly pulling apart, and there's a ripple of laughter around the room. I definitely didn't see this coming, and definitely not this soon, but fuck, if it doesn't feel good to finally feel like she's mine.

BY THE TIME Raf gets back, Lainey, Charlie and Adam are ready to leave. They have a couple of hours on the road ahead of them thanks to traffic, and I have no doubt Lainey will use that time to sleep off some of this wine.

"I hope we did a good job of keeping you company and taking away any stress you're feeling about the guardianship process. Everything will be great, big brother. Julia will be here soon and it'll be amazing." My little sister smiles sleepily at me. "I want to come for a visit, but only when you're ready, okay? Settle into your little family first, then let us come shower her with love." Lainey hugs me and whispers so only I can hear, "I'm so happy for you, O." I squeeze my drunk little sister a little tighter and let her go, making sure Adam's got a hold of her because she's about to topple over.

After saying our goodbyes, Maeve sways next to me, and I wonder if it isn't about time she sleeps this wine off as well. I crouch down and scoop her up in a firefighter's carry, which gets her giggling again. I drop her down gently on her bed.

"All right, blondie. Time for you to sleep this off before you end up marrying somebody else today." I pull a blanket up to cover her up, but she throws it off, pulling me onto the bed with her.

"I only ever wanted to marry you, Owen. No matter how tipsy I might get, it was only ever going to be you. I knew that when I was nineteen, and I still know it now." She smiles, cradling my face in her hands, and kisses me softly. I want to believe what she said, but she's had a lot of wine. Still, my heart beats wildly with the hope of the truth behind her words.

"Will you stay with me?"

Fact: I would like nothing more. But again, a lot of wine was consumed.

"Let me get you some water and some aspirin before you fall asleep, all right?" She nods, but there's mischief in her bright blue eyes.

"Then you'll get in here and remind me what it feels like to be fucked by Owen James, yeah?" I take in a sharp breath. Again, there's nothing I'd like more. I don't answer her and get up to grab the water and painkillers.

When I step back into her room, she's under the covers, but I take in the clothes scattered next to the bed. When I step closer, her bra and panties are also on the floor.

Fuck. Me. I'm gonna have to deny my wife, aren't I?

"Maevey. What are you doing?" I set the glass and pills on the nightstand and straighten.

"I want you, Owen. Please?" She starts to move the covers down her body, and I, being the fool that I am, stop her and tuck her in tighter.

"Not yet. Soon. I promise." Her eyes go glassy with tears, and I regret everything I've just said.

"You don't want me?" Her voice cracks as she whines, and it's actually a little bit adorable. How could she think I don't want her?

Right. She's drunk.

"Hey, no. It's not because I don't want you. I do. So much. But I need you to sleep off this wine first, okay?" I brush some of the hair off her forehead, and she wiggles.

I lay down next to her, above the covers, and she burrows her face into my chest, taking a deep breath. I run my hand up and down her back, and she closes her eyes tightly, then relaxes as she takes another deep inhale. Within seconds, her breathing evens out, a soft snore occasionally slipping out. For a few minutes, I allow myself to savor the feel of her against me like this for the second time today. Then, I get up quietly and walk out, shutting the door gently behind me.

38 /
fuck first. food later.

maeve

I **OPEN** my eyes to find that it's still light outside.

Or did I sleep through the night? No...that's not possible, is it?

Based on the warmth of the sunshine, I'm assuming it's sunset, not sunrise. I sit up to find myself quite naked, which is surprising for a moment, until the memories come back to me. Me begging Owen to shag me, getting undressed under the covers, nearly crying when he said no—for good reason, of course. I was properly sloshed.

I can't even bring myself to be embarrassed. I'm not sure I would have acted differently had I not had that many glasses of wine in me. I'm so wound up for him, I'm not sure I can go another day without feeling his weight on me.

Better not get too caught up in those thoughts right now, though.

I reach for the water and painkillers on the nightstand, and down the tablets. There's a dull ache in my head, but thankfully it's not too bad. Walking over to the attached bathroom, I get in the shower, thoroughly enjoying the hot water on my skin.

· · ·

DRESSED in sleep shorts and a tank top, I leave the bedroom as the scent of garlic and something like bacon hits my nostrils, making me moan. If Owen is in the kitchen cooking, I can't be held responsible for my actions. Few things in this world are hotter than a man cooking. I haven't even seen him yet, and the thought of him has my skin heating. I'm quite willing to beg him again to get naked and get inside me.

Sure enough, there he is, moving something around a pan as it sizzles on the stove. He turns in time to see me walking in and a huge smile spreads across his face, making my stomach flip. It's his boyish smile, his sweet I-don't-know-I'm-smiling smile. It's my favorite.

"Hey, Maevey. Good nap?" How can this man be asking me about my nap when he's walking around this kitchen in low-slung sweats and a T-shirt that clings to his every muscle?

I don't give a shit about my nap!

"Oh. Okay. Sorry I asked?" He turns back to the stove and moves the pan from the hot element.

I said the thing about the nap out loud then. Right. Great. Bloody hell.

"Are you all right?" He's giving me his full attention now, nothing is visibly being cooked anymore.

"All my thoughts are coming out of my mouth, and just the sight of you standing there is making me hornier than I've ever been in my entire life, so no. I am, in fact, not all right." I tug at the hem of my tank top simply to give my hands something to do. "I'm not opposed to begging when I'm sober, Owen."

Before I get the chance to speak again, he's in front of me, hands on his hips, eyes on my lips. "You never have to beg me for anything, Maevey. You want me to take you to my bed and fuck you until you can't remember your name?" I nod so big and so fast that my vision blurs. Owen lifts me off the floor, and I wrap my legs around him. My back hits the wall, and I gasp. "I was making us dinner. You don't want to eat first?"

"Fuck first. Food later," I say against his lips.

"As you wish." Both of his hands give my ass a strong squeeze, then we're on the move again. I expect my back to hit the bed next, but instead, my feet hit the floor. "This is probably gonna go too fast, but I promise I'm gonna take my time on the next round, all right?" He pulls off his T-shirt with one hand, then pushes his pants and boxer briefs to the floor in one swoop. He steps off the heap of clothes on the floor and opens the drawer on his nightstand, pulling out a condom.

"*No*," I say, causing him to stop and look back at me. "I mean no to the condom. I haven't been with anyone in a long time, and I've been tested. I'm on the pill. I don't want anything between us." That gets him to look at me.

"Me too. Uh, the not being with anyone and being tested, I mean." While he's facing me, I take the opportunity to let my eyes roam all over him. At the new tattoos on his chest, at the way his muscles move, at how different yet the same he looks since last time.

"Take off your clothes, Maeve." I shake my head, and his green eyes narrow. I see nothing but desire in them, and my heartbeat pounds between my ears and between my legs at the thought of us finally being together like this again.

"I want you to take them off for me."

He walks to me slowly, predatorily, and I fucking love it.

"Lift your arms and leave them there." I do as I'm told, loving the stern tone in his voice. He lifts up the hem of my tank top at a painfully unhurried speed, letting his fingers roam over my stomach, my ribs, the sides of my breasts. He stops to cup each of them, weighing them in his hands, and a pained groan leaves his mouth while his thumbs brush back and forth over my nipples.

When I gasp at the sensation traveling straight to my clit, my arms start to drop, and he stops all movement.

"Arms up, Maevey." I mouth *yes*, and straighten my arms above my head again. "Such a good girl." I moan at his praise. He knows exactly what those words did to me all those years ago, and he doesn't seem surprised that they have the same effect on me now. I fight the urge to melt into a puddle on the floor, and force my limbs to remain upright.

He continues his movement, hands skimming my arms as he pulls my top over my head. I let my arms drop and his eyes narrow again at my bratty behavior.

"I'm gonna need you to stay still for this next part. Think you can do that? That means no touching me." I nod my response, which seems to be enough for him. He kneels down in front of me, hands going to my hips. He pulls down the band of my shorts and suddenly stops. I know why. He traces the tattoo on my hip bone with one of his fingers. It's just tiny numbers, but he traces each number with his fingertip, as if branding the date further into my skin, into my soul.

"It's the day we—"

"I know what day we met, Maeve." His head swivels up, and his eyes meet mine. Everything stills in that moment. "When did you get this?"

"Almost ten years ago," I answer. He looks back at the tattoo then plants a hot, open-mouthed kiss on it, and I suck in so much air I become lightheaded. The urge to run my fingers through his hair, to pull him up to me, is so strong, but I don't. His smirk tells me he knows just how much I'm having to hold back, and he loves it.

He grabs the waistband of my shorts with both hands again, and his strong fingers dig into my skin as he slowly pulls them down my legs. His warm palms skim over my backside before he lets go.

"Spread your legs." I step out of my shorts, widening both

of my legs as I do. Owen runs his nose up one inner thigh, and his hand up the other. My breath starts coming in shorter spurts as he gets closer to exactly where I want him. But a nagging thought makes me stiffen, and of course, he notices.

"What's the matter?" I shake my head and close my eyes.

Not now, not now, not now!

"Maeve? Talk to me." I can see he's about to get up, and I really, *really* don't want him to.

"It's just...I wasn't expecting this, and I didn't, um, prepare." I curse myself for not getting a wax before coming here, then suck in a sharp breath as Owen runs both hands up and down my legs in a soothing motion. "I swear I normally keep things a little tidier down there and I—" All the air rushes out of my lungs as Owen's fingers part my lips open. I look down to find him staring intently at my core, not a trace of disappointment on his face.

"I like you just like this, sunshine. Fuck, look at you. You're dripping for me. You're perfect. Your body is perfect. Do you hear me?" I nod, unable to take my eyes off him as I watch his hand moving. His fingers move deftly over me, cautiously avoiding my clit. "Say it. Say your body is perfect."

"My body is perfect. Ahh!" I feel two fingers plunge into me as his thumb applies pressure to my clit and there's no way I can stand up straight much longer. My moans are loud, and my hands are in fists next to me as I do everything I can not to lean on him.

"Good girl. You can put your hands on me now. I think you're gonna need to hold on." Both hands land on his shoulders at the same time with a loud clap. His hot tongue meets my clit, his fingers curl inside of me, and then he sucks. Hard. The blazing heat travels from my core out to my fingers and toes as I slump forward whimpering Owen's name. Everything moves in slow motion as my orgasm takes over, the lava traveling slowly through my veins to reach every last inch of my body.

As my breathing slows, Owen stands, bringing one arm around my waist to hold me up. His hand, the one that was just busy sending me to oblivion, comes up between us, and he takes the two fingers that were just inside me into his mouth. His eyes close, and he moans as he licks and sucks his fingers clean. My breathing quickens again, and I already have that desperate ache to have him inside me come rushing back.

Sensing exactly what I need, Owen picks me up and sets me on the bed delicately.

"I thought you said this time would be quick." I can't help but tease him.

"As much as I want to bury myself inside you and fuck you mercilessly, I never want to hurt you. I had to make sure you were ready for me. And I really needed to taste you again." He brushes his nose against mine as he adjusts himself between my legs.

"All good reasons," I say before I bring my lips to his, tasting myself on him, already writhing beneath him as I look for friction.

Finally, finally, I feel the head of his cock nudge at my entrance, and I gasp at the feel of him being there with no barriers between us. I've never not used protection with anyone and this is why. It needed to be with him.

I let out a shaky breath, and he brings his knuckles to my cheek. "Okay?" God, this question. Nothing sets me off balance and rights me back up more than this question from his lips. The way his brows furrow as he takes me in, and the way the love sounds in his voice every time he says that one little word is my absolute undoing. Tears sting the backs of my eyes, but I smile through it. Not because I feel I should, but because smiling with him comes so naturally again.

"Yes, my darling," I whisper against his lips, and he pushes further into me. Our eyes meet as he pulls almost all the way out, then further in, and again until he's fully seated. "Now give me what I've missed for seven long years, Owen. Fuck me like you mean it."

He smirks and his green eyes light up with the challenge. "Maevey, whether I'm making love to you slow or fucking you hard and fast, I'm always gonna mean it. For fucking ever." He doesn't give me a chance to respond as he lifts my hips and thrusts into me so hard that I scream with the all-encompassing pleasure of it. This angle has him hitting a perfect spot inside me, and I don't think I can hold off another orgasm much longer, but I want this to last forever.

"Look at you, my perfect wife. Taking everything I'm giving you." I open my eyes to find him looking down at where we connect, and I moan again as I feel myself clench around him. Watching him watching us is so hot. "Now tell me, who gets to make you come?"

"Y-you. You do."

He lowers his head to take a nipple into his mouth. When his teeth graze the hard peak, and his tongue flicks over it at the same pace as he's fucking me, my eyes roll to the back of my head.

Owen pulls back and I miss his mouth on me instantly, but fuck, his words spur me on in a whole other way. "That's right. And what am I to you, *wife*?"

I can hardly string words together as he keeps up his punishing rhythm. "M-my husband."

He growls, and I watch as his muscles tense. "So again. Who gets to make you come?"

I'm a mess of moans and whimpers, but I manage to give him the answer. "My husband. Only my husband gets to make me come." I tighten around him as I sit on the precipice of my orgasm.

He hisses in a breath. "Yeah, I feel that. I feel every bit of this cunt gripping me and I want more. So, you're gonna come for me now, *fengári mou*."

He presses his thumb to my clit, moving with expert precision. No one has ever known my body as well as Owen James. No one ever will. And sparks fly all around me. Our sparks still fly, just like they always have. Because they never stopped.

The words coming out of my mouth are unintelligible. My body shakes, and I cling on to Owen as his thrusts become shallower and more erratic. Owen tenses as he holds on to me, too. With our faces buried in each other's necks, he takes a deep breath, then runs his nose along my jaw, and across my cheek until we're nose-to-nose, breathing one another's air.

When his lips touch mine, they're soft and searching. Nothing like the man who just ordered me to climax. He's still holding himself up with one arm, only letting me feel some of his weight, and when he starts to lift off, I wrap my legs around him, pulling him back down.

"Wait. Just a little while longer like this. Please." He doesn't say anything, he just goes back to kissing me, letting me take delight in the way he feels above me, inside me.

We stay like that for a long time, neither one of us making the move to separate. The pressure of our bodies together, the feel of him still connected to me, all of it equates to a perfect moment. Just like last time. And I hate what that thought does to me. I hate that my instinct is to immediately push him off and be the first to lie and say this means nothing.

just like the tides.

maeve

I DON'T GET the chance to push him off me because he deepens our kiss, his tongue seeking out mine, making me almost forget the possibility that history will repeat itself. It's as if Owen can read my feelings, and he knows exactly how to settle them.

He moves above me, and he hardens again as he shifts his hips. His cock moves inside me easily, the delicious friction causing a whimper to leave my lips.

"You need me to prove to you that this is nothing like last time, Maevey? Because I'm gonna do that." He moves again, pulling almost all the way out of me and pushing back in so fast it makes my eyes roll to the back of my head. "I'll show you every day that I won't make the same mistake twice." Again, he pulls out slowly and rams himself back into me. "I'll show you that this isn't just for one night. It never was. You're my forever. Do you hear me, sunshine?" He does it again, pushing even harder this time, and all of my nerve endings come to life. I whimper a response that sounds vaguely like a yes.

"Now say it with me." He continues his slow movements followed by hard and fast thrusts as he hits that perfect spot inside me. But it's not enough. I need faster. I whimper again, moving my hips, urging him to speed up. "I'm yours. Only yours." He kisses my neck and whispers in my ear, "Say it."

"You're mine. Only mine." His green eyes meet mine, and the heat in his gaze is the only response I need. He likes that I didn't just repeat the exact words he said to me but turned them back on him.

"Fuck, yes, I am. Now say you're mine. Only mine." He doesn't take his eyes off me, and it's obvious that keeping up this slow pace is difficult for him. Surely, he wants more, too.

"I'm yours. Only yours." The words come out clearly. There's not a shred of doubt in my heart that they're true.

"And this time it's forever." He pulls back further, keeping his eyes locked on mine. "Say the words, Maeve." My brain knows that his words should not have this kind of effect on me. They're just words. But my body doesn't care. Every command out of Owen's mouth is mine to fulfill.

"This time it's forever." He grunts a response and picks up the pace, but only ever so slightly. I brush the hair off my face, but before I can bring my hand back to his shoulder, he covers my hand with his, linking our fingers together on the bed.

"Now say it all again for me." His jaw is so tight I'm afraid he'll hurt himself. It's visible that he's holding back, and it pains him to do so. I want everything from him, almost as much as I want to know that the words I'm about to say again are true.

"You're mine." He speeds up, keeping his movements controlled. "I'm yours." My whimpers get louder as his thrusts get faster and harder. "Forever," I scream, over and over as he pushes me over the edge again, our eyes and hands locked together as I come. His grip on my hand tightens as he grunts out his release.

"Forever," he whispers as he collapses next to me, pulling me with him so my head lands on his chest. I listen as his quickened heartbeat begins to slow, his breathing going along with it. He drops a kiss to the top of my head, then another, and then he whispers again, "Forever, *fengári mou*. You and me forever."

I shut my eyes tightly, willing the tears to remain where they are. I inhale a deep breath and nod into his chest. We stay like that, with nothing but the sounds of our slowing breaths and his heartbeat in my ear. I let myself believe the lie. Just for now.

Eventually, I can no longer ignore my bladder and the stickiness of our bodies becomes more obvious and less hot, so I speak up.

"Hey, O?"

"Mmm?" He runs a hand through my hair, and it's damp, and right now, I'm not sure if it's from my shower earlier or from all of the sex.

"I really need the loo. And a shower." He chuckles and kisses the top of my head again.

"All right Maevey. Meet you in there."

I'm about to shower with Owen. With my husband. Who I basically just committed to staying married to while he rammed himself into me. And I loved it so much I came…again! This might be the best day of my life.

I extricate myself from his bed and walk awkwardly to the bathroom with my thighs sticking together.

I take in Owen's bathroom for the first time. There are two separate vanities, a gigantic soaker tub I vow to slip my way into one day, and a shower big enough for the two of us and…activities. The toilet is in its own room, which I love, and as I flush, I hear the water running in the shower.

A very naked, very beautiful Owen James is standing before me, gathering clean towels to hang on the towel warmer as steam fills the room.

Yep. Best day of my life.

He opens the shower door and steps inside, leaving it open as he looks up at me. "Coming?"

Dear God, I'm not sure I can, but I wouldn't hate it if I did.

As if he can read my mind, he chuckles and extends his hand toward me. "I meant into the shower, sunshine. Come here." I feel my face heat as I step closer to him. He takes my hand and pulls me in, letting me have the stream of perfectly hot water. I gladly stand under it, letting the water run down my back, sighing as my muscles relax. When I look up, I'm met with a pair of hungry green eyes. Owen is standing under the other shower head, which I know for a fact isn't running as hot as this one. My gaze roams over his body, really taking all of him in for the first time in proper lighting.

My eyes snag on the tattoos across his chest, and I reach out a hand to touch the moon at the center of it. On his left pec is a woman riding a horse. She has a crescent moon above her head and a veil blowing in the wind. Behind them are ocean waves that look like they're almost reaching for her. As the waves fade over his shoulder, origami swans swim along calm waters, and a lump forms in my throat at the memory of the day we met, the tiny origami swans on the table, the one he played with that day.

The water morphs into lines that wrap around his upper arm. The tattoos that travel down his right arm are all ones I've seen before. The eagle with *semper fidelis* on ribbons. He's always had that one. It's a Marine Corp motto, meaning *always faithful*. On the inside of his bicep, is his dad's favorite Irish saying, which Bon also has a tattoo of.

"What's with the horse lady and the moon?" He sighs, looking down at me. He places his hand over mine, over his heart.

"Selene is the goddess of the moon in Greek mythology. She's the personification of the moon itself. *Fengári.*" My breath hitches in my throat, and I force down a swallow.

"*Fengári mou.* That's what you call me. Your moon." He smiles, and his heart rate speeds up beneath my hand. "I, uh, looked it up once."

"My moon. That's what you've always been, Maeve. My moon. The one whose gravitational pull I can't stay away from. I'm always drawn to you. To where you are." His hand drops and he brushes some hair off my forehead with his index finger, letting his hand linger there.

"Like the ocean tides?" He nods, and his smile widens.

"Yeah, Maevey. Just like the tides." I'm thankful for the droplets of water running down my face. Hopefully, he can't tell there are tears mixed in, too. But of course, he swipes a thumb across my cheek as his brows furrow.

"And the swans?" I ask.

He swallows, keeping his hand on my face. "I took one with me the day we met. I used to take it with me everywhere, take it out when I needed to feel you close to me, which was…a lot. Eventually, the thing just sort of disintegrated." He sighs, like the memory of losing a piece of scrap paper is painful to him.

"How long?" I ask, knowing he'll understand I need to know when he got these tattoos for me.

"Started about eight years ago. I got the swans once the paper one you made fell apart." He cradles my face in his hands, still smiling down at me like he didn't just tell me he marked his body with tattoos explicitly meant to be of me—for me—on his chest. As if he didn't mark his body with something to remember the day we met, just like I did. Tattoos he got before we had even slept together for the first time.

"Oh," is all I manage to croak out. Owen pulls me into him, and my head rests next to where my hand still covers his heart as he holds me close.

"You've always been my end-game, Maeve. I've known that for a long time." I nod and let it sink in. These aren't just words he's saying. He means it. As I let everything he's said implant, I know I need to keep chasing this happiness. I know I have to move on from the hurt of the past and be here. Be present. Because maybe this isn't just for now. Maybe this really could be forever.

40 /

ours.

owen

SHE SAID SHE'S MINE. She said forever. But my brain won't let go of the fact that maybe it was just a product of the moment. She hasn't said she loves me, and I won't push her into it. But fuck, if I'm not dying to hear her say the words. To say them to her myself.

I'm just finishing up dinner while she dries her hair. She didn't want to go to sleep with wet hair. And even though my body feels suddenly empty without hers next to me, I got the feeling that she needed a little space. Maybe I did too? We're not used to being around one another yet. I'm not used to being around anyone these days.

The pasta is ready when I hear her padding into the kitchen. She comes up behind me, wrapping her arms around my waist. I feel her leave a kiss on my back before she burrows her face into my T-shirt. "Hello, darling."

Fuck everything I just said about needing space. I need no space. I need this. Every fucking day.

I turn off the heat and turn around in her arms, bringing my hand to her chin, and tipping her face up to mine. "I really like hearing you call me that." I lower my lips down to hers, because being able to be this close to Maeve and kiss her is the greatest gift I've ever been given. Her contented sigh is followed by the loud rumble of my stomach, and we both laugh as we pull our bodies apart.

"Let's eat?" She phrases it as a question, which is adorable because if it weren't for the fact that this carbonara has to be eaten fresh, I'd take her back into my bedroom and watch her fall apart for me over and over again.

"Yeah, Maevey. Let's eat." I pull one of her hands to my lips and kiss her palm. "You mind getting us some drinks while I serve this?" Her eyes light up, and I watch as her freckles move up her cheeks with her smile.

"I don't mind at all. You want a beer?" She walks to the cupboard, and I watch her tiny frame reach up for a glass.

"Just water is great. Thank you." Concentrating back on the pasta, my face stretches into a smile. This is such a normal thing for us to do, something so domestic and borderline boring. We're just having dinner. But it's not normal or boring. It's monumental. It's us finally being an *us* and getting to do things together. In the same room. Not just me watching her prep her tea through a computer screen, or her listening to me tell her about our morning routines on base.

I shake my head and top our plates with parmesan before realizing she's not at the table, but at the kitchen island with two glasses of water, napkins and forks.

Setting our plates down, she sticks her nose to the plate, and takes a deep breath in. I chuckle, having seen her do this so many times now with everything she eats. Maeve finds the joy in the smallest things, like smelling her food before she eats it.

She looks up at me, fork in hand, as if asking me if we can dig in. I pick up my fork, but before I take a bite, I watch as she takes hers. She moans, rolling her head back and setting her fork down loudly. Then she takes a drink of water and stands up.

Maeve shocks the shit out of me when she climbs onto my lap and straddles me, then kisses me. Hard. That gets me dropping my fork with a loud clang on the plate because I need both hands to pull her into me. She moans into my mouth, her hands roaming all over my hair, neck, and shoulders.

"Thank you," she whispers against my lips. As quickly as she got there, she's gone. She hops back up on her stool and takes another forkful of pasta, moaning again. "This is the greatest thing I've ever tasted."

My laugh explodes out of me as I watch her and adjust the erection now begging for attention in my pants. "I get all that just for making you pasta?"

"Not just any pasta, Owen. My favorite pasta. My favorite meal. And it's perfect." She moans again, wiggling in her seat.

"Keep making those noises, and I'll carry you back to bed to remind you what else makes you moan like that." Her cheeks turn pink as she swallows.

"Don't you dare. Not until I've eaten every last bite of this." Her tone is serious, but the playfulness in her eyes has me laughing again. "Seriously, O. Wow." Those are her last words until every last bit of her meal is gone from her plate.

AS WE'RE WASHING UP, my phone rings and I look down to see that it's one of the social workers calling. Maeve looks up and smiles, nodding for me to take it.

"Hello?" There's silence, then someone clears their throat.

"Hi, Mr. James?"

"Yes?"

"Oh, hi. It's Jessica, one of the social workers on Julia's case" Her voice is familiar now. She has a melodic voice that stands out.

"Hi, Jessica. How are you?"

"Oh, I'm fine. Thanks so much for asking." She clears her

throat again before continuing, "It looks like everything is set for Julia to go home with you in a couple of days, but I wanted to make a final call and see if you'd like to visit with her before the court hearing."

"Yes. Yes, I would like that very much." My voice is maybe a little louder than it needs to be, which has Maeve spinning to face me with eyebrows raised as she rinses a dish.

Jessica lets out a sigh. "Oh, good. I'm very pleased to hear that. Is tomorrow afternoon all right for you to come see her? Then the court hearing will be the following day, and you'll be able to take Julia home."

I swallow a sudden lump in my throat at the thought of Julia being here, and I pace into the next room. "That's completely fine. I'm ready." I wait for the words to sour on my tongue like a lie, but they don't.

"Oh, that's wonderful! I'm happy you'll have a chance to start getting to know one another and bond. She's still so young." She pauses and takes a deep breath. "Please let me know if there's anything we can do to help."

"I will, Jessica. Thank you."

We say our goodbyes, and I stand there for a minute, watching Maeve as she loads the dishwasher with a small smile on her face.

As I walk back into the kitchen, she straightens and faces me. "Did something happen? Is Julia all right?" She reaches out and pulls me to her by my T-shirt and I cage her to the countertop, letting her warmth push away the doubt that's circling me like a school of sharks.

Can I do this? Will Maeve and I be okay?

I shut down the thoughts so I can answer her. "Julia's all right. That was Jessica, the social worker." She nods, urging me on. "She just wanted to ask if I'd like to visit with Julia tomorrow before the court hearing in a couple of days." Her face softens, and she nods again.

"Can I come with you?" Somehow, I love her even more

for having this reaction when she could have chosen to feel slighted to have this come up when we've just started to figure *us* out.

I do the only thing I can think of. I kiss her completely senseless. I let my kiss say everything I don't think I can right now. How grateful I am for her. How happy I am that she's here. How I hope she never leaves.

When we're both good and breathless, I pull back and run my fingers through her hair, completely cognizant of the fact that I've wanted this for a decade. I've wanted her, the feel of her next to me, her hair in between my fingers, for ten years.

She smiles up at me, resting her chin on my chest. "So, I can go with you, right?" Maeve giggles, and a peace settles over my heart.

"The answer to that is always yes, Maevey."

How am I ever going to let her go, if that's still what she wants?

I HELP her finish with the dishes, and we make a plan to go back to the guesthouse in the morning to get whatever she needs, although she is adamant that she won't go inside if the bats are anywhere where she can see them. I send a quick text to the owner of the house I rented last time I stayed in San Diego, so Maeve and I don't have to fly back and forth before bringing Julia home.

We watch reruns of *The Office*, one or both of us occasionally saying a line along with the actors. Sitting on the couch, watching TV is even more mundane than prepping dinner with her earlier, and I absolutely love it. I soak up every second.

Before I feel too tired, I get up to shut off all the lights and double check the security system. Maeve is rustling around in the bedroom she had been staying in. I knock twice on the open door to let her know I'm there.

She stands quickly from where she was bent over her suitcase.

"Owen Agamemnon James! You packed me absolutely no knickers!" I wince at her use of my middle name as she stands to face me, hands on her hips. "I thought I just hadn't looked hard enough before, but no. There aren't any here, are there?"

I pull my lips between my teeth to keep myself from smiling or laughing and shake my head. She huffs out a breath and crosses her arms, which I love because it does wonderful things to her tits.

"One," I start, "I didn't want to go through your private things." I walk toward her slowly as she rolls her eyes like it's a bullshit reason. "And two, I knew you wouldn't need any. I sure don't mind the lack of extra layers between you and me, *fengári mou*." I stand in front of her and watch as her arms relax at her sides. She rolls her eyes again, but this time, she smiles.

Wrapping an arm around her waist, I pull her to me. Her arms come up around my neck and her smile widens. "Well, I will need some tomorrow. I do not want to meet the wonderful Julia with no knickers on!"

I chuckle. "Deal." I watch as she licks her bottom lip, fingers playing with the hair at the nape of my neck. "Are you ready for bed?" At my question, her grip tightens on my neck, and she looks over at the bed next to us.

"Oh. Yeah. I can sleep in here if you'd rather have your bed to yourself." She tries to back up, but I don't let her, holding her close to me.

"Not a fucking chance, Maevey. You wanna sleep here? Then I'm sleeping here, too. But as far as I'm concerned, that bed in the other room is ours now." I punctuate the statement with a kiss to her lips, and she sighs, relaxing her body and her hold on me.

"You sure know how to make a girl swoon." She smirks and drops a chaste kiss on my lips.

"So where will it be?" I rub my thumb in circles along her waist and she smiles a little wider.

"Ours."

Fuck. Yes.

I pick her up and throw her over my shoulder, hitting the light switch on my way out of this room and walk us into *our* bedroom to sleep on *our* bed.

41 /

a direct flight to my pussy.

maeve

I USED to hug one of my pillows at night and fall asleep pretending it was Owen's chest I was laying on. On the nights when I felt sad, or I hadn't talked to him in a while, and even in those early days when I still allowed myself to think that he would call after everything that happened between us, it was such a source of comfort. But nothing, and I mean not a single thing, could have prepared me for the absolute bliss that is falling asleep and waking up wrapped around Owen James. I'm more on him than next to him when I pry one eye open to see that the sun is rising, but given that he pulls me back to him when I try to slip away, it seems he doesn't mind.

"I feel like I've waited my whole life for this right here." His gravelly, sleepy voice goes straight to my chest, then travels down, right to my core. He wraps both arms around me and kisses the top of my head, exhaling a happy sigh. "I used to hug a pillow and pretend it was you waking up next to me, and now you're here."

"What?" I sit up, needing to see his face and analyze whether he's serious or if I was doing the thinking out loud thing again, but his cheeks are red, and he looks embarrassed.

He's serious?

"Well, that was super embarrassing to admit in my semi-conscious state the first time I wake up next to my wife. Should we just get up so I can punch myself in the face for being such a loser?" He sits up, throwing his legs over the side of the bed. I'm properly stunned at his admission, and by the time I catch up to what's just happened and get up, he's in the bathroom brushing his teeth. I brought my toothbrush here last night, so I drop some toothpaste on it and start brushing.

We brush in silence for a couple of minutes, and as he's rinsing, I decide it's now my time to speak. "I dod dat too. An I rearry rike it ren yu caw muh dat." He turns, eyebrows furrowed as he looks down at me.

"Pardon?" I spit into the sink and rinse my mouth quickly as Owen watches me curiously.

"I did that, too. And I really like it when you call me that. *My wife,*" I say the last two words in a deep voice that sounds absolutely nothing like Owen. "I used to fall asleep hugging a pillow wishing it was you, so when you said that it just sort of stunned me a bit because after that night, I didn't think you thought of me like that." I straighten up and run a hand through my hair which is looking a bit like a rat's nest at the moment. "When you call me your wife, my heart feels like it's going to beat out of my chest, you know? I get these funny tingles all over my body. It's like those two words take a direct flight to my pussy. Anyway, I really like it." My heart beats wildly, and I feel it in my temples, hear it in my ears. Maybe admitting these embarrassing things was a horrible idea.

Bloody idiot! Of course it was a horrible idea. You have no idea what you're doing!

I look up to find a smiling Owen, those crinkled eyes full of something dark and naughty. All traces of embarrassment are gone from his face. "That sounds like a flight I wanna be on, Maevey."

In a swift move, he picks me up and places me on the countertop, spreading my legs with his hips as he moves closer to me. His fingers skim my inner thighs, and he toys with the hem of my shorts. I'm so needy for him that I have to bite the inside of my cheek to keep from moaning at the simple touch. I've no knickers on, and his fingers are so close to where I want him. It's blissful torture.

He continues his exploration, his fingers closer to finding evidence of what he makes me feel. "Where exactly do you feel it when I call you my wife?" He runs a finger up my slit, through the wetness there and stops at the entrance. "Here?" Then his fingers move up and up until one digit is resting on my clit. "Or here?" He asks as his finger slides back and forth. I prop my arms behind me so I can hold myself up, trying to move my hips for more friction. "Which one is it, *wife*?"

"Th-the second one. B-both. I-I don't know." I moan loudly as he increases speed and pressure. I'm so close already, I might come just from these simple touches and his words, but then he takes his hand away and grips the waist-band of my shorts with both hands.

"Lift." And I do. I move instinctually as he shoves my shorts down my legs and drops them to the floor. As he kneels in front of me, he looks into my eyes and says, "Now, I want to taste exactly what being called *my wife* does to you." He spreads my legs further, propping one of my feet on his shoulder as his tongue does its best work.

Owen has me screaming within minutes, using nothing but his mouth, but the thing that sends me over the edge? His growly voice as he says, "Fuck, *my wife* tastes so good. Like honey. So sweet."

I can hardly hold myself up when my orgasm subsides. Owen leaves tender kisses on my thighs and stomach, then stands to his full height, wiping his glistening lips on the back of his hand. My mouth waters as I see the bulge in his boxer briefs. He shoves them down his legs, and I let my eyes take in every detail. The blond hair that leads from his belly button to his rigid cock. The way his abs flex when he gives himself one slow stroke. Just the memory of him inside me has my pussy aching.

Owen's arm wraps around me, and he helps me down from the countertop. Slowly, silently, he turns me around and steps closer so that his front is flush with my back. Just like the day in the gym.

"You remember how much I liked having you close to me like this, Maevey?" He runs a finger down the column of my neck until his fingers splay between my shoulder blades. Owen pushes me, so I'm bent over the counter. "I liked it so much I had to have a cold shower, but it didn't help." His hands are soothing as they travel lower, leaving goosebumps in their wake. "So, I ended up jerking myself off to the thought of you. Again. And then you caught me."

All thoughts leave my brain as I focus on feeling. I feel Owen's words, feel his careful touches as he takes gentle control, moving my body the way he wants. He always seems to know exactly what to do, the exact way to take charge without making me feel like I have to submit to his whims.

He pushes my feet apart with his own, and I whimper, feeling his hot, hard cock behind me. "Owen, I–"

"You don't have to ask me, sunshine. I know what you want." And with that, the head of his cock teases my entrance. I whimper again, the need to have him fill me enough to set my skin on fire. Just when I think he's going to give me what I want, he gives me what I need, instead.

"It's always been you, Maeve." He moves himself to rub my clit with his length and my head drops, chin hitting my chest. "Always been you my heart beats for." He gathers my hair into a ponytail and uses it to lift my head, so our eyes meet in the mirror. "Always been you I want to come home to." And with that, he thrusts all the way inside me while those dark green eyes bore into mine.

He doesn't start slow this time. His pace is immediately hard and fast, and once he sees I'm not looking away from him through the mirror, he lets my hair go. I miss the possessive hold, but he replaces it with firm hands going to my hips, where he pushes me back onto him at the perfect pace.

"My wife loves this cock, doesn't she?" I gasp, unable to answer as the force of his thrusts and his words send shocks of pleasure all over my body. Owen raises one eyebrow, waiting for my response.

"Yes," I mumble.

"Yes, what, *fengári mou*?" Still not breaking eye contact, I moan, unsure whether I'll be able to get actual words out as his cock hits my G-spot.

But I'm no quitter. "Yes, I love my husband's cock." I nearly come just from saying the words. Owen's pupils dilate through the mirror, sweat dripping down his temple.

"Good girl. Now let me watch you fall apart for me, wife." Unsurprisingly, my body complies. Our gazes are unwavering as I tense around him, and he pulses inside me. When I prop my hand on the mirror, Owen's much larger one lands over it, linking our fingers together as if he needs one more way for us to be connected. I need it too. I need to be connected to him in all ways. Always.

As we both come down from our high, Owen lowers to pepper kisses all across my back, whispering words I can't hear because my pulse is still too loud in my ears. But I feel the words. I feel the love, and reverence, and cherishing in his words. I don't need to hear them.

Owen pulls me up, turning me to face him once again. So he can kiss me with that tenderness I adore. He kisses my nose, my cheeks and my forehead before finally pulling back with a sigh. I watch him move to get a washcloth, watch him run it under warm water before he gets on his knees and starts to wipe my inner thighs.

Once we're both cleaned up and dressed, we head to the guesthouse, so I can make sure I have undergarments and collect a few more of my things before someone comes to take care of the creatures living in the attic.

I quickly change from my leggings and sports bra into a flowy white linen dress with buttons down the front. I slip on a pair of simple brown leather sandals, gold hoop earrings and a few bangles around my wrist. I'm about to put on a necklace when I notice Owen standing in the doorway of our bedroom with arms crossed as he leans into the frame, watching me.

I struggle with the clasp and huff out an annoyed breath. "Would you mind?" I hold out the necklace in his direction, and he smiles. His typical outfit is slightly more polished today. Dark denim with shoes that don't look like they've been battered and a polo shirt that hugs his biceps perfectly. He looks good enough to eat. He always does.

He walks behind me and takes the delicate gold chain from my fingers. He waits as I move my hair out of the way, and when I do, he leans down and leaves a trail of kisses along my neck. My head rolls back onto his chest, and I squeeze my thighs together, because Owen's open-mouthed kisses are my undoing. He stops at my earlobe, pulling it between his teeth. I arch into him, feeling the evidence of what these kisses are doing to his body, too.

"Do you want me to put this necklace on or not?" When I grunt out a response, he laughs. "You look perfect, *fengári mou*. You always do."

"Owen, basically all you've seen me in since I got to Ojai is workout gear, pajamas and your clothes." He finishes doing up the clasp and pulls my back to his front, wrapping his arms around me.

"Perfect," he whispers. I turn in his arms, placing both

hands on his chest. As I'm about to speak, he stops me with a finger to my lips. "Everything is going to be fine. We don't have to just pretend to like each other anymore. I'm not worried. And I love you. Okay?"

Tears immediately spring up in my eyes, and I nod my response. Even if I'm not entirely convinced everything is indeed going to be fine, his words do help. And my own *I love you* sits right at the tip of my tongue, ready to jump out, but I hold back again, not wanting to think about why that is.

"WHY ARE WE STOPPING HERE?" I ask as Owen parks on the street in front of a black building with nothing on it other than a neon *Open* sign in a small window.

"Gotta pick up my daily order." He smiles as he reaches over the center console to cup my jaw and give me a quick kiss on the lips. "Be right back."

I watch him walk into the building, noticing how good his bum looks in those jeans, but also how he literally seems to have an extra bounce in his step. The thought that maybe I put that there makes me smile.

Within a couple of minutes, Owen is back with a box I now know well. He hands it to me as he steps back inside, and I open it up, inhaling a deep breath as the smell of fresh donuts and icing fill my lungs.

"Do you even like these?" I ask.

"I started liking them when you told me they were your favorite." He smiles easily at me before looking back at the road, pulling into Ojai traffic as we drive toward the Santa Barbara airport. I swallow down the lump in my throat. The one that grows every time I learn just how much Owen was paying attention all those years ago.

I take a bite of a donut then offer it to him so he can have a bite, too. I giggle as sprinkles fall over his chin and land on his lap. Owen turns the volume up and Carrie Underwood's voice fills the cabin, and we enjoy the drive while singing along to our old country favorites.

He smiles for the whole journey, and I swear, it's as if I'm seeing his smile for the first time every time. It never gets old, looking at him to find him smiling at me, or just smiling because we're together.

Owen had thought about driving all the way to San Diego, but we would have had to drive through predictably horrendous LA traffic. Instead, he chartered a flight from Santa Barbara directly to San Diego. He didn't want Julia in a car for too long when he brings her back to Ojai, and he was told it's safe for her to fly since it's not a commercial flight.

We get settled in the plane with sparkling water, the box of donuts sitting on a table nearby. I take my shoes off, and Owen quickly pulls my feet up onto his lap in the seat across from mine.

"So. You left the Marine Corps, then what? You started Aegis right away?" Owen doesn't seem surprised by my sudden question about his past.

"Sort of, yeah. I was still in therapy once or twice a week then, but I was doing way better than before. Raf really wanted to do the personal security thing, and knowing Adam obviously helped. I focused on the cyber stuff and started developing an app almost right away. It took a few years, but once it was finished, and we worked all the kinks out, there was a lot of interest, which is why I ended up selling it. I figured I could help Raf with the business here on the West Coast, but he's got everything handled. He's very good at what he does." I nod my agreement. Raf really is one of the best. It's why we became friends after I hired him. He's professional, but kind and funny.

"And you?" Owen asks. "You came out here and got your big break? How did that happen?" There's genuine curiosity in his question. It seems that as much as I avoided talking about him with Elaina, he must have avoided talking about me, too.

"Yeah. Five years ago, I got a supporting role in a film that took place in a post-apocalyptic world. I thought it was going to be a total flop, like everything else I had worked on previously, but it really took off." I smile, remembering the shock of hearing the opening week box office numbers. I bought a bottle of wine, not a box, and celebrated with Bon.

"I know. I saw it." I look up, the smile erased from my face. He runs a hand up my bare calf, squeezing lightly. "I knew nothing about the story. I just needed a way to unwind one day, so I went to see a movie alone, and there you were. I walked out at the end and bought another ticket for the next showing just so I could see more of you." He cocks his head to the side as he studies the shocked expression on my face.

"Wow," I respond.

Owen's soft laughter sends vibrations through his body, causing mine to mirror the movement. "Yeah. I knew I still had a lot of work to do before I could see you. Before I could apologize. But damn, it was good to see you like that, doing what you had always set out to do. I was really proud of you, Maeve. I *am* really proud of you." The sincerity in his voice is crystal clear, without a ripple of dishonesty, and it warms my entire body.

"Thank you. I was really proud of me, too. It was really starting to feel like nothing was going to happen after those first few years of navigating the New York acting scene and then trying to figure it out in LA. A near decade of boxed wine and ramen is a long time, you know?" A wistful smile graces my lips as cherished memories flood back, ones that have slowly faded from my mind but are still filled with pure joy.

"And in all those years, you never...I don't know...had any serious relationships?" My question has Owen's hand moving a little higher up my leg, squeezing a little tighter.

"No," is his simple answer.

"Not even *one*?" I know my tone is incredulous. I mean, how could he not have had even *one* long term girlfriend in a decade?

"No," he repeats as he squeezes again, sending a shiver up my spine. "A lot changed in my life, Maeve, but a lot stayed the same, too. I still watch *The Office*. I still listen to country music. I'm still in love with you. My circumstances didn't change any of that."

"Right," I say. "So fundamentally, you're still the same Owen, then." I try for a light comment, but I don't think it comes off that way. I don't know how to respond to him when he says these things to me.

He nods, eyes never leaving mine. "And what's changed for you?"

I purse my lips and shake my head, trying to think of all the ways I'm different now. "I suppose not a lot has changed for me either. I'm not as much of a dreamer as I used to be, but I suppose all my fundamental elements are still the same, too."

I'm still in love with you, too!

I want to scream it, but the words stay lodged somewhere between my heart and my mouth.

"Hmm." Owen's hands switch to my other leg, spreading more of his warmth over my skin.

"How are you feeling about Julia? About seeing her today, taking her home tomorrow?" The subject change has this conversation going from charged to strained, all thanks to me.

"Good. I'm excited to see her. Nervous as hell to have a little person to take care of. I don't know what the fuck I'm doing, even after all the books I've been reading." His hands go still, and I can feel the tension building in his body. I hate that I caused it.

"You'll be great, Owen. You've prepared as much as you could in a short amount of time. And…I mean, I can help you.

I don't know a ton about babies either, but we could…we could figure it out, for now." I shrug, immediately feeling stupid for my suggestion. I know nothing about babies or motherhood. But I don't suppose I'm going to be her mother anyway because this will end soon. It has to. I'm not the person Owen deserves. He deserves a sweet wife and a loving mother for his children. I can't be that. It's genetically impossible.

"Hey," Owen says as he squeezes my leg again. "Don't overthink it. This is whatever you want it to be, remember?" I wince. Not because his words are harsh. He literally says the perfect thing to appease my worries all the time, but because I know what I want it to be. I just can't get past how I could ever become the woman his family deserves. So, I say the thing I know he deserves to hear.

"For the record, Owen, you're going to be a great dad. The kind that teaches his kids to play whatever sports they're into, who creates a safe space for them to be creative and fully themselves. You're going to be the kind of dad you had growing up, O. That legacy is going to live on, and I'm really happy I'm going to get to watch that happen." Even if from afar, I don't say.

The tension in his body evaporates, and he leans in, laying a warm kiss on my shin. "Thank you, Maevey."

The remainder of the flight is less intense, as we choose lighter topics to talk about. Places we've traveled to, funny stories about Bon and Raf and I chat about Charlie and her plans to take a break from her life in London. It doesn't surprise me at all that my twin is finding herself while I'm attempting to do the same.

I somehow manage to enjoy our time together rather than dwelling too much on how much this brand-new dynamic of ours is about to change. I'm excited for him. He's so ready for this, and he's going to be a great dad to this little girl.

. . .

WHEN WE LAND in San Diego, there's a blacked-out SUV waiting for us. Owen gets into the driver's seat, blowing out a long breath as he adjusts the seat and mirrors. I peek into the back seat and notice there's a car seat already set up, just like the one in his truck in Ojai. It feels so real, now. This baby girl is about to become a part of Owen's family. There's a whole lifetime of worrying and making choices. A whole person to nurture and help grow. It's terrifying.

On the drive, he takes my hand, placing it on my lap with our fingers intertwined. He occasionally looks over at me, a small smile always on his face.

We eventually make it to a parking lot, and once the car is stopped, Owen pulls my hand to his lips, lays a kiss on it and lets me go so we can exit the vehicle.

As we step up to the brown building, I take Owen's hand back in mine, and he gives it a squeeze. I turn my face toward him, ready to reassure him as he's been reassuring me this whole time.

The words are right there.

I love you. Whatever happens, we've got this. I'm not going anywhere.

But the front door opens, and the social worker steps out with a bright smile on her face.

she. loves. me.

owen

I'M nervous as all fuck, but I've been trying really hard not to let it show. And Maeve's been amazing. We've talked about things we've missed out on during our time apart. Even if we hadn't been touching every second of this trip, I would have felt comforted just by having her here. Everything makes sense as long as she's around.

Hand-in-hand, we walk up to the Health and Human Services building where we can spend time with Julia before the court guardianship hearing tomorrow.

Maeve puts on her best celebrity smile, and Jessica, the young social worker, eats it right up. "Hello again, Jessica." If Jessica was, or is, star-struck at all, she does not show it, and I like that about her. It makes this whole thing a lot less stressful.

As we step inside, Julia's little coos fill my ears and Maeve's head perks up at the sound, too. She looks at me with brows raised and an excited smile on her face.

"Oh, she's been a bit fussy today," Jessica says with apologetic eyes.

Someone else is holding Julia, who doesn't seem to be

settling. Maeve takes a few steps toward Julia with me but stops just behind me as I place a gentle hand on Julia's little blonde head.

"Is somebody having a tough day?" I attempt the soft, soothing tone I heard my dad use on me and Lainey as kids. The kind that always made me feel a little more settled. Julia continues to scream, and my heart lurches as doubt creeps in. Maeve's hand rests on my arm, and she squeezes lightly. It's enough to keep me grounded, enough to encourage me to keep trying.

"May I?" I ask the social worker, who nods and begins to hand Julia over to me. I cradle Julia gently in my arms, smiling down at her. I tuck her blanket a little tighter around her, so her arms don't flail too much.

I look down at Maeve, who is watching silently as Julia continues to grizzle. "I read the other day that when they're this little, they like to be held close, and because they can't control their limbs yet, you sort of have to do it for them." Once it feels like she's a little more snug in my arms, I start to bounce a little. "And they like movement, because it mimics what it felt like when they were in the mom's belly, and some-times shushing works, too." Julia's cries get louder for a moment, so I look back down at her, hoping with everything I've got that this works. "We'll try this for a few minutes and see how you like it, all right?" Julia doesn't respond, but Maeve smiles encouragingly.

"You're doing great, O." She looks at Julia, brushing the little wisps of hair on her head. "And so are you, poppet."

"Poppet? I like that." Maeve blushes and shrugs, running a finger over Julia's little button nose. I lean down to kiss Maeve's forehead, but Julia screams again, so I start making shushing sounds as I bounce around the room.

She feels so small, but she's so strong because she's trying and almost succeeding at breaking out of the blanket. I walk around for a few minutes as Jessica looks on with a pleased look on her face, and Maeve watches with a warmth in her eyes I don't think I've ever seen before. It's hard to decide whether I want to watch Julia's facial expressions or Maeve's right now.

As Julia settles down, the room grows quiet, and I clear my throat. "I uh, think it's working?" Maeve nods with a proud smile on her face. Jessica and the other woman both smile, looking pretty pleased with how I've handled my crying baby.

My baby. She's about to be mine.

We spend about an hour with Julia, and even though she sleeps most of the time, I love every minute of watching her, getting to know the little noises she makes. She'll stay with the emergency foster parents she was placed with until everything gets signed off by the courts tomorrow.

We got into the building with no issues, but when we leave, there are a handful of photographers outside. They shouldn't be here. This is private, so no one should know about it.

I immediately sense Maeve tense next to me, so I put my arm around her as we walk out toward the car.

They fire questions at us, from wanting to know about our wedding, to the wedding night, to what our plans are for where we'll live. Maeve keeps a straight face and continues walking. We're only a few feet from the car when one particular question has her stopping in her tracks.

"Maeve, how did you end up going from dating a major celebrity to marrying a deadbeat dad who needs to settle his shit in court?"

"Excuse me?" Her blue eyes look like they could shoot fire at this poor idiot's face right now. I assume she's going to keep walking, but she doesn't. "There is nothing deadbeat about my husband. If you need to know one thing about him, it should be this: he loves so very well. He loves in big ways, with grand actions, like buying his wife a whole stable filled with horses. And he loves small, with quiet actions, like making sure my favorite snacks are always stocked, and my tea is made the way I like in the mornings." She swings her arms out as she speaks, chest heaving as she flies through this monologue. "If anyone was ever made to be a father, it's this man. He had the best examples of unconditional love growing up, and now he lives those examples daily. I see it. I feel it. And I only hope I can show even a fraction of that love and devotion back to him. So, *you*, asshole, you do not get to sell him short. Not even for one moment. I may not deserve his love, but people like you don't even deserve to breathe the same air as Owen James."

Her chest is heaving, but she's done talking, so I guide her into the car and rush to the driver's side. Maeve isn't one to lose control, but that back there was her absolutely relinquishing it.

She doesn't say anything until we get to the end of the road.

"I'm so, so sorry, Owen. I'll never forgive myself if I messed everything up. I didn't know what else to say. That was so horrible, and I couldn't let him speak about you like that. But I'm sorry if this sets you back. I swear I'll do anything to set things straight. It's probably best if we divorce now, right? I mean, it's probably best if you're not married to whoever that lunatic was out there. That clip is going to be everywhere."

I can't bring myself to say anything. I keep replaying her words over and over in my head—the ones she said back at the Health and Human Services parking lot, not the nonsense she's talking about now.

She fucking loves me. I know she does. Even if the exact words didn't come out, what just happened out there? That was all love. She. Loves. Me.

It's the only thought in my brain for the entire ten-minute drive to the house we're staying in for the night, and when I pull into the garage, I get out of the truck the second the ignition is off. I shut the garage door and round the vehicle to get to her side. Maeve hasn't moved, and she turns quickly when I open her door. There are unshed tears in her eyes, and I feel a little bit guilty about that, but I couldn't focus on this during the drive. I need to feel her and look her in the eyes, so I help her out and when the door is shut, I push her back against it. Her big doe eyes are on me, looking so sad and confused. I take each of her cheeks in my hands and kiss her. Just a soft, tender kiss. She relaxes into me, her hands coming up to my chest, fisting my shirt.

"Maeve, listen carefully. Are you listening?" I keep her face in my hands tipped up so I can see her.

"Yes," she responds in a raspy voice.

"You have nothing to be sorry for. You spoke up for me. I don't care about what some asshole thinks. I care about what *you* think. And you seem to think I love you a whole lot, which tells me I'm doing my job right." She nods, eyes filling back up with tears. "And I think you were also saying something else back there, which is that you're not deserving of this love, and I can't have that. I won't hear it, you got me?" A tear slips down her cheek. "We were made for each other, Maevey. There was never any other option but this. But us." She nods again and brings her hands up to my shoulders, standing on her tiptoes to reach my lips. I lean down and take her mouth, and this time the kiss is feral. It's tongues and teeth and moans and *fuck*, I need her.

"I'd love to be the guy who carries you to bed right now and makes slow, sweet love to you, but I'm not gonna be that guy. I need to be inside you now. Fuck, I need it so badly I'm about to burst out of my own skin. And it's not a physical need. It's more than that. It's because the only way I feel whole is when I'm connected to you, *fengári mou*. And right now, I need to feel that more than anything. Is that okay?"

We're both panting by the time I finish talking, her hands digging into my shoulders.

"Yes, Owen. Please." Her voice is steady and her eyes clear, despite the lust coursing through both of us right now.

I start pulling the front of her dress up until it's all bunched at her waist. "Take off your panties, Mrs. James." Her eyes widen as she lowers her hands to hook her thumbs into her silky underwear, letting them fall to the ground. "Now pull out my cock." Her hands work quickly to undo my belt, steady through every motion as she lowers my zipper, lowers my pants and boxer briefs together. She lets out a quiet moan as she looks at my erection between us, upright and aching for her.

"Always such a good girl. Now, hold this." I hand her the fabric of her dress that's in my hand and she takes it. My hands go to the backs of her thighs, and I lift her, feeling how wet she already is for me on my lower abdomen. She gasps at the contact and brings her hands back to my shoulders, the dress now trapped between us.

"Say you want this, Maevey." I repeat the words I said to her that first night. "All of this. Even when it's messy and hard. Say you want me."

"I want this. All of it. I want you. I've never wanted anything more than I've wanted you for the last ten years, Owen." She brings her lips to mine, pulling my lower lip between hers. I lower her, so she feels the head of my cock nudging her, and she bites down on my lip. I want to sink into her hard and fast, but I don't want to hurt her.

Knowingly, she says, "You won't hurt me darling. We were made for each other, remember?" She smirks, and I pull her down to me, burying myself in to the hilt. Her pussy's got such a tight grip on me in this position, and I could live like this forever, feeling her squeeze me, hearing her whimpers.

I pull almost all the way out, but I don't make her wait. I plunge back in hard and fast, and I can tell she's close already.

"I love seeing you like this, Maevey. Love seeing you come undone for me. Love the way you sound when it's just you and me loving each other like this." She whimpers and pulls at my hair, moving her hips as she chases her own pleasure. "That's it, *wife*. Take what you need. Take everything. I'm yours."

She grinds on me while I hold her up, loving the feel of her body seeking pleasure from mine. I don't know if I'll ever get enough of us like this.

Her movements become more frantic, and her moans get louder. "Owen…I need…"

"I know what you need, Maeve. You need me to fuck you harder." I take over again, keeping my movements fast and steady. "You need me to tell you how fucking perfect you are. You need to hear your husband say how much he loves this pussy. How fucking good it feels to know that this is forever. That we're forever. That I'm gonna fuck you so good until my last breath. Is that what you need?"

"Yes, Owen!" Her nails dig into the skin on my shoulder, her body taut all over as she rides out her orgasm. I pump into her mercilessly, wanting her to ride it for as long as possible, and when she finally relaxes, I let myself go over the edge. Maeve holds on to me tightly, tucking her face into my neck and leaving kisses there as I groan out my release with her name on my lips. Always her name.

We stay like that for a few heartbeats, just soaking one another up, holding on through the adrenaline drop and matching one another's slowing breaths. This is what I used to dream about when I was isolated, going without food or water for days on end. The feel of her in my arms, her breath on my skin, my heart so full it almost hurts. This is the feeling I would imagine during that dark time, but the real thing? It's far better than anything I ever dreamed of.

She trails kisses along my jaw, and I feel the smile on her face. As I disconnect our bodies, I take off my shirt, handing it to her so she doesn't have our mess dripping down her legs. I lean down to kiss her as I help her clean up, steadying her on her still wobbly legs.

Her eyes are on my face as I lower the hem of her dress back down, and she giggles. Looking at her with an arched brow, I silently ask what she's laughing at.

"I don't imagine many married couples are rushing home to have sex up against the car in the garage, do you?" With an arm still around her waist, I bring her closer so we're nose-to-nose.

"Well, they might if they waited seven years for it."

Those big doe eyes meet mine again, and she smiles. "You sure have a way with words, Mr. James."

"I mean every single one, Mrs. James." Our lips meet again in a kiss that I hope tells her that I really do mean it all. I mean every touch, look, word, everything. There was never going to be another option for me. If it wasn't Maeve, it would be no one.

———

OUT OF DUE DILIGENCE, given what happened yesterday, I go into the courthouse alone while Maeve waits at the house. She spends most of that time talking to her publicist, who gave her shit for her little meltdown yesterday, but who also congratulated her for standing up for her man.

Once everything's signed, and I'm officially Julia's guardian, the social workers help me with the car seat I had installed in the rental. I reassure them I already have a base installed in my SUV at home, and then we're off.

On the way to the airport, Maeve sits in the backseat with Julia, who cries almost the entire way. She must not like the car seat, or maybe just cars in general.

In the plane, she seems to settle for a few minutes, but as soon as we're in the air, she's crying again.

"Maybe she needs a fresh nappy?" Maeve looks over at me as I try to feed Julia a bottle she's not interested in at all. She must see the confusion on my face because she sighs and says, "Diaper. Sorry."

"Oh. Uh. Right. Shit. I've never done that before." I look around for a place to set Julia down, but Maeve is already on it. She opens up the diaper bag and takes out a little mat that was folded in there. Then she gets a diaper and puts it down with the wipes next to it. "Great. Thanks, Maevey."

I put Julia on the mat and start to take her zippered one-piece thing off. At least this isn't a complicated outfit, but it's hard to take her tiny legs out of it without feeling like I'm going to hurt her.

"Um, let me know if I can help." Maeve stands next to me, watching everything I'm doing with curiosity and something like contentment in her eyes. "You're doing great," she says encouragingly.

I nod and continue to attempt to keep Julia on the mat. Her cries have quieted a bit, but she's still unhappy. "How does this come off? Is there like a string you pull or some-thing?" I notice the little tabs at the front and try to pull one, and the whole side comes undone. Thank fuck. I repeat the same thing on the other side and slide the diaper off. Thank-fully it's just wet. I wave it around for a second, not knowing what to do with it. Maeve takes it and rushes over to a garbage bin, but she's back next to me in seconds.

"What's next?" she asks. "Wipes?" She opens up the plastic container with wet wipes inside and pushes it closer to me.

"Right. Yeah. Thanks." I take one, then another, then another and wipe down as much as I can while Julia squirms and cries. She must hate this. She must hate me by now, given how much she's cried. "Okay, she's good, right?"

"That's great, Owen. You're doing really well." Maeve nods along beside me, every bit as clueless as I am, but damn, it's nice to have her doing this with me. "Here's a clean diaper." She hands me the thing, but it looks nothing like what I just took off Julia. I'm too scared to take my hand off Julia in case she falls off or something, so I just stand there, staring at the diaper like an idiot. "Do you want me to open it up for you?" Maeve offers.

"Would you, please? I need eight more hands to do this safely." She giggles and takes the diaper, opening it up.

"Here, you lift up her bum, and I'll put this under her. The sticky tab things were on the back and then wrapped around the front, yeah?" Maeve looks down at the diaper in her hand, flipping it over a couple of times.

"Yeah, I think you got it." I lift Julia's little body, and Maeve slides the diaper underneath her. As I hold her legs, Maeve flips the other part of the diaper over her body and holds it in place while I get the sticky tabs in place. Julia is still crying when I get her little legs back into her pajamas, and I quickly scoop her up to try to soothe her again.

I let out a long breath, placing Julia on my chest and holding her there with one hand. I use my free hand to pull Maeve to me. I kiss her forehead, and when she looks up at me, I kiss her lips, just a press of our mouths together for a few seconds. "Thank you," I whisper.

"Of course, darling. I'm here for you." She lifts a hand, placing it over mine, which is currently splayed across Julia's tiny back. I know at this moment that she means it. That as scared as she is, as unsure as she might be about all of this, right now, in this moment, she's here for me. For us. Neither of us know what to do, but we work as a team, and that feels really fucking good.

fatal. to my panties, that is.

maeve

WE'VE MADE IT HOME, and Owen has taken Julia to every room of the house, describing each one to her. His final stop is the nursery, where he walks her around to her crib, the rocking chair and changing table. I've never really been in this room before, but it's clear the love that Owen has put into getting this together—with the help of his mum and sister. Once he's finished the tour, he stands in the middle of the room looking down at her with so much love in his eyes, I feel myself teetering.

Owen James is devastating on a good day, with his worn jeans and tight T-shirts that leave no muscle on his taut body to the imagination. Owen James wearing all that, smiling, *and* holding a baby? Catastrophic. Disastrous. Fatal. To my panties, that is.

He catches me staring and somehow, his smile grows even wider, then he looks down at a sleeping Julia in his arms and when he looks up, there are tears in his eyes. Actual tears. I will play back this moment in slow motion in my mind again and again for years to come. I just know it.

"You all right?" I lay a hand on his forearm and take a

peek at the little bundle who's finally fallen asleep in his arms.

"Yeah. Yeah. I just think Clay and Monica would be really happy she's here. You know?" He sniffles, and I can't help it, I do too. This little girl started out life with such tragedy, losing both parents before she even got to lay eyes on either of them. And now, she's here, about to start a life with a man who will be the best father he can be.

Standing here now, seeing his devotion to her, and knowing exactly how he feels about me, I almost wonder if it's not too late for that dream I had once upon a time to become a reality.

The thought of raising children with Owen feels…consequential, weighty in a way I hadn't experienced when I let go of my hopes of ever being with him. I think it's because he's so very loving, so kind, and open with his feelings, while I feel like I'm still sorting myself out in a lot of ways. That makes me feel like maybe I'm not enough yet. Like maybe he was given this responsibility for a reason. Because I didn't grow up with the same kind of warmth and unconditional love he was surrounded by.

My childhood home wasn't filled with warm hugs, a mum who made my favorite foods, and a dad who was proud of everything I did, no matter how small. No. My house was nothing but a shelter for Char and me. It had a revolving door of men whose only qualifier for being there was how much money they were willing to give my mum until either they got bored of her or she was done with them. It was a place where the children had to parent themselves. Where two sisters learned to lean on one another at the tender age of three, because there was no one else.

This is so not the time for these thoughts.

"Of course they'd be happy, darling. They chose you for a reason." He hums a response, and I'm not even sure he heard me because he's already busy staring at Julia's changing facial expressions again. I can't say I blame him.

"It's really beautiful out. Do you want to come sit out on the deck? I can put Julia in that little basket thing my mom got for her, or we can just hold her? Do you think she'd like that? What do you think is better for her?" His eyes dart back and forth between my face and hers.

My god, he's adorable.

"I think she looks perfectly content in your arms, O. But why don't I get the portable bassinet and bring it out with us, just in case?" His creased forehead relaxes at my question, and he nods. "I'll see you out there in a minute."

Owen is quietly speaking to Julia when I walk out to the back deck. They're swinging on the big swing that I've been meaning to come sit on but haven't had a chance to until now. I set the bassinet down beside me and then sit, joining them both in the gentle swinging.

"This is nice. I can't believe I've never come out here before." I look out at the mountains, noting that here, signs of spring are much more obvious than in LA. The colors are getting brighter, and it's nice to see things growing, flowers blooming. There's a field of lavender off to the side, and the smell is drifting over to where we are. It's perfect.

"Wait until you see the sunset. It's a pretty great view from out here." He looks up at me briefly, but he's only got eyes for Julia right now.

And I'm not so sure the view can get better than this, to be honest.

"She seems to have settled a bit." I lay a gentle hand on Julia's back. She's lying on Owen's chest, as it seems to be her favorite spot these past few hours.

"Yeah. She's still squirmy and not really sleeping for long. Maybe she can sense a new place? New people? I don't know." He kisses the top of her head. The movement is natural, as if he's done it a million times before. "I just hope she feels safe enough here to rest, you know? Babies are supposed to sleep a lot, and she's been so restless."

"I'm sure she feels safe, O. Look at her, all tucked into your chest. It's a very safe and comfortable place to be. Trust me." I look up at him, and my lips involuntarily curl into a smile. As I meet his gaze, I see that he is also smiling, his dimples deepening and eyes crinkling in response to mine.

As the sun begins its descent, Owen cradles Julia in his arms. They both exude a sense of calm and contentment, seeming much more at ease in each other's company.

When it's finally dark, we go back inside, and Owen sets her down in her crib. I can tell it's difficult for him to leave the room, but he does—with the monitor in a tight grip in his hands.

"I'm sorry. I didn't even let you hold her. I just feel like I've missed so much time with her already, and—"

"It's all right, O. I know you two haven't had the opportunity to bond yet, and I don't mind seeing you snuggle a baby." I place a reassuring hand on his forearm, and he leans into me, running his fingers through my hair.

"I feel like we should talk about this. We haven't really discussed how we're going to do this now that Julia's home. And I'm sorry that I haven't brought it up before now. We've kind of gone from zero to a hundred." His touch is soothing, but something in his tone has the blood running a little colder in my veins. "I know this wasn't part of whatever plans you had for yourself. I understand your career is demanding, so—"

Owen doesn't get to finish his thought because Julia's screaming interrupts him. We both rush into her room, and Owen scoops her up.

"She must be hungry. She didn't eat very much last time I gave her a bottle. Do you mind holding her while I get another one ready?" I take Julia in my arms, her little face already turning red from crying. All the bobbing and shushing isn't working as we wait for Owen to get back.

The minutes feel like hours, and when he comes back, he gently touches the bottle to her lips and she happily takes it, seeming to calm almost instantly. Her brown eyes pop open and latch onto mine, making my heart lurch inside my rib cage.

"There you are, poppet. Was someone feeling hangry? Hmm? I understand. I'm not very nice on an empty stomach either, you know?" She makes a rather satisfied gurgling noise as she gulps down the bottle, and I laugh, looking up to find Owen watching us.

His eyes are glistening, and his lips part as he takes a deep breath in. I'd like to tell myself he's looking at me like that because he sees our future like this, raising kids together. I'd like to believe that the reason that tears are about to roll down his cheeks is because he wants this life with me, even if it's not starting the way either of us initially pictured it. But my dumb brain gives my heart a swift kick into reality. Maybe he looks like he's about to cry because it's sinking in that I'll never be able to be a present mum with the way I work. Maybe this look is nothing more than deep disappointment in what is versus what could have been.

He takes a step toward us, and Julia shakes her head, spilling some milk on her cheeks as she goes back to crying, but this time it's more of a screechy scream than a regular cry. Owen's eyebrows bunch up and he wipes at my face quickly before cleaning up the formula on Julia's cheek and neck.

"She feels a bit warm, maybe I'll take her out of her sleeper and see if she's more comfortable?" I move toward the changing table, but Owen's face is still serious, full of worry. "Or would you rather…?"

He nods, taking her to the table and carefully removing her clothing as she screams bloody murder. I try not to over-think the fact that he wants to care for her versus having me do it. I try not to go to that place that tells me I could never be a mum because I never had one who loved me the way a child should be loved.

Undressing her seems to make things worse as she thrashes her little body. Owen handles the whole thing calmly, but there's tension building in his shoulders. He changes her diaper, speaking calmly to her the whole time, as if he's explaining to her what he's doing. It's so sweet, the way he gives her a full play-by-play of tossing her wet diaper and putting a new one on.

She doesn't let up, though. Her crying only gets more and more desperate, and I try to reassure Owen that babies just cry sometimes. Anytime I say anything, he nods and takes a deep breath, keeping himself calm. It's impressive how little he's freaking out considering he's never dealt with a screaming infant before.

AFTER TWO HOURS of Owen doing everything he can to soothe her, still nothing has worked. He's done skin-to-skin, given her a bath, tried feeding her again, swaddled her, and still it's been nonstop crying. I ask him if he'd like a break, to get some fresh air or a drink. He accepts, and as soon as I take her little body in my hands, I know something is wrong. She's far too warm. I look at Owen, and he seems to sense my inner panic.

"What is it? What's wrong?" I wish I knew.

"I don't know, but something definitely is. Do you have a baby thermometer?" Owen nods and opens up the cupboard, taking out a well-stocked first aid kit for babies and small children. He really is prepared.

He touches the thermometer to her forehead, and I gasp when I take in the number. 101.

I carry Julia back to the change table and start to change her into a zippered sleeper.

"What are you doing? What's happening?" I angle my head, but I don't look him in the eyes.

"I think we need to take her to the hospital, O. I'm going to get her dressed. Can you pack a bag with lots of diapers, formula and a few extra clothes?" He doesn't ask questions; he just starts moving quickly around the room. He's like a ping-pong ball, bouncing from corner to corner, getting what Julia needs.

Once she's dressed, and Owen has the bag ready, I get Julia into her car seat, then I take the truck keys and walk outside. He looks at me like I've sprouted a second head.

"You're in no shape to drive, Owen. Sit in the back with her. I'll drive." He still says nothing, just goes through the motions of locking up the house and getting into the truck.

My heart is beating in my throat like it's trying to claw its way out of my body, but I will myself to calm the fuck down. Taking a few deep breaths, I adjust the driver's seat and search for the hospital address in the map app on my phone. I hear Owen's seatbelt click, and I put the truck into drive. It's time to show the fuck up for Owen. For Julia.

44 /

don't you know what a bloody indicator is?

owen

WHAT THE FUCK, *what the fuck, what the fuck? How is this happening? I finally bring Julia home and end up at the hospital? This is so fucked up. What the hell did I do wrong?*

Maeve's growl takes me out of my thoughts and back into the moment. "Fuck right off, you wanker! Don't you know what a bloody indicator is?" She blows out an annoyed breath. "Honestly, some people shouldn't be allowed on the road."

Julia is still crying, arms flailing in front of her as her face keeps getting redder and redder. I'm trying to soothe her, but nothing is helping.

Maeve passes the car in front of us as she shakes her fist at the driver. "The speed limit is forty! Even my granny drives faster than you!" She keeps her eyes on the road, stopping at every stop sign while muttering *comeoncomeoncomeon* at every red light. She's being perfectly safe while unleashing her road rage on every act of incompetent driving she comes across. If I could muster up the energy to laugh, I would. But the stress of this situation has my body completely rigid, and I'm barely able to breathe, let alone laugh. Still, I'm thankful for her. For the fact that she's here, that she offered to drive, that she even knew what that damn number I can't erase from my mind meant.

101. That's obviously a high temperature for a newborn?

"Get off your phone, you irresponsible twat! Ugh! The nerve of some people!" Maeve's eyes meet mine in the rearview mirror, and she gives me a tight smile. "You all right, O? We're almost there."

"Yeah," I answer, but my voice is all gravelly, and my tongue is like sandpaper.

Maeve pulls into the ER entrance and motions for me to get out. "Go on. I'll park and meet you inside."

"Maeve, you can't. People will see you. They'll recognize you." I'm torn between staying with Maeve and taking Julia inside, but Julia lets out a wail that I feel in my bones, and I think Maeve feels it, too.

"I'll figure it out. You've got to take her in, Owen." I hate this. I wish Raf was here, so he could stay with her. I wish I didn't have to choose between them right now. Maeve nods, and I get out, throwing the backpack over my shoulder as I round the car to get the car seat out.

"I'll make some calls. Get some guys here as soon as possible. If you need to stay in the car, I understand, okay?" She nods, and as I walk up to the ER doors, she gives me a small wave before driving away toward the parking lot. The feeling in my stomach that she shouldn't leave is strong, but I ignore it so I can get Julia what she needs.

mummy dearest.

maeve

I KNOW it makes him uneasy, leaving me to fend for myself. I have no idea who I'll run into or what'll happen once I set foot inside the hospital, how long it'll be before someone has their phone in my face. Truthfully, I don't really care because Owen is my family.

I don't get the chance to find out whether anyone would recognize me, though, because as I'm parking the truck, my phone rings, and rather than checking who's calling, I pick up right away. I look at the screen once I've already accepted the call, and my stomach flips as nausea hits me hard.

It doesn't ease up when her shrill voice comes through the speaker. "Aren't you going to say hello to Mummy dearest?" Her voice is like nails on a chalkboard, immediately bringing back childhood memories of being told to be quiet, go away, to be more like my sister. Catherine never should have had children.

Children should be seen, not heard, she used to say.

I consider just hanging up the phone. I can go back to ignoring her, but I know she won't go away. "What do you want, Mum?"

"Some greeting after months of not speaking to me and ignoring my calls, Maeve." She scoffs before continuing, "I called because it's what a mother does when her daughter gets married. Were you ever planning on telling me?"

"Considering I haven't told you anything about my life since I was eighteen, no. I was not." My temples are immediately throbbing. This conversation couldn't have come at a worst time. "Is there something you want? I'm busy."

"Yes. Well. You always are." I can hear her rolling her eyes even through the phone. It's one more thing we have in common, and I hate how that fact scrapes at my insides. She always thought my career choice was ridiculous until I made it big, and she started calling expecting me to "pay her back" for having raised me.

"I'm at the hospital, Mum. I really need to go."

"Why?"

I don't know what makes me answer her. Maybe it's the slight concern in her voice, maybe it's the fact that I'm not thinking straight because of this whole situation. Whatever the reason, my stupid mouth works faster than my brain. "We picked up Owen's daughter today and she's sick."

"You two couldn't even take care of a baby for a few hours and you already have her at the hospital?" Cue instant regret, and a bowling ball of guilt hitting me in the gut. Her comment renders me speechless, and she takes advantage. "Honestly, Maeve, what were you thinking? Marrying a man who's gone to court to get custody of a baby? You always were so stupid with men. I've always told you that you take after me. I left Geoff, that pathetic loser, by the way. He was gambling away all our money, so I got out before he could lose it all." I don't engage. I don't care about her loser husband or what he does with his money. "But he did gamble quite a lot of it away. I kept the house, but there wasn't much leftover after the divorce was finalized." Again, I don't respond. I'm not even sure I so much as blink or breathe as she speaks. I know she wants money, but she won't ask for it. She always waits for us to offer it, so it seems like it's our idea. Not this time.

"Is that why you called, Mum? To call me stupid and ask for money?" I start to gather my things in the truck. I don't want to waste any more time on her.

"Just, you know, a little something to tide me over. I have a lifestyle to maintain. Remember how your father left me with nothing and I had to start over? I'm too old for that now, Maeve." I scoff at her words.

The only father I've ever known left her with plenty of money to raise us girls and keep a roof over our heads when Charlie and I were three years old. After he found out we weren't actually his, he couldn't stay, and I don't completely blame him, even if I wish we had been able to go with him. He left us each a trust that we were able to access at eighteen, and that's when Char and I left for NYU. It's how we afforded school and got away from our toxic mother. Mum tried to take that away from us, too, though.

"I'm not giving you money." I keep my voice even, and I swear I can hear the moment she switches from *Mummy dearest* to the cruel woman she is.

"Oh? Is that so?" Her elevated tone tells me she's about to hit me with something that she thinks will hurt me. "And you think you can stay there, playing house with your *first husband* and a baby that isn't even yours? You think you're not just like me, Maeve? You're not built for motherhood any more than I was. Being a sweet, devoted wife isn't in your DNA, dearie." Her words drip with venom as her tone drops to a menacing whisper, her snarky comment turning into a cruel attack in the blink of an eye.

I want to hide or run like I used to as a child when she told me I'd never amount to anything worthwhile because Charlie was the smart one. I feel my knees tremble and my heart thrash inside my chest as I brace myself for more of her cruelty.

"You'll never be able to let go of your big dreams. You'll resent that man and that baby in no time. This isn't your calling, Maeve. You don't have a single nurturing bone in your body. You could hardly comfort your own twin when your dad left, for God's sake." I flinch at her mention of Charlie. She's not wrong. I didn't know how to comfort Char at first, when we were kids. It didn't come naturally to me. Like it didn't come naturally to Mum, a detail she conveniently fails to mention now.

Seemingly satisfied, she takes a deep breath, surely feeling the impact of her words even though she's thousands of miles away.

"I've got to go, Mum. Don't call me again." My voice remains flat, though inside, my head is at war with my heart, and both are losing. I think about Bon and how we've always called her the Mum in our group. She had Eva as an example of how to love, and she loves big. So does Owen.

"You'll be the one calling me when this is all over and you need advice. I'll be waiting." I don't wait for her to say anything else. I don't say goodbye. I end the call and sit in Owen's truck, numb. I don't move to exit the vehicle. I can't. My legs may as well be made of lead, because they refuse to carry me to Owen, even if all my heart wants is to run to him. How easy it would be to find comfort in Owen right now, but I'm not the one who needs comforting. He is. And I can't provide that for him. Not after having my future laid out for me by my mother.

I make a phone call, and within fifteen minutes, Arthur is here, with a look on his face that tells me just how much he hates helping me without telling his friend and…boss? I'm not sure. Anyway, he's obvious about not being pleased about the situation. And I'm vague with my reason for leaving, blaming it on being recognized if I entered the hospital. The lie tastes rotten in my mouth. I couldn't care less about being recognized.

"Owen is going to hate this, Maeve. So is Rafael." He glances at me as he runs a hand down his face.

"I know, but hopefully Julia just has a fever, and they can sort it out quickly, then he'll know everything, and it'll be fine." I swallow, hoping that I'm right. Hoping that she's okay and he is too. "And I'm calling Raf next. Don't worry."

I call Owen on the way back to his house, but it goes to voicemail. He's obviously busy with Julia. I'll just try again later.

PACKING DOESN'T TAKE LONG, and within an hour of leaving the hospital, I'm in my car with the local bodyguard Raf sent over. He's driving me back home to LA. Home. That's where I'm going because this was a nice little daydream, but it's not my real life, is it? I can't even be there to help Owen with the baby.

The dream I've lived these last few days falls to the ground, and I watch it shatter into a million tiny pieces. Owen was never mine to keep. We said forever, but forever was only ever possible inside that little bubble, and that's not real.

I sniffle, and Luke, the very tall, dark and handsome middle-aged man with kind eyes driving me, pulls a handkerchief out of his pocket and hands it to me.

"Here you go, Ms. Howard. It's going to be all right, miss. You go on and cry as much as you need to." He gives me a reassuring look before settling his eyes back on the road, and I feel the impact of tonight's events settle like a weighted blanket on my body, only there's no comfort in it. It's much too heavy. Suffocating. Every breath is a struggle as I try to push back against the heaviness, but it only seems to grow stronger. The darkness outside mirrors the growing weight inside, and I am consumed by the overwhelming sense of dread and sadness.

The loud sobs that overtake my body, the sounds I make, feel and sound foreign. Like it's happening to someone else, because I can't be living through this pain again, can I? Losing Owen once was enough. Once nearly wrecked me.

46 /

are you her father?

owen

HER FEVER IS EVEN HIGHER NOW. The nurse looked at me like I was an absolute imbecile when I stammered that she just started crying and wouldn't stop.

"Are you her father?" The question is simple enough, but the answer gets lodged in my throat, and I can't force it out. "Sir?"

"N-no. No, I'm not. I'm her guardian. I just got her today." The two nurses at the desk exchange worried glances, like they don't know what to do next.

Welcome to the club.

"Can you please just take care of her? I'll pay whatever it costs, just please… Please help her." Julia is still screaming as one of the nurses and I see the thick substance on her ear at the same time. She puts on a glove and wipes it, and it looks like there's blood, too. My head instantly starts to pound, every possible worst-case scenario slamming into my skull like a highway pile-up.

I take a few deep breaths as the nurses ask all kinds of questions about Julia, what medication she's taken, if any, and I answer everything in the same way: I don't know. I feel like such a fuck-up. Doing my best to explain the situation to them, they seem to believe that I've only been with her a few hours, and I reiterate that in that time all she's had is formula.

Julia's taken away for scans, and one of the nurses reassures me she'll be well cared for. I've called a pediatrician in town, and I was going to take Julia in next week to see her, but we haven't even had time for that, so the ER was the best option.

Reaching into my back pocket to call Maeve and let her know where I am in the hospital, I find it empty. Of course. Of course I remembered every little thing Julia could have needed, but forgot my phone in the house.

I walk back to the front desk and explain to the nurses that Maeve might be coming in looking for me, and they all look at me like they can see a few loose screws in my head. I don't even blame them. I came in with a sick baby, who isn't mine, and now I'm telling them one of the most well-known actresses in the world might be coming to look for me. Yeah, they're not letting me leave this place without getting my head checked.

A LITTLE OVER two hours later, I'm still in the waiting room. Julia is in intensive care, but I can't stay there with her yet. She has a terrible ear infection, which was made worse by the air pressure in the airplane. I've been responsible for her for only a few hours, and I managed to fuck up already.

I'm about to crawl out of my skin. I don't know where the hell Maeve is, or if she's been trying to contact me. I can't call anyone, and my heart feels like it might actually beat right through my rib cage.

I've felt this panic before. I know this feeling, of being trapped and feeling like there's no way out, except this time it's not a place I'm trapped in, it's this loop of not knowing what's next. It feels like there's always another shoe about to drop these days, and I'm not sure I can handle any more.

"Owen!" A deep male voice sounds down the hall, and I turn around to see who's calling me. I round the corner at breakneck speed and nearly collide with Arthur. Raf, walking a few steps behind his brother, comes to a sudden stop just before we all crash into each other. He quickly places his hands on my shoulders, halting my momentum as my body jolts forward. "There you are," he says with concern in his voice. I hardly even register his face as my eyes roam the hallway and front doors, willing Maeve to appear there.

"Look at me, James," Raf's voice is commanding. I normally only hear him like this on the job or on the field. I do as he's asking me. "Maeve's all right. She's safe." Then the fucker hugs me. Tight. And he doesn't let go. Not until my breathing settles and my shoulders relax. Then he slaps me on the back and pulls back.

"How's the littlest baby girl doing?" I shake my head, and he understands that I don't have any answers.

"Where is she?" My voice trembles and cracks as I try to speak. My stomach churns, a sour taste filling my mouth. It feels like I'm losing hold of something precious. It's slipping through my fingers like sand.

Raf lets out a breath, and I know he doesn't want to tell me. "She's in LA." He lets the words sink in for two seconds before he continues, "Luke's with her, and he's updating me every hour. And no, I will not ask him to also update you. You have enough on your mind here. You worry about Julia. We've got Maeve." I swallow my protests down because I know he's right, but it doesn't make it any easier to accept. She left. Not just the hospital. She left Ojai. She left. Us.

"Why?" I ask Rafael, but it's Arthur who clears his throat as if to answer.

"I think she's running away, Owen." Art's eyes flick to his brother as they exchange a look of sympathy or some other bullshit sentiment I don't care for right now. "She wouldn't tell me much when I asked her what's going on, but I could see it all over her face. She looked…spooked. I'm sorry."

I feel my brows furrow as I listen to my friend's words, and the tension in my stomach intensifies as I try to imagine what my wife could be running away from. My fists clench and my heart races as I think about her walking away without a word. Is it anger, disappointment, or frustration coursing through me? Maybe all three. I thought she was coming around to the idea of us. I thought we were moving forward. But she left. Why now, when I need her the most?

I walk back to the waiting room, not wanting a nurse or doctor to not find me there if they ever decide to tell me what's happening. The guys follow silently.

My thoughts are a jumbled mess. I need Maeve here. I want her here.

But she doesn't want to be here, does she?

The three of us sit down, and I remember my lack of a phone.

"Hey, would you mind going by my house and getting my phone? I forgot it when we rushed out with Julia, and I need… I gotta know what's going on directly from Maeve." I swallow as I rub at my eyes because I'm exhausted, but I'm also on the verge of ugly crying right here in this hospital waiting room. "I need to call my mom. I need to call Lainey. I need…"

Maeve. I need Maeve. I can't lose both of my girls on the same night. I can't.

do you want to take a pregnancy test now?

maeve

I SPENT the whole night staring at my phone. Waiting. Hoping. Needing news that Owen is okay, that Julia is okay. But I haven't gotten any. I'm watching the sunrise from my bedroom in a house that doesn't feel like home quite like Owen's did, and it only makes my heart ache more. His house felt more like home in a week than my own has for months.

Every call and text that isn't Owen just makes my chest feel a little bit tighter, and I can't bring myself to respond to any.

I miss them. We hardly had any time together in that little bubble, but God, it was perfect, and all I want is to go back there.

"Maeve Charlotte Howard, I know you're in here!" Bon's voice booms from somewhere in my house, and the relief and dread battle inside of me as I wait for her to find me. It's early, and she hates mornings, so I know this is out of love. I know she's worried.

Sure enough, a minute later, she's standing in the doorway to my bedroom with her hair in a nest atop her head, wearing a cropped T-shirt and what must be Adam's sweatpants because they're about six sizes too big for her.

"Cheese on rice, Mae. You have us all worried sick! If it wasn't for Raffy telling us you were here and safe, I think I would have broken down your gate to get to you sooner." She huffs out a breath, sounding properly winded. "I've been calling you and Owen all night. Well, most of the night, because I somehow fell asleep while sitting at the dining room table with my phone in my hand. Adam found me when he got home this morning from a redeye flight. Can you believe that?" She's already in my bed, tucking her legs under my covers. "Anyway, I must be coming down with something because as soon as I got up from my perch at the table, I ran to the bathroom to throw up. I don't think I'll be eating chicken pot pie for a little while, which is such a shame because Adam has gotten so good at making them for me." She sits up quickly and scoots farther from me on the bed. "Oh fuck, what if I'm contagious? I wasn't even thinking. I'm so sorry, I'll go, I—"

I place a hand on my best friend's clammy one and pull her back in. "I don't think what you have is contagious, Bon. Come here." My sweet, clueless Elaina is pregnant, but I'm not about to tell her as much.

We sit in silence for a few minutes, but the little wheel is spinning faster and faster in Elaina's brain as all the questions she's begging to ask run through her mind. I'm the first to ask a question though.

"Have you heard from O?" My voice cracks at even just the mention of him. Every part of me is as brittle as the sugar glass we use on set. Just one touch and I'll crack into a million tiny pieces.

Bon heaves out a sigh. "Yeah. Raf and Arthur are there now. They've got him." She bites her bottom lip, and I know she has more to say. "From someone who has left the love of her life in the middle of the night herself, why did you run,

Mae? I'm not judging. It's not my place to. I just want to understand." There's not a single thread of doubt in me that she means every word.

"It's just easier this way. I would have caused too much of a commotion, and Julia's health is the most important thing right now." She nods, but also narrows her eyes at me. I can see that my answer isn't sufficient for her, and I don't blame her for wanting to question me further. Honestly, it's not quite enough for me either, but the small voice in my head gets louder with every passing minute. It keeps telling me that I won't be enough, that he'll be settling if he commits to a life with me. That one day, he'll see that I'm not wife or mother material. Just like my mum.

"You're not even going to ask me how I know Owen is the love of your life?" My stomach drops and splatters on the floor beneath us. I didn't even catch what she had said. "Because he is, Maeve. And if you seriously think you're doing him some kind of favor by distancing yourself from him and Julia, you're wrong." Elaina never pushes like this. She's normally softer with her delivery. This feels more like Charlie than Bon right now. "I've watched you two since we were nineteen. You became reluctant friends, forced together by me because you love me so much you were willing to befriend my deployed brother so he'd have someone else to talk to." She huffs out a small laugh.

"I'm not stupid enough to think you did it all for me. I knew it was for you, too, but you agreed because I asked you. I asked because, even then, I could see the connection between you two. Like the string that bound you both together suddenly glowed when you were in the same room, begging to never be pulled apart again." Her glassy green eyes go to the window as a tear rolls down her cheek. "I know those years when we didn't hear from him were hard, and I'm sorry I never talked to you about it. I couldn't, back then. I know seeing him again after so long was hard on you, and I love and appreciate you so much for not once complaining about having to be close to Owen again. You're the most selfless person I know, Mae, and I'm so grateful to you." Her eyes remain on something else in the room, and I know she has more to say. "I could never ask you to settle for a life you don't want, but I also could never watch you give up on your biggest dream just because you're scared you won't be enough. You're always enough. Just as you are. Always."

It doesn't surprise me that she knows my heart so well. I know hers intimately, and I understand how it feels to see your best friend, your chosen sister, hurting.

"Do you think I'd make a good enough mum? I mean, I know I'll never be like Eva, or the kind of mum you'll be. I know I don't have that natural maternal sensitivity like you, but do you think I could learn?" Tears run fast and hot down my cheeks, pooling on the bed sheet crumpled in my lap before sinking quickly into the fabric. I watch as my sadness and confusion are soaked up and wonder if it can be that easy to let your fears be soaked up by something else, too.

"Mae. Where is this coming from? How could you think you're not maternal? Do you know that Owen sent me a voice memo bragging about how you were there to help him with Julia? He didn't say anything about what you did, but how you did it. How you went straight into action and told him he was doing a great job even when he had no clue what he was doing. How you stayed calm, right by his side the entire time." Bon moves so that we're face-to-face, her watery green eyes looking straight into mine. "Who do we go to when we don't know what to do? You, Maeve. You get shit done. Sure, I bake muffins, but you act in a moment of crisis. You have maternal instincts, Maeve Howard. You don't need to be taught. You've taken care of me and Charlie hundreds of times. Hear me when I say this, Maeve. You are *not* your mother."

And that's when the dam breaks. My tears come out in a torrential downpour, and my sobs rack my body, which my best friend readily hugs.

Deep down, I've always known that I'm not like Catherine, but she played right into my deepest insecurities. Except, I know Bon is right. I'm capable of love. I've loved Elaina since the day I met her. I've loved Charlie my whole life. I've loved Owen for ten years. I already love this little baby who I've only just met.

I can't find the words to respond to her just yet, but my resolve is kicking in. I can't let Owen go through this alone. Not when he's already been through such a scary time all on his own. I know that my love for him is enough to make me want to be there for him, even if, in the end, he doesn't want my complicated mess. Even if I turn out not to be enough, or I turn out to be too much, Owen deserves to feel loved and supported. I never should have left, but fear drove me here, away from him and back to familiar feelings. Now, I'll let love drive me back to him.

"Want to come to Ojai with me? We can call Char and she can come with?" Bon's eyes widen as she pulls back to look at me, and she nods furiously, eyes welling with tears. Jen helped Charlie find a place in LA, so she's close by. "Okay. Do you want to take the pregnancy test now, or would you rather do it at home with Adam?"

"W-what?" Bon blinks, and her tears stream down her cheeks, hands trembling as she shakes her head.

"Bestie, your boobs have always been fabulous, but they look like they're ready to pop out of that top and make my A-cups shrivel up in jealousy. You threw up chicken pot pie? That's not normal. Not for you. And you haven't fallen asleep at a table since our uni days. You will always seek out a sofa or a bed, but you were tired enough to pass out with the lights on, sitting on a hard chair." Her tears are free falling down her cheeks when she brings her hands to them, and a small sob shakes her shoulders.

"You think so? Oh God, Mae, this is awful timing." My heart stops beating as I consider the possibility that this wouldn't make her happy.

"Bon, do you not want a baby?"

"I do. I mean we didn't plan for it to happen so fast, but we knew we wanted this eventually. I had my IUD taken out because we're getting married soon, but I didn't think anything would happen so fast. We haven't really been careful lately, and I haven't been tracking my cycles. But I had wine that day at Owen's so I can't be pregnant, right? Because that would be bad for a baby. And Owen needs me. I need to be able to be there for him and for you, and will I be able to do that if I'm this tired all the time? And, fuck, my boobs hurt so fucking badly."

"Bon, breathe. Look at me." She takes a shaky inhale and looks at me with sad eyes. "I could be wrong, but, my sweet friend, if I'm right, we're going to celebrate because I could never feel anything but pure joy knowing you're going to bring a life into this world, and I know everyone will feel the same. So, what do you say we go find out?" I squeeze her still shaking hand and she smiles. I want this for her and Adam, and even if it's not today, I look forward to celebrating this milestone with them. But I'm pretty sure this is it.

ONCE WE'RE in the bathroom, I guide Elaina through the process of taking a pregnancy test. I read the instructions and relay them to her because she's too anxious to look. I've never been more thankful for my neurotic publicist, who insists all her clients have pregnancy tests at home. According to her, there's nothing worse than dealing with a celebrity being caught at a 24-hour drugstore with a box of tests in her hand.

I stand against the bathroom door, talking into it as if the door itself is my best friend in her very delicate current state of shock and surprise. She insisted on taking two tests, so we're going with the pee-in-a-cup method.

"Okay, so just pee in the plastic cup," I say, "then dip the ends of the sticks in for however many seconds the packaging says. I think it's like ten seconds. Then lay them flat on the counter."

"Fucking goddamn it, I still got pee on my hand!" I laugh on my side of the door, and she does the same on her side, which is a relief given how scared she looked just minutes ago. "Okay, and now I just wait?" I hear her shuffling inside the bathroom and the water running.

"Yep," I say as she opens the door, hugging me tightly around my neck. It's always been our thing since she's a few inches taller than me.

"Thanks for doing this with me, Mae." Her voice breaks, and she squeezes me a little tighter. "I'm so grateful for you."

"I'm so grateful you trusted me to do this with you, Bon." I pull back and take in her still glassy emerald eyes, seeing so much of her brother in that color that it makes my heart constrict just a little more. "Thank you for trusting me with Owen, too." We exchange watery smiles and I squeeze her hand.

Wanting to distract myself from thoughts of missing Owen, I peek over her shoulder dramatically, pretending to look at the tests sitting on the vanity behind her.

"That should be long enough. You ready?" I widen my eyes at her. Bonnie nods at me, and I walk to the vanity, knowing she won't want to be the one to see the results first. It doesn't take me more than two steps to see the two bright pink lines on one test, and I step closer, the other's tiny screen says *pregnant*.

"Ha!" I hold up both tests at her eye level. "You're a mum, Bon!"

She screams and starts to jump up and down, fresh new

tears of joy streaming down both of our cheeks, and I jump with her. With every hop, I feel all of the bad feelings finally leave my body. All the doubt and insecurities that my mum tried to drill into me scatter across the floor like a school of tiny fish. They dart and flit about, never settling in one place, always looking for water to dive into, but I'm solid now. I'm no longer permeable and able to let them make a home inside of me.

48 /

his name is owen james, and he's my husband!

owen

MY MOM'S on her way here. It only took one word from me for her to say *I'm on my way*. That word was *Mamá*. That's literally all I said, and her decision was made.

I started to explain the situation with Julia and Maeve, but at one point, Raf had to take over as I sat on a chair with my head between my knees. I know these feelings. I know this panic well.

It sounds like there's a jet plane taking off in my ears, the thumping of my heart equally loud as I taste iron in my mouth, which is fitting because with every swallow, it feels like there are nails dragging down my throat. The vice wrapped around my lungs and heart gets tighter with every inhale. I need water. I need air. I need Maeve.

I've lost count of how many times I've had that thought in the hours since I last saw her. I couldn't bring myself to call her. Couldn't make myself hear all the reasons why she left and went back to LA. Not over the phone. I need to see her face when she tells me she doesn't want me. Us. This. Just the thought of that very thing happening has my breathing coming in faster in shallow spurts.

I've been allowed to go see Julia. She looks so fragile in her little incubator. All I could do was put my hand through the opening to touch her. I came back to the waiting room, so I'm not alone in the NICU room. The machines beeping and everyone whispering was only making me more anxious.

Raf and Arthur have sat with me in the silence for hours, neither leaving at the same time, even if it's just to get a cup of shitty hospital coffee, and I appreciate these Machado brothers more by the minute.

I'm sure the sun is getting ready to set again by now, but I haven't left this room for more hours than I care to think about. It feels like there are ants crawling all over my skin. I can't shake the feeling that something horrible is happening and there's nothing I can do to stop it.

I should have known better. I'm responsible for her, and I didn't even know she was in pain. Just like I was responsible for them, and I couldn't get them all out of that hellhole.

No, this isn't the same. I'm not locked in a cage. No one's dying trying to save me. Not again.

My breathing picks up, and I feel that familiar pressure in my chest. I try to take a breath in, but the air gets lodged in my throat and won't make it to my lungs. What little air I'm pulling in comes through shallow, quick breaths that aren't enough. I open my mouth, gasping for air. Nothing. Panic creeps up my spine, moving quickly to my limbs that now feel like they're made of lead. Alarms are sounding in my head, telling me that if I don't get a hold of this soon, I'm going to black out. I catch Raf's head whip toward me, but he doesn't get the chance to say or do anything because we both hear her at the same time.

"His name is Owen James, and he's my husband!" There's more, something about her needing to find me but I can't move, paralyzed by the fear that this is another mirage.

"Maevey! We're here," Raf calls out into the hall. I still

haven't moved. I haven't breathed. I won't until I see it's really her. That, or I'll pass the fuck out.

She rounds the corner, blonde hair whipping across her face as her wide blue eyes scan the room. When they land on me, they soften in the way that they used to ten years ago, in that way I've seen again these last few days.

Maeve doesn't walk, she sprints across the tiny room and directly into my arms, straddling me on the tiny love seat I didn't think was actually big enough for two people.

She touches her forehead to mine, cradling my face in her hands gently, fingers moving to massage my scalp. I would close my eyes, but they're trained on her. My lungs are begging for air, but I can't seem to remember how to get it to them.

"I'm here. I'm not going anywhere." Maeve continues to run her fingers through my hair, her words landing in a breathy whisper on my lips. "I love you, Owen. Breathe. It's okay. Just breathe."

And I do. In a loud gasp, I suck in a breath, and instantly, it's as if the grip around my chest loosens, the panic subsides, and all feeling comes back to my hands and feet. I wrap my arms around Maeve, pulling her body closer to mine, not giving a shit about where we are. I take in a few more lungfuls of air before I try to say anything.

Once our breathing is in sync, I play back the words Maeve said. *I'm here. I'm not going anywhere. I love you.*

"You love me." It's not a question, but even I can hear the awe in my voice at the statement.

"I never stopped. Not even for a minute. I was yours from the moment you caught me from falling." Her voice is soft, a tone I've only heard when she speaks to Julia, and now to me.

"Which time?" I ask and the smile blooms on her face, taking over every inch as her cheek dimples and her eyes crinkle at the edges.

"Does it matter? Are we really going to discuss the semantics of my clumsiness?" Her teasing tone works its way through me, untying all of the knots in my muscles, and sending a warm, soothing comfort where the tightness used to be. Her smirk settles me further, but I can see the hint of worry in her eyes. She's putting on a brave face for me. She's here for *me*. And it's not lost on me that she obviously had to work through some shit to get to this point.

"I knew you loved me. I've always known it." I rub small circles on her lower back, and she relaxes into me.

"This is not the time to get cocky, Mr. James." The corners of my lips tug upward at her words.

"That's not what this is. I knew it because I felt it. I saw it. In the way you held Julia, in your road rage, in the way you looked at me. When Raf and Art said you left, I thought maybe I saw what I wanted to see. I thought it was all in my head, but I know you, Maeve. I know how it feels to be loved by you." I wrap my arms a little tighter around her. "The hard part isn't saying the words. We've loved each other for years. I've said the words to you in my head a thousand times. The hard part is this. It's what happens when things get rough. When running away seems like the only choice, but instead you come back and stick around for the messy parts. This is how I know you love me."

Twin tears roll down her cheeks as she gives me a wobbly smile, her eyes shining with love. There are no masks here today, and that's exactly how I want it to be. Forever.

49 /
the easiest thing
i've ever done.

maeve

THE EASIEST THING I've ever done is tell Owen I love him. I didn't even have to think about the words, they've just always lived inside me, and there was no effort needed to let them out. The hard part, like he said, is when shit gets hard. And right now? It's hard.

Owen was on the brink of a massive panic attack when I walked in here, and he's still tense. We've been to see Julia together, and it looks like we can take her home soon. She needed fluids to get her body temperature back to normal. The pediatrician explained that she had an ear infection, and it likely wasn't a bad infection, but that flying may have exacerbated it.

After spending some time just watching Julia sleep, we agree to head back to the waiting area to let everyone know how she's doing.

Owen's face is a mixture of guilt and defeat, his eyes are downcast as he fiddles with the hem of his shirt. His shoulders slump forward, and his lips are pressed into a tight line.

I stop him in a quiet hallway with a touch on his forearm. "Hey, O?" He turns toward me, but his eyes are still lowered.

I stand closer to him, pushing my face into his line of sight. "It wasn't your fault." He winces at my words. "You heard the doctor. We couldn't have known. Yeah, she was fussy, but that's not uncommon for a baby that's only a few weeks old."

His eyes finally meet mine, and he gives me a few quick nods. "I'm glad you were there. That you noticed she felt warm. If you hadn't been—"

"But I was. We were together, and Julia is fine. And that's how it's going to stay. Okay?" The conviction in my voice still surprises me, given that just this morning, I was still feeling like I couldn't handle these new roles, this new life. "Uh, my mum called. Just before I left." I clear my throat, and Owen's eyebrows raise in question. "She said a lot of things. That I'm just like her, how my first marriage is going to end in divorce, just like all of hers have, and that I'm not fit to be a wife or mum."

"Maevey…That's why you left?" I nod, and now it's my turn to wince.

"I know it wasn't the right thing to do, and I'm so sorry. I let her get to me. I'd already been so scared and unsure of whether I could do this, if I could be what you and Julia deserve…" I huff out a breath and see Owen shaking his head. "I once dreamed of this, Owen. Of you and I being married, having a family, getting our happily ever after. But that was a fairytale. It didn't seem possible given how I was raised. At least, not for me. So, I replaced that dream with my career dreams. I thought that if I could be driven and dedicated to my goals, I'd never end up like my mother and my grandmother, who used men until they had nothing left. I wanted to make my own life. Have my own money. And I made that happen. But the older I got, the more I started to see that I was becoming like her in other ways—selfish, incapable of loving, focused on getting what I wanted and nothing else. Forgoing a family in the process." I rub at a spot on my forehead as if to wipe away thoughts of my mum and the toxic lies that she's tried to make me believe my whole life.

"And now? What do you dream of now?" Owen's eyes are serious, the crease between his brows deep as he takes me in.

"You, darling. I don't know that I ever really stopped dreaming of this fairytale life with you. I just denied the truth hard enough to make myself believe the lies, but—"

Owen cuts me off with a kiss, his hands cupping my face. Instinctively, I open up for him, and his tongue strokes mine in a way that leaves me breathless and wanting more. I whimper embarrassingly loudly when he pulls away, bringing our foreheads together.

"You're nothing like them, nothing like your mother. You made shit happen for yourself, and you did it while loving your sister, my sister, and everyone else you met. You did it while somehow loving me, even when I didn't deserve it. You built your career while building a family for yourself and Charlie, because that's what your friends are to you. Lainey, me, Raf and Adam. We're your family." He shakes his head, and his thumbs gently wipe at the tears on my cheeks. "And I think you know that now. I think you figured it out and that's why you came back."

I nod again, swallowing down the tears so I can say this to him as clearly as possible. "You're my family, Owen. You're my home. My heart. My dream."

"Yeah. And you're mine, *fengári mou*. You always were." Owen kisses me again, gentler this time. Just a series of presses of his mouth against mine as my face still sits cradled in his hands. Every kiss is a silent *I love you* that I feel down to my bones.

Once my tears are dry, we make our way back to the waiting room, which has turned into a small family gathering, as Raf, Charlie, Bon and Adam all refuse to leave the hospital. Eva is on her way from Marblehead to support Owen, and

Arthur offered to go pick her up from the airport so that we can all stay together, or he'd be here, too.

Raf walks into the room with a tray of coffee and tea in his hand. He hands one to Charlie, which she accepts without any smart remarks. They must have some sort of truce going, given our reason for being here. The moment he passes a cup to Bon, her eyes widen, and her hand flies to her mouth. She shakes her head, but Raf doesn't understand what's happening. She's clearly having an aversion to coffee. Poor thing. First her beloved pot pie, now coffee?

She stands and bolts to the nearest trash can where she empties whatever she had in her stomach, which can't have been much. Adam is next to her in the blink of an eye, holding her hair and rubbing her back.

"Raf, get those coffees out of here, please?" Adam's voice is a perfect mix of stern and kind, and my chest warms at the thought of him using this dad tone on their child. Rafael nods dumbly and pivots out of the room, Charlie on his tail, likely going to dump her tea.

By the time Bon rights herself, Raf and Charlie are back, both looking concerned, but Adam looks… oddly calm.

"Lainey, I think we need to tell them." He takes her hand and gingerly guides her back to a chair where he sits first, guiding her down onto his lap.

"Tell *them*?" she asks, seemingly coming back to life. "I haven't even told *you*!" She instinctively puts a hand on her stomach, and Owen, Charlie and Raf all gasp at the same time. It's kind of cute.

"Baby, your body's changed, you're tired all the time, and last week you said you didn't want strawberries because they tasted like blue cheese, which then made you want cheese, and we went to the store and bought eight different kinds. Remember?" Adam remains calm, completely unfazed by what's happening. Bon's eyes water, and she lets out a sob.

"I wanted to put a bun in the oven and have you open it

as a surprise. It was going to be so cute. I was going to get your reaction on video and everything. It was going to be perfect!" He wipes her tears away, a crooked smile playing on his lips.

"This is perfect. I mean, I hate that you're sick and so tired, but you're growing a life, my love. That we made together. What's more perfect than that? You're going to be an amazing mom, just like yours." Adam's words are sweet and so perfectly the exact thing my bestie needs to hear right now. My own doubts and insecurities about motherhood creep in, slowly, like black smoke infiltrating a bright room.

Owen's hand moves up along my spine, fingers wrapping around the back of my neck where my muscles have tensed. He leans into me and whispers, "I love you." And just like that, those nagging feelings evaporate into thin air.

I know that the insecurities, the fear, the guilt, the shame, and whatever nasty sentiment wants to rear its ugly head will be back. I know they're not gone forever, but I have Owen by my side to help shoo them away. To bring me back to the reality that what we have is wonderful, and that we can lean on each other when things get hard.

Rafael practically jumps out of his skin as Adam whispers something to Bon. She nods, and they both smile.

"We're having a baby!" Bon jumps up and exclaims, as if we didn't all already clue into that very fact. But gosh, she's sweet. Immediately we're all rushing the happy couple, Rafael going to his best friend and wrapping him in one of his famous bear hugs. Owen hugs them both, and I stand back and take it all in. Their joy, the little bit of fear lingering in their eyes, the excitement buzzing in the air.

if there are no objections...

maeve

EVA CAME by the hospital to say a quick hello and to give Owen one of her infamous motherly hugs before heading to the house. We managed to convince them all to spend the night there and not at the hospital. Owen and I took turns napping on the rocking chairs in the NICU, holding Julia for skin-to-skin contact to help with her body temperature and just watching her. We hardly slept, but I think I can speak for Owen when I say that we're just so happy she's all right, it doesn't even matter.

Julia's fever finally subsided overnight, and we received the good news that there were no complications from the procedure to remove the blockage in her ear. With the green light to take her back home, we were relieved and grateful. When the doctor declared Julia healthy enough to leave the hospital, we let out a collective sigh of relief. Smiles spread across our faces, and tears of joy glimmered in our eyes as we packed up our belongings and prepared to take the little one home. The feeling of happiness and contentment was almost tangible in the air.

Everyone is waiting for us at Owen's house when we

arrive. We get Julia settled in her *Yia-Yia's* arms as our family surrounds us, coming together to make coffee, gather snacks and take care of the precious little girl I hope to call mine one day.

Owen pulls me aside, as his phone rings in his hand. He shows me the screen, and I recognize his lawyer's name. We lock eyes for a moment, and I smile, communicating to him that it's okay to take the call, that I'm here and we're doing this together.

"Hi, John." He puts the call on speaker as we walk out to the front porch, away from the commotion. "I've got you on speaker. Maeve is here."

"Lovely to finally talk to you, Mrs. James." His tone is jovial, and I immediately like him. Also, I just really like being called Mrs. James.

"Hello! Given your cheerful tone, I sure hope you have something good to say, otherwise my husband will be firing you." I mean it, too. If he has bad news after that greeting, he's done.

John's response is a throaty laugh. "Just going to cut right to the chase, huh? I like you. Of course I have good news. I know you were a bit worried about what this hospital visit meant for your guardianship, Owen. The social workers have confirmed with the doctors that you couldn't have known Julia had a blockage in her ear since they didn't know themselves, and it's not anyone's fault that this happened." He pauses as my heart stops beating. Owen's grip loosens as he lets out the breath he must have been holding. "Now, the guardianship papers only have Owen's name on them, and I can put the adoption paperwork through as soon as possible, but I wanted to ask whether anything has changed with that before we continue. Are we adding a name to the paperwo—"

"Yes!" My answer is loud. Too loud. Owen's grip on my hand tightens again, and I look up at him. "I mean, yes, please. If that's okay. If there are no objections. I'd really like to be added to the official paperwork as Julia's mmm… as Julia's mm—" Sobbing. I am sobbing. I bury my face in Owen's chest to muffle the sounds as surely John thinks I've lost it.

"As Julia's mum. Please add Maeve's name to the paperwork as Julia's mother, John." Owen's steady voice does nothing to help with my crying. In fact, it just makes me cry harder.

A sniffle comes through the phone speaker, and it makes me like John a little more.

"Consider it done. I won't congratulate you prematurely on the adoption, even though I know it'll go through with no issues, but let me congratulate you both on taking this step. I'm very happy for you." Another sniffle. I did not expect John, the lawyer, to be such a softie, but I'm here for it.

I'm still a mess, so Owen takes over. "Thanks John. Talk soon."

The call ends, and Owen's arms wrap around me tightly. He kisses the top of my head as his chest moves with a deep breath, and everything suddenly calms. My tears stop and my breathing slows. As I pull away from Owen to wipe at my face, he cradles it in his hands.

"Are you sure, Maevey?" His eyes roam over my face, likely looking for any sign of regret over what I've just asked for. "Are you sure this is the life you want? With me? With Julia?"

We lock eyes, and I can see the specks of doubt swimming in them. Owen needs reassurance. He always has. So I freely give it to him. "Yes, Owen. I want this. I want you. I want this life. This is my dream come true. My biggest, wildest, most beautiful dream. The one I thought I had to let go of. The one I was certain would never come true. And here you are, making it real."

He closes his eyes, a slow breath exhaling out of him as he touches his forehead to mine.

"I love you," we both whisper at the same time. A quiet giggle builds in my chest, and Owen's shoulder shakes lightly with his own laughter. The sounds are filled with relief, joy, more love than I know what to do with.

I wipe at the tears on his face in the gentle way he always does mine, and he leans into my touch, turning his face to kiss the middle of my palm before bringing our hands to the middle of his chest.

"Always," he says.

"Always," I echo.

51 /
this is it.

owen

THIS IS IT. This is how we begin. Out on the front porch. Not in a moment of lust, not in passing, but looking into each other's eyes, wholly present.

I might not remember reciting our vows in Vegas, but I'll never forget this. I'll never forget how it feels to have the woman I've loved for a decade commit herself to me in a way I wouldn't even allow myself to daydream of. It's real. It's really happening.

Once we both stop crying, we make our way back to the living room. All eyes are on us as we walk in, including Mamá's worried ones.

"We're going to be Julia's parents," I open with.

"Well, Owen was always planning to adopt her…" Maeve looks at the floor, a small smile playing on her lips, telling me without words to continue.

"But Maeve's name is officially going on the adoption paperwork, and—" I stop, because the whole room breaks into whispered cheers as Julia sleeps soundly.

"Oh, sweetheart." My mom hugs Maeve as tightly as she can with Julia cradled to her chest, pulling back to pat

Maeve's cheek, as she always does. "Two of my girls are becoming moms. What a beautiful day this is." She moves to take Maeve's hand in her own, eyeing the rings there with tears in her eyes. "These suit you, Mae. They're perfect. That green, it's…"

"My favorite color," Maeve finishes for her, and they both nod in agreement. "I couldn't have picked a better ring myself, Eva. Thank you."

Jesus, how did I get this lucky?

My sister practically rams into me, hugging me tightly around the waist. "Thanks for making my best friend my real sister, O." And goddamnit, my eyes are stinging with tears again. Rafael is usually the crier, but I think I'm about to fight him for that title.

Everyone, Charlie included, congratulates us with hugs, and as the party calms down, my sister claps and bounces on the spot.

"Welcome to the family, Mrs. James. Permanently," Elaina says right as my mother sobs behind me. We all turn to her, worried something is wrong.

"I'm sorry." Ma quickly wipes at her tears. "I'm just so happy. Mrs. James. Oh, it's just…" Another sob. Raf quickly wraps an arm around her shoulders, pulling her into him as he rubs her back.

"All right, Mom and Dad. What can we do to help you today? We've got lunch ready, and Adam's prepping dinner." Rafael turns to the kitchen and waves at Adam, completely unaware of what he's just done. Unaware that my heart just nearly burst in my chest at hearing his words.

Mom and Dad.

There's a mix of sadness that my friend and his wife aren't here, but gratitude for the fact that Maeve and I are. I teeter between grief and glee, knowing Julia's real mom and dad can't be the ones to comfort her, to watch her grow. But there's also immense joy in the fact that Maeve and I will happily step into those roles and do everything we can to give her the best life. To be called her dad is so bittersweet right now, but I know that one day the word will bring me nothing but pure joy. I know I'll earn that title and make my friends proud.

Maeve looks up at me, eyes shining with tears again and a wide smile on her face.

"This is more than enough. Thank you. Thanks for showing up for us." I squeeze my wife's hand as we take in this family that Julia is going to be so lucky to be a part of.

We eat lunch, and Rafael, Charlie, Lainey, and Adam leave shortly after to get back to LA. Arthur somehow managed to get the bat situation taken care of so my mom can stay in the guesthouse. She doesn't want to impose on newlywed and new-parent life, but she wants to make sure we know that she's there for support if we need it. I think we both feel relieved to have her here for a few days, especially knowing Julia is still recovering.

BRINGING her home was such a massive relief that, by the time evening came, I passed out. I hadn't really slept for two days, and both Maeve and my mom forced me into the bedroom to sleep.

The sun is shining brightly when I open my eyes and, I roll over, expecting to feel Maeve there, but the bed is empty. I'm alone.

When I open our bedroom door, I hear her off-key singing so clearly, and it makes me chuckle. She's across the hall, a sleeping Julia in her arms as she sways to the lullaby I recognize as "Lavender's Blue." They're beautiful, my girls. I had no idea this much love could fit into one person's heart.

Maeve sits her down in her crib, smiling down at our sleeping baby. When she turns around, she jumps, bringing a hand to her heart as she swears under her breath. When she reaches the door, she scowls at me, but it's not until the door clicks shut that she slaps my pec.

"You scared me, O!" I catch her wrist in my hand and bring her palm to my lips, kissing the sensitive skin there.

"I'm sorry. How can I make it up to you, Mrs. James?" I smile, watching as my wife softens for me. I'll never take for granted having these little moments with her.

"Don't you get all swoony and seductive on me, sir. We have things to talk about." She points a finger toward the bedroom, and my eyebrows twitch, rising skyward as my smile widens. "No, no, no. I really do mean talk. Come on."

I feign annoyance, but the truth is, I could sit and do nothing with her, and I'd be perfectly content. We can talk, or not. I'm happy.

"First of all, I want you to know that I intend to be here with you and Julia. While you were sleeping, I moved some things around for work, and we can sort out what childcare will look like when I get back to filming in a few weeks. I know it's not ideal, but you could both come with me? I don't know. We can talk about it." She's pacing around the room, and I let her walk off her pent-up energy. "But I'm in this with you. In case that wasn't clear."

"Okay, Maevey. I'm not worried. We'll figure it out." Her step falters, and she stops, taking in my words. She nods, softening for a second before her body goes rigid again. She sits on the edge of the bed and crosses her arms.

"You bought a house for me, O? With horses and a lavender field? A *house*?" My stomach falls to the floor. She looks pissed. Fuck. She hates it. I bought the wrong house.

I don't say anything. My hand nervously scratches the back of my neck as I think of something to say. I'm about to tell her we can move when I hear her sniffle. I fall to my knees in front of her.

"Maevey, no, I—"

"It's perfect, Owen James. Don't you dare think for a

moment that you didn't do the right thing. I couldn't love this house more than I already do, but knowing you chose it for me? For us?" A sob makes her shoulders shake, but she's determined to keep going. "All I wanted was you, Owen. You and me. But you had to go and buy us a house, marry me, and give me a daughter. I know the circumstances are awful, but I look at her, and she already feels like she's ours. You made all of my dreams come true with a drunken night in Vegas." Another sob breaks free, but it morphs into a laugh. "How dare you be so annoyingly perfect?"

I laugh, too, thankful that she loves the house I chose with her in mind. "Arthur told you, didn't he?" I ask, already knowing the answer, and she hesitates for only a second before smiling. My favorite blue eyes meet mine, those baby blues swimming with love and devotion. "And to be honest, the lavender field was mostly for me. I could never find anything that smelled like you other than the flower itself, so..."

Her head shakes from side to side. "God, you are insufferably romantic. I love it so much. Can we live happily ever after now?"

"We already are, Maevey."

epilogue

owen

one month later

"HEY MAEVEY?" I'm playing with her hair the way I always hoped I'd get to. Her head is resting on my chest. We just had unhurried sex for the first time in weeks because Lainey and Adam took Julia for the afternoon. Maeve starts shooting in a little over a week, and though Julia and I will be living close to the set with her, we know it's going to be an adjustment.

It's a bit strange, being at Maeve's house in LA, in her moody bedroom with plum walls instead of our sunny, cream-colored one in Ojai. It's like she lived a different life when it was just her in this big house.

"Mmm?" I almost feel bad for what I'm about to ask given how relaxed she is, but I can't hold it in anymore.

"Aren't you due to have your period at some point?" I keep up my movements, not wanting to startle her.

"What do you mean?" Her nose scrunches, and she looks up at me, confusion painted on her face.

I lick my lips nervously. "It's just that we've been together every day for like six weeks and you haven't had one. I don't want to pretend to be some expert on women's health, and I'm not questioning you, I swear. I just figured it's important for me to know that in case you need anything or—"

"Oh, my god. Oh, my god. OH, MY GOD!" She bolts upright in bed, the sheets sliding off her body. "Owen! Why didn't you say something sooner?" Climbing over my body, she runs naked to the bathroom, and I hear her opening doors and fidgeting with something. "I'm taking a pregnancy test," she shouts at me.

I can't see her, but I hear her moving around and it sounds like she's turning the place upside down. I put on my boxer briefs and grab my T-shirt to offer to her once she's done.

"Ah! Fuck. Bon was right. There's no way to do this without pissing on your own hand." She flushes, and soon, I hear the water running at the sink. I assume it's safe to approach her, so I walk to the bathroom door, watching as she focuses on the suds on her hands, clearly avoiding the test on the counter. As she dries her hands, I hand her my shirt, and she slips it on. She also avoids looking at me, so I give her some time. I've thought about this, considered it as a possibility, but she obviously has not.

Hands wringing together in front of her, she opens her mouth, closes it, opens it again. "I'm so sorry, darling. I… I'm on birth control. I've only been on it for a couple of months after removing an IUD. I guess I still wasn't used to taking the pill every day, and I know I missed a couple of days when we first got together, with that whole bat situation and my things being split between the guesthouse and the main house. I did bleed a little, but just assumed it was a super light period. I —" She sighs, looking up at me with teary eyes. "I'm sorry."

I walk over to my wife, brushing the hair off her forehead, tucking a few strands behind her ear. With my other hand, I reach for the small pink test stick and pick it up, taking in the two bright pink stripes, feeling the smile explode across my cheeks. I know what this means. I also looked up how pregnancy tests work, and what the results look like. I like to be prepared, what can I say?

"I'm not, Maevey. I'm not sorry at all." I turn the test toward her, and she brings her hand to her mouth as a sob shakes her shoulders. "Guess we're getting started on that football team right away, huh?" Another sob, then another. I'm about to panic at her reaction when the sobs start to sound more like laughter.

"We're going to have another baby!" She jumps up, and I catch her just in time for her legs to wrap around me as she laughs with tears rolling down her cheeks. She kisses me, but pulls away too soon, and that's when I see the worry wash across her face.

"No, *fengári mou*. Don't doubt for one second that you can do this. That we can do this." She shakes her head, blue eyes watery still.

"How am I going to love another baby as much as I love Julia? Is that even possible?" I smile, thankful that her doubt has nothing to do with her abilities as a mum, because she's an absolutely incredible one.

"I have a pretty good feeling that you'll figure out a way. We both will."

She nods, bringing her forehead to mine. "I love you, Owen. Thank you for making all my dreams come true."

"I love you, sunshine." I kiss her sweetly, feeling the way her body molds to mine, the way we fit together. It'll never get old.

WE GET DRESSED in our comfies, and while Maeve calls Jen to arrange a discreet OB-GYN appointment, I go to the kitchen to start on Maeve's afternoon cup of tea. When I get to the pantry for her digestives, I see a stack of mail sitting on the counter, and an envelope with red and pink hearts on it draws my attention. It's addressed to both of us, which is strange, since I've never given out this address.

I open the envelope to find a postcard with a handwritten note.

Dear Mr. and Mrs. James,

You left this behind on your wedding day, so we took the liberty to mail it to you because these memories should be cherished forever. We wish you many happy years of marriage. You were one of our most memorable couples yet!

All our love,
- Mary and the HEA Chapel team

I empty the envelope, and along with hundreds of little pieces of heart-shaped confetti, a USB flash drive comes tumbling out. I get back to the kitchen, gather the tea and cookies, and take them to the living room. There, I turn the TV on, pop open my laptop, and insert the drive into it. Of course, I check it for viruses. You can't ever be too safe, but when it comes back clean, I open the video file, casting it to the TV.

The video is just starting when I hear Maeve walk into the room. "Do you think I'll be showing soon? We're going to have to hide my bump for a while. What if my boobs get huge? I'll need to ask the doctor about that next week." She sits down next to me, reaching for a biscuit on the coffee table. "Thanks, darling. What's this?" she asks as she points to the TV.

I don't say anything as I hit play and watch as the shaky video begins. It's me on the screen, standing in front of an all-white altar decorated with thousands of white silk flowers.

"Owen? What…what is this?" Her cookie gets tossed back on the plate as she watches with unwavering attention, waiting for what we both can safely guess comes next.

Shania Twain's "Still The One" starts to play, and the camera quickly pans to where Maeve stands at the end of an aisle, her raven wig is still on her head as her Docs peek out beneath the hem of her white dress. She's smiling so big, I swear she might be the only source of light in the entire room. And she's looking at me. At where I'm standing at the end of that aisle. She mouths the lyrics, telling me I'm still the one she loves and dreams of as she walks toward where I am. The camera stops as she stands in front of me, bouncing on her toes with excitement.

The officiant smiles kindly at us both and begins the cere-mony. The entire time, Maeve and I only have eyes for each other. *"I understand you'd like to say your own vows. Owen, please go ahead."*

I hear my voice come through the speakers then, clear and sure. *"Maeve. My Maevey. You are my moon and my sunshine. You've been the brightest thing in my life, day or night, since the moment I laid eyes on you. When I look at you, I see my future, my life, and it's so full of love that sometimes it doesn't feel like I can hold it all inside my chest. I'm so honored to know you. To be known by you, this fierce, protective, sassy, smart, kind, wonderful woman that you are. The years we've spent apart have been hard, but I know that I'm the man I always wanted to be for you now."* I take Maeve's hand in mine and watch her as she listens to me recite my vows, which are truly impressive given how drunk I was. No amount of alcohol can dilute my love for her. She turns to me, and we look into each other's watery eyes as we continue to listen. *"My hope is that I can spend the rest of my life making up for lost time with you, showing you every day that I've never, and will never love anyone but you."*

The memory comes rushing back to me, and I say aloud,

together with the recording, *"In this lifetime and in all others, you are my first, my last, my only, my truest love."*

Maeve's tiny sob comes out through smiling lips as she whispers my name. We both hear her sniffle on the screen and turn back, knowing her vows will come next.

"Wow," my bride says on the screen, *"I'm not sure how to follow that up."* She takes a deep breath and lets it out by blowing raspberries and we both laugh, then and now. Maeve's face grows serious again, and she begins, *"Owen, I have dreamed of this since I was nineteen years old. I had no idea a man this good, kind, generous, and loving existed until I met you. I don't know what kind of life we'll have or what kinds of hardships we'll go through, but I know that together, we can do anything because I have never felt stronger or safer than I do when I'm with you. Being apart from you was the hardest thing I've ever had to do, and I don't wish to ever do it again. I am yours. I am so very completely yours. I always have been, and I always will be. You are my whole heart. I love you. I will choose you always, my darling."* She sniffles again as the officiant blows out a breath, wiping away a tear.

We turn to face one another again, listening as we take traditional vows and exchange the golden rings neither of us has taken off since that day. I take Maeve's left hand and kiss her ring finger, and she, in a very typical Maeve move, lunges herself onto my lap, wrapping her arms around my neck.

"I love you. I love you. I love you," she chants into my neck. She pulls away and lets her tears freely flow down her cheeks. Looking into my eyes, she says, "I do, Owen. I choose you forever. Always." I nod my agreement, not yet able to find words. "I can't believe we managed those vows in our state." A wet laugh escapes her as she runs her fingers through my hair.

"I do, too, Maeve. You're my only choice. Always," I whisper and now it's her turn to nod. I lift her up and reach for my phone, pulling up the same song I chose for us that night, then I bring her to her feet as "You" by Dan + Shay begins to play. Without hesitation, Maeve wraps her arms back around my neck, and we dance to our song.

————

maeve

seven months later

"Mama, poppet. I'm Mama," I tell my sweet Julia. She's nearly nine months old and the absolute light of our lives.

"Dada!" the chubby-cheeked little angel exclaims, hands springing up in the air as her Cheerios fly off her highchair tray and onto the floor. With eyes the color of chocolate like Monica's, and dirty blonde hair I know she gets from Clay, but looks just like Owen's, Julia has been the missing puzzle piece in my life I didn't even know I needed. Is it hard some days, caring for a baby while being pregnant, and trying to remain relevant in my career? Hell. Yes. But I'm not doing it alone. I have a husband who supports us in every way, who's a partner in everything and who encourages me when I feel like I can't do it all. He believes in me relentlessly.

Ojai is home, but we kept the house in LA, so we don't have to worry about things for Julia when we're there overnight, or when we extend our stay there for shoots or events.

We also have family rallying around us, supporting us, and loving us in each of their unique ways unconditionally. Eva even moved to California. She said she could hardly stand to be away from her babies for so long; she knew she wouldn't be able to handle it for her grandbabies. Watching her be a *Yia-Yia* to Julia has been incredible. They have such a beautiful relationship. So much so that *Yia-Yia* was Julia's first word. Dada was the second. Now I'm trying to make Mama happen. She doesn't actually seem to know what any of these mean as she parrots everything we say, but I'm still dying to hear her say Mama.

"Dada's right here, *moro mou*." Owen walks in, arms full of grocery bags, and I let my eyes delight in the wet dream that is my husband, with his biceps flexed and tattoos peeking out. His blonde hair peeks beneath his baseball cap, and his back muscles ripple as he sets everything down. I must be drooling because he chuckles when he catches me ogling. "You got your fill, Mrs. James?"

"Never," I shoot back without hesitation. He walks to me, fingers wrapping around my jaw as he tips my head up and kisses me so hard it makes me dizzy.

"Hey, Maevey," he whispers against my lips. I reach up to kiss him again, but our daughter has other ideas.

"Dada! Dada!" Little hands slap the tray, now almost devoid of cereal, whereas the floor is sprinkled with it.

Owen and I both laugh at her call for attention from her favorite person. I don't even mind the fact that she favors Owen. I get it. He's my favorite person, too.

He lowers himself and kisses her sticky cheek with a loud smack while simultaneously placing a gentle hand on my now very swollen belly.

"I see my girls are having a good day, but how's my boy?" He kneels next to me, bringing his lips to my belly as his hand moves over it, making Douglas push against the pressure. Once Bon and Adam had their baby girl, we asked if she would mind if we named our boy after her and Owen's late dad, and her response was laughter mixed with tears as she leapt up to hug us both, so we knew she didn't mind at all. Eva's reaction was nearly identical.

"We're all great, my darling." My fingers play with the hair at the nape of his neck. "Did you happen to stop by Jo's on your way out of Ojai, by any small chance?" Owen's chuckle reverberates through me.

"I think Mama is craving honey sticks again, Jules. What do you think?"

"Ya. Mmmama." She wiggles in her seat, making grabby hands at me. "Mama! Mama!" Immediately, tears roll down my cheeks, and I stand to pick Julia up, remembering to undo the buckle holding her in.

"Yes, my sweet Julia. Mama!" I hug her close to me, then pull back as she wiggles against me, kicking her brother in the process.

"Mama! Dada!" She makes grabby hands at Owen now, and he steps in so, we're in a three-way embrace, our baby boy kicking gently between us all. No moment has ever felt more perfect.

THE END

acknowledgments

It's hard to know where to start with this one because there are so many people to thank. If this was an award speech, I'd be the girl taking out a handwritten note filled with names, and I'd definitely have the mic shut off and the music playing to get me off the stage. I'm so sorry that I'm *that* girl.

Like with the first book, this one couldn't have been written without the love and support of my husband. Love and support aren't even strong enough words. That man is my rock, my safe place, and my home even when we're displaced and uncertain. During a time when I had more hard days than not, you have remained my constant and my best friend, babe. I love you so stupidly much.

My children have also been adorable little cheerleaders, always asking about my books and the characters. They were the first to plant the idea in my head for a Christmas book, so it turns out I'm raising little masterminds. Boys, you might never read this, but I love you endlessly. You make me better every single day.

Mãe, Pai, Diego and Sarah - thanks for always asking about my books, for following me online even when it probably makes you a little uncomfortable, and for walking alongside me as I make yet another career shift.

Meg. What the fuck do I even say? You've lifted me up on countless occasions, been the wind beneath my wings, and the exact friend I needed when writing felt impossible. I never want to write a book without you as my sounding board. Please don't make me, okay? I love you, friend.

Natasha, Sabrina, Sarah, Megan, Cami, Marylou, Melly, Lemmy, Amanda, Jess, Janine (I'm probably missing someone) - your endless support warms me from the inside out. More than once I have asked myself how I got so lucky to have you in my corner. I still don't have an answer, but I'm so incredibly grateful for you.

Alpha/Beta readers, the ones who saw me through changing storylines and a very messy draft and stuck around anyway - I love you. Every single one of you.

Kristen, thank you for each and every unhinged comment you left during copy edits. Thank you for helping me make this story and these characters stronger and better. I hope you know how much I admire and appreciate you.

Katie, where do I start? The voice notes, the kid videos, the tears, the fact that I've known since you were an ARC reader for *Lost Love Found* that I needed you to edit my books. All of it. I'm so happy to have you in my life as an editor and as a friend.

If you have ever messaged me to tell me you read my book, thank you. You probably made me cry, and it made my day, and I've probably forced you to be friends with me now, so you're stuck with me!

And now to you, reader. Thanks for making it this far. Thanks for giving my characters a chance. Thanks for making my dream a reality.

xoxo,
-Cristina

about the author

Cristina Santos is a mom of two little boys who hopefully will never read this book. She is married to the man of her dreams and lives lakeside with all her wild boys (pup included) in Nova Scotia, Canada. She loves a good sunset and will forever and ever and ever believe in the power of playlists, 90's romantic comedies and love stories.

This is Cristina's second book.

cristinasantosauthor.com

instagram.com/cristinasantosauthor
tiktok.com/@cristinasantosauthor

also by cristina santos

Please note that though these are interconnected, they can all be read as standalones. Remember to check content warnings.

there's more...

Want to keep in touch? Learn more about Cristina's books?

Head to cristinasantosauthor.com!

———

Flip the page to read chapter 1 of *Out of Focus*, book 3 in the
Love in LA Series

out of focus

book 3 in the love in la series

1 / ouch. that's going to leave a mark.

charlie

now

"STOP CALLING ME, Robert. I'm not your girlfriend. I never was. You made that perfectly clear." I breathe in a lungful of the warm Los Angeles air and immediately regret it. I came outside to clear my head. To go for a walk and forget about London and Robert for a bit. And now, I'm acutely aware of everything around me yet again.

What is that smell? And why does the bottom of my shoe feel sticky?

"You said you needed space. How much more space could you need? We're on opposite sides of the planet!" His words instantly make my temples throb.

"You know that's not what I meant. We agreed that you would give me time." I huff out a breath, unsure of how many more ways I can find to tell him that I need him to leave me alone.

"Charlotte, stop acting like a petulant child. Come home."

A few weeks ago, I would have.

I would have said I was a shoo-in for CFO at the company

Robert and I work for. Worked for? I haven't formally quit, but the thought has crossed my mind more than a handful of times in the seven months since my last visit to LA. I've earned this hypothetical promotion, though, and that's why I haven't handed in my resignation. As their VP of Finance, I helped Robert Thorpe, the current CFO, and voice at the end of the line, reduce costs and address operational inefficiencies. A job he has proven to be completely inept at. Now, Robert's father is stepping down as CEO, and he's gunning for the job. Instead of staying and fighting for my place as the company's first female with a C-level executive position in its seventy-three-year lifespan, I asked for a leave of absence. Effective immediately. And then I got on a plane to LA. Again.

"Charlotte? Are you even listening to me?" Ugh. I hate that he keeps calling me by my full name. My mother calls me that. Well, my mother *and* Robert, who refuses to be called anything else. The Thorpes only do full names or obnoxious nicknames. There's no in-between. My thoughts are slipping away again, so I know what the answer to his question is.

Nope. So not listening.

Squinting against the harsh sunlight, I realize that I forgot my sunglasses yet again on my way out the door. The sunglasses that are sitting on the kitchen counter, next to my to-do list, which includes a reminder to change my phone plan while I'm here because, this time, I am staying. This won't be like last time when I only stayed for a few days before running back to Robert and whatever emergency he was feigning.

I wonder how much this call is costing me. And did I close the balcony door before I left?

I take a breath and decide that it's fine. I'll tackle the list later, and it's okay if the door was left open. The flat is on the seventh floor, so it's not like anyone can break in, and it rarely rains here, anyway.

Despite the circumstances, I couldn't have come to LA at a

better time. It's been two weeks since I told my twin, Maeve, that I was finally ready for the change I claimed to need all those months ago. Last time I was here, she had just accidentally married the love of her life and then decided to officially adopt the baby who had been placed in her husband's care. Owen's gone through a lot, and a drunken Vegas wedding was apparently what they both needed to start their lives together.

Since then, both Maeve and our best friend Elaina announced pregnancies just weeks apart. Elaina and Adam had their baby girl on New Year's Day, just two years and a day after they met. I've missed so much over the years, and it feels good to be here and witness all of the joy in Maeve and Elaina's lives. They're the two most important people in my world, and while they've been falling in love and growing babies, I've been living a monotonous routine of work, take-out, and a standing three-night-a-week date with my vibrator. I'm not jealous of what they have because I'm truly so happy they have found such joy, but I'm tired of hearing about everything over phone calls while I feel stuck living a life that isn't exciting anymore. I want more for myself, and I know I deserve it.

Between our mum's latest man drama and the announcement at the firm, I was being suffocated in London. I've always loved the city, but lately, everything there has felt wrong. Including Robert. Maybe, especially him. And that's why I'm here. I need space, clarity, and to make sense of my life.

Thanks to my twin's endless connections in Los Angeles, I was able to sublet a furnished place as soon as I got here. Maeve and Elaina have lived in LA since we graduated from NYU eight years ago. They asked me to come then, too, but the thought of living in another strange city just four years after moving from London to New York was completely overwhelming to me. Once I got the scholarship to Oxford for my master's degree, it was time to head back to England and eventually back to London after I graduated.

LA made sense for them. They were pursuing jobs in Hollywood, and they've both made names for themselves in their respective careers. I'm immensely proud of them. I suppose I've done the same, just in London and in a career I'm not entirely sure suits me anymore. A career I picked because it seemed like the right thing to do. It was safe. Predictable, yet challenging. It seemed so perfect. And I'm so damn good at my job, but is all of that enough?

I must make some sort of noise because Robert sighs and continues. "Oh, good. You're still there. Charlotte, you've got to come back. My father won't step down until I prove I've settled down. We've talked about this. We're the dream team. CEO and CFO power couple. Please, Lottie." He's the one sounding like a petulant child now. A spoiled rich boy who's always gotten his way, and that has unfortunately included with me as well. Right down to the fact that I let him call me that ridiculous nickname, which he reserves for when he wants something from me.

He latched on to me the moment I started impressing our professors at Oxford. I caught his attention, intriguing him with my brain. My mistake was thinking he'd be interested in other parts of my body, but all he's ever done is allude to the fact that he's not ready to take that step yet. He loves to tell me how someday we'll be the ultimate power couple, married and running the company his great-grandfather founded. Once he's done enjoying being a bachelor, that is, because he'd hate to resent the woman he spends his life with. And I've understood it.

We met at twenty-two, and I didn't want to get married then, either. I wanted to focus on school and my career. So when Robert said he wanted to wait until we were both ready for that final commitment, it made sense to me. And it made me feel like I had a safety net ready to catch me. I figured marrying the right man was worth the wait. And despite his many faults, Robert mostly understands me and accepts me as I am.

We decided years ago that an open relationship was the best thing for us. We knew we wanted to eventually fully commit to one another. Robert wanted to make sure we both got dating other people well out of our systems before we became exclusive.

Maeve doesn't understand it, but for me, it always made perfect sense. I got the security of knowing I'd found my person, and I could choose to date other people if and when I wanted to. Though for the past couple of years, I haven't wanted to, and Robert and I have spent almost no time together as a couple.

"Lottie. Babe. I'm ready now. What do I have to say to make you believe me?" His whiny voice cuts through the noise, and I shake my head, attempting to focus.

"Nothing. I've already told you I need a break. That's why I'm taking this leave of absence. I need you to respect that this time." My voice is firm, even if inside, I'm completely falling apart. "Two months ago you said that we're not in a relationship. Now you want me to commit to being with you permanently because your dad is giving you an ultimatum?" My heart is racing, and my nerves are completely shot. Have I just left behind my one chance at the two things I've always wanted? A top position in my field and a husband. Those are the next goals to be achieved.

A husband.

Something both my best friend and sister have now. Well, Elaina will soon. She's been engaged to Adam for over a year, but her pregnancy was so rough on her that she couldn't bring herself to plan a wedding at the same time.

"Well, yes, Charlotte. I'm ready now because the CEO position is ready now. We both said we wanted to meet career goals before committing. We both agreed. We've waited years for this, and you know you're the only one I could ever marry." This fact is what had kept me going. Kept me waiting. I always thought Robert was a good guy for not pressuring me into a relationship when I wasn't ready. He once told me that he knew the first time I smiled at him that I was the one. I don't even remember the moment. Don't remember the smile since it was probably fake. Likely because I was trying so hard to look like I belonged in the room, rather than fighting off the urge to put on headphones or leave and quiet my mind with a book or a walk. I had my mask on when I gave him that smile, but he doesn't know that. Most people don't.

"How long?" Robert's voice barely registers among all the noise. In my head. Out here. I need to find somewhere quiet.

"What?" I ask, not even sure what he's going on about.

"How long do you need?" His tone's changed from cajoling to slightly annoyed.

"I'm not sure. Perhaps until Lainey and Adam are married? Once Maeve gives birth? I don't know. I need space, Robert. I need space from *you*." There. I said it. It might feel as though my heart is about to gallop out of my chest, but I said the words.

Robert clears his throat. "Oh. I didn't realize. All these years, I thought, well, I thought you wanted this. Me."

"I did. I..." I can't force myself to say I do because I'm not sure that's true any longer. "I did. I still might. But I can't figure that out when you tell me we're not together and then two weeks later decide you want to marry me because your dad has a position ready for you. Where am I in all of this? When do my feelings start to count?" I take an exasperated breath. "We made this decision years ago when neither of us were ready, and I'm still not sure that I am. I need to see for myself what the best thing for me is. Personally and professionally. And my sister might need me here. It's a delicate time. There's so much going on. I don't want to miss it all." My temples throb as the words pour out of me.

"I'm trying to understand, Lottie." This time, when I hear the nickname that only he uses, my muscles relax. The familiarity is soothing. This is the conundrum I always find myself in with him. One moment he overwhelms me, and the next, he's the familiar presence I need to calm down. But it never lasts with Robert. One way or the other.

"Thank you. Are you all right?" The words stick in my throat. I know I need to do this, but Robert has been a constant in my life for years. Other than Maeve and Elaina, he's the person who knows me best. Who mostly understands my need to get away; my difficulty with sensory overwhelm. It's hard to simply let a person like that go, especially when I'm not very good at letting people in.

"Yeah. Fine." His voice is a bit harder again, and I'm back on the Robert roller coaster. Is it too much to ask for to simply be understood? Fully? "Is this you trying to get back at me? Because we agreed to an open relationship until we were married, Charlotte. It's not my fault you chose to stop dating other people, and I didn't. But if what you need is for us to be broken up so you can shag some LA boys before you come home to me, then fine. Get it out of your system." He's completely serious, too.

It's never bothered him to think of me with other people. I thought it was sort of progressive, even if it did always feel like a bit of red flag hanging limply between us. Now that red flag is practically glowing, waving aggressively and warning me to stay away.

He's partially right, though. It's not his fault I chose to stop dating, but now, I feel completely unprepared for the possibility of a permanent relationship. With anyone.

"I should go. I'll call you when I'm ready, all right?" I'm about to say goodbye when I hear the telltale sound of the call ending. He hung up. I keep the phone to my ear, embarrassed.

Do the people around me know I was just hung up on? Can they tell? I say goodbye, pretending that didn't happen and willing the burning sensation in my cheeks away.

It doesn't work. The whole interaction throws me off, and I end up pacing back and forth on the sidewalk for several minutes. My phone is clutched to my chest like a security blanket as I dwell on every single word we just said to one another. My heart rate is still accelerated, the whooshing sound loud in my ears. Sweat is trickling down the back of my neck, making me itchy. Tears sting my eyes, but I can't let them fall. There are too many people, and I can sense their eyes on me, so I start walking.

What am I doing here? I should have stayed in London. What if I go back and they don't want me? I won't have a job. How will I make money?

I should have moved to LA a long time ago. I haven't been happy in London for ages. Have I ever been happy? Why don't I know the answer to that? What is wrong with me?

What if working in finance is my entire purpose, and I've just messed it up? I should go back. But what if I hate it? Do I have to do it for the next several decades?

I owe it to myself to figure this out. That's why I'm here. But what if I don't? Do I have to suffer through living in this limbo forever?

Why am I so indecisive that I can't just pick something and someone and live a happy life? Why am I so stupid and unable to handle simple things like everyone else can?

When I find myself in front of a small park, I spot a woman running, and I remember the reason I left the apartment to begin with: to escape. While the world of finance is where I've always excelled, writing is what brings me home.

On my walks, I often get lost in the characters I'm reading or writing about. What started as a hobby, quickly turned into a hyper-fixation, and has now morphed into an all-consuming, secret side hustle. I write the love stories I wish I lived myself. I write the happy endings I hope everyone gets to have. The one I never saw my mum get because she was so selfish and always seemed to pick unavailable men. I live in both worlds, but this one that I've created, with flawed but beautiful characters, I get to keep to myself. I get to control it.

I tuck my phone into the pocket of my pants and take in my surroundings. The relief is almost immediate as the thoughts fall away, and I focus on my breathing and the movement of my legs.

Soon, my thoughts trail to the characters I'm writing. I get lost in the mental planning of the settings, the mood, and how I want things to feel. I let myself get lost in getting to know these people.

I walk for so long that my legs are almost numb, but I can't stop now. Not when my mind finally clears. I need to hang on to this feeling.

I close my eyes for a second. Just a second. And my body comes in full contact with a wall. Then, the pavement. I open my eyes just in time to feel my elbow hit the sidewalk.

Ouch. That's going to leave a mark.

I lay my head back on the floor and drape one arm over my face to hide from the embarrassment of walking with my eyes closed. I'm acutely aware of the shooting pain in my other elbow and the soreness in my lower back since I landed mostly on it. Words are leaving my mouth, but I couldn't tell you what they are. And is someone talking to me?

"Can you tell me where you're hurt?" The voice is soothing and sounds a little closer now.

"I think it's mostly my ego if I'm honest. I'm so very sorry. I was just getting into this groove, and I closed my eyes for only a second, I swear—"

"So, you *did* have your eyes closed." My whole body tenses. Recognition hits me harder than the pavement beneath me. I know the sass in that tone. I can practically see the arrogant smirk painted on the face of the jerk it belongs to.

Rafael Machado.

You have got to be bloody joking me.

———

Out of Focus is available on e-book, Kindle Unlimited and paperback.